Patricia Cornwell's first novel, *Postmortem*, is the only novel to have won the Edgar, John Creasey, Anthony and MacAvity awards, and the Prix du Roman d'Aventure in one year. Her other novels, *Body of Evidence*, *All That Remains* and *Cruel and Unusual* (which won the Crime Writers' Association Gold Dagger Award), attracted equal critical acclaim and became international bestsellers, establishing the author as one of the top crime writers. A former crime reporter for the *Charlotte Observer*, Patricia Cornwell worked for over six years as a computer analyst in the Chief Medical Examiner's office in Virginia. She is also the author of *A Time for Remembering*, a biography of Ruth Bell Graham, the wife of the evangelist. She lives in Richmond, Virginia.

Patricia Cornwell

THE BODY
FARM

WARNER BOOKS

A *Warner* Book

First published in the United States in 1994
by Charles Scribner's Sons
First published in Great Britain in 1994
by Little, Brown and Company

This edition published by Warner Books in 1995

A CIP catalogue record for this book
is available from the British Library.

ISBN 0 7515 1221 4

Typeset by Hewer Text Composition Services, Edinburgh
Printed and bound in Great Britain by
Clays Ltd, St. Ives plc

Warner Books
A Division of
Little, Brown and Company (UK)
Brettenham House
Lancaster Place
London WC2E 7EN

They that go down to the sea in ships, that do business in great waters; These see the works of the Lord, and his wonders in the deep.

Psalm 107:23–24

To Senator Orrin Hatch of Utah
for his tireless fight against crime

1

On the sixteenth of October, shadowy deer crept to the edge of dark woods beyond my window as the sun peeked over the cover of the night. Plumbing above and below me groaned, and one by one other rooms went bright as sharp tattoos from ranges I could not see riddled the dawn. I had gone to sleep and gotten up to the sound of gunfire.

It is a noise that never stops in Quantico, Virginia, where the FBI Academy is an island surrounded by Marines. Several days a month I stayed on the Academy's security floor, where no one could call me unless I wanted them to or follow me after too many beers in the Boardroom.

Unlike the Spartan dormitory rooms occupied by new agents and visiting police, in my suite were TV, kitchen, telephone, and a bathroom I did not have to share. Smoking and alcohol were not allowed, but I suspected that the spies and protected witnesses

typically sequestered here obeyed the rules about as
well as I did.

As coffee heated in the microwave, I opened my
briefcase to retrieve a file that had been waiting for me
when I had checked in last night. I had not reviewed
it yet for I could not bring myself to wrap my mind
around such a thing, to take such a thing to bed. In
that way I had changed.

Since medical school, I had been accustomed to
exposing myself to any trauma at any hour. I had
worked around the clock in emergency rooms and
performed autopsies alone in the morgue until dawn.
Sleep had always been a brief export to some dark,
vacant place I rarely later recalled. Then gradually over
the years something perniciously shifted. I began to
dread working late at night, and was prone to bad
dreams when terrible images from my life popped up
in the slot machine of my unconscious.

Emily Steiner was eleven, her dawning sexuality a
blush on her slight body, when she wrote in her diary
two Sundays before, on October 1:

Oh, Im' so happy! Its almost 1 in the morning and
Mom doesnt know Im' writing in my dairy because
Im' in bed with the flash light. We went to the
cover dish supper at the church and Wren was
there! I could tell he noticed me. Then he gave
me a fireball! I saved it while he wasnt looking.
Its in my secret box. This afternoon we have youth
group and he wants me to meet him early and not
tell anyone!!!

At three-thirty that afternoon, Emily left her house in Black Mountain, just east of Asheville, and began the two-mile walk to the church. After the meeting, other children recalled seeing her leave alone as the sun slipped below the foothills at six P.M. She veered off the main road, guitar case in hand, and took a shortcut around a small lake. Investigators believed it was during this walk she encountered the man who hours later would steal her life. Perhaps she stopped to talk to him. Perhaps she was unaware of his presence in the gathering shadows as she hurried home.

In Black Mountain, a western North Carolina town of seven thousand people, local police had worked very few homicides or sexual assaults of children. They had never worked a case that was both. They had never thought about Temple Brooks Gault of Albany, Georgia, though his face smiled from Ten Most Wanted lists posted across the land. Notorious criminals and their crimes had never been a concern in this picturesque part of the world known for Thomas Wolfe and Billy Graham.

I did not understand what would have drawn Gault there or to a frail child named Emily who was lonely for her father and a boy named Wren. But when Gault had gone on his murderous spree in Richmond two years before, his choices had seemed just as devoid of rationality. In fact, they still did not make sense.

Leaving my suite, I passed through sun-filled glass corridors as memories of Gault's bloody career in Richmond seemed to darken the morning. Once he had been within my reach. I literally could have touched him, for a flicker, before he had fled through a window and was gone. I had not been armed on that occasion, and it was not my business to go around shooting people anyway. But I had not been able to shake the chill of doubt that had settled over my spirit back then. I had not stopped wondering what more I could have done.

Wine has never known a good year at the Academy, and I regretted drinking several glasses of it in the Boardroom the night before. My morning run along J. Edgar Hoover Road was worse than usual.

Oh, God, I thought. *I'm not going to make it.*

Marines were setting up camouflage canvas chairs and telescopes on roadsides overlooking ranges. I felt bold male eyes as I slowly jogged past, and knew the gold Department of Justice crest on my navy T-shirt was duly noted. The soldiers probably assumed I was a female agent or visiting cop, and it disturbed me to imagine my niece running this same route. I wished Lucy had picked another place to intern. Clearly, I had influenced her life, and very little frightened me quite as much as that did. It had become my habit to worry about her during workouts when I was in agony and aware of growing old.

HRT, the Bureau's Hostage Rescue Team, was out on maneuvers, helicopter blades dully batting air. A pickup truck hauling shot-up doors roared past, followed by another caravan of soldiers. Turning around, I began the one-and-a-half-mile stretch back to the Academy, which could have passed for a modern tan brick hotel were it not for its rooftops of antennas and location out in the middle of a wooded nowhere.

When at last I reached the guard booth, I veered around tire shredders and lifted my hand in a weary salute to the officer behind glass. Breathless and sweating, I was contemplating walking the rest of the way in when I sensed a car slowing at my rear.

"You trying to commit suicide or something?" Captain Pete Marino said loudly across the Armor-Alled front seat of his silver Crown Victoria. Radio antennas bobbed like fishing rods, and despite countless lectures from me, he wasn't wearing his seat belt.

"There are easier ways than this," I said through his open passenger's window. "Not fastening your seat belt, for example."

"Never know when I might have to bail out of my ride in a hurry."

"If you get in a wreck, you'll certainly bail out in a hurry," I said. "Probably through the windshield."

An experienced homicide detective in Richmond, where both of us were headquartered, Marino recently had been promoted and assigned to the First Precinct, the bloodiest section of the city. He had been involved with the FBI's Violent Criminal Apprehension Program, or VICAP, for years.

In his early fifties, he was a casualty of concentrated doses of tainted human nature, bad diet, and drink, his face etched by hardship and fringed with thinning gray hair. Marino was overweight, out of shape, and not known for a sweet disposition. I knew he was here for the Steiner consultation, but wondered about the luggage in his backseat.

"Are you staying for a while?" I asked.

"Benton signed me up for Street Survival."

"You and who else?" I asked, for the purpose of Street Survival was not to train individuals but task forces.

"Me and my precinct's entry team."

"Please don't tell me part of your new job description is kicking in doors."

"One of the pleasures of being promoted is finding your ass back in uniform and out on the street. In case you haven't noticed, Doc, they ain't using Saturday Night Specials out there anymore."

"Thank you for the tip," I said dryly. "Be sure to wear thick clothing."

"Huh?" His eyes, blacked out by sunglasses, scanned mirrors as other cars crept past.

"Paint bullets hurt."

"I don't plan on getting hit."

"I don't know anyone who plans on it."

"When did you get in?" he asked me.

"Last night."

Marino slid a pack of cigarettes from his visor. "You been told much?"

"I've looked at a few things. Apparently the detectives from North Carolina are bringing in most of the case records this morning."

"It's Gault. It's gotta be."

"Certainly there are parallels," I said cautiously.

Knocking out a Marlboro, he clamped it between his

lips. "I'm going to nail that goddam son of a bitch if I have to go to hell to find him."

"If you find out he's in hell, I wish you'd just leave him there," I said. "Are you free for lunch?"

"As long as you're buying."

"I always buy." I stated a fact.

"And you always should." He slipped the car into drive. "You're a goddam doctor."

I trotted and walked to the track, cut across it and let myself into the back of the gym. Inside the locker room three young, fit women in various stages of nudity glanced at me as I walked in.

"Good morning, ma'am," they said in unison, instantly identifying themselves. Drug Enforcement Administration agents were notorious around the Academy for their annoyingly chivalrous greetings.

I self-consciously began taking off wet clothes, having never grown accustomed to the rather male militaristic attitude here, where women did not think twice about chatting or showing off their bruises with nothing on but the lights. Clutching a towel tightly, I hurried to the showers. I had just turned on the water when a pair of familiar green eyes peeked around the plastic curtain, startling me. The soap shot out of my hands and skidded across the tile floor, stopping near my niece's muddy Nikes.

"Lucy, can we chat *after* I get out?" I yanked the curtain shut.

"Geez, Len just about killed me this morning," she said happily as she booted the soap back into the stall.

"It was great. Next time we run the Yellow Brick Road I'll ask him if you can come."

"No, thank you." I massaged shampoo into my hair. "I have no desire for torn ligaments and broken bones."

"Well, you really should run it once, Aunt Kay. It's a rite of passage up here."

"Not for me it isn't."

Lucy was silent for a moment, then uncertain when she said, "I need to ask you something."

Rinsing my hair and pushing it out of my eyes, I gathered the curtain and looked out. My niece was standing back from the stall, filthy and sweaty from head to toe, blood smudging her gray FBI T-shirt. At twenty-one, she was about to graduate from the University of Virginia, her face honed into a beautiful sharpness, her short auburn hair brightened by the sun. I remembered when her hair was long and red, when she wore braces and was fat.

"They want me to come back after graduation," she said. "Mr. Wesley's written a proposal and there's a good chance the Feds will approve."

"What's your question?" Ambivalence kicked in hard again.

"I just wondered what you thought about it."

"You know there's a hiring freeze."

Lucy looked closely at me, trying to read information I did not want her to have.

"I couldn't be a new agent straight out of college anyway," she said. "The point is to get me into ERF now, maybe through a grant. As for what I'll do after that"—she shrugged—"who knows?"

ERF was the Bureau's recently built Engineering Research Facility, an austere complex on the same grounds as the Academy. The workings within were classified, and it chagrined me a little that I was the chief medical examiner of Virginia, the consulting forensic pathologist for the Bureau's Investigative Support Unit, and had never been cleared to enter hallways my young niece passed through every day.

Lucy took off her running shoes and shorts, and pulled her shirt and sports bra over her head.

"We'll continue this conversation later," I said as I stepped out of the shower and she stepped in.

"Ouch!" she complained as spray hit her injuries.

"Use lots of soap and water. How did you do that to your hand?"

"I slipped coming down a bank and the rope got me."

"We really should put some alcohol on that."

"No way."

"What time will you leave ERF?"

"I don't know. Depends."

"I'll see you before I head back to Richmond," I promised as I returned to the lockers and began drying my hair.

Scarcely a minute later, Lucy, not given to modesty either, trotted past me wearing nothing but the Breitling watch I'd given her for her birthday.

"Shit!" she said under her breath as she began

yanking on her clothes. "You wouldn't believe every-thing I've got to do today. Repartition the hard disk, reload the whole thing because I keep running out of space, allocate more, change a bunch of files. I just hope we don't have any more hardware problems." She complained on unconvincingly. Lucy loved every minute of what she did every day.

"I saw Marino when I was out running. He's up for the week," I said.

"Ask him if he wants to do some shooting." She tossed her running shoes inside her locker and shut the door with an enthusiastic clang.

"I have a feeling he'll be doing plenty of that." My words followed her out as half a dozen more DEA agents walked in, dressed in black.

"Good morning, ma'am." Laces whipped against leather as they took off their boots.

By the time I was dressed and had dropped my gym bag back in my room, it was quarter past nine and I was late.

Leaving through two sets of security doors, I hurried down three flights of stairs, boarded the elevator in the gun-cleaning room, and descended sixty feet into the Academy's lower level, where I routinely waded through hell. Inside the conference room, nine police investigators, FBI profilers, and a VICAP analyst sat at a long oak table. I pulled out a chair next to Marino as comments caromed around the room.

"This guy knows a hell of a lot about forensic evidence."

"And anybody who's served time does."

"What's important is he's extremely comfortable with this type of behavior."

"That suggests to me he's *never* served time."

I added my file to other case material going around the room and whispered to one of the profilers that I wanted a photocopy of Emily Steiner's diary.

"Yeah, well, I disagree," Marino said. "The fact someone's done time don't mean he fears he's going to do time again."

"Most people would fear it—you know, the proverbial cat on the hot stove."

"Gault ain't most people. He likes hot stoves."

I was passed a stack of laser prints of the Steiners' ranch-style house. In back, a first-floor window had been pried open, and through it the assailant had entered a small laundry room of white linoleum and blue-checked walls.

"If we consider the neighborhood, the family, the victim herself, then Gault's getting bolder."

I followed a carpeted hallway into the master bedroom, where the decor was pastel prints of tiny bouquets of violets and loose flying balloons. I counted six pillows on the canopied bed and several more on a closet shelf.

"We're talking about a real small window of vulnerability here."

The bedroom with its little girl decor belonged to Emily's mother, Denesa. According to her police statement, she had awakened at gunpoint around two A.M.

11

"He may be taunting us."

"It wouldn't be the first time."

Mrs. Steiner described her attacker as of medium height and build. Because he was wearing gloves, a mask, long pants, and a jacket, she was uncertain about race. He gagged and bound her with blaze orange duct tape and put her in the closet. Then he went down the hall to Emily's room, where he snatched her from her bed and disappeared with her in the dark early morning.

"I think we should be careful about getting too hung up on this guy. On Gault."

"Good point. We need to keep an open mind."

I interrupted. "The mother's bed is made?"

The counterpunctal conversation stopped.

A middle-aged investigator with a dissipated, florid face said, "Affirmative," as his shrewd gray eyes alighted, like an insect, on my ash-blond hair, my lips, the gray cravat peeking out of the open collar of my gray-and-white-striped blouse. His gaze continued its surveillance, traveling down to my hands, where he glanced at my gold Intaglio seal ring and the finger that bore no sign of a wedding band.

"I'm Dr. Scarpetta," I said, introducing myself to him without a trace of warmth as he stared at my chest.

"Max Ferguson, State Bureau of Investigation, Asheville."

"And I'm Lieutenant Hershel Mote, Black Mountain Police." A man crisply dressed in khaki and old enough to retire leaned across the table to offer a big calloused hand. "Sure is a pleasure, Doc. I've heard right much about ya."

"Apparently"—Ferguson addressed the group—"Mrs. Steiner made her bed before the police arrived."

"Why?" I inquired.

"Modesty, maybe," offered Liz Myre, the only woman profiler in the unit. "She's already had one stranger in her bedroom. Now she's got cops coming in."

"How was she dressed when the police got there?" I asked.

Ferguson glanced over a report. "A zip-up pink robe and socks."

"This was what she had worn to bed?" a familiar voice sounded behind me.

Unit Chief Benton Wesley shut the conference room door as he briefly met my eyes. Tall and trim, with sharp features and silver hair, he was dressed in a single-breasted dark suit and was loaded down with paperwork and carousels of slides. No one spoke as he briskly took his chair at the head of the table and jotted several notes with a Mont Blanc pen.

Wesley repeated, without looking up, "Do we know if this was the way she was dressed when the assault took place? Or did she put on the robe after the fact?"

"I'd call it more a gown than a robe," Mote spoke up. "Flannel material, long sleeves, down to her ankles, zipper up the front."

"She didn't have on nothing under it except panties," Ferguson offered.

"I won't ask you how you know that," Marino said.

13

"Panty line, no bra. The state pays me to be observant. The Feds, for the record"—he looked around the table—"don't pay me for shit."

"Nobody should pay for your shit unless you eat gold," Marino said.

Ferguson got out a pack of cigarettes. "Anybody mind if I smoke?"

"I mind."

"Yeah, me, too."

"Kay." Wesley slid a thick manila envelope my way. "Autopsy reports, more photos."

"Laser prints?" I asked, and I was not keen on them, for like dot matrix images, they are satisfactory only from a distance.

"Nope. The real McCoy."

"Good."

"We're looking for offender traits and strategies?" Wesley glanced around the table as several people nodded. "And we have a viable suspect. Or I'm assuming we're assuming we do."

"No question in my mind," Marino said.

"Let's go through the crime scene, then the victimology," Wesley went on as he began perusing paperwork. "And I think it's best we keep the names of known offenders out of the mix for the moment." He surveyed us over his reading glasses. "Do we have a map?"

Ferguson passed out photocopies. "The victim's house and the church are marked. So is the path we think she took around the lake on her way home from the church meeting."

Emily Steiner could have passed for eight or nine with her tiny fragile face and form. When her most recent school photograph had been taken last spring, she had worn a buttoned-up kelly green sweater; her flaxen hair was parted on one side and held in place with a barrette shaped like a parrot.

To our knowledge, no other photographs were taken of her until the clear Saturday morning of October 7, when an old man arrived at Lake Tomahawk to enjoy a little fishing. As he set up a lawn chair on a muddy ledge close to the water, he noticed a small pink sock protruding from nearby brush. The sock, he realized, was attached to a foot.

"We proceeded down the path," Ferguson was saying, and he was showing slides now, the shadow of his ballpoint pen pointing on the screen, "and located the body here."

"And that's how far from the church and her house?"

"About a mile from either one, if you drive. A little less than that as a crow flies."

"And the path around the lake would be as a crow flies?"

"Pretty much."

Ferguson resumed. "She's lying with her head in a northernly direction. We have a sock partially on the left foot, a sock on the other. We have a watch. We have a necklace. She was wearing blue flannel pajamas and panties, and to this day they have not been found. This is a close-up of the injury to the rear of her skull."

The shadow of the pen moved, and above us

15

through thick walls muffled gunshots sounded from the indoor range.

Emily Steiner's body was nude. Upon close inspection by the Buncombe County medical examiner, it was determined that she had been sexually assaulted, and large dark shiny patches on her inner thighs, upper chest, and shoulder were areas of missing flesh. She also had been gagged and bound with blaze orange duct tape, her cause of death a single small-caliber gunshot wound to the back of the head.

Ferguson showed slide after slide, and as images of the girl's pale body in the rushes flashed in the dark, there was silence. No investigator I'd ever met had ever gotten used to maimed and murdered children.

"Do we know the weather conditions in Black Mountain from October one through the seventh?" I asked.

"Overcast. Low forties at night, upper fifties during the day," Ferguson replied. "Mostly."

"Mostly?" I looked at him.

"On the average," he enunciated slowly as the lights went back on. "You know, you add the temperatures together and divide by the number of days."

"Agent Ferguson, any significant fluctuation matters," I said with a dispassion that belied my growing dislike of this man. "Even one day of unusually high temperatures, for example, would alter the condition of the body."

Wesley began a new page of notes. When he paused, he looked at me. "Dr. Scarpetta, if she was killed shortly after she was abducted, how decomposed should she have been when she was found on October seventh?"

"Under the conditions described, I would expect her to be moderately decomposed," I said. "I also would expect insect activity, possibly other postmortem damage, depending on how accessible the body was to carnivores."

"In other words, she should be in a lot worse shape than this"—he tapped photographs—"if she'd been dead six days."

"More decomposed than this, yes."

Perspiration glistened at Wesley's hairline and had dampened the collar of his starched white shirt. Veins were prominent in his forehead and neck.

"I'm right surprised no dogs got to her."

"Well, now, Max, I'm not. This ain't the city, with mangy strays everywhere. We keep our dogs penned in or on a leash."

Marino indulged in his dreadful habit of picking apart his Styrofoam coffee cup.

Her body was so pale it was almost gray, with greenish discoloration in the right lower quadrant. Fingertips were dry, the skin receding from the nails. There was slippage of her hair and the skin of her feet. I saw no evidence of defense injuries, no cuts, bruises, or broken nails that might indicate a struggle.

"The trees and other vegetation would have shielded her from the sun," I commented as vague shadows drifted over my thoughts. "And it doesn't appear that her wounds bled out much, if at all, otherwise I would expect more predator activity."

"We're assuming she was killed somewhere else,"

Wesley interpolated. "Absence of blood, missing clothing, location of the body, and so on would indicate she was molested and shot elsewhere, then dumped. Can you tell if the missing flesh was done postmortem?"

"At or around the time of death," I replied.

"To remove bite marks again?"

"I can't tell you that from what I have here."

"In your opinion, are the injuries similar to Eddie Heath's?" Wesley referred to the thirteen-year-old boy Temple Gault had murdered in Richmond.

"Yes." I opened another envelope and withdrew a stack of autopsy photographs bound in rubber bands. "In both cases we have skin excised from shoulder, upper inner thigh. And Eddie Heath was shot in the head, his body dumped."

"It also strikes me that despite the gender differences, the body types of the girl and boy are similar. Heath was small, prepubescent. The Steiner girl is very small, almost prepubescent."

I pointed out, "A difference worth noting is that there are no crisscrosses, no shallow cuts at the margins of the Steiner girl's wounds."

Marino explained to the North Carolina officers, "In the Heath case, we think Gault first tried to eradicate bite marks by slicing through them with a knife. Then he figures that's not doing the job so he removes pieces of skin about the size of my shirt pocket. This time, with the little girl he's snatched, maybe he just cuts out the bite marks and is done with it."

"You know, I *really* am uncomfortable with these assumptions. We can't assume it's Gault."

18

"It's been almost two years, Liz. I doubt Gault got born again or has been working for the Red Cross."

"You don't know that he hasn't. Bundy worked in a crisis center."

"And God talked to the Son of Sam."

"I can assure you God told Berkowitz nothing," Wesley said flatly.

"My point is that maybe Gault—if it's Gault—just cut out the bite marks this time."

"Well, it's true. Like in anything else, these guys get better with practice."

"Lord, I hope this guy don't get any better." Mote dabbed his upper lip with a folded handkerchief.

"Are we about ready to profile this thing?" Wesley glanced around the table. "Would you go for white male?"

"It's a predominantly white neighborhood."

"Absolutely."

"Age?"

"He's logical and that adds years on."

"I agree. I don't think we're talking about a youthful offender here."

"I'd start with twenties. Maybe late twenties."

"I'd go with late twenties to mid-thirties."

"He's very organized. His weapon of choice, for example, is one he brought with him versus something he found at the scene. And it doesn't look as if he had any trouble controlling his victim."

"According to family members and friends, Emily wouldn't have been hard to control. She was shy, easily frightened."

"Plus, she had a history of being sick, in and out of doctors' offices. She was accustomed to being compliant with adults. In other words, she pretty much did what she was told."

"Not always." Wesley's face was expressionless as he perused the pages of the dead girl's diary. "She didn't want her mother to know she was up at one A.M., in bed with a flashlight. Nor does it appear she planned to tell her mother she was going to the church meeting early that Sunday afternoon. Do we know if this boy, Wren, showed up early as planned?"

"He didn't show until the meeting started at five."

"What about Emily's relationships with other boys?"

"She had typical eleven-year-old relationships. Do you love me? Circle yes or no."

"What's wrong with that?" Marino asked, and everybody laughed.

I continued arranging photographs in front of me like tarot cards as my uneasiness grew. The gunshot wound to the back of the head had entered the right parietal-temporal region of the skull, lacerating the dura and a branch of the middle meningeal artery. Yet there was no contusion, no subdural or epidural hematomas. Nor was there vital reaction to injuries of the genitalia.

"How many hotels are there in your area?"

"I reckon around ten. Now a couple are bed-and-breakfast places, homes where you can get a room."

"Have you been keeping up with registered guests?"

"To tell you the truth, we hadn't thought about that."

"If Gault's in town, he's got to be staying some-where."

Her laboratory reports were equally perplexing: vitreous sodium level elevated to 180, potassium 58 milliequivalents per liter.

"Max, let's start with the Travel-Eze. In fact, if you'll do it, I'll hit the Acorn and Apple Blossom. Might want to try the Mountaineer, too, though that's a little farther down the road."

"Gault's most likely to stay in a place where he has maximum anonymity. He's not going to want the staff noticing his coming and going."

"Well, he's not going to have a whole lot of choice. We don't have nothing all that big."

"Probably not the Red Rocker or Blackberry Inn."

"I wouldn't think so, but we'll check 'em out anyway."

"What about Asheville? They must have a few large hotels."

"They got all kinds of things since they passed liquor by the drink."

"You thinking he took the girl to his room and killed her there?"

"No. Absolutely not."

"You can't hold a little kid hostage like that somewhere and not have someone notice. Like housekeeping, room service."

"That's why it would surprise me if Gault's staying in a hotel. The cops started looking for Emily right after she was kidnapped. It was all over the news."

The autopsy had been performed by Dr. James

21

Jenrette, the medical examiner who had been called to the scene. A hospital pathologist in Asheville, Jenrette was under contract with the state to perform forensic autopsies on the rare occasion such a need might arise in the cloistered foothills of western North Carolina. His summary that "some findings were unexplained by the gunshot wound to the head" was simply not enough. I slipped off my glasses and rubbed the bridge of my nose as Benton Wesley spoke.

"What about tourist cabins, rental properties in your area?"

"Yes, sir," Mote answered. "Lots and lots of them." He turned to Ferguson. "Max, I reckon we'd better check them, too. Get a list, see who's been renting what."

I knew Wesley sensed my troubled mood when he said, "Dr. Scarpetta? You look like you have something to add."

"I'm perplexed by the absence of vital reaction to any of her injuries," I said. "And though the condition of her body suggests she has been dead only several days, her electrolytes don't fit her physical findings. . . ."

"Her what?" Mote's expression went blank.

"Her sodium is high, and since sodium stays fairly stable after death, we can conclude that her sodium was high at the time of her death."

"What does that mean?"

"It could mean she was profoundly dehydrated," I said. "And by the way, she was underweight for her age. Do we know anything about a possible eating disorder? Had she been sick? Vomiting? Diarrhea? A history of taking diuretics?" I scanned the faces around the table.

When no one replied, Ferguson said, "I'll run it by the mother. I gotta talk to her anyway when I get back."

"Her potassium is elevated," I went on. "And this also needs to be explained, because vitreous potassium becomes elevated incrementally and predictably after death as cell walls leak and release it."

"Vitreous?" Mote asked.

"The fluid of the eye is very reliable for testing because it's isolated, protected, and therefore less subject to contamination, putrefaction," I answered. "The point is, her potassium level suggests she's been dead longer than her other findings indicate."

"How long?" Wesley asked.

"Six or seven days."

"Could there be any other explanation for this?"

"Exposure to extreme heat that would have escalated decomposition," I replied.

"Well, that's not going to be it."

"Or an error," I added.

"Can you check it out?"

I nodded.

"Doc Jenrette thinks the bullet in her brain killed her instantly," Ferguson announced. "Seems to me you get killed instantly and there's not going to be any vital reaction."

"The problem," I explained, "is this injury to her brain should not have been instantly fatal."

"How long could she have survived with it?" Mote wanted to know.

"Hours," I replied.

"Other possibilities?" Wesley said to me.

"*Commotio cerebri*. It's like an electrical short circuit—you get a bang on the head, die instantly, and we can't find much if any injury." I paused. "Or it could be that *all* of her injuries are postmortem, including the gunshot wound."

Everybody let that sink in for a moment.

Marino's coffee cup was a small pile of Styrofoam snow, the ashtray in front of him littered with wadded gum wrappers.

He said, "You find anything to indicate maybe she was smothered first?"

I told him I had not.

He began clicking his ballpoint pen open and shut. "Let's talk about her family some more. What do we know about the father besides he's deceased?"

"He was a teacher at Broad River Christian Academy in Swannanoa."

"Same place Emily went?"

"Nope. She went to the public elementary school in Black Mountain. Her daddy died about a year ago," Mote added.

"I noticed that," I said. "His name was Charles?"

Mote nodded.

"What was his cause of death?" I asked.

"I'm not sure. But it was natural."

Ferguson added, "He had a heart condition."

Wesley got up and moved to the whiteboard.

"Okay." He uncapped a black Magic Marker and began writing. "Let's go over the details. Victim's

24

from a middle-class family, white, age eleven, last seen by her peers around six o'clock in the afternoon of October 1 when she walked home alone from a church meeting. On this occasion, she took a shortcut, a path that follows the shore of Lake Tomahawk, a small man-made lake.

"If you look at your map, you'll see there is a clubhouse on the north end of the lake and a public pool, both of which are open only in the summer. Over here you've got tennis courts and a picnic area that are available year-round. According to the mother, Emily arrived home shortly after six-thirty. She went straight to her room and practiced guitar until dinner."

"Did Mrs. Steiner say what Emily ate that night?" I asked the group.

"She told me they had macaroni and cheese and salad," Ferguson said.

"At what time?" According to the autopsy report, Emily's stomach contents consisted of a small amount of brownish fluid.

"Around seven-thirty in the evening is what she told me."

"That would have been digested by the time she was kidnapped at two in the morning?"

"Yes," I said. "It would have cleared her stomach long before then."

"It could be that she wasn't given much in the way of food and water while held in captivity."

"Thus accounting for her high sodium, her possible dehydration?" Wesley asked me.

"That's certainly possible."

25

He wrote some more. "There's no alarm system in the house, no dog."

"Do we know if anything was stolen?"

"Maybe some clothes."

"Whose?"

"Maybe the mother's. While she was taped up in the closet, she thought she heard him opening drawers."

"If so, he was right tidy. She also said she couldn't tell if anything was missing or disturbed."

"What did the father teach? Did we get to that?"

"Bible."

"Broad River's one of these fundamentalist places. The kids start the day singing 'Sin Shall Not Have Dominion Over Me.'"

"No kidding."

"I'm serious as a heart attack."

"Jesus."

"Yeah, they talk about Him a lot, too."

"Maybe they could do something with my grandson."

"Shit, Hershel, nobody could do nothing with your grandson because you spoil him rotten. How many minibikes he's got now? Three?"

I spoke again. "I'd like to know more about Emily's family. I assume they are religious."

"Very much so."

"Any other siblings?"

Lieutenant Mote took a deep, weary breath. "That's what's really sad about this one. There was a baby some years back, a crib death."

"Was this also in Black Mountain?" I asked.

26

"No, ma'am. It was before the Steiners moved to the area. They're from California. You know, we got folks from all over."

Ferguson added, "A lot of foreigners head to our hills to retire, vacation, attend religious conventions. Shit, if I had a nickel for every Baptist I wouldn't be sitting here."

I glanced at Marino. His anger was as palpable as heat, his face boiled red. "Just the kind of place Gault would get off on. The folks there read all the big stories about the son of a bitch in *People* magazine, *The National Enquirer*, *Parade*. But it never enters no one's mind the squirrel might come to town. To them he's Frankenstein. He don't really exist."

"Don't forget they did that TV movie on him, too," Mote spoke again.

"When was that?" Ferguson scowled.

"Last summer, Captain Marino told me. I don't recollect the actor's name, but he's been in a lot of those Termination movies. Isn't that right?"

Marino didn't care. His private posse was thundering through the air. "I think the son of a bitch's still there." He pushed his chair back and added another wad of gum to the ashtray.

"Anything's possible," Wesley said matter-of-factly.

"Well." Mote cleared his throat. "Whatever you boys want to do to help out would be mighty appreciated."

Wesley glanced at his watch. "Pete, you want to cut the lights again? I thought we'd run through these earlier cases, show our two visitors from North Carolina how Gault spent his time in Virginia."

PATRICIA CORNWELL

For the next hour horrors flashed in the dark like
disjointed scenes from some of my very worst dreams.
Ferguson and Mote never took their wide eyes off
the screen. They did not say a word. I did not see
them blink.

2

Beyond windows in the Boardroom plump ground-hogs sunned themselves on the grass as I ate salad and Marino scraped the last trace of the fried chicken special off his plate.

The sky was faded denim blue, trees hinting of how brightly they would burn when fall reached its peak. In a way I envied Marino. The physical demands of his week would almost seem a relief compared to what waited for me, perched darkly over me, like a huge insatiable bird.

"Lucy's hoping you'll find time to do some shooting with her while you're here," I said.

"Depends on if her manners have improved." Marino pushed his tray away.

"Funny, that's what she usually says about you."

He knocked a cigarette out of his pack. "You mind?"

"It doesn't matter because you're going to smoke it anyway."

29

"You never give a fella any credit, Doc." The cigarette wagged as he talked. "It's not like I haven't cut back." He fired up his lighter. "Tell the truth. You think about smoking every minute."

"You're right. Not a minute goes by that I don't wonder how I stood doing anything so unpleasant and antisocial."

"Bullshit. You miss it like hell. Right now you wish you was me." He exhaled a stream of smoke and gazed out the window. "One day this entire joint's going to end up a sinkhole because of these friggin' groundhogs."

"Why would Gault have gone to western North Carolina?" I asked.

"Why the hell would he go anywhere?" Marino's eyes got hard. "You ask any question about that son of a bitch and the answer's the same. *Because he felt like it.* And he ain't gonna stop with the Steiner girl. Some other little kid—some woman, man, hell, it don't matter—is going to be in the wrong place at the wrong time when Gault gets another itch."

"And you really think he's still there?"

He tapped an ash. "Yeah, I really think he is."

"Why?"

"Because the fun's just begun," he said as Benton Wesley walked in. "The greatest goddam show on earth and he's sitting back watching, laughing his ass off as the Black Mountain cops run around in circles trying to figure out what the hell to do. They average one homicide a year there, by the way."

30

I watched Wesley head for the salad bar. He ladled soup into a bowl, placed crackers on his tray, and dropped several dollars in a paper plate set out for customers when the cashier wasn't around. He did not indicate that he had seen us, but I knew he had a gift for taking in the smallest details of his surroundings while seeming in a fog.

"Some of Emily Steiner's physical findings make me wonder if her body was refrigerated," I said to Marino as Wesley headed toward us.

"Right. I'm sure it was. At the hospital morgue." Marino gave me an odd look.

"Sounds like I'm missing something important," Wesley said as he pulled out a chair and sat down.

"I'm contemplating that Emily Steiner's body was refrigerated before it was left at the lake," I said.

"Based on what?" A gold Department of Justice cuff link peeked out of his coat sleeve as he reached for the pepper shaker.

"Her skin was doughy and dry," I answered. "She was well preserved and virtually unmolested by insects or animals."

"That pretty much shoots down the idea of Gault staying in some tourist trap motel," Marino said. "He sure as hell didn't stash the body in his minibar."

Wesley, always meticulous, spooned clam chowder away from him and raised it to his lips without spilling a drop.

"What's been turned in for trace?" I asked.

"Her jewelry and socks," Wesley replied. "And the duct tape, which unfortunately was removed before

31

being checked for prints. It was pretty cut up at the morgue."

"Christ," Marino muttered.

"But it's distinctive enough to hold promise. In fact, I can't say I've ever seen blaze orange duct tape before." He was looking at me.

"I certainly haven't," I said. "Do your labs know anything about it yet?"

"Nothing yet except there's a pattern of grease streaks, meaning the edges of the roll the tape came from are streaked with grease. For whatever that's worth."

"What else do the labs have?" I asked.

Wesley said, "Swabs, soil from under the body, the sheet and pouch used to transport her from the lake."

My frustration grew as he continued to talk. I wondered what had been missed. I wondered what microscopic witnesses had been silenced forever.

"I'd like copies of her photographs and reports, and lab results as they come in," I said.

"Whatever's ours is yours," Wesley replied. "The labs will contact you directly."

"We got to get time of death straight," Marino said. "It ain't adding up."

"It's very important we sort that out," Wesley concurred. "Can you do some more checking?"

"I'll do what I can," I said.

"I'm supposed to be in Hogan's Alley." Marino got up from the table as he glanced at his watch. "In fact, I guess they've started without me."

"I hope you plan to change your clothes first," Wesley said to him. "Wear a sweatshirt with a hood."

"Yo. So I get dropped by heat exhaustion."

"Better than getting dropped by nine-millimeter paint bullets," Wesley said. "They hurt like hell."

"What? You two been discussing this or something?"

We watched him leave. He buttoned his blazer over his big belly, smoothed his wispy hair, rearranged his trousers as he walked. Marino had a habit of self-consciously grooming himself like a cat whenever he made an entrance or an exit.

Wesley stared at the dirty ashtray where Marino had been sitting. He turned his eyes to me, and I thought they seemed uncommonly dark, his mouth set as if it had never known how to smile.

"You've got to do something about him," he said.

"I wish I had that power, Benton."

"You're the only one who comes close to having that power."

"That's frightening."

"What's frightening is how red his face got during the consultation. He's not doing a goddam thing he's supposed to do. Fried foods, cigarettes, booze." Wesley glanced away. "Since Doris left he's gone to hell."

"I've seen some improvement," I said.

"Brief remissions." He met my eyes again. "In the main he's killing himself."

In the main, Marino was and had been all of his life. And I did not know what to do about it.

"When are you going back to Richmond?" he asked,

and I wondered what went on behind his walls. I wondered about his wife.

"That depends," I answered. "I was hoping to spend a little time with Lucy."

"She's told you we want her back?"

I stared out at sunlit grass and leaves stirring in the wind. "She's thrilled," I said.

"You're not."

"No."

"I understand. You don't want Lucy to share your reality, Kay." His face softened almost imperceptibly. "I suppose it should relieve me that in one department, at least, you are not completely rational or objective."

I was not completely rational or objective in more than one department, and Wesley knew this all too well.

"I'm not even certain what she's doing over there," I said. "How would you feel if it were one of your children?"

"The same way I always feel when it's my children. I don't want them in law enforcement or the military. I don't want them familiar with guns. And yet I want them involved in all of these things."

"Because you know what's out there," I said, my eyes again on his and lingering longer than they should.

He crumpled his napkin and placed it on his tray. "Lucy likes what she's doing. So do we."

"I'm glad to hear it."

"She's remarkable. The software she's helping us develop for VICAP is going to change everything. We're not talking about that much time before it's possible for us to track these animals around the globe. Can you imagine if Gault had murdered the Steiner girl in Australia? Do you think we'd know?"

"Chances are we wouldn't," I said. "Certainly not this soon. But we don't know it's Gault who killed her."

"What we do know is that time is more lives." He reached for my tray and stacked it on top of his.

Both of us got up from the table.

"I think we should drop in on your niece," he said.

"I don't think I'm cleared."

"You're not. But give me a little time and I'll bet I can remedy that."

"I would love it."

"Let's see, it's one o'clock now. How about meeting me back here at four-thirty?" he said as we walked out of the Boardroom.

"How's Lucy getting along in Washington, by the way?" He referred to the least-sought-after dormitory, with its tiny beds and towels too small to cover anything that mattered. "I'm sorry we couldn't have offered her more privacy."

"Don't be. It's good for her to have a roommate and suitemates, not that she necessarily gets along with them."

"Geniuses don't always work and play well with others."

"The only thing she ever flunked on her report card," I said.

* * *

35

I spent the next several hours on the phone, unsuccessfully trying to reach Dr. Jenrette, who apparently had taken the day off to play golf.

My office in Richmond, I was pleased to hear, was under control, the day's cases thus far requiring only views, which were external examinations with body fluids drawn. Blessedly, there had been no homicides from the night before, and my two court cases for the rest of the week had both settled. At the appointed time and place, Wesley and I met.

"Put this on." He handed me a special visitor's pass, which I clipped to my jacket pocket next to my faculty name tag.

"No problems?" I asked.

"It was a stretch, but I managed to pull it off."

"I'm relieved to know I passed the background check," I said ironically.

"Well, just barely."

"Thanks a lot."

He paused, then lightly touched my back as I preceded him through a doorway.

"I don't need to tell you, Kay, that nothing you see or hear at ERF leaves the building."

"You're right, Benton. You don't need to tell me."

Outside the Boardroom, the PX was packed with National Academy students in red shirts browsing at everything imaginable emblazoned with "FBI." Fit men and women politely passed us on steps as they headed to class, not a single blue shirt to be found in the color-coded crowd, for there had been no new agent classes in over a year.

We followed a long corridor to the lobby, where a digital sign above the front desk reminded guests to keep visitor's passes properly displayed. Beyond the front doors, distant gunfire peppered the perfect afternoon.

The Engineering Research Facility was three beige concrete-and-glass pods with large bay doors and high chain-link fences. Rows of parked cars bore testament to a population I never saw, for ERF seemed to swallow its employees and send them away at moments when the rest of us were unconscious.

At the front door, Wesley paused by a sensor module with a numeric keypad that was attached to the wall. He inserted his right thumb over a reading lens, which scanned his print as the data display instructed him to type in his Personal Identification Number. The biometric lock was released with a faint click.

"Obviously, you've been here before," I commented as he held the door for me.

"Many times," he said.

I was left to wonder what business typically brought him here as we followed a beige-carpeted corridor, softly lit and silent, and more than twice the length of a football field. We passed laboratories where scientists in somber suits and lab coats were busily engaged in activities I knew nothing of and could not identify at a glance. Men and women worked in cubicles and over countertops scattered with tools, hardware, video displays, and strange devices. Behind windowless double doors a power saw whined through wood.

At an elevator, Wesley's fingerprint was required

again before we could access the rarefied quiet where Lucy spent her days. The second floor was, in essence, an air-conditioned cranium enclosing an artificial brain. Walls and carpet were muted gray, space precisely partitioned like an ice cube tray. Each cubicle contained two modular desks with sleek computers, laser printers, and piles of paper. Lucy was easy to spot. She was the only analyst wearing FBI fatigues.

Her back was to us as she talked into a telephone headset, one hand manipulating a stylus over a computerized message pad, the other typing on a keyboard. If I had not known better, I might have thought she was composing music.

"No, no," she said. "One long beep followed by two short ones and we're probably talking about a malfunction with the monitor, maybe the board containing the video chips."

She swiveled around in her chair when her peripheral vision picked us up.

"Yes, it's a huge difference if it's just one short beep," she explained to the person on the line. "Now we're talking about a problem in a system board. Listen, Dave, can I get back with you?"

I noticed a biometric scanner on her desk, half buried beneath paper. On the floor and filling a shelf overhead were formidable programming manuals, boxes of diskettes and tapes, stacks of computer and software magazines, and a variety of pale blue bound publications stamped with the Department of Justice seal.

"I thought I'd show your aunt what you're up to," Wesley said.

Lucy slipped off the headset, and if she was happy to see us I could not tell.

"Right now I'm up to my ears in problems," she said. "We're getting errors on a couple four-eighty-six machines." She added for my benefit, "We're using PCs to develop the Crime Artificial Intelligence Network known as CAIN."

"*CAIN?*" I marveled. "That's a rather ironic acronym for a system designed to track violent criminals."

Wesley said, "I suppose you could look at it as the ultimate act of contrition on the part of the world's first murderer. Or maybe it simply takes one to know one."

"Basically," Lucy went on, "our ambition is for CAIN to be an automated system that models the real world as much as possible."

"In other words," I said, "it's supposed to think and act the way we do."

"Exactly." She resumed typing. "The crime analysis report you're accustomed to is right here."

Appearing on the screen were queries from the familiar fifteen-page form I had been filling out for years whenever a body was unidentified or the victim of an offender who probably had murdered before and would again.

"It's been condensed a little." Lucy brought up more pages.

"The form's never really been the problem," I pointed out. "It's getting the investigator to complete the darn thing and send it in."

"Now they'll have choices," Wesley said. "They can

have a dumb terminal in their precinct that will allow them to sit down and fill in the form on-line. Or for the true Luddite, we have paper—a bubble form or the original one, which can be sent off as usual or faxed."

"We're also working with handwriting recognition technology," Lucy went on. "Computerized message pads can be used while the investigator's in his car, the squad room, waiting around for court. And anything we get on paper—handwritten or otherwise—can be scanned into the system.

"The interactive part comes when CAIN gets a hit or needs supplementary information. He'll actually communicate with the investigator by modem, or by leaving messages in voice or by electronic mail."

"The potential's enormous," Wesley said to me.

I knew the real reason he had brought me here. This cubicle felt far removed from inner-city field offices, bank robberies, and drug busts. Wesley wanted me to believe if Lucy worked for the Bureau, she would be safe. Yet I knew better, for I understood the ambushes of the mind.

The clean pages my young niece was showing me in her pristine computer would soon carry names and physical descriptions that would make violence real. She would build a data base that would become a landfill of body parts, tortures, weapons and wounds. And one day she would hear the silent screams. She would imagine the faces of victims in crowds she passed.

"I assume what you're applying to police investigators will also have meaning for us," I said to Wesley.

"It goes without saying that medical examiners will be part of the network."

Lucy showed us more screens and elaborated on other marvels in words difficult even for me. Computers were the modern Babel, I had decided. The higher technology reached, the greater the confusion of tongues.

"That's the thing about Structure Query Language," she was explaining. "It's more declarative than navigational, meaning the user specifies *what* he wants accessed from the data base instead of *how* he wants it accessed."

I had begun watching a woman walking in our direction. She was tall, with a graceful but strong stride, a long lab coat flowing around her knees as she slowly stirred a paintbrush in a small aluminum can.

"Have we decided what we're going to run this on eventually?" Wesley continued chatting with my niece. "A mainframe?"

"Actually, the trend is toward downsized client/data base server environments. You know, minis, LANs. Everything gets smaller."

The woman turned into our cubicle, and when she looked up, her eyes went straight to mine and held for a piercing instant before shifting away.

"Was there a meeting scheduled that I didn't know about?" she said with a cool smile as she set the can on her desk. I got the distinct impression she was displeased by the intrusion.

"Carrie, we'll have to take care of our project a little later. Sorry," Lucy said. She added, "I assume you've met Benton Wesley. This is Dr. Kay Scarpetta, my aunt. And this is Carrie Grethen."

"A pleasure to meet you," Carrie Grethen said to me, and I was bothered by her eyes.

I watched her slide into her chair and absently smooth her dark brown hair, which was long and pinned back in an old-fashioned French twist. I guessed she was in her mid-thirties, her smooth skin, dark eyes, and cleanly sculpted features giving her face a patrician beauty both remarkable and rare.

As she opened a file drawer, I noted how orderly her work space was compared to my niece's, for Lucy was too far gone into her esoteric world to give much thought to where to store a book or stack paper. Despite her ancient intellect, she was very much the college kid who chewed gum and lived with clutter.

Wesley spoke. "Lucy? Why don't you show your aunt around?"

"Sure." She seemed reluctant as she exited a screen and got up.

"So, Carrie, tell me exactly what you do here," I heard him say as we walked away.

Lucy glanced back in their direction, and I was startled by the emotion flickering in her eyes.

"What you see in this section is pretty self-explanatory," she said, distracted and quite tense. "Just people and workstations."

"All of them working on VICAP?"

"There's only three of us involved with CAIN. Most of what's done up here is tactical"—she glanced back again. "You know, tactical in the sense of using computers to get a piece of equipment to operate better. Like various electronic collection devices and some of the robots Crisis Response and HRT use."

Her mind was definitely elsewhere as she led me to the far end of the floor, where there was a room secured by another biometric lock.

"Only a few of us are cleared to go in here," she said, scanning her thumb and entering her Personal Identification Number. The gunmetal-gray door opened onto a refrigerated space neatly arranged with workstations, monitors, and scores of modems with blinking lights stacked on shelves. Bundled cables running out the backs of equipment disappeared beneath the raised floor, and monitors swirling with bright blue loops and whorls boldly proclaimed "CAIN." The artificial light, like the air, was clean and cold.

"This is where all fingerprint data are stored," Lucy told me.

"From the locks?" I looked around.

"From the scanners you see everywhere for physical access control and data security."

"And is this sophisticated lock system an ERF invention?"

"We're enhancing and troubleshooting it here. In fact, right now I'm in the middle of a research project pertaining to it. There's a lot to do."

She bent over a monitor and adjusted the brightness of the screen.

"Eventually we'll also be storing fingerprint data from out in the field when cops arrest somebody and use electronic scanning to capture live fingerprints," she went on. "The offender's prints will go straight into CAIN, and if he's committed other crimes from which latent prints were recovered and scanned into the system, we'll get a hit in seconds."

"I assume this will somehow be linked to automated fingerprint identification systems around the country."

"Around the country and hopefully around the world. The point is to have all roads lead here."

"Is Carrie also assigned to CAIN?"

Lucy seemed taken aback. "Yes."

"So she's one of the three people."

"That's right."

When Lucy offered nothing further, I explained, "She struck me as unusual."

"I suppose you could say that about everybody here," my niece answered.

"Where is she from?" I persisted, for I had taken an instant dislike to Carrie Grethen. I did not know why.

"Washington State."

"Is she nice?" I asked.

"She's very good at what she does."

"That doesn't quite answer my question." I smiled.

"I try not to get into the personalities of this place. Why are you so curious?" Defensiveness crept into her tone.

"I'm curious because she made me curious," I simply said.

"Aunt Kay, I wish you'd stop being so protective.

44

Besides, it's inevitable in light of what you do professionally that you're going to think the worst about everyone."

"I see. I suppose it's also inevitable, in light of what I do professionally, that I'm going to think everyone is dead," I said dryly.

"That's ludicrous," my niece said.

"I was simply hoping you'd met some nice people here."

"I would appreciate it if you would also quit worrying about whether I have friends."

"Lucy, I'm not trying to interfere with your life. All I ask is that you're careful."

"No, that isn't all you ask. You *are* interfering."

"It is not my intention," I said, and Lucy could make me angrier than anyone I knew.

"Yes, it is. You really don't want me here."

I regretted my next words even as I said them. "Of course I do. I'm the one who got you this damn internship."

She just stared at me.

"Lucy, I'm sorry. Let's not argue. Please." I lowered my voice and placed my hand on her arm.

She pulled away. "I've got to go check on something."

To my amazement, she abruptly walked off, leaving me alone in a high-security room as arid and chilly as our encounter had become. Colors eddied on video displays, and lights and digital numbers glowed red and green as my thoughts buzzed dully like the pervasive white noise. Lucy was the only child of

45

my irresponsible only sister, Dorothy, and I had no children of my own. But my love for my niece could not be explained by just that.

I understood her secret shame born of abandonment and isolation, and wore her same suit of sorrow beneath my polished armor. When I tended to her wounds, I was tending to my own. This was something I could not tell her. I left, making certain the door was locked behind me, and it did not escape Wesley's notice when I returned from my tour without my guide. Nor did Lucy reappear in time to say good-bye.

"What happened?" Wesley asked as we walked back to the Academy.

"I'm afraid we got into another one of our disagreements," I replied.

He glanced over at me. "Someday get me to tell you about my disagreements with Michele."

"If there's a course in being a mother or an aunt, I think I need to enroll. In fact, I wish I had enrolled a long time ago. All I did was ask her if she'd made any friends here and she got angry."

"What's your worry?"

"She's a loner."

He looked puzzled. "You've alluded to this before. But to be honest, she doesn't impress me as a loner at all."

"What do you mean?"

We stopped to let several cars pass. The sun was low and warm against the back of my neck, and he had taken off his suit jacket and draped it over his arm.

He gently touched my elbow when it was safe to

46

cross. "I was at the Globe and Laurel several nights ago and Lucy was there with a friend. In fact, it may have been Carrie Grethen, but I'm really not sure. But they seemed to be having a pretty good time."

My surprise couldn't have been much more acute had Wesley just told me Lucy had hijacked a plane.

"And she's been up in the Boardroom a number of late nights. You see one side of your niece, Kay. What's always a shock to parents or parental figures is that there's another side they don't see."

"The side you're talking about is completely foreign to me," I said, and I did not feel relieved. The idea that there were elements of Lucy I did not know was only more disconcerting.

We walked in silence for a moment, and when we reached the lobby I quietly asked, "Benton, is she drinking?"

"She's old enough."

"I realize that," I said.

I was about to ask him more when my heavy preoccupations were aborted by the simple, swift action of his reaching around and snapping his pager off his belt. He held it up and frowned at the number in the display.

"Come on down to the unit," he said, "and let's see what this is about."

3

Lieutenant Hershel Mote could not keep the note of near hysteria out of his voice when Wesley returned his telephone call at twenty-nine minutes past six P.M.

"You're where?" Wesley asked him again on the speaker phone.

"In the kitchen."

"Lieutenant Mote, take it easy. Tell me exactly where you are."

"I'm in SBI Agent Max Ferguson's kitchen. I can't believe this. I've never seen nothing like this."

"Is there anybody else there?"

"It's just me here alone. Except for what's upstairs, like I told you. I've called the coroner and the dispatcher's seeing who he can raise."

"Take it easy, Lieutenant," Wesley said again with his usual unflappability.

I could hear Mote's heavy breathing.

I said to him, "Lieutenant Mote? This is Dr. Scarpetta.

48

I want you to leave everything exactly the way you found it."

"Oh, Lordy," he blurted. "I done cut him down. . . ."

"It's okay. . . ."

"When I walked in I . . . Lord have mercy, I couldn't just leave him like that."

"It's all right," I reassured him. "But it's very important that nobody touches him now."

"What about the coroner?"

"Not even him."

Wesley's eyes were on me. "We're heading out. You'll see us no later than twenty-two hundred hours. In the meantime, you sit tight."

"Yes, sir. I'm just going to sit right in this chair till my chest stops hurting."

"When did this start?" I wanted to know.

"When I got here and found him. I started having these pains in my chest."

"Have you ever had them before?"

"Not that I recollect. Not like this."

"Describe where they are," I said with growing alarm.

"Right in the middle."

"Has the pain gone to your arms or neck?"

"No, ma'am."

"Any dizziness or sweating?"

"I'm sweating a bit."

"Does it hurt when you cough?"

"I've not been coughing. So I don't reckon I can say."

"Have you ever had any heart disease or high blood pressure?"

"Not that I know of."

"And you smoke?"

"I'm doing it now."

"Lieutenant Mote, I want you to listen to me carefully. I want you to put out your cigarette and try to calm down. I'm very concerned because you've had a terrible shock, you're a smoker, and that's a setup for a coronary. You're down there and I'm up here. I want you to call an ambulance right now."

"The pain's settling down a little. And the coroner should be here any minute. He's a doctor."

"That would be Dr. Jenrette?" Wesley inquired.

"He's all we got 'round here."

"I don't want you fooling around with chest pains, Lieutenant Mote," I said firmly.

"No, ma'am, I won't."

Wesley wrote down addresses and phone numbers. He hung up and made another call.

"Is Pete Marino still running around out there?" he asked whoever had answered the phone. "Tell him we've got an urgent situation. He's to grab an overnight bag and meet us over at HRT as fast as he can get there. I'll explain when I see him."

"Look, I'd like Katz in on this one," I said as Wesley got up from his desk. "We're going to want to fume everything we can for prints, in the event things aren't the way they appear."

"Good idea."

"I doubt he'd be at The Body Farm this late. You might want to try his pager."

"Fine. I'll see if I can track him down," he said of my forensic scientist colleague from Knoxville.

When I got to the lobby fifteen minutes later, Wesley was already there, a tote bag slung over his shoulder. I had had just enough time in my room to exchange pumps for more sensible shoes, and to grab other necessities, including my medical bag.

"Dr. Katz is leaving Knoxville now," Wesley told me. "He'll meet us at the scene."

Night was settling beneath a distant slivered moon, and trees stirring in the wind sounded like rain. Wesley and I followed the drive in front of Jefferson and crossed a road dividing the Academy complex from acres of field offices and firing ranges. Closest to us, in the demilitarized zone of barbecues and picnic tables shaded by trees, I spotted a familiar figure so out of context that for an instant I thought I was mistaken. Then I recalled Lucy once mentioning to me that she sometimes wandered out here alone after dinner to think, and my heart lifted at the chance of making amends with her.

"Benton," I said, "I'll be right back."

The faint sound of conversation drifted toward me as I neared the edge of the woods, and I wondered, bizarrely, if my niece were talking to herself. Lucy was perched on top of a picnic table, and as I drew closer I was about to call her name when I saw she was speaking to someone seated below her on the bench. They were so close to each other their silhouettes were one, and I froze in the darkness of a tall, dense pine.

51

"That's because you always do that," Lucy was saying in a wounded tone I knew well.

"No, it's because you always assume I'm doing that." The woman's voice was soothing.

"Well, then, don't give me cause."

"Lucy, can't we get past this? *Please*."

"Let me have one of those."

"I wish you wouldn't start."

"I'm not starting. I just want a puff."

I heard the spurt of a match striking, and a small flame penetrated the darkness. For an instant, my niece's profile was illuminated as she leaned closer to her friend, whose face I could not see. The tip of the cigarette glowed as they passed it back and forth. I silently turned and walked away.

Wesley resumed his long strides when I got back to him. "Someone you know?" he asked.

"I thought it was," I said.

We walked without speaking past empty ranges with rows of target frames and steel silhouettes eternally standing at attention. Beyond, a control tower rose over a building constructed completely of tires, where HRT, the Bureau's Green Berets, practiced maneuvers with live ammunition. A white-and-blue Bell JetRanger waited on the nearby grass like a sleeping insect, its pilot standing outside with Marino.

"We all here?" the pilot asked as we approached.

"Yes. Thanks, Whit," Wesley said.

Whit, a perfect specimen of male fitness in a black flight suit, opened the helicopter's doors to help us board. We strapped ourselves in, Marino and I in back,

Wesley up front, and put on headsets as blades began to turn, the jet engine warming.

Minutes later, the dark earth was suddenly far beneath our feet as we rose above the horizon, air vents open and cabin lights off. Our transmitted voices blurted on and off in our ears as the helicopter sped south toward a tiny mountain town where another person was dead.

"He couldn't have been home long," Marino said. "We know . . . ?"

"He wasn't." Wesley's voice cut in from the copilot's seat. "He left Quantico right after the consultation. Flew out of National at one."

"We know what time his plane got to Asheville?"

"Around four-thirty. He could have been back to his house by five."

"In Black Mountain?"

"Right."

I spoke. "Mote found him at six."

"Jesus." Marino turned to me. "Ferguson must've started beating off the minute he hit—"

The pilot cut in, "We got music if anybody wants it."

"Sure."

"What flavor?"

"Classical."

"Shit, Benton."

"You're outvoted, Pete."

"Ferguson hadn't been home long. That much is clear no matter who or what's to blame," I resumed our jerky conversation as Berlioz began in the background.

"Looks like an accident. Like autoeroticism gone bad. But we don't know."

Marino nudged me. "Got any aspirins?"

I dug in my pocketbook in the dark, then got a mini Maglite out of my medical bag and rooted around some more. Marino muttered profanities when I motioned I could not help him, and I realized he was still in the sweatpants, hooded sweatshirt, and lace-up boots he had been wearing at Hogan's Alley. He looked like a harddrinking coach for some bush-league team, and I could not resist shining the light over incriminating red paint stains on his upper back and left shoulder. Marino had gotten shot.

"Yeah, well, you ought to see the other guys," his voice abruptly sounded in my ears. "Yo, Benton. Got any aspirins?"

"Airsick?"

"Having too much fun for that," said Marino, who hated to fly.

The weather was in our favor as we chopped a path through the clear night at around a hundred and five knots. Cars below us glided like bright-eyed waterbugs as the lights of civilization flickered like small fires in the trees. The vibrating darkness might have soothed me to sleep were my nerves not running hot. My mind would not stay still as images clashed and questions screamed.

I envisioned Lucy's face, the lovely curve of her jaw and cheek as she leaned into the flame cupped by her girlfriend's hands. Their impassioned voices sounded in my memory, and I did not know why I was stunned.

I did not know why it should matter. I wondered how much Wesley was aware. My niece had been interning at Quantico since fall semester had begun. He had seen her quite a lot more than I had.

There was not a breath of wind until we got into the mountains, and for a while the earth was a pitch-black plain.

"Going up to forty-five hundred feet," our pilot's voice sounded in our headsets. "Everybody all right back there?"

"I don't guess you can smoke in here," Marino said.

At ten past nine, the inky sky was pricked with stars, the Blue Ridge a black ocean swelling without motion or sound. We followed deep shadows of woods, smoothly turning with the pitch of blades toward a brick building that I suspected was a school. Around a corner, we found a football field with police lights flashing and flares burning copper in an unnecessary illumination of our landing zone. And the Nightsun's thirty million peak candlepower blazed down from our belly as we made our descent. At the fifty-yard line, Whit settled us softly like a bird.

"'Home of the War Horses,'" Wesley read from bunting draped along the fence. "Hope they're having a better season than we are."

Marino gazed out his window as the blades slowed down. "I haven't seen a high school football game since I was in one."

"I didn't know you played football," I remarked.

"Yo. Number twelve."

"What position?"

"Tight end."

"That figures," I said.

"This is actually Swannanoa," Whit announced. "Black Mountain's just east."

We were met by two uniformed officers from the Black Mountain Police. They looked too young to drive or carry guns, their faces pale and peculiar as they tried not to stare. It was as if we had arrived by spacecraft in a blaze of gyrating lights and unearthly quiet. They did not know what to make of us or what was happening in their town, and it was with very little conversation that they drove us away.

Moments later, we parked along a narrow street throbbing with engines and emergency lights. I counted three cruisers in addition to ours, one ambulance, two fire trucks, two unmarked cars, and a Cadillac.

"Great," Marino muttered as he shut the car door. "Everybody and his cousin Abner's here."

Crime-scene tape ran from the front porch posts to shrubbery, fanning out on either side of the beige two-story aluminum-sided house. A Ford Bronco was parked in the gravel drive ahead of an unmarked Skylark with police antennas and lights.

"The cars are Ferguson's?" Wesley asked as we mounted concrete steps.

"The ones in the drive, yes, sir," the officer replied. "That window up in the corner's where he's at."

I was dismayed when Lieutenant Hershel Mote suddenly appeared in the front doorway. Obviously, he had not followed my advice.

"How are you feeling?" I asked him.

"I'm holding on." He looked so relieved to see us I almost expected a hug. But his face was gray. Sweat ringed the collar of his denim shirt and shone on his brow and neck. He reeked of stale cigarettes.

We hesitated in the foyer, our backs to stairs that led to the second floor.

"What's been done?" Wesley asked.

"Doc Jenrette took pictures, lots of 'em, but he didn't touch nothing, just like you said. He's outside talking to the squad if you need him."

"There's a lot of cars out there," Marino said. "Where is everybody?"

"A couple of the boys are in the kitchen. And one or two's poking around the yard and in the woods out back."

"But they haven't been upstairs?"

Mote let out a deep breath. "Well, now, I'm not going to stand here and lie to you. They did go on up and look. But nobody's messed with anything, I can promise you that. The Doc's the only one who got close."

He started up the stairs. "Max is . . . he's . . . Well, goddam." He stopped and looked back at us, his eyes bright with tears.

"I'm not clear on how you discovered him," Marino said.

We resumed climbing steps as Mote struggled for composure. The floor was covered in the same dark red carpet I had seen downstairs, the heavily varnished pine paneling the color of honey.

He cleared his throat. "About six this evening I

stopped by to see if Max wanted to go out for some supper. When he didn't come to the door, I figured he was in the shower or something and came on in."

"Were you aware of anything that might have indicated he had a history of this type of activity?" Wesley delicately asked.

"No, sir," Mote said with feeling. "I can't imagine it. I sure don't understand. . . . Well, I've heard tell of people rigging up weird things. I can't say I know what it's for."

"The point of using a noose while masturbating is to place pressure on the carotids," I explained. "This constricts the flow of oxygen and blood to the brain, which supposedly enhances orgasm."

"Also known as going while you're coming," Marino remarked with his typical subtlety.

Mote did not accompany us as we moved forward to a lighted doorway at the end of the hall.

SBI Agent Max Ferguson had a manly, modest bedroom with pine chests of drawers and a rack filled with shotguns and rifles over a rolltop desk. His pistol, wallet, credentials, and a box of Rough Rider condoms were on the table by the quilt-covered bed, the suit I'd seen him wearing in Quantico this morning neatly draped over a chair, shoes and socks nearby.

A wooden bar stool stood between the bathroom and closet, inches from where his body was covered with a colorful crocheted afghan. Overhead, a severed nylon cord dangled from an eye hook screwed into the wooden ceiling. I got gloves and a thermometer out of my medical bag. Marino swore under his breath as

I pulled the afghan back from what must have been Ferguson's worst nightmare. I doubted he would have feared a bullet half as much.

He was on his back, the size-D cups of a long-line black brassiere stuffed with socks that smelled faintly of musk. The pair of black nylon panties he had put on before he died had been pulled down around his hairy knees, and a condom still clung limply to his penis. Magazines nearby revealed his predilection for women in bondage with spectacularly augmented breasts and nipples the size of saucers.

I examined the nylon noose tightly angled around the towel padding his neck. The cord, old and fuzzy, had been severed just above the eighth turn of a perfect hangman's knot. His eyes were almost shut, his tongue protruding.

"Is this consistent with him sitting on the stool?" Marino looked up at the segment of rope attached to the ceiling.

"Yes," I said.

"So he was beating off and slipped?"

"Or he may have lost consciousness and then slipped," I answered.

Marino moved to the window and leaned over a tumbler of amber liquid on the sill. "Bourbon," he announced. "Straight or close to it."

The rectal temperature was 91 degrees, consistent with what I would have expected had Ferguson been dead approximately five hours in this room, his body covered. Rigor mortis had started in the

59

small muscles. The condom was a studded affair with a large reservoir that was dry, and I went over to the bed to take a look at the box. One condom was missing, and when I stepped into the master bathroom I found the purple foil wrapper in the wicker trash basket.

"That's interesting," I said as Marino opened dresser drawers.

"What is?"

"I guess I assumed he would have put on the condom while he was rigged up."

"Makes sense to me."

"Then wouldn't you expect the wrapper to be near his body?" I picked it out of the trash, touching as little of it as possible, and placed it inside a plastic bag.

When Marino didn't respond, I added, "Well, I guess it all depends on when he pulled down his panties. Maybe he did that before he put the noose around his neck."

I walked back into the bedroom. Marino was squatting by a chest of drawers, staring at the body, a mixture of incredulity and disgust on his face.

"And I always thought the worst thing that could happen is you croak on the john," he said.

I looked up at the eye bolt in the ceiling. There was no way to tell how long it had been there. I started to ask Marino if he had found any other pornography when we were startled by a heavy thud in the hallway.

"What the hell . . . ?" Marino exclaimed.

He was out the door, and I was right behind him.

Lieutenant Mote had collapsed near the stairs. He was facedown and motionless on the carpet. When I knelt beside him and turned him over, he was already blue.

"He's in cardiac arrest! Get the squad!" I pulled Mote's jaw forward to make sure his airway was unobstructed.

Marino's feet thundered down the stairs as I placed my fingers on Mote's carotid and felt no pulse. I thumped his chest but his heart would not answer. I began CPR, compressing his chest once, twice, three times, four, then tilted his head back and blew once into his mouth. His chest rose, and one-two-three-four I blew again.

I maintained a rhythm of sixty compressions per minute as sweat rolled down my temples and my own pulse roared. My arms ached and were becoming as unwilling as stone when I began the third minute and the noise of paramedics and police swelled up from the stairs. Someone gripped my elbow and guided me out of the way as many pairs of gloved hands slapped on leads, hung a bottle of IV fluid, and started a line. Voices barked orders and announced every activity in the loud dispassion of rescue efforts and emergency rooms.

As I leaned against the wall and tried to catch my breath, I noticed a short, fair young man incongruously dressed for golf watching the activity from the landing. After several glances in my direction, he approached me shyly.

61

"Dr. Scarpetta?"

His earnest face was sunburned below his brow, which obviously had been spared by a cap. It occurred to me that he probably belonged to the Cadillac parked out front.

"Yes?"

"James Jenrette," he said, confirming my suspicions. "Are you all right?" He withdrew a neatly folded handkerchief and offered it to me.

"I'm doing okay, and I'm very glad you're here," I said sincerely, for I could not turn over my latest patient to someone who was not an M.D. "Can I entrust Lieutenant Mote to your care?" My arms trembled as I wiped my face and neck.

"Absolutely. I'll go with him to the hospital." Jenrette next handed me his card. "If you have any other questions tonight, just page me."

"You'll be posting Ferguson in the morning?" I asked.

"Yes. You're welcome to assist. Then we'll talk about all this." He looked down the hall.

"I'll be there. Thank you." I managed a smile.

Jenrette followed the stretcher out, and I returned to the bedroom at the end of the hall. From the window, I watched lights pulse blood red on the street below as Mote was placed inside the ambulance. I wondered if he would live. I sensed the presence of Ferguson in his flaccid condom and stiff brassiere, and none of it seemed real.

The tailgate slammed. Sirens whelped as if in protest before they began to scream. I was not aware that

Marino had walked into the room until he touched my arm.

"Katz is downstairs," he informed me.

I slowly turned around. "We'll need another squad," I said.

4

It had long been a theoretical possibility that latent fingerprints could be left on human skin. But the likelihood of recovering them had been so remote as to discourage most of us from trying.

Skin is a difficult surface, for it is plastic and porous, and its moisture, hairs, and oils interfere. On the uncommon occasion that a print is successfully transferred from assailant to victim, the ridge detail is far too fragile to survive much time or exposure to the elements.

Dr. Thomas Katz was a master forensic scientist who had maniacally pursued this elusive evidence for most of his career. He also was an expert in time of death, which he researched just as diligently with ways and means that were not commonly known to the hoi polloi. His laboratory was called The Body Farm, and I had been there many times.

He was a small man with prepossessed blue eyes, a great shock of white hair, and a face amazingly benevolent for the atrocities he had seen. When I met him at the top of the stairs, he was carrying a box window fan, a tool chest, and what looked like a section of vacuum cleaner hose with several odd attachments. Marino was behind him with the rest of what Katz called his "Cyanoacrylate Blowing Contraption," a double-decker aluminum box fitted with a hot plate and a computer fan. He had spent hundreds of hours in his East Tennessee garage perfecting this rather simple mechanical implement.

"Where are we heading?" Katz asked me.

"The room at the end of the hall." I relieved him of the window fan. "How was your trip?"

"More traffic than I bargained for. Tell me what all's been done to the body."

"He was cut down and covered with a wool afghan. I have not examined him."

"I promise not to delay you too much. It's a lot easier now that I'm not bothering with a tent."

"What do you mean, *a tent*?" Marino frowned as we entered the bedroom.

"I used to put a plastic tent over the body and do the fuming inside it. But too much vapor and the skin gets too frosted. Dr. Scarpetta, you can set the fan in that window." Katz looked around. "I might have to use a pan of water. It's a bit dry in here."

I gave him as much history as we had at this point.

"Do you have any reason to think this is something other than an accidental autoerotic asphyxiation?" he asked.

"Other than the circumstances," I replied, "no."

"He was working that little Steiner girl's case."

"That's what we mean by circumstances," Marino said.

"Lord, if that hasn't been in the news all over."

"We were in Quantico this morning meeting about that case," I added.

"And he comes straight home and then this." Katz looked thoughtfully at the body. "You know, we found a prostitute in a Dumpster the other week and got a good outline of a hand on her ankle. She'd been dead four or five days."

"Kay?" Wesley stepped into the doorway. "May I see you for a minute?"

"And you used this thing on her?" Marino's voice followed us into the hall.

"I did. She had painted fingernails, and as it turns out, they're real good, too."

"For what?"

"Prints."

"Where does this go?"

"Doesn't matter much. I'm going to fume the entire room. I'm afraid it's going to mess up the place."

"I don't think he's gonna complain."

Downstairs in the kitchen, I noticed a chair by the phone where I supposed Mote had sat for hours waiting for us to arrive. Nearby on the floor was a glass of water and an ashtray crammed with cigarette butts.

"Take a look," said Wesley, who was accustomed to searching for odd evidence in odd places.

He had filled the double sink with foods he had

gotten out of the freezer. I moved closer to him as he opened the folds of a small, flat package wrapped in white freezer paper. Inside were shrunken pieces of frozen flesh, dry at the edges and reminiscent of yellowed waxy parchment.

"Any chance I'm thinking the wrong thing?" Wesley's tone was grim.

"Good God, Benton," I said, stunned.

"They were in the freezer on top of these other things. Ground beef, pork chops, pizza." He nudged packages with a gloved finger. "I was hoping you'd tell me it's chicken skin. Maybe something he uses for fish bait or who knows what."

"There are no feather holes, and the hair is fine like human hair."

He was silent.

"We need to pack this in dry ice and fly it back with us," I said.

"That won't be tonight."

"The sooner we can get immunological testing done, the sooner we can confirm it's human. DNA will confirm identity."

He returned the package to the freezer. "We need to check for prints."

"I'll put the tissue in plastic and we'll submit the freezer paper to the labs," I said.

"Good."

We climbed the stairs. My pulse would not slow down. At the end of the hallway, Marino and Katz stood outside the shut door. They had threaded a hose through the hole where the doorknob had been, the contraption humming as it pumped Super Glue vapors into Ferguson's bedroom.

Wesley had yet to mention the obvious, so finally I did. "Benton, I didn't see any bite marks or anything else someone may have tried to eradicate."

"I know," he said.

"We're almost done," Katz told us when we got to them. "A room this size and you can get by with less than a hundred drops of Super Glue."

"Pete," Wesley said, "we've got an unexpected problem."

"I thought we'd already reached our quota for the day," he said, staring blandly at the hose pumping poison beyond the door.

"That should do it," said Katz, who was typically impervious to the moods of those around him. "All I got to do now is clear out the fumes with the fan. That will take a minute or two."

He opened the door and we backed away. The overpowering smell didn't seem to bother him in the least.

"He probably gets high off the stuff," Marino muttered as Katz walked into the room.

"Ferguson's got what appears to be human skin in his freezer." Wesley went straight to the point.

"You want to run that one by me again?" Marino said, startled.

"I don't know what we're dealing with here," Wesley added as the window fan inside the room began to whir. "But we got one detective dead with incriminating evidence found with his frozen hamburgers and pizza. We got another detective with a heart attack. We've got a murdered eleven-year-old girl."

"Goddam," Marino said, his face turning red.

"I hope you brought enough clothes to stay for a while," Wesley added to both of us.

"Goddam," Marino said again. "That son of a bitch."

He looked straight at me and I knew exactly what he was thinking. A part of me hoped he was wrong. But if Gault wasn't playing his usual malignant games, I wasn't certain the alternative was better.

"Does this house have a basement?" I asked.

"Yes," Wesley answered.

"What about a big refrigerator?" I asked.

"I haven't seen one. But I haven't been in the basement."

Inside the bedroom, Katz turned off the window fan. He motioned to us that it was all right to come in.

"Man, try getting this shit off," Marino said as he looked around.

Super Glue dries white and is as stubborn as cement. Every surface in the room was lightly frosted with it, including Ferguson's body. With flashlight angled, Katz sidelighted smudges on walls, furniture, windowsills, and the guns over the desk. But it was just one he found that brought him to his knees.

"It's the nylon," our friendly mad scientist said with pure delight as he knelt by the body and leaned close to Ferguson's pulled-down panties. "You know, it's a good surface for prints because of the tight weave. He's got some kind of perfume on."

He slipped the plastic sheath off his Magna brush, and the bristles fell open like a sea anemone. Unscrewing the lid from a jar of Delta Orange magnetic powder, Katz dusted a very good latent print that someone had left on the dead detective's shiny black nylon panties. Partial prints had materialized around Ferguson's neck, and Katz used contrasting black powder on them. But there wasn't enough ridge detail to matter. The strange frost everywhere I looked made the room seem cold.

"Of course, this print on his panties is probably his own," Katz mused as he continued to work. "From when he pulled them down. He might have had something on his hands. The condom's probably lubricated, for example, and if some of that transferred to his fingers, he could have left a good print. You're going to want to take these?" He referred to the panties.

"I'm afraid so," I said.

He nodded. "That's all right. Pictures will do." He got out his camera. "But I'd like the panties when you're finished with them. As long as you don't use scissors, the print will hold up fine. That's the good thing about Super Glue. Can't get it off with dynamite."

"How much more do you need to do here tonight?" Wesley said to me, and I could tell he was anxious to leave.

"I want to look for anything that might not survive the body's transport, and take care of what you found in the freezer," I said. "Plus we need to check the basement."

He nodded and said to Marino, "While we take care

of these things, how about your being in charge of securing this place?"

Marino didn't seem thrilled with the assignment.

"Tell them we'll need security around the clock," Wesley added firmly.

"Problem is, they don't got enough uniforms in this town to do anything around the clock," Marino said sourly as he walked off. "The damn bastard's just wiped out half the police department."

Katz looked up and spoke, his Magna brush poised midair. "Seems like you're pretty certain who you're looking for."

"Nothing's certain," Wesley said.

"Thomas, I'm going to have to ask for another favor," I said to my dedicated colleague. "I need you and Dr. Shade to run an experiment for me at The Farm."

"*Dr. Shade?*" Wesley said.

"Lyall Shade is an anthropologist at the University of Tennessee," I explained.

"When do we start?" Katz loaded a new roll of film into his camera.

"Immediately, if possible. It will take a week."

"Fresh bodies or old?"

"Fresh."

"That really is the guy's name?" Wesley went on.

It was Katz who answered as he took a photograph. "Sure is. Spelled L-Y-A-L-L. Goes all the way back to his great-grandfather, a surgeon in the Civil War."

5

Max Ferguson's basement was accessible by concrete steps in back of his house, and I could tell by dead leaves drifted against them that no one had been here for a while. But I could be no more exact than that, for fall had peaked in the mountains. Even as Wesley tried the door, leaves spiraled down without a sound as if the stars were shedding ashes.

"I'm going to have to break the glass," he said, jiggling the knob some more as I held a flashlight.

Reaching inside his jacket, he withdrew the Sig Sauer nine-millimeter pistol from its shoulder holster and sharply tapped the butt against a large pane in the center of the door. The noise of glass shattering startled me even though I was prepared for it, and I half expected police to rapidly materialize from the dark. But no footfall or human voice was carried on the wind, and I imagined the existentialist terror Emily Steiner must have felt before she died. No matter where that might have been, no one

72

had heard her smallest cry, no one had come to save her.

Tiny glass teeth left in the mullion sparkled as Wesley carefully put his arm through the opening and found the inside knob.

"Damn," he said, pushing against the door. "The latch bolt must be rusted."

Working his arm in farther to get a better grip, he was straining against the stubborn lock when suddenly it gave. The door flew open with such force that Wesley spilled into the opening, knocking the flashlight out of my hand. It bounced, rolled, and was extinguished by concrete as I was hit by a wall of cold, foul air. In complete darkness, I heard broken glass scrape as Wesley moved.

"Are you all right?" I blindly inched forward, hands held out in front of me. *"Benton?"*

"Jesus." He sounded shaky as he got to his feet.

"Are you okay?"

"Damn, I can't believe this." His voice moved farther away from me.

Glass crunched as he groped along the wall, and what sounded like an empty paint bucket clanged dully as he knocked it with his foot. I squinted when a naked bulb went on overhead, my eyes adjusting to a vision of Benton Wesley dirty and dripping blood.

"Let me see." I gently took hold of his left wrist as he scanned our surroundings, rather dazed. "Benton, we need to get you to a hospital," I said as I examined multiple lacerations on his palm. "You've got glass embedded in several of these cuts, and you're going to need stitches."

"You're a doctor." The handkerchief he wrapped around his hand instantly turned red.

"You need a hospital," I repeated as I noticed blood spreading darkly through the torn fabric of his left trouser leg.

"I hate hospitals." Behind his stoicism, pain smoldered in his eyes like fever. "Let's look around and get out of this hole. I promise not to bleed to death in the meantime."

I wondered where the hell Marino was.

It did not appear that SBI Agent Ferguson had entered his basement in years. Nor did I see any reason why he should have unless he had a penchant for dust, cobwebs, rusting garden tools, and rotting carpet. Water stained the concrete floor and cinderblock walls, and body parts of crickets told me that legions had lived and died down here. As we wandered corner to corner, we saw nothing to make us suspicious that Emily Steiner had ever been a visitor.

"I've seen enough," said Wesley, whose bright red trail on the dusty floor had come full circle.

"Benton, we've got to do something about your bleeding."

"What do you suggest?"

"Look that way for a moment." I directed him to turn his back to me.

He did not question why as he complied, and I quickly stepped out of my shoes and hiked up my skirt. In seconds, I had my panty hose off.

"Okay. Let me have your arm," I told him next.

I tucked it snugly between my elbow and side as any physician in similar circumstances might. But as I wrapped the panty hose around his injured hand, I could feel his eyes on me. I became intensely aware of his breath touching my hair as his arm touched my breast, and a heat so palpable I feared he felt it, too, spread up my neck. Amazed and completely flustered, I quickly finished my improvised dressing of his wounds and backed away.

"That should hold you until we can get to a place where I can do something more serious." I avoided his eyes.

"Thank you, Kay."

"I suppose I should ask where we're going next," I went on in a bland tone that belied my agitation. "Unless you're planning on our sleeping in the helicopter."

"I put Pete in charge of accommodations."

"You do live dangerously."

"Usually not this dangerously." He flipped off the light and made no attempt to relock the basement door.

The moon was a gold coin cut in half, the sky around it midnight blue, and through branches of far-off trees peeked the lights of Ferguson's neighbors. I wondered if any of them knew he was dead. On the street, we found Marino in the front seat of a Black Mountain Police cruiser, smoking a cigarette, a map spread open in his lap. The interior light was on, the young officer behind the wheel no more relaxed than he had seemed hours earlier when he had picked us up at the football field.

"What the hell happened to you?" Marino said to Wesley. "You decide to punch out a window?"

"More or less," Wesley replied.

Marino's eyes wandered from Wesley's panty-hose bandage to my bare legs. "Well, well, now ain't that something," he muttered. "I wish they'd taught that when I was taking CPR."

"Where are our bags?" I ignored him.

"They're in the trunk, ma'am," said the officer.

"Officer T. C. Baird here's going to be a Good Samaritan and drop us by the Travel-Eze, where yours truly's already taken care of reservations," Marino went on in the same irritating tone. "Three deluxe rooms at thirty-nine ninety-nine a pop. I got us a discount because we're cops."

"I'm not a cop." I looked hard at him.

Marino flicked his cigarette butt out the window. "Take it easy, Doc. On a good day, you could pass for one."

"On a good day, so can you," I answered him.

"I think I've just been insulted."

"No, I'm the one who's just been insulted. You know better than to misrepresent me for discounts or any other reason," I said, for I was an appointed government official bound by very clear rules. Marino knew damn well that I could not afford the slightest compromise of scrupulosity, for I had enemies. I had many of them.

Wesley opened the cruiser's back door. "After you,"

he quietly said to me. Of Officer Baird he asked, "Do we know anything further about Mote?"

"He's in intensive care, sir."

"What about his condition?"

"It doesn't sound too good, sir. Not at this time."

Wesley climbed in next to me, delicately resting his bandaged hand on his thigh. He said, "Pete, we've got a lot of people to talk to around here."

"Yeah, well, while you two was playing doctor in the basement, I was already working on that." Marino held up a notepad and flipped through pages scribbled with illegible notes.

"Are we ready to go?" Baird asked.

"More than ready," Wesley answered, and he was losing patience with Marino, too.

The interior light went off and the car moved forward. For a while, Marino, Wesley, and I talked as if the young officer wasn't there as we passed over unfamiliar dark streets, cool mountain air blowing through barely opened windows. We sketched out our strategy for tomorrow morning. I would assist Dr. Jenrette with the autopsy of Max Ferguson while Marino talked to Emily Steiner's mother. Wesley would fly back to Quantico with the tissue from Ferguson's freezer, and the results of these activities would determine what we did next.

It was almost two A.M. when we spotted the Travel-Eze Motel ahead of us on U.S. 70, its sign neon yellow against the rolling dark horizon. I couldn't have been happier had our quarters been a Four Seasons, until we were informed at the registration desk that the restaurant had closed, room service had ended, and there was no bar. In fact, the clerk advised in his North Carolina accent, at this hour we would be better off looking forward to breakfast instead of looking back at the dinner we had missed.

"You got to be kidding," Marino said, thunder gathering in his face. "If I don't get something to eat my gut's going to turn inside out."

"I'm mighty sorry, sir." The clerk was but a boy with rosy cheeks and hair almost as yellow as the motel's sign. "But the good news is there's vending machines on each floor." He pointed. "And a Mr. Zip no more'n a mile from here."

"Our ride just left." Marino glared at him. "What? I'm supposed to walk a mile at this hour to some joint called *Mr. Zip*?"

The clerk's smile froze, fear shining in his eyes like tiny candles as he looked to Wesley and me for reassurance. But we were too worn out to be much help. When Wesley rested his bloody panty-hose wrapped hand on the counter, the lad's expression turned to horror.

"Sir! Do you need a doctor?" His voice went up an octave and cracked.

"Just my room key will be fine," Wesley replied.

The clerk turned around and nervously lifted three keys from their consecutive hooks, dropping two of them to the carpet. He stooped to pick them up and dropped one of them again. At last, he presented them to us, the room numbers stamped on the attached plastic medallions big enough to read at twenty paces.

"You ever heard of security in this joint?" Marino said as if he had hated the boy since birth. "You're supposed

78

to write the room number on a piece of paper which you *privately* slip to the guest so every drone can't see where he keeps the wife and Rolex. In case you ain't keeping up with the news, you had a murder real close to here just a couple weeks back."

In speechless bewilderment the clerk watched Marino next hold up his key as if it were a piece of incriminating evidence.

"No minibar key? Meaning forget having a drink in the room at this hour, too?" Marino raised his voice some more. "Never mind. I don't want no more bad news."

As we followed a sidewalk to the middle of the small motel, TV screens flickered blue and shadows moved behind filmy curtains over plate-glass windows. Alternating red and green doors reminded me of the plastic hotels and homes of Monopoly as we climbed stairs to the second floor and found our rooms. Mine was neatly made and cozy, the television bolted to the wall, water glasses and ice bucket wrapped in sanitary plastic.

Marino repaired to his quarters without bidding us good-night, shutting his door just a little too hard.

"What the hell's eating him?" Wesley asked as he followed me into my room.

I did not want to talk about Marino, and pulling a chair close to one of the double beds, I said, "Before I do anything we need to clean you up."

"Not without painkiller."

Wesley went out to fill the ice bucket and removed a fifth of Dewar's from his tote bag. He fixed drinks while I spread a towel on the bed and arranged it with forceps, packets of Betadine, and 5-O nylon sutures.

"This is going to hurt, isn't it." He looked at me as he took a big swallow of Scotch.

I put on my glasses and replied, "It's going to hurt like hell. Follow me." I headed into the bathroom.

For the next several minutes, we stood side by side at the sink while I washed his wounds with warm soapy water. I was as gentle as possible and he did not complain, but I could feel him flinch in the small muscles of his hand. When I glanced at his face in the mirror, he was perspiring and pale. He had five gaping lacerations in his palm.

"You're just lucky you missed your radial artery," I said.

"I can't tell you how lucky I feel."

Looking at his knee, I added, "Sit here." I lowered the toilet lid.

"Do you want me to take my pants off?"

"Either that or we cut them."

He sat down. "They're ruined anyway."

With a scalpel, I sliced through the fine wool fabric of his left trouser leg while he sat very still, his leg fully extended. The cut on his knee was deep, and I shaved around it and washed it thoroughly, placing towels on the floor to blot bloody water dripping everywhere. As I led Wesley back into the bedroom, he limped over to the bottle of Scotch and refilled his glass.

"And by the way," I told him, "I appreciate the thought, but I don't drink before surgery."

"I guess I should be grateful," he answered.

"Yes, you should be."

He seated himself on the bed, and I took the chair, moving it close. I tore open foil packets of Betadine and began to swipe his wounds.

"Jesus," he said under his breath. "What is that, battery acid?"

"It's a topical antibacterial iodine."

"You keep that in your medical bag?"

"Yes."

"I didn't realize first aid was an option for most of your patients."

"Sadly, it isn't. But I never know when I might need it." I reached for the forceps. "Or when someone else at a scene might—like you." I withdrew a sliver of glass and placed it on the towel. "I know this may come as a great shock to you, Special Agent Wesley, but I started out my career with living patients."

"And when did they start dying on you?"

"Immediately."

He tensed as I extracted a very small sliver.

"Hold still," I said.

"So what's Marino's problem? He's been a total ass lately."

I placed two more slivers of glass on the towel and stanched the bleeding with gauze. "You'd better take another swallow of your drink."

"Why?"

"I've gotten all of the glass."

"So you're finished and we're celebrating." He sounded the most relieved I had ever heard him.

"Not quite." I leaned close to his hand, satisfied that

I had not missed anything. Then I opened a suture packet.

"Without Novocain?" he protested.

"As few stitches as you need to close these cuts, numbing you would hurt as much as the needle," I calmly explained, gripping the needle with the forceps.

"I'd still prefer Novocain."

"Well, I don't have any. It might be better if you don't look. Would you like me to turn on the TV?"

Wesley stoically stared away from me as he answered between clenched teeth, "Just get it over with."

He did not utter a protest while I worked, but as I touched his hand and leg I could feel him tremble. He took a deep breath and began to relax when I dressed his wounds with Neosporin and gauze.

"You're a good patient." I patted his shoulder as I got up.

"Not according to my wife."

I could not remember the last time he had referred to Connie by name. On the rare occasion he mentioned her at all, it was a fleeting allusion to a force he seemed conscious of, like gravity.

"Let's sit outside and finish our drinks," he said.

The balcony beyond my room door was a public one that stretched the entire length of the second floor. At this hour the few guests who might have been awake were too far away to hear our conversation. Wesley arranged two plastic chairs close together. We had no table between us, so he set our drinks and bottle of Scotch on the floor.

"Do you want more ice?" he asked.

"This is fine."

He had turned off lamps inside the room, and beyond us the barely discernible shapes of trees began to move in concert the longer I stared at them. Headlights were small and sporadic along the distant highway.

"On a scale of one to ten, how awful would you rank this day?" he spoke quietly in the dark.

I hesitated, for I had known many awful days in my career. "I suppose I'd give it a seven."

"Assuming ten's the worst."

"I have yet to have a ten."

"What would that be?" I felt him look at me.

"I'm not sure," I said, superstitious that naming the worst might somehow manifest it.

He fell silent and I wondered if he was thinking about the man who had been my lover and his best friend. When Mark had been killed in London several years before, I had believed there could be no pain worse than that. Now I feared I was wrong.

Wesley said, "You never answered my question, Kay."

"I told you I wasn't sure."

"Not that question. I'm talking about Marino now. I asked you what his problem is."

"I think he's very unhappy," I answered.

"He's always been unhappy."

"I said *very*."

He waited.

"Marino doesn't like change," I added.

"His promotion?"

83

"That and what's going on with me."

"Which is?" Wesley poured more Scotch into our glasses, his arm brushing against me.

"My position with your unit is a significant change."

He did not agree or disagree but waited for me to say more.

"I think he somehow perceives that I've shifted my alliances." I realized I was getting only more vague. "And that is unsettling. Unsettling for Marino, I mean."

Still, Wesley offered no opinion, ice cubes softly rattling as he sipped his drink. We both knew very well what part of Marino's problem was, but it was nothing that Wesley and I had done. Rather, it was something Marino sensed.

"It's my opinion that Marino's very frustrated with his personal life," Wesley said. "He's lonely."

"I believe both of those things are true," I said.

"You know, he was with Doris for thirty-some years and then suddenly finds himself single again. He's clueless, has no idea how to go about it."

"Nor has he ever really dealt with her leaving. It's stored up. Waiting to be ignited by something unrelated."

"I've worried about that. I've worried about what that something unrelated might be."

"He still misses her. I believe he still loves her," I said, and the hour and the alcohol made me feel sad for Marino. I rarely could stay angry with him long.

Wesley shifted his position in his chair. "I guess that would be a ten. At least for me."

"To have Connie leave you?" I looked over at him.

"To lose someone you're in love with. To lose a child you're at war with. To not have closure." He stared straight ahead, his sharp profile softly backlit by the moon. "Maybe I'm kidding myself, but I think I could take almost anything as long as there's resolution, an ending, so I can be free of the past."

"We are never free of that."

"I agree that we aren't entirely." He continued staring ahead when he next said, "Marino has feelings for you that he can't handle, Kay. I think he always has."

"They're best left unacknowledged."

"That sounds somewhat cold."

"I don't mean it coldly," I said. "I would never want him to feel rejected."

"What makes you assume he doesn't already feel that way?"

"I'm not assuming he doesn't." I sighed. "In fact, I'm fairly certain he's feeling pretty frustrated these days."

"Actually, *jealous* is the word that comes to mind."

"Of you."

"Has he ever tried to ask you out?" Wesley went on as if he had not heard what I just said.

"He took me to the Policeman's Ball."

"Umm. That's pretty serious."

"Benton, let's not joke about him."

"I wasn't joking," he said gently. "I care very much about his feelings and I know you do." He paused. "In fact, I understand his feelings very well."

85

"I understand them, too."

Wesley set down his drink.

"I guess I should go in and try to get at least a couple hours' sleep," I decided without moving.

He reached over and placed his good hand on my wrist, his fingers cool from holding his glass. "Whit will fly me out of here when the sun is up."

I wanted to take his hand in mine. I wanted to touch his face.

"I'm sorry to leave you."

"All I need is a car," I said as my heart beat harder.

"I wonder where you rent one around here. The airport, maybe?"

"I guess that's why you're an FBI agent. You can figure out things like that."

His fingers worked their way down to my hand and he began to stroke it with his thumb. I had always known our path one day would lead to this. When he had asked me to serve as his consultant at Quantico, I had been aware of the danger. I could have said no.

"Are you in much pain?" I asked him.

"I will be in the morning, because I'm going to have a hangover."

"It is the morning."

I leaned back and shut my eyes as he touched my hair. I felt his face move closer as he traced the contours of my throat with his fingers, then his lips. He touched me as if he had always wanted to, while darkness swept in from the far reaches of my brain and light danced across my blood. Our kisses were stolen like fire. I knew I had found the unforgivable sin I had never been able to name, but did not care.

We left our clothes where they landed and went to bed. We were tender with his wounds but not deterred by them, and made love until dawn began to catch around the horizon's edge. Afterward I sat on the porch watching the sun spill over the mountains, coloring the leaves. I imagined his helicopter lifting and turning like a dancer in air.

6

In the center of downtown, across the street from the Exxon station, was Black Mountain Chevrolet, where Officer Baird delivered Marino and me at 7:45 A.M.

Apparently, the local police had been spreading word throughout the business community that the "Feds" had arrived and were staying "under cover" at the Travel-Eze. Though I did not feel quite the celebrity, neither did I feel anonymous when we drove off in a new silver Caprice while it seemed that everyone who had ever thought of working for the dealership stood outside the showroom and watched.

"I heard some guy call you *Quincy*," Marino said as he opened a steak biscuit from Hardee's.

"I've been called worse. Do you have any idea how much sodium and fat you're ingesting right now?"

"Yeah. About one third of what I'm going to ingest. I got three biscuits here, and I plan to eat every damn one of them. In case you've got a problem with your short-term memory, I missed dinner last night."

"You don't need to be rude."

"When I miss food and sleep, I get rude."

I did not volunteer that I had gotten less sleep than Marino, but I suspected he knew. He would not look me in the eye this morning, and I sensed that beneath his irritability he was very depressed.

"I didn't sleep worth a damn," he went on. "The acoustics in that joint suck."

I pulled down the visor as if that somehow would alleviate my discomfort, then turned the radio on and switched stations until I landed on Bonnie Raitt. Marino's rental car was being equipped with a police radio and scanner and would not be ready until the end of the day. I was to drop him off at Denesa Steiner's house and someone would pick him up later. I drove while he ate and gave directions.

"Slow down," he said, looking at a map. "This should be Laurel coming up on our left. Okay, you're going to want to hang a right at the next one."

We turned again to discover a lake directly ahead of us that was no bigger than a football field and the color of moss. Its picnic areas and tennis courts were deserted, and it did not appear that the neatly maintained clubhouse was currently in use. The shore was lined with trees beginning to brown with the wane of fall, and I imagined a little girl with guitar case in hand heading home in the deepening shadows. I imagined an old man fishing on a morning like this and his shock at what he found in the brush.

"I want to come out here later and walk around," I said.

"Turn here," Marino said. "Her house is at the next corner."

"Where is Emily buried?"

"About two miles over that way." He pointed east. "In the church cemetery."

"This is the church where her meeting was?"

"Third Presbyterian. If you view the lake area as being sort of like the Washington Mall, you got the church at one end and the Steiner crib at the other with about two miles in between."

I recognized the ranch-style house from the photographs I had reviewed at Quantico yesterday morning. It seemed smaller, as so many edifices do when you finally see them in life. Situated on a rise far back from the street, it was nestled on a lot thick with rhododendrons, laurels, sourwoods, and pines.

The gravel sidewalk and front porch had been recently swept, and clustered at the edge of the driveway were bulging bags of leaves. Denesa Steiner owned a green Infiniti sedan that was new and expensive, and this rather surprised me. I caught a glimpse of her arm in a long black sleeve holding the screen door for Marino as I drove away.

The morgue in Asheville Memorial Hospital was not unlike most I had seen. Located in the lowest level, it was a small bleak room of tile and stainless steel with but one autopsy table that Dr. Jenrette had rolled close to a sink. He was making the Y incision on Ferguson's body when I arrived at shortly after nine. As blood became exposed to air, I detected the sickening sweet odor of alcohol.

"Good morning, Dr. Scarpetta," Jenrette said, and he seemed pleased to see me. "Greens and gloves are in the cabinet over there."

I thanked him, though I would not need them, for the young doctor would not need me. I expected this autopsy to be all about finding nothing, and as I looked closely at Ferguson's neck, I got my first validation. The reddish pressure marks I had observed late last night were gone, and we would find no deep injury to underlying tissue and muscle. As I watched Jenrette work, I was humbly reminded that pathology is never a substitute for investigation. In fact, were we not privy to the circumstances, we would have no idea why Ferguson had died, except that he had not been shot, stabbed, or beaten, nor had he succumbed to some disease.

"I guess you noticed the way the socks smell that he had stuffed in his bra," Jenrette said as he worked. "I'm wondering if you found anything to correspond with that, like a bottle of perfume, some sort of cologne?"

He lifted out the block of organs. Ferguson had a mildly fatty liver.

"No, we didn't," I replied. "And I might add that fragrances are generally used in scenarios like this when there's more than one person involved."

Jenrette glanced up at me. "Why?"

"Why bother if you're alone?"

"I guess that makes sense." He emptied the stomach contents into a carton. "Just a little bit of brownish fluid," he added. "Maybe a few nutlike particles. You say he flew back to Asheville not long before he was found?"

"That's right."

"So maybe he ate peanuts on the plane. And drank. His STAT alcohol's point one-four."

"He probably also drank when he got home," I said, recalling the glass of bourbon in the bedroom.

"Now, when you talk about there being more than one person in some of these situations, is this gay or straight?"

"Often gay," I said. "But the pornography is a big clue."

"He was looking at nude women."

"The magazines found near his body featured nude women," I restated his remark, for we had no way of knowing what Ferguson had been looking at. We knew only what we had found. "It's also important that we didn't see any other pornography or sexual paraphernalia in his house," I added.

"I guess I would assume there would be more of it," Jenrette said as he plugged in the Stryker's saw.

"Usually, these guys keep trunkloads of it," I said. "They never throw it out. Frankly, it bothers me quite a lot that we found only four magazines, all of them current issues."

"It's like he was really new at this."

"There are many factors that suggest he was inexperienced," I replied. "But mostly what I'm seeing is inconsistency."

"Such as?" He incised the scalp behind the ears,

folding it down to expose the skull, and the face suddenly collapsed into a sad, slack mask.

"Just as we found no bottle of perfume to account for the fragrance he had on, we found no women's clothing in the house except what he had on," I said. "There was only one condom missing from the box. The rope was old, and we found nothing, including other rope, that might be the origin of it. He was cautious enough to wrap a towel around his neck, yet he tied a knot that's extremely dangerous."

"As the name suggests," said Jenrette.

"Yes. A hangman's knot pulls very smoothly and won't let go," I said. "Not exactly what you want to use when you're intoxicated and perched on top of a varnished bar stool, which you're more likely to fall off of than a chair, by the way."

"I wouldn't think many people would know how to tie a hangman's knot," Jenrette mused.

"The question is, did Ferguson have reason to know?" I said.

"I guess he could have looked it up in a book."

"We found no books about knot tying, no nautical-type books or anything like that in his house."

"Would it be hard to tie a hangman's knot? If there were instructions, let's say?"

"It wouldn't be impossible, but it would take a little practice."

"Why would someone be interested in a knot like that? Wouldn't a slip knot be easier?"

"A hangman's knot is morbid, ominous. It's neat,

precise. I don't know." I added, "How is Lieutenant Mote?"

"Stable, but he'll be in the ICU for a while."

Dr. Jenrette turned on the Stryker's saw. We were silent as he removed the skull cap. He did not speak again until he had removed the brain and was examining the neck.

"You know, I don't see a thing. No hemorrhage to the strap muscles, hyoid's intact, no fractures of superior horns of the thyroid cartilage. The spine's not fractured, but I don't guess that happens except in judicial hangings."

"Not unless you're obese, with arthritic changes of the cervical vertebrae, and get accidentally suspended in a weird way," I said.

"You want to look?"

I pulled on gloves and moved a light closer.

"Dr. Scarpetta, how do we know he was alive when he was hanged?"

"We can't really know that with certainty," I said. "Unless we find another cause of death."

"Like poisoning."

"That's about the only thing I can think of at this point. But if that's the case, it had to be something that worked very fast. We do know he hadn't been home long before Mote found him dead. So the odds are against the bizarre and in favor of his death being caused by asphyxia due to hanging."

"What about manner?"

"Pending," I suggested.

When Ferguson's organs had been sectioned and

returned to him in a plastic bag placed inside his chest cavity, I helped Jenrette clean up. We hosed down the table and floor while a morgue assistant rolled Ferguson's body away and tucked it into the refrigerator. We rinsed syringes and instruments as we chatted some more about what was happening in an area of the world that initially had attracted the young doctor because it was safe.

He told me he had wished to start a family in a place where people still believed in God and the sanctity of life. He wanted his children in church and on athletic fields. He wanted them untainted by drugs, immorality, and violence on TV.

"Thing is, Dr. Scarpetta," he went on, "there really isn't any place left. Not even here. In the past week I've worked an eleven-year-old girl who was sexually molested and murdered. And now a State Bureau of Investigation agent dressed in drag. Last month I got a kid from Oteen who overdosed on cocaine. She was only seventeen. Then there are the drunk drivers. I get them and the people they smash into all the time."

"Dr. Jenrette?"

"You can call me Jim," he said, and he looked depressed as he began to collect paperwork from a countertop.

"How old are your children?" I asked.

"Well, my wife and I keep trying." He cleared his throat and averted his eyes, but not before I saw his pain. "How about you? You got children?"

"I'm divorced and have a niece who's like my own,"

I said. "She's a senior at UVA and currently doing an internship at Quantico."

"You must be mighty proud of her."

"I am," I replied, my mood shadowed again by images and voices, by secret fears about Lucy's life.

"Now I know you want to talk to me some more about Emily Steiner, and I've still got her brain here if you want to see it."

"I very much do."

It is not uncommon for pathologists to fix brains in a ten percent solution of formaldehyde called formalin. The chemical process preserves and firms tissue. It makes further studies possible, especially in cases involving trauma to this most incredible and least understood of all human organs.

The procedure was sadly utilitarian to the point of indignity, should one choose to view it like that. Jenrette went to a sink and retrieved from beneath it a plastic bucket labeled with Emily Steiner's name and case number. The instant Jenrette removed her brain from its formalin bath and placed it on a cutting board, I knew the gross examination would tell me only more loudly that something was very wrong with this case.

"There's absolutely no vital reaction," I marveled, fumes from the formalin burning my eyes.

Jenrette threaded a probe through the bullet track.

"There's no hemorrhage, no swelling. Yet the bullet didn't pass through the pons. It didn't pass through the basal ganglia or any other area that's vital." I looked up at him. "This is not an immediately lethal wound."

"I can't argue that one."

"We should look for another cause of death."

"I sure wish you'd tell me what, Dr. Scarpetta. I've got tox testing going on. But unless that turns up something significant, there's nothing I can think of that could account for her death. Nothing but the gunshot to her head."

"I'd like to look at a tissue section of her lungs," I said.

"Come on to my office."

I was considering that the girl might have been drowned, but as I sat over Jenrette's microscope moments later moving around a slide of lung tissue, questions remained unanswered.

"If she drowned," I explained to him as I worked, "the alveoli should be dilated. There should be edema fluid in the alveolar spaces with disproportionate auto-lytic change of the respiratory epithelium." I adjusted the focus again. "In other words, if her lungs had been contaminated by fresh water, they should have begun decomposing more rapidly than other tissues. But they didn't."

"What about smothering or strangulation?" he asked.

"The hyoid was intact. There were no petechial hemorrhages."

"That's right."

"And more importantly," I pointed out, "if someone tries to smother or strangle you, you're going to fight like hell. Yet there are no nose or lip injuries, no defense injuries whatsoever."

He handed me a thick case file. "This is everything," he said.

While he dictated Max Ferguson's case, I reviewed every report, laboratory request, and call sheet pertaining to Emily Steiner's murder. Her mother, Denesa, had called Dr. Jenrette's office anywhere from one to five times daily since Emily's body had been found. I found this rather remarkable.

"The decedent was received inside a black plastic pouch sealed by the Black Mountain Police. The seal number is 445337 and the seal is intact—"

"Dr. Jenrette?" I interrupted.

He removed his foot from the pedal of the dictating machine. "You can call me Jim," he said again.

"It seems her mother has called you with unusual frequency."

"Some of it is us playing telephone tag. But yes." He slipped off his glasses and rubbed his eyes. "She's called a lot."

"Why?"

"Mostly she's just terribly distraught, Dr. Scarpetta. She wants to make sure her daughter didn't suffer."

"And what did you tell her?"

"I told her with a gunshot wound like that, it's probable she didn't. I mean, she would have been unconscious . . . uh, probably was when the other things were done."

He paused for a moment. Both of us knew that Emily Steiner had suffered. She had felt raw terror. At some point she must have known she was going to die.

"And that's it?" I asked. "She's called this many times to find out if her daughter suffered?"

"Well, no. She's had questions and information.

Nothing of particular relevance." He smiled sadly. "I think she just needs someone to talk to. She's a sweet lady who's lost everyone in her life. I can't tell you how badly I feel for her and how much I pray they catch the horrible monster who did this. That Gault monster I've read about. The world will never be safe as long as he's in it."

"The world will never be safe, Dr. Jenrette. But I can't tell you how much we want to catch him, too. Catch Gault. Catch anybody who does something like this," I said as I opened a thick envelope of glossy eight-by-ten photographs.

Only one was unfamiliar, and I studied it intensely for a long time as Dr. Jenrette's unemphatic voice went on. I did not know what I was seeing because I had never seen anything quite like this, and my emotional response was a combination of excitement and fear. The photograph showed Emily Steiner's left buttock, where there was an irregular brownish blotch on the skin no bigger than a bottle cap.

"The visceral pleura shows scattered petechiae along the interlobar fissures—"

"What is this?" I interrupted Dr. Jenrette's dictation again.

He put down the microphone as I came around to his side of the desk and placed the photograph in front of him. I pointed out the mark on Emily's skin as I smelled Old Spice and thought of my ex-husband, Tony, who had always worn too much of it.

"This mark on her buttock is not covered in your report," I added.

99

"I don't know what that is," he said without a trace of defensiveness. He simply sounded tired. "I just assumed it was some sort of postmortem artifact."

"I don't know of any artifact that looks like that. Did you resect it?"

"No."

"Her body was on something that left that mark." I returned to my chair, sat down, and leaned against the edge of his desk. "It could be important."

"Yes, if that's the case, I could see how it might be important," he replied, looking increasingly dejected.

"She's not been in the ground long." I spoke quietly but with feeling.

He stared uneasily at me.

"She's never going to be in better shape than she is now," I went on. "I really think we ought to take another look at her."

He did not blink as he wet his lips.

"Dr. Jenrette," I said, "let's get her up *now*."

Dr. Jenrette flipped through cards in his Rolodex and reached for the phone. I watched him dial.

"Hello, Dr. James Jenrette here," he said to whoever answered. "I wonder if Judge Begley might be in?"

The Honorable Hal Begley said he would see us in his chambers in half an hour. I drove while Jenrette gave directions, and I parked on College Street with plenty of time to spare.

The Buncombe County Courthouse was an old dark brick building that I suspected had been the tallest edifice downtown until not too many years before.

100

Its thirteen stories were topped by the jail, and as I looked up at barred windows against a bright blue sky, I thought of Richmond's overcrowded jail, spread out over acres, with coils of razor wire the only view. I believed it would not be long before cities like Asheville would need more cells as violence continued to become so alarmingly common. "Judge Begley's not known for his patience," Dr. Jenrette warned me as we climbed marble steps inside the old courthouse. "I can promise he's not going to like your plan."

I knew that Dr. Jenrette did not like my plan, either, for no forensic pathologist wants a peer digging up his work. Dr. Jenrette and I both knew that implicit in all of this was that he had not done a good job.

"Listen," I said as he headed down a corridor on the third floor, "I don't like the plan, either. I don't like exhumations. I wish there were another way."

"I guess I just wish I had more experience in the kinds of cases you see every day," he added.

"I don't see cases like this every day," I said, touched by his humility. "Thank God, I don't."

"Well, I'd be lying to you, Dr. Scarpetta, if I said that it wasn't real hard on me when I got called to that little girl's scene. Maybe I should have spent a little more time."

"I think Buncombe County is extremely lucky to have you," I said sincerely as we opened the judge's outer office door. "I wish I had more doctors like you in Virginia. I'd hire you."

He knew I meant it and smiled as a secretary as old as any woman I'd ever met who was still employed peered up at us through thick glasses. She used an electric typewriter instead of a computer, and I surmised from the numerous gray steel cabinets lining walls that filing was her forte. Sunlight seeped wanly through barely opened venetian blinds, a galaxy of dust suspended in the air. I smelled Rose Milk as she rubbed a dollop of moisturizing cream into her bony hands.

"Judge Begley's expecting you," she said before we introduced ourselves. "You can just go on in. That door there." She pointed to a shut door across from the one we had just come through. "Now just so you know, court's adjourned for lunch and he's due back at exactly one."

"Thank you," I said. "We'll try not to keep him long."

"Won't make any difference if you try."

Dr. Jenrette's shy knock on the judge's thick oak door was answered by a distracted "Come in!" from the other side. We found His Honor behind a partner's desk, suit jacket off as he sat erectly in an old red leather chair. He was a gaunt, bearded man nearing sixty, and as he glanced over notes in a legal pad, I made a number of telling assessments about him. The orderliness of his desk told me that he was busy and quite capable, and his unfashionable tie and soft-soled shoes bespoke someone who did not give a damn how people like me assessed him.

"Why do you want to violate the sepulchre?" he asked in slow Southern cadences that belied a quick mind as he turned a page in a legal pad.

"After going over Dr. Jenrette's reports," I replied,

"we agree some questions were not answered by the first examination of Emily Steiner's body."

"I know of Dr. Jenrette but don't believe I know you," Judge Begley said to me as he placed the legal pad on the desk.

"I'm Dr. Kay Scarpetta, the chief medical examiner of Virginia."

"I was told you had something to do with the FBI."

"Yes, sir. I am the consulting forensic pathologist for the Investigative Support Unit."

"Is that like the Behavioral Science Unit?"

"One and the same. The Bureau changed the name several years ago."

"You're talking about the folks who do the profiling of these serial killers and other aberrant criminals who until recently we didn't have to worry about in these parts." He watched me closely, lacing his fingers in his lap.

"That's what we do," I said.

"Your Honor," Dr. Jenrette said. "The Black Mountain Police has requested the assistance of the FBI. There's some fear that the man who murdered the Steiner girl is the same man who killed a number of people in Virginia."

"I'm aware of that, Dr. Jenrette, since you were so kind as to explain some of this when you called earlier. However, the only item on the agenda right now is your wish for me to grant you the right to dig up this little girl.

"Before I let you do something as upsetting and disrespectful as that, you're going to have to give me a powerfully good reason. And I do wish the two of you would sit down and make yourselves comfortable. That's why I have chairs on that side of my desk."

"She has a mark on her skin," I said as I seated myself.

"What sort of mark?" He eyed me with interest as Dr. Jenrette slipped a photograph out of an envelope and set it on the judge's blotter.

"You can see it in the photograph," Jenrette said.

The judge's eyes dropped to the photograph, his face unreadable.

"We don't know what the mark is," I explained. "But it may tell us where the body lay. It may be some type of injury."

He picked up the photograph, squinting as he examined it more closely. "Aren't there studies of photographs you can do? Seems to me there's all sorts of scientific things they do these days."

"There are," I answered. "But the problem is, by the time we finish conducting any studies, the body will be in such poor condition that we'll no longer be able to tell anything from it if we still need to exhume it. The longer the interval gets, the harder it is to distinguish between an injury or other significant mark on the body and artifacts due to decomposition."

"There are a lot of details about this case that make it very odd, Your Honor," Dr. Jenrette said. "We just need all the help we can get."

"I understand the SBI agent working the case was

found hanged yesterday. I saw that in the morning paper."

"Yes, sir," Dr. Jenrette said.

"Are there odd details about his death, too?"

"There are," I replied.

"I hope you're not going to come back here a week from now and want to dig him up."

"I can't imagine that," I said.

"This little girl has a mama. And just how do you think she's going to feel about what you've got in mind?"

Neither Dr. Jenrette nor I replied. Leather creaked as the judge shifted in his chair. He glanced past us at a clock on the wall.

"See, that's my biggest problem with what you're asking," he went on. "I'm thinking about this poor woman, about what all she's been through. I have no interest whatsoever in putting her through anything else."

"We wouldn't ask if we didn't think it was important to the investigation of her daughter's death," I said. "And I know Mrs. Steiner must want justice, Your Honor."

"You go get her mama and bring her to me," Judge Begley said as he got up from his chair.

"Excuse me?" Dr. Jenrette looked bewildered.

"I want her mama brought to me," the judge repeated. "I should be freed up by two-thirty. I'll expect to see you back here."

"What if she won't come?" Dr. Jenrette asked, and both of us got up.

"Can't say I'd blame her a bit."

"You don't need her permission," I said with calm I did not feel.

"No, ma'am, I don't," said the judge as he opened the door.

7

Dr. Jenrette was kind enough to let me use his office while he disappeared into the hospital labs, and for the next several hours I was on the phone.

The most important task, ironically, turned out to be the easiest. Marino had no trouble convincing Denesa Steiner to accompany him to the judge's chambers that afternoon. More difficult was figuring out how to get them there, since Marino still did not have a car.

"What's the holdup?" I asked.

"The friggin' scanner they put in don't work," he said irritably.

"Can't you do without that?"

"They don't seem to think so."

I glanced at my watch. "Maybe I'd better come get you."

"Yeah, well, I'd rather get there myself. She's got a pretty decent ride. In fact, there are some who say an Infiniti's better than a Benz."

"That's moot, since I'm driving a Chevrolet at the moment."

"She said her father-in-law used to have a Benz a lot like yours and you ought to think of switching to an Infiniti or Legend."

I was silent.

"Just food for thought."

"Just get here," I said shortly.

"Yeah, I will."

"Fine."

We hung up without good-byes, and as I sat at Dr. Jenrette's cluttered desk I felt exhausted and betrayed. I had been through Marino's bad times with Doris. I had supported him as he had begun venturing forth into the fast, frightening world of dating. In return, he had always telegraphed judgments about my personal life without benefit of having been asked.

He had been negative about my ex-husband, and very critical of my former lover, Mark. He rarely had anything nice to say about Lucy or the way I dealt with her, and he did not like my friends. Most of all, I felt his cold stare on my relationship with Wesley. I felt Marino's jealous rage.

He was not at Begley's office when Dr. Jenrette and I returned at half past two. As minutes crept by inside the judge's chambers, my anger grew.

"Tell me where you were born, Dr. Scarpetta," the judge said to me from the other side of his immaculate desk.

"Miami," I replied.

"You certainly don't talk like a Southerner. I would have placed you up north somewhere."

"I was educated in the North."

"It might surprise you to know that I was, too," he said.

"Why did you settle here?" Dr. Jenrette asked him.

"I'm sure for some of the very same reasons that you did."

"But you're from here," I said.

"Going back three generations. My great-grandfather was born in a log cabin around here. He was a teacher. That was on my mother's side. On my father's side we had mostly moonshiners until about halfway into this century. Then we had preachers. I believe that might be them now."

Marino opened the door, and his face peeked in before his feet did. Denesa Steiner was behind him, and though I would never accuse Marino of chivalry, he was unusually attentive and gentle with this rather peculiarly put together woman whose dead daughter was our reason for gathering. The judge rose, and out of habit so did I, as Mrs. Steiner regarded each of us with curious sadness.

"I'm Dr. Scarpetta." I offered my hand and found hers cool and soft. "I'm terribly sorry about this, Mrs. Steiner."

"I'm Dr. Jenrette. We've talked on the phone."

"Won't you be seated," the judge said to her very kindly.

Marino moved two chairs close together, directing her to one while he took the other. Mrs. Steiner was in her mid- to late thirties and dressed entirely in black. Her skirt was full and below her knees, a sweater buttoned to her chin. She wore no makeup, her only jewelry a plain gold wedding ring. She looked the part of a spinster missionary, yet the longer I studied her, the more I saw what her puritanical grooming could not hide.

She was beautiful, with smooth pale skin and a generous mouth, and curly hair the color of honey. Her nose was patrician, her cheekbones high, and beneath the folds of her horrible clothes hid a voluptuously well formed body. Nor had her attributes successfully eluded anything male and breathing in the room. Marino, in particular, could not take his eyes off her.

"Mrs. Steiner," the judge began, "the reason I wanted you to come here this afternoon is these doctors have made a request I wanted you to hear. And let me say right off how much I appreciate your coming. From all accounts, you've shown nothing but courage and decency during these unspeakably trying hours, and I have no intention whatsoever of adding to your burdens unnecessarily."

"Thank you, sir," she said quietly, her tapered, pale hands clasped tightly in her lap.

"Now, these doctors have found a few things in the photographs taken after little Emily died. The things they've found are mysterious and they want to take another look at her."

"How can they do that?" she asked innocently in a voice steady and sweet, and not indigenous to North Carolina.

110

"Well, they want to exhume her," the judge replied.

Mrs. Steiner did not look upset but baffled, and my heart ached for her as she fought back tears.

"Before I say yes or no to their request," Begley went on, "I want to see how you might feel about this."

"You want to dig her up?" She looked at Dr. Jenrette, then me.

"Yes," I answered her. "We would like to examine her again immediately."

"I don't understand what you might find this time that you didn't find before." Her voice trembled.

"Maybe nothing that will matter," I said. "But there are a few details I noticed in photographs that I'd like to get a closer look at, Mrs. Steiner. These mysterious things might help us catch whoever did this to Emily."

"Do you want to help us snatch the SOB who killed your baby?" the judge asked.

She nodded vigorously as she wept, and Marino spoke with fury. "You help us, and I promise we're going to nail the goddam bastard."

"I'm sorry to put you through this," said Dr. Jenrette, who would forever be convinced he had failed.

"Then may we proceed?" Begley leaned forward in his chair as if poised to spring, for like everyone in his chambers, he felt this woman's horrible loss. He felt her abject vulnerability in a manner that I was convinced would forever change the way he viewed offenders with hard luck stories and excuses who approached his bench.

Denesa Steiner nodded again because she could not

speak. Then Marino helped her out of the room, leaving Jenrette and me.

"Dawn will come early and there are plans to make," Begley said.

"We need to coordinate a lot of people," I concurred.

"Which funeral home buried her?" Begley asked Jenrette.

"Wilbur's."

"That's in Black Mountain?"

"Yes, Your Honor."

"The name of the funeral director?" The judge was taking notes.

"Lucias Ray."

"What about the detective working this case?"

"He's in the hospital."

"Oh, that's right." Judge Begley looked up and sighed.

I was not sure why I went straight there, except that I had said I would, and I was mad at Marino. I was irrationally offended by, of all things, his allusion to my Mercedes, which he had unfavorably compared to an Infiniti.

It wasn't that his comment was right or wrong, but that its intent was to cause irritation and insult. I would not have asked Marino to go with me now had I believed in Loch Ness monsters, creatures from lagoons, and the living dead. I would have refused had he begged, despite my secret fear of water snakes. Actually, of all snakes great and small.

112

There was enough light left when I reached Lake Tomahawk to retrace what I had been told were Emily's last steps. Parking by a picnic area, I followed the shoreline with my eyes as I wondered why a little girl would walk out here as night began to fall. I recalled how fearful I had been of the canals when I was growing up in Miami. Every log was an alligator and cruel people loitered along the isolated shores.

As I got out of my car, I wondered why Emily had not been afraid. I wondered if there might be some other explanation for why she had chosen this route.

The map Ferguson had passed around during the consultation at Quantico indicated that on the early evening of October 1, Emily had left the church and veered off the street at the point where I was standing. She had passed picnic tables and turned right on a dirt trail that appeared to have been worn by foot traffic rather than cleared, for the path was well defined in some spots and imperceptible in others as it followed the shore through woods and weeds.

I briskly passed riotous clumps of tall grasses and brush as the shadow of mountain ranges deepened over water and the wind picked up, carrying the sharp promise of winter. Dead leaves crackled beneath my shoes as I drew upon the clearing marked on the map with a tiny outline of a body. By now, it had gotten quite dark.

I dug inside my handbag for my flashlight, only to recall that it was broken and still inside Ferguson's basement. I found one book of matches left from my smoking days, and it was half empty.

113

"Damn," I exclaimed under my breath as I began to feel fear.

I slipped out my .38 and tucked it in a side pocket of my jacket, my hand loose around its grips as I stared at the muddy ledge at the water's edge where Emily Steiner's body had been found. Shadows compared to photographs I recalled indicated that surrounding brush had recently been cut back, but any other evidence of recent activity had been gently covered by nature and the night. Leaves were deep. I rearranged them with my feet to look for what I suspected the local police might not.

I had worked enough violent crimes in my career to have learned one very important truth. A crime scene has a life of its own. It remembers trauma in soil, insects altered by body fluids, and plants trampled by feet. It loses its privacy just as any witness does, for no stone is left undisturbed, and the curious do not stop coming just because there are no further questions to ask.

It is common for people to continue visiting a scene long after there is a reason. They take souvenirs and photographs. They leave letters, cards, and flowers. They come in secret and leave that way, for it is shameful to stare just because you cannot help it. It seems a violation of something sacred even to leave a rose.

I found no flowers in this spot as I swept leaves out of the way. But my toe did strike several small, hard objects that dropped me to my hands and knees, eyes straining. After much rooting around, I recovered what appeared to be four gumballs still in plastic wrappers. It

114

was not until I held them close to a lighted match that I realized the candies were jawbreakers, or Fireballs, as Emily had called them in her diary. I got up, breathing hard.

Furtively, I glanced around, listening to every sound. The noise of my feet crashing through leaves seemed horrendously loud as I followed a path that I now could not see at all. Stars were out, the half moon my only guide, my matches long since spent. I knew from the map that I was not far from the Steiners' street, and it was closer to pick my way there than attempt returning to my car.

I was perspiring beneath my coat and terrified of tripping, for in addition to not having a flashlight, I also had failed to bring my portable phone. It occurred to me that I would not want any of my colleagues to see me now, and if I injured myself, I might have to lie about how it happened.

Ten minutes into this awful journey, bushes grabbed my legs and destroyed my hose. I stubbed my toe on a root and stepped in mud up to my ankles. When a branch stung my face, barely missing my eye, I stood still, panting and frustrated to the point of tears. To my right, between the street and me, was a dense expanse of woods. To my left was the water.

"Shit," I said rather loudly.

Following the shore was the lesser danger, and as I continued I actually got somewhat more adept at it. My eyes adapted better to moonlight. I became more surefooted and intuitive, and could sense from shifts in dampness and temperature of air when I was nearing dryer ground or mud or straying too far from the path. It was as if I were instantly evolving into a nocturnal creature in order to keep my species alive.

Then, suddenly, streetlights were ahead as I reached the end of the lake opposite where I had parked. Here the woods had been cleared for tennis courts and a parking lot, and as Emily had done several weeks before, I veered off the path and momentarily was on pavement again. As I walked along her street, I realized I was trembling.

I remembered the Steiner house was two down on the left, and as I got closer to it I wasn't certain what I would say to Emily's mother. I had no desire to tell her where I had been or why, for the last thing she needed was more upset. But I knew no one else in this area and could not imagine knocking on a stranger's door to use the phone.

No matter how hospitable anyone in Black Mountain might be, I would be asked why I looked as if I had been lost in a wilderness. It was possible someone might even find me frightening, especially if I had to explain what I did for a profession. As it turned out, my fears were invalidated by an unexpected knight who suddenly rode out of the dark and nearly ran me down.

I got to the Steiners' driveway as Marino was backing out of it in a new midnight-blue Chevrolet. As I waved at him in the beam of his headlights, I could see the blank expression on his face as he abruptly hit the brakes. His mood shifted from incredulity to rage.

"God damn sonofabitch, you practically gave me a heart attack. I coulda run you over."

I fastened my shoulder harness and locked the door.

"What the fuck're you doing out here? Shit!"

"I'm glad you finally got your car and that the scanner works. And I very much need a very strong Scotch and I'm not sure where one finds anything like that around here," I said as my teeth began to chatter. "How do you turn the heat on?"

Marino lit a cigarette, and I wanted one of those, too. But there were some vows I would never break. He turned the heat on high.

"Jesus. You look like you've been mud wrestling," he said, and I couldn't remember when I had seen him so rattled. "What the hell've you been doing? I mean, are you okay?"

"My car's parked by the clubhouse."

"What clubhouse?"

"On the lake."

"The lake? What? You've been *out there* after dark? Have you lost your friggin' mind?"

"What I've lost is my flashlight, and I didn't remember that until it was a little late." As I spoke, I slipped my .38 out of my coat pocket and returned it to my handbag, a move that Marino did not miss. His mood worsened.

"You know, I don't know what the fuck's your problem. I think you're losing it, Doc. I think it's all caught up with you and you're getting goofy as a shithouse rat. Maybe you're going through the change."

"If I were going through 'the change' or anything else so personal and so none-of-your-business, you can rest assured I would not discuss it with you. If for no other reason than your vast male dullness or sensitivity of a fence post—which may or may not be gender related, I have to add, to be fair. Because I wouldn't want to assume that all men are like you. If I did, I know I would give them up entirely."

"Maybe you should."

"Maybe I will!"

"Good! Then you can be just like your bratty niece! Hey. Don't think it ain't obvious which way she swings."

"And that is yet one more thing that isn't your goddam business," I said furiously. "I can't believe you're stooping so low as to stereotype Lucy, to dehumanize her just because she doesn't make the exact choices you would."

"Oh yeah? Well maybe the problem is that she does makes the exact same choices I would. I date women."

"You don't know the first thing about women," I said, and it occurred to me that the car was an oven and I had no idea where we were going. I flipped the heat down and glared out my window.

"I know enough about women to know you'd drive anybody crazy. And I can't believe you were out walking around the lake after dark. *By yourself.* So just what the hell would you have done if *he* was out there, too?"

"Which he?"

"Goddam I'm hungry. I saw a steakhouse on Tunnel Road when I was up this way earlier. I hope they're still open."

"Marino, it's only six forty-five."

"Why did you go out there?" he asked again, and both of us were calming down.

"Someone left candy on the ground where her body was discovered. Fireballs." When he made no reply, I added, "The same candy she mentioned in her diary."

"I don't remember that."

"The boy she had a crush on. I think his name was Wren. She wrote that she had seen him at a church supper and he gave her a Fireball. She saved it in her secret box."

"They never found it."

"Found what?"

"Whatever this secret box was. Denesa couldn't find it either. So maybe Wren left the Fireballs at the lake."

"We need to talk to him," I said. "It would appear that you and Mrs. Steiner are developing a good rapport."

"Nothing like this should ever have happened to someone like her."

"Nothing like this should ever happen to anyone."

"I see a Western Sizzler."

"No, thank you."

"How about Bonanza?" He flipped on his turn signal.

"Absolutely not."

Marino surveyed brightly lighted restaurants lining

119

Tunnel Road as he smoked another cigarette. "Doc, no offense, but you've got an attitude."

"Marino, don't bother with the 'no offense' preamble. All it does is telegraph that I'm about to be offended."

"I know there's a Peddler around here. I saw it in the Yellow Pages."

"Why were you looking up restaurants in the Yellow Pages?" I puzzled, for I'd always known him to shop for restaurants the same way he did for food. He cruised without a list and took what was easy, cheap, and filling.

"I wanted to see what was in the area in case I wanted something nice. How about calling so I know how to get there?"

I reached for the car phone and thought of Denesa Steiner, for I was not who Marino had hoped he would be taking to the Peddler this night.

"Marino," I told him quietly. "Please be careful."

"Don't start in about red meat again."

"That's not what worries me most," I said.

8

The cemetery behind Third Presbyterian Church was a rolling field of polished granite headstones behind a chain link fence choked with trees.

When I arrived at 6:15, dawn bruised the horizon and I could see my breath. Ground spiders had put up their webbed awnings to begin the business of the day, and I respectfully stepped around them as Marino and I walked through wet grass toward Emily Steiner's grave.

She was buried in a corner close to woods where the lawn was pleasantly mingled with cornflowers, clover, and Queen Anne's lace. Her monument was a small marble angel, and to find it we simply followed the scraping noise of shovels digging dirt. A truck with a winch had been left running at the site, and its headlights illuminated the progress of two leathery old men in overalls. Shovels glinted, the surrounding grass bleached of color, and I smelled damp earth as it fell from steel blades to a mound at the foot of the grave.

121

Marino turned on his flashlight, and the tombstone stood in sad relief against the morning, wings folded back and head bent in prayer. The epitaph carved in its base read:

> There is no other in the World—
> Mine was the only one

"Jeez. Got any idea what that means?" Marino said close to my ear.

"Maybe we can ask him," I replied as I watched the approach of a startlingly large man with thick white hair.

His long dark overcoat flowed around his ankles as he walked, giving the eerie impression from a distance that he was several inches off the ground. When he got to us, I saw he had a Black Watch scarf wrapped around his neck, black leather gloves on his huge hands, and rubbers pulled over his shoes. He was close to seven feet tall, with a torso the size of a barrel.

"I'm Lucias Ray," he said, and enthusiastically shook our hands as we introduced ourselves.

"We were wondering about the significance of the epitaph," I said.

"Mrs. Steiner sure did love her little girl. It's just pitiful," the funeral director said in a thick drawl that sounded more Georgian than North Carolinian. "We have a whole book of verses you can look through when you're deciding on what to have inscribed."

"Then Emily's mother got this from your book?" I asked.

"Well, to tell you the truth, no. I believe she said it's Emily Dickinson."

The grave diggers had put down their shovels, and it was light enough now for me to see their faces, wet with sweat and as furrowed as a farmer's fields. Heavy chain clanked as they unwound it from the winch's drum. Then one of the men stepped down into the grave. He secured the chain to hooks on the sides of the concrete vault as Ray went on to tell us that more people had shown up for Emily Steiner's funeral than he had ever heard of around here.

"They were outside the church, on the lawn, and it took close to two hours for all of them to walk past the casket to pay their respects."

"Did you have an open casket?" Marino asked in surprise.

"No, sir." Ray watched his men. "Now, Mrs. Steiner wanted to, but I wouldn't hear of it. I told her she was distraught and would thank me later for saying 'no. Why, her little girl wasn't in any kind of shape for a thing like that. I knew a lot of folks would show up just to stare. Course, a lot of rubberneckers showed up anyway, seeing as how there was so much in the news."

The winch strained loudly and the truck's diesel engine throbbed as the vault was slowly lifted from the earth. Soil rained down in chunks as the concrete burial chamber rocked higher in the air with each turn of the crank, and one of the men stood by like a member of a ground crew to direct with his hands.

At almost the precise moment the vault was free of

its grave and lowered to the grass, we were invaded by television crews with cameras mounted and reporters and photographers. They swarmed around the gaping wound in the earth and the vault so stained with red clay that it almost looked bloody.

"Why are you exhuming Emily Steiner?" one of them called out.

"Is it true the police have a suspect?" yelled another.

"Dr. Scarpetta?"

"Why has the FBI been called in?"

"Dr. Scarpetta?" A woman pushed a microphone close to my face. "It sounds like you're second-guessing the Buncombe County medical examiner."

"Why are you desecrating this little girl's grave?"

And above the fray Marino suddenly bellowed as if he had been wounded, "Get the fuck out of here now! You're interfering with an investigation! You hear me, goddam it?" He stomped his feet. "Leave now!"

The reporters froze with shocked faces. They stared at him with open mouths as he continued to rail against them, complexion crimson, blood vessels bulging in his neck.

"The only one desecrating anything around here is you assholes! And if you don't leave right now, I'm gonna start breaking cameras and anything else in my reach, including your goddam ugly heads!"

"Marino," I said, and I placed my hand on his arm. He was so tense he had turned to iron.

"All my goddam career I've been dealing with you assholes and I've had it! You hear me! I've goddam had

*it, you bunch of motherfuckinsonofabitch BLOODSUCKIN'
PARASITES!"*

"Marino!" I pulled him by the wrist as fear electrified
every nerve in my body. Never had I seen him in such a
rage. *Dear Lord*, I thought. *Don't let him shoot anyone.*

I got in front of him to make him look at me, but his
eyes danced wildly above my head. "Marino, listen to
me! They're leaving. Please calm down. Marino, take it
easy. Look, every last one of them is leaving right now.
See them? You've certainly made your point. They're
almost running."

The journalists were gone as suddenly as they had
appeared, like some phantom band of marauders that
had materialized and vanished in the mist. Marino
stared across the empty expanse of gently rolling lawn
with its sprigs of plastic flowers and perfect rows of
gray markers. The clarion sound of steel striking steel
rang out again and again. With hammer and chisel the
diggers broke the vault's coal tar seal, then lowered the
lid to the earth as Marino hurried into the woods. We
pretended not to notice the hideous grunts and groans
and gagging sounds coming from mountain laurels as
he vomited.

"Do you still have a bottle of each of the fluids
you used for embalming?" I asked Lucias Ray, whose
reaction to the advancing troops of media and Marino's
outburst seemed more quizzical than bothered.

"I may have half a bottle left of what I used on her,"
he said.

"I'll need chemical controls for toxicology," I explained.

"It's just formaldehyde and methanol with a trace

of lanoline oil—as common as chicken soup. Now, I did use a lower concentration because of her small size. Your detective friend sure don't look too good," he added as Marino emerged from the woods. "You know, the flu's going around."

"I don't think he has the flu," I said. "How did the reporters find out we were here?"

"Now, you got me on that one. But you know how folks are." He paused to spit. "Always someone who's got to run his yap."

Emily's steel casket was painted as white as the Queen Anne's lace that had grown around her plot, and the diggers did not need the winch to lift it out of the vault and gently lower it to the grass. The casket was small like the body inside it. Lucias Ray slipped a radio out of a coat pocket and spoke into it.

"You can come on now," he said.

"Ten-four," a voice came back.

"No more reporters, I sure hope like heck?"

"They're all gone."

A shiny black hearse glided through the cemetery's entrance and drove half in the woods and half on the grass, miraculously dodging graves and trees. A fat man wearing a trench coat and porkpie hat got out to open the tailgate, and the diggers slid the casket inside while Marino watched from a distance, mopping his face with a handkerchief.

"You and I need to talk." I had moved close and spoke quietly to him as the hearse went on its way.

"I don't need nothing right now." His face was pale.

126

"I've got to meet Dr. Jenrette at the morgue. Are you coming?"

"No," he said. "I'm going on back to the Travel-Eze. I'm gonna drink beer until I puke again, then I'm gonna switch to bourbon. And after that I'm gonna call Wesley's ass and ask him when the shit we can get out of this armpit town, because I tell you, I don't have another decent shirt here and I just ruined this one. I don't even have a tie."

"Marino, go lie down."

"I'm living out of a bag this big," he went on, holding his hands not too far apart.

"Take Advil, drink as much water as you can hold, and eat some toast. I'll check on you when we finish at the hospital. If Benton calls, tell him I'll have my portable phone with me or he can call my pager."

"He's got those numbers?"

"Yes," I said.

Marino glanced at me over his handkerchief as he mopped his face again. I saw the hurt in his eyes before it slipped back behind its walls.

9

Dr. Jenrette was doing paperwork in the morgue when I arrived as the hearse did shortly before ten. He smiled nervously at me as I took off my suit jacket and put a plastic apron over my clothes.

"Would you have a guess as to how the press found out about the exhumation?" I asked, unfolding a surgical gown.

He looked startled. "What happened?"

"About a dozen reporters showed up at the cemetery."

"That's a real shame."

"We need to make sure nothing more gets out," I said, tying the gown in back and doing my best to sound patient. "What happens here needs to remain here, Dr. Jenrette."

He said nothing.

"I know I am a visitor and I wouldn't blame you if you resented the hell out of my presence. So please don't think I'm insensitive to the situation or indifferent to

128

your authority. But you can rest assured that whoever murdered this little girl keeps up with the news. Whenever something gets leaked, *he* finds out about it, too."

Dr. Jenrette, pleasant person that he was, did not look the least bit offended as he listened carefully. "I'm just trying to think of who all knew," he said. "The problem is by the time word got around that could have been a lot of people."

"Let's make sure word doesn't get around about anything we might find in here today," I said as I heard our case arrive.

Lucias Ray walked in first, the man in the porkpie hat right behind him pulling the church cart bearing the white casket. They maneuvered their cargo through the doorway and parked close to the autopsy table. Ray slipped a metal crank out of his coat pocket and inserted it in a small hole at the casket's head. He began cranking loose the seal as if he were starting a Model-T.

"That should do it," he said, dropping the crank back into his pocket. "Hope you don't mind my waiting around to check on my work. It's an opportunity I don't usually get, since we're not in the habit of digging up people after we bury 'em."

He started to open the lid, and if Dr. Jenrette hadn't placed his hands on top of it to stop him, I would have.

"Ordinarily that wouldn't be a problem, Lucias," Dr. Jenrette said. "But it's really not a good idea for anyone else to be here right now."

"I think that's being a might bit touchy." Ray's smile

got tight. "It's not like I haven't seen this child before. Why I know her inside and out better than her own mama."

"Lucias, we need you to go on now so Dr. Scarpetta and I can get this done," Dr. Jenrette spoke in his same sad soft tone. "I'll call you when we're finished."

"Dr. Scarpetta"—Ray fixed his eyes on me—"I must say it does appear folks are a little less friendly since the Feds came to town."

"This is a homicide investigation, Mr. Ray," I said. "Perhaps it would be best not to take things personally since nothing has been intended that way."

"Come on, Billy Joe," the funeral director said to the man in the porkpie hat. "Let's go get something to eat."

They went out. Dr. Jenrette locked the door.

"I'm sorry," he said, pulling on gloves. "Lucias can be overbearing sometimes, but he really is a good person."

I was suspicious we would find that Emily had not been properly embalmed or had been buried in a fashion that did not reflect what her mother had paid. But when Jenrette and I opened the casket's lid, I saw nothing that immediately struck me as out of order. The white satin lining had been folded over her body, and on top of it I found a package wrapped in white tissue paper and pink ribbon. I started taking photographs.

"Did Ray mention anything about this?" I handed the package to Jenrette.

"No." He looked perplexed as he turned it this way and that.

The smell of embalming fluid wafted up strongly as I opened the lining. Beneath it Emily Steiner was well preserved in a long-sleeve, high-collar dress of pale blue velveteen, her braided hair in bows of the same material. A fuzzy whitish mold typically found on bodies that have been exhumed covered her face like a mask and had started on the tops of her hands, which were on her waist, clasped around a white New Testament. She wore white knee socks and black patent leather shoes. Nothing she had been dressed in looked new.

I took more photographs; then Jenrette and I lifted her out of the casket and placed her on top of the stainless steel table, where we began to undress her. Beneath her sweet, little girl clothes hid the awful secret of her death, for people who die gracefully do not bear the wounds she had.

Any honest forensic pathologist will admit that autopsy artifacts are ghastly. There is nothing quite like the Y incision in any premortem surgical procedure, for it looks like its name. The scalpel goes from each clavicle to sternum, runs the length of the torso, and ends at the pubis after a small detour around the navel. The incision made from ear to ear at the back of the head before sawing open the skull is not attractive, either.

Of course, injuries to the dead do not heal. They can only be covered with high lacy collars and strategically coiffed hair. With heavy makeup from the funeral home and a wide seam running the length of her small body, Emily looked like a sad rag doll stripped of its frilly clothes and abandoned by its heartless owner.

Water drummed into a steel sink as Dr. Jenrette and I scrubbed away mold, makeup, and the flesh-colored putty filling the gunshot wound to the back of the head and the areas of the thighs, upper chest, and shoulders where skin had been excised by her killer. We removed eye caps beneath eyelids and took out sutures. Our eyes watered and noses began to run as sharp fumes rose from the chest cavity. Organs were breaded with embalming powder, and we quickly lifted them out and rinsed some more. I checked the neck, finding nothing that my colleague hadn't already documented. Then I wedged a long thin chisel between molars to open the mouth.

"It's stubborn," I said in frustration. "We're going to have to cut the masseters. I want to look at the tongue in its anatomical position before getting at it through the posterior pharynx. But I don't know. We may not be able to."

Dr. Jenrette fitted a new blade into his scalpel. "What are we looking for?"

"I want to make certain she didn't bite her tongue."

Minutes later I discovered that she had.

"She's got marks right there at the margin," I pointed out. "Can you get a measurement?"

"An eighth of an inch by a quarter."

"And the hemorrhages are about a quarter of an inch deep. It looks like she might have bitten herself more than once. What do you think?"

"It looks to me like maybe she did."

"So we know she had a seizure associated with her terminal episode."

132

"The head injury could do that," he said, fetching the camera.

"It could, but then why doesn't the brain show that she survived long enough to have a seizure?"

"I guess we've got the same unanswered question."

"Yes," I said. "It's still very confusing."

When we turned the body, I absorbed myself in studying the peculiar mark that was the point of this grim exercise as the forensic photographer arrived and set up his equipment. For the better part of the afternoon we took rolls of infrared, ultraviolet, color, high-contrast, and black-and-white film, with many special filters and lenses.

Then I went into my medical bag and got out half a dozen black rings made of acrylonitrile-butadiene-styrene plastic, or more simply, the material that commonly composes pipes used for water and sewage lines. Every year or two I got a forensic dentist I knew to cut the three-eighth-inch-thick rings with a band saw and sand them smooth for me. Fortunately, it wasn't often I needed to pull such an odd trick out of my bag, for rarely was it necessary to remove a human bite mark or other impression from the body of someone murdered.

Deciding on a ring three inches in diameter, I used a machinist's die punch to stamp Emily Steiner's case number and location markers on each side. Skin, like a painter's canvas, is on a stretch, and in order to support the exact anatomical configuration of the mark on Emily's left buttock during and after its removal, I needed to provide a stable matrix.

133

"Have you got Super Glue?" I asked Dr. Jenrette.

"Sure." He brought me a tube.

"Keep taking photographs of every step, if you don't mind," I instructed the photographer, a slight Japanese man who never stood still.

Positioning the ring over the mark, I fixed it to the skin with the glue and further secured it with sutures. Next I dissected the tissue around the ring and placed it *en bloc* in formalin. All the while I tried to figure out what the mark meant. It was an irregular circle incompletely filled with a strange brownish discoloration that I believed was the imprint of a pattern. But I could not make out what, no matter how many Polaroids we looked at from how many different angles.

We did not think about the package wrapped in white tissue paper until the photographer had left and Dr. Jenrette and I had notified the funeral home that we were ready for their return.

"What do we do about this?" Dr. Jenrette asked.

"We have to open it."

He spread dry towels on a cart and set the gift on top of them. Carefully slicing the paper with a scalpel, he exposed an old box from a pair of size-six women's loafers. He cut through many layers of Scotch tape and removed the top.

"Oh my," he said under his breath as he stared in bewilderment at what someone had intended for a little girl's grave.

Shrouded in two sealed freezer bags inside the box was a dead kitten that could not have been but a few months old. It was as stiff as plyboard when I lifted it out, its delicate ribs protruding. The cat was a female, black with white feet, and she wore no collar. I saw no evidence of what had killed her until I took her into the X-ray room, and a little later was mounting her films on a light box.

"Her cervical spine is fractured," I said as a chill pricked up the hair on the back of my neck.

Dr. Jenrette frowned as he moved closer to the light box. "It looks like the spine's been moved out of the usual position here." He touched the film with a knuckle. "That's weird. It's displaced laterally? I don't think that could happen if she got hit by a car."

"She wasn't hit by a car," I told him. "Her head's been twisted clockwise by ninety degrees."

I found Marino eating a cheeseburger in his room when I returned to the Travel-Eze at almost seven P.M. His gun, wallet, and car keys were on top of one bed and he was on the other, shoes and socks scattered across the floor as if he had walked out of them. I could tell he had probably gotten back here not too long before I did. His eyes followed me as I went to the television and turned it off.

"Come on," I said. "We have to go out."

The "gospel truth" according to Lucias Ray was that Denesa Steiner had placed the package in Emily's casket. He had simply assumed that beneath the gift wrapping was a favorite toy or doll.

"When did she do this?" Marino asked as we walked briskly through the motel's parking lot.

"Right before the funeral," I replied. "Have you got your car keys?"

"Yeah."

"Then why don't you drive."

I had a nasty headache I blamed on formalin fumes and lack of food and sleep.

"Have you heard from Benton?" I asked as casually as possible.

"There should have been a bunch of messages at the desk for you."

"I came straight to your room. And how would you know if I had a lot of messages?"

"The clerk tried to give 'em to me. He figured between the two of us I look like the doctor."

"That's because you look like a man." I rubbed my temples.

"It's mighty white of you to notice."

"Marino, I wish you wouldn't talk like such a racist, because I really don't think you are one."

"How do you like my ride?"

His car was a maroon Chevrolet Caprice, fully loaded with flashing lights, a radio, telephone, scanner. It had even come equipped with a mounted video camera and a Winchester stainless steel Marine twelve-gauge shotgun. Pump action, it held seven rounds and was the same model the FBI used.

"My God," I said in disbelief as I got into the car. "Since when do they need riot guns in Black Mountain, North Carolina?"

"Since now." He cranked the engine.

"Did you request all this?"

"Nope."

"Would you like to explain to me how a ten-person police force can be better equipped than the DEA?"

"Because maybe the people who live around here really understand what community policing's all about. This community's got a bad problem right now, and what's happening is area merchants and concerned citizens are donating shit to help. Like the cars, phones, the shotgun. One of the cops told me some old lady called up just this morning and wanted to know if the federal agents that had come to town to help would like to have Sunday dinner with her."

"Well, that's very nice," I said, baffled.

"Plus, the town council's thinking about making the police department bigger, and I have a suspicion that helps explain some things."

"What things?"

"Black Mountain's gonna need a new chief."

"What happened to the old one?"

"Mote was about as close to a chief as they had."

"I'm still not clear on where you're going with this."

"Hey, maybe where I'm going is right here in this town, Doc. They're looking for an experienced chief and treating me like I'm 007 or something. It don't take a rocket scientist to figure it out."

"Marino, what in God's name is going on with you?" I asked very calmly.

He lit a cigarette. "What? First you don't think I look like a doctor? Now I don't look like a chief, either? I guess to you I don't look like nothing but a Dogtown slob who still talks like he's eating spaghetti with the mob back in Jersey and only takes out women in tight sweaters who tease their hair."

He blew out smoke furiously. "Hey, just because I like to bowl don't mean I'm some tattooed redneck. And just because I didn't go to all these Ivy League schools like you did don't mean I'm a dumb shit."

"Are you finished?"

"And another thing," he railed on, "there's a lot of really good places to fish around here. They got Bee Tree and Lake James, and except for Montreat and Biltmore, the real estate's pretty cheap. Maybe I'm just sick as shit of drones shooting drones and serial killers costing more to keep alive in the pen than I friggin' get paid to lock their asses up. *If* the assholes even stay in the pen, and that's the biggest 'if' of all."

We had been parked in the Steiner driveway for five minutes now. I stared out at the house lit up wondering if she knew we were here and why.

"Now are you finished?" I asked him.

"No, I ain't finished. I'm just sick of talking."

"In the first place, I didn't go to Ivy League schools. . . ."

"Well, what do you call Johns Hopkins and Georgetown?"

"Marino, goddam it, shut up."

He glared out the windshield and lit another cigarette.

"I was a poor Italian brought up in a poor Italian neighborhood just like you were," I said. "The difference is that I was in Miami and you were in New

Jersey. I've never pretended to be better than you, nor have I ever called you stupid. In fact, you're anything but stupid, even if you butcher the English language and have never been to the opera.

"My list of complaints about you all go back to one thing. You're stubborn, and when you're at your worst, you're bigoted and intolerant. In other words, you act toward others the way you suspect they're acting toward you."

Marino jerked up the door handle. "Not only do I not got time for a lecture from you, I ain't interested in one." He threw down his cigarette and stamped it out.

We walked in silence to Denesa Steiner's front door, and I had a feeling when she opened it she could sense Marino and I had been fighting. He would not look my way or acknowledge me in any way as she led us to a living room that was unnervingly familiar because I had seen photographs of it before. The decor was country, with an abundance of ruffles, plump pillows, hanging plants, and macramé. Behind glass doors, a gas fire glowed, and numerous clocks did not argue time. Mrs. Steiner was in the midst of watching an old Bob Hope movie on cable.

She seemed very tired as she turned off the television and sat in a rocking chair. "This hasn't been a very good day," she said.

"Well, now, Denesa, there's no way it could have been." Marino sat in a wing chair and gave her his full attention.

"Did you come here to tell me what you found?"

she asked, and I realized she was referring to the exhumation.

"We still have a lot of tests to conduct," I told her.

"Then you didn't find anything that will catch that man." She spoke with quiet despair. "Doctors always talk about tests when they don't know anything. I've learned that much after all I've been through."

"These things take time, Mrs. Steiner."

"Listen," Marino said to her. "I really am sorry to bother you, Denesa, but we've got to ask you a few more questions. The Doc here wants to ask you some."

She looked at me and rocked.

"Mrs. Steiner, there was a gift-wrapped package in Emily's casket that the funeral director says you wanted buried with her," I said.

"Oh, you're talking about Socks," she said matter-of-factly.

"Socks?" I asked.

"She was a stray kitten who started coming around here. I guess that would have been a month or so ago. And of course Emily was such a sensitive thing she started feeding it and that was it. She did love that little cat." She smiled as her eyes teared up.

"She called her Socks because she was pure black except for these perfect white paws." She held out her hands, splaying her fingers. "It looked like she had socks on."

"How did Socks die?" I carefully asked.

"I don't really know." She pulled tissues from a pocket and dabbed her eyes. "I found her one

morning out in front. This was right after Emily . . .
I just assumed the poor little thing died of a broken
heart." She covered her mouth with the tissues and
sobbed.

"I'm going to get you something to drink." Marino
got up and left the room.

His obvious familiarity with both the house and
its owner struck me as extremely unusual, and my
uneasiness grew.

"Mrs. Steiner," I said gently, leaning forward on the
couch. "Emily's kitten did not die of a broken heart. It
died of a broken neck."

She lowered her hands and took a deep, shaky
breath. Her eyes were red-rimmed and wide as they
fixed on me. "What do you mean?"

"The cat died violently."

"Well, I guess it got hit by a car. That's such a pity.
I told Emily I was afraid of that."

"It wasn't hit by a car."

"Do you suppose one of the dogs around here
got it?"

"No," I said as Marino returned with what looked
like a glass of white wine. "The kitten was killed by a
person. Deliberately."

"How could you know such a thing as that?" She
looked terrified, and her hands trembled as she took
the wine and set it on the table next to her chair.

"There were physical findings that make it clear the
cat's neck was wrung," I continued to explain very
calmly. "And I know it's awful for you to hear
details like this, Mrs. Steiner, but you must know

the truth if you are to help us find the person responsible."

"You got any idea who might have done something like that to your little girl's kitten?" Marino sat back down and leaned forward again, forearms resting on his knees, as if he wanted to assure her that she could depend on and feel safe with him.

She silently struggled for composure. Reaching for her wine, she took several unsteady sips. "I do know I've gotten some calls." She took a deep breath. "You know, my fingernails are blue. I'm such a wreck." She held out a hand. "I can't settle down. I can't sleep. I don't know what to do." She dissolved into tears again.

"Denesa, it's all right," Marino said kindly. "You just take your time. We're not going anywhere. Now tell me about the phone calls."

She wiped her eyes and went on. "It's been men mostly. Maybe one woman who said if I'd kept my eye on my little girl like a good mother, this wouldn't have . . . But one sounded young, like a boy playing pranks. He said something. You know. Like he'd seen Emily riding her bike. This was after . . . So it couldn't have been. But this other one, he was older. He said he wasn't finished." She drank more wine.

"He wasn't finished?" I asked. "Did he say anything else?"

"I don't remember." She shut her eyes.

"When was this?" Marino asked.

"Right after she was found. Found by the lake." She reached for her wine again and knocked it over.

"I'll get that." Marino abruptly got up. "I need to smoke."

"Do you know what he meant?" I asked her.

"I knew he was referring to what happened. To who did this to her. I felt he was saying it wasn't the end of bad things. And I guess it was a day later I found Socks."

"Captain, maybe you could fix me some toast with peanut butter or cheese. I feel like my blood sugar's getting low," said Mrs. Steiner, who seemed oblivious to the glass on its side and the puddle of wine on the table by her chair.

He left the room again.

"When the man broke into your house and abducted your daughter," I said, "did he speak to you at all?"

"He said if I didn't do exactly what he said, he'd kill me."

"So you heard his voice."

She nodded as she rocked, her eyes not leaving me.

"Did it sound like the voice on the phone that you were just telling us about?"

"I don't know. It might have. But it's hard to say."

"Mrs. Steiner . . . ?"

"You can call me Denesa." Her stare was intense.

"What else do you remember about him, the man who came into your house and taped you up?"

"You're wondering if he might be that man in Virginia who killed the little boy."

I said nothing.

"I remember seeing pictures of the little boy and his

143

family in *People* magazine. I remember thinking back then how awful it was, that I couldn't imagine being his mother. It was bad enough when Mary Jo died. I never thought I'd get past that."

"Is Mary Jo the child you lost to SIDS?"

Interest sparked beneath her dark pain, as if she were impressed or curious that I would know this detail. "She died in my bed. I woke up and she was next to Chuck, dead."

"Chuck was your husband?"

"At first I was afraid he might have accidentally rolled on top of her during the night and smothered her. But they said no. They said it was SIDS."

"How old was Mary Jo?" I asked.

"She'd just had her first birthday." She blinked back tears.

"Had Emily been born yet?"

"She came a year later, and I just knew the same thing was going to happen to her. She was so colicky. So frail. And the doctors were afraid she might have apnea, so I had to constantly check on her in her sleep. To make sure she was breathing. I remember walking around like a zombie because I never had a night's sleep. Up and down all night, night after night. Living with that horrible fear."

She closed her eyes for a moment and rocked, brow furrowed by grief, hands clenching armrests.

It occurred to me that Marino did not want to hear me question Mrs. Steiner because of his anger, and that was why he was out of the room so much. I knew then his emotions had wrestled him into the ropes. I feared he would no longer be effective in this case.

Mrs. Steiner opened her eyes and they went straight to mine. "He's killed a lot of people and now he's here," she said.

"Who?" I was confused by what I had been thinking.

"Temple Gault."

"We don't know for a fact he's here," I said.

"I know he is."

"How do you know that?"

"Because of what was done to my Emily. It's the same thing." A tear slid down her cheek. "You know, I guess I should be afraid he'll get me next. But I don't care. What do I have left?"

"I'm very sorry," I said as kindly as I could. "Can you tell me anything more about that Sunday? The Sunday of October first?"

"We went to church in the morning like we always did. And Sunday school. We ate lunch, then Emily was in her room. She was practicing guitar some of the time. I didn't see her much, really." She stared the wide stare of remembering.

"Do you recall her leaving the house early for her youth group meeting?"

"She came into the kitchen. I was making banana bread. She said she had to go early to practice guitar and I gave her some change for the collection like I always did."

"What about when she came home?"

"We ate." She was not blinking. "She was unhappy. And wanted Socks in the house and I said no."

145

"What makes you think she was unhappy?"

"She was difficult. You know how children can get when they're in moods. Then she was in her room awhile and went to bed."

"Tell me about her eating habits," I said, recalling that Ferguson had intended to ask Mrs. Steiner this after he returned from Quantico. I supposed he'd never had the chance.

"She was picky. Finicky."

"Did she finish her dinner Sunday night after her meeting?"

"That was part of what we got into a fuss about. She was just pushing her food around. Pouting." Her voice caught. "It was always a struggle. . . . It was always hard for me to get her to eat."

"Did she have a problem with diarrhea or nausea?"

Her eyes focused on me. "She was sick a lot."

"Sick can mean a lot of different things, Mrs. Steiner," I said patiently. "Did she have frequent diarrhea or nausea?"

"Yes. I already told Max Ferguson that." Tears flowed freely again. "And I don't understand why I have to keep answering these same questions. It just opens up things. Opens up wounds."

"I'm sorry," I said with a gentleness that belied my surprise. When had she told Ferguson this? Did he call her after he left Quantico? If so, she must have been one of the last people to talk to him before he died.

"This didn't happen to her because she was sickly," Mrs. Steiner said, crying harder. "It seems people should be asking questions that would help catch *him*."

"Mrs. Steiner—and I know this is difficult—but where were you living when Mary Jo died?"

"Oh God, please help me."

She buried her face in her hands. I watched her try to compose herself, shoulders heaving as she wept. I sat numbly as she got still, little by little, her feet, her arms, her hands. She slowly lifted her eyes to me. Through their bleariness gleamed a strange cold light that oddly made me think of the lake at night, of water so dark it seemed another element. And I felt fretful the way I did in my dreams.

She spoke in a low voice. "What I want to know, Dr. Scarpetta, is do you know that man?"

"What man?" I asked, and then Marino walked back in with a peanut butter and jelly sandwich on toast, a dish towel, and a bottle of chablis.

"The man who killed the little boy. Did you ever talk to Temple Gault?" she asked as Marino set her glass upright and refilled it, and placed the sandwich nearby.

"Here, let me help with that." I took the dish towel from him and wiped up spilled wine.

"Tell me what he looks like." She shut her eyes again.

I saw Gault in my mind, his piercing eyes and light blond hair. He was sharp featured, small and quick. But it was the eyes. I would never forget them. I knew he could slit a throat without flinching. I knew he had killed all of them with that same blue stare.

"Excuse me," I said, realizing Mrs. Steiner was still talking to me.

147

"Why did you let him get away?" she repeated her question as if it were an accusation, and began crying again.

Marino told her to get some rest, that we were leaving. When we got into the car, his mood was horrible.

"Gault killed her cat," he said.

"We don't know that for a fact."

"I ain't interested in hearing you talk like a lawyer right now."

"I am a lawyer," I said.

"Oh yeah. Excuse me for forgetting you got that degree, too. It just slips my mind that you *really are* a doctor-lawyer-Indian chief."

"Do you know if Ferguson called Mrs. Steiner after he left Quantico?"

"Hell, no, I don't know."

"He mentioned in the consultation he intended to ask her several medical questions. Based on what Mrs. Steiner said to me, it sounds like he did, meaning he must have talked to her shortly before his death."

"So maybe he called her as soon as he got home from the airport."

"And then he goes straight upstairs and puts a noose around his neck?"

"No, Doc. He goes straight upstairs to beat off. Maybe talking to her on the phone put him in the mood."

That was possible.

"Marino, what's the last name of the little boy Emily liked? I know his first name was Wren."

148

"Why?"

"I want to go see him."

"In case you don't know much about kids, it's almost nine o'clock on a school night."

"Marino," I said evenly, "answer my question."

"I know he don't live too far from the Steiners' crib." He pulled off on the side of the road and turned on his interior light. "His last name's Maxwell."

"I want to go to his house."

He flipped through his notepad, then glanced over at me. Behind his tired eyes I saw more than resentment. Marino was in terrific pain.

The Maxwells lived in a modern log cabin that was probably prefabricated and had been built on a wooded lot in view of the lake.

We pulled into a gravel drive lit by floodlights the color of pollen. It was cool enough for rhododendron leaves to begin to curl, and our breath turned to smoke as we waited on the porch for someone to answer the bell. When the door opened, we faced a young, lean man with a thin face and black-rimmed glasses. He was dressed in a dark wool robe and slippers. I wondered if anyone stayed up past ten o'clock in this town.

"I'm Captain Marino and this is Dr. Scarpetta," Marino said in a serious police tone that would fill any citizen with dread. "We're working with the local authorities on the Emily Steiner case."

"You're the ones from out of town," the man said.

"Are you Mr. Maxwell?" Marino asked.

"Lee Maxwell. Please come in. I guess you want to talk about Wren."

We entered the house as an overweight woman in a pink sweatsuit came downstairs. She looked at us as if she knew exactly why we were there.

"He's up in his room. I was reading to him," she said.

"I wonder if I might speak to him," I said in as nonthreatening a voice as possible, for I could tell the Maxwells were upset.

"I can get him," the father said.

"I'd rather go on up, if I might," I said.

Mrs. Maxwell absently fiddled with a seam coming loose on a cuff of her sweatshirt. She was wearing small silver earrings shaped like crosses that matched a necklace she had on.

"Maybe while the doc does that," Marino spoke up, "I can talk to the two of you?"

"That policeman who died already talked to Wren," said the father.

"I know." Marino spoke in a manner that told them he didn't care who had talked to their son. "We promise not to take up too much of your time," he added.

"Well, all right," Mrs. Maxwell said to me.

I followed her slow, heavy progress up uncarpeted stairs to a second floor that had few rooms but was so well lit my eyes hurt. There didn't seem to be a corner inside or out of the Maxwells' property that wasn't flooded with light. We walked into Wren's bedroom and the boy was in pajamas and standing in the middle of the floor. He stared at us as if we'd caught him in the middle of something we weren't supposed to see.

"Why aren't you in bed, son?" Mrs. Maxwell sounded more weary than stern.

"I was thirsty."

"Would you like me to get you another glass of water?"

"No, that's okay."

I could see why Emily would have found Wren Maxwell cute. He had been growing in height faster than his muscles could keep up, and his sunny blond hair wouldn't stay out of his dark blue eyes. Lanky and shaggy, with a perfect complexion and mouth, he had chewed his fingernails to the quick. He wore several bracelets of woven rawhide that could not be taken off without cutting, and they somehow told me he was very popular in school, especially with girls, whom I expected he treated quite rudely.

"Wren, this is Dr."—she looked at me—"I'm sorry, but you're going to have say your last name again."

"I'm Dr. Scarpetta." I smiled at Wren, whose expression turned to bewilderment.

"I'm not sick," he quickly said.

"She's not that kind of doctor," Mrs. Maxwell told her son.

"What kind are you?" By now his curiosity had overcome his shyness.

"Well, she's a doctor sort of like Lucias Ray is one."

"He ain't a doctor." Wren scowled at his mother. "He's an undertaker."

"Now you go on and get in bed, son, so you don't

catch cold. Dr. Scarletti, you can pull up that chair and I'll be downstairs."

"Her name's *Scarpetta*," the boy fired at his mother, who was already out the door.

He climbed into his twin bed and covered himself with a wool blanket the color of bubble gum. I noticed the baseball theme of the curtains drawn across his window, and the silhouettes of trophies behind them. On pine walls were posters of several sports heroes, and I recognized none of them except Michael Jordan, who was typically airborne in Nikes like some magnificent god. I pulled a chair close to the bed and suddenly felt old.

"What sport do you play?" I asked him.

"I play for the Yellow Jackets," he answered brightly, for he had found a co-conspirator in his quest to stay up past bedtime.

"The Yellow Jackets?"

"That's my Little League team. You know, we beat everybody around here. I'm surprised you haven't heard of us."

"I'm certain I would have heard of your team if I lived here, Wren. But I don't."

He regarded me as if I were some exotic creature behind glass in the zoo. "I play basketball, too. I can dribble between my legs. I bet you can't do that."

"You're absolutely right. I can't. I'd like you to tell me about your friendship with Emily Steiner."

His eyes dropped to his hands, which were nervously fiddling with the edge of the blanket.

"Had you known her a long time?" I continued.

"I've seen her around. We're in the same youth group at church." He looked at me. "Plus, we're both in the sixth grade but we have different homeroom teachers. I have Mrs. Winters."

"Did you get to know Emily right after her family moved here?"

"I guess so. They came from California. Mom says they have earthshakes out there because the people don't believe in Jesus."

"It seems Emily liked you a great deal," I said. "In fact, I'd say she had a big crush on you. Were you aware of that?"

He nodded, eyes cast down again.

"Wren, can you tell me about the last time you saw her?"

"It was at church. She came in with her guitar because it was her turn."

"Her turn for what?"

"For music. Usually Owen or Phil plays the piano, but sometimes Emily would play guitar. She wasn't very good."

"Were you supposed to meet her at church that afternoon?"

Color mounted his cheeks and he sucked in his lower lip to keep it from trembling.

"It's all right, Wren. You didn't do anything wrong."

"I asked her to meet me there early," he quietly said.

"What was her reaction?"

"She said she would but not to tell anybody."

"Why did you want her to meet you early?" I continued to probe.

"I wanted to see if she would."

"Why?"

Now his face was very red and he was working hard to hold back tears. "I don't know," he barely said.

"Wren, tell me what happened."

"I rode my bike to the church just to see if she was there."

"What time would this have been?"

"I don't know. But it was at least an hour before the meeting was supposed to start," he said. "And I saw her through the window. She was inside sitting on the floor practicing guitar."

"Then what?"

"I left and came back with Paul and Will at five. They live over there." He pointed.

"Did you say anything to Emily?" I asked.

Tears spilled down his cheeks, and he impatiently wiped them away. "I didn't say nothing. She kept staring at me but I pretended not to see her. She was upset. Jack asked her what was wrong."

"Who's Jack?"

"The youth leader. He goes to Montreat Anderson College. He's real fat and's got a beard."

"What was her reply when Jack asked what was wrong?"

"She said she felt like she was getting the flu. Then she left."

"How long before the meeting was over?"

"When I was getting the basket off the top of the piano. 'Cause it was my turn to take up the collection."

"This would have been at the very end of the meeting?"

"That's when she ran out. She took the shortcut." He bit his lower lip and gripped the blanket so hard that the small bones of his hands were clearly defined.

"How do you know she took a shortcut?" I asked.

He looked up at me and sniffed loudly. I handed him several tissues, and he blew his nose.

"Wren," I persisted, "did you actually *see* Emily take the shortcut?"

"No, ma'am," he meekly said.

"Did anybody see her take the shortcut?"

He shrugged.

"Then why do you think she took it?"

"Everybody says so," he replied simply.

"Just as everybody has said where her body was found?" I was gentle. When he did not respond, I added more forcefully, "And you know exactly where that is, don't you, Wren?"

"Yes, ma'am," he said almost in a whisper.

"Will you tell me about that place?"

Still staring at his hands, he answered, "It's just this place where lots of colored people fish. There's a bunch of weeds and slime, and huge bullfrogs and snakes hanging out of the trees, and that's where she was. A colored man found her, and all she had on was her socks, and it scared him so bad he turned white as you are. After that Dad put in all the lights."

"Lights?"

"He put all these lights in the trees and everywhere.

It makes it harder for me to sleep, and then Mom gets mad."

"Was it your father who told you about the place at the lake?"

Wren shook his head.

"Then who did?" I asked.

"Creed."

"Creed?"

"He's one of the janitors at school. He makes toothpicks, and we buy them for a dollar. Ten for a dollar. He soaks them in peppermint and cinnamon. I like the cinnamon best 'cause they're real hot like Fireballs. Sometimes I trade him candy when I run out of lunch money. But you can't tell anybody." He looked worried.

"What does Creed look like?" I asked as a quiet alarm began to sound in the back of my brain.

"I don't know," Wren said. "He's a greaser 'cause he's always wearing white socks with boots. I guess he's pretty old." He sighed.

"Do you know his last name?"

Wren shook his head.

"Has he always worked at your school?"

He shook his head again. "He took Albert's place. Albert got sick from smoking, and they had to cut his lung out."

"Wren," I asked, "did Creed and Emily know each other?"

He was talking faster and faster. "We used to make her mad by saying Creed was her boyfriend 'cause one time he gave her some flowers he picked. And he would give her candy 'cause she didn't like toothpicks. You know, a lot of girls would rather have candy than toothpicks."

"Yes," I answered with a grim smile, "I suspect a lot of girls would."

The last thing I asked Wren was if he had visited the place at the lake where Emily's body had been found. He claimed he had not.

"I believe him," I said to Marino as we drove away from the Maxwells' well-lit house.

"Not me. I think he's lying his little ass off so his old man don't whip the shit out of him." He turned down the heat. "This ride heats up better than any one I've ever had. All it's missing is heaters in the seats like you got in your Benz."

"The way he described the scene at the lake," I went on, "tells me he's never been there. I don't think he left the candy there, Marino."

"Then who did?"

"What do you know about a custodian named Creed?"

"Not a damn thing."

"Well," I said, "I think you'd better find him. And I'll tell you something else. I don't think Emily took the shortcut around the lake on her way home from the church."

"Shit," he complained. "I hate it when you get like this. Just when pieces start to fall in place you shake the hell out of them like a damn puzzle in a box."

"Marino, I took the path around the lake myself. There's no way an eleven-year-old girl—or anybody else, for that matter—would do that when it's getting dark. And it would have been almost completely dark by six P.M., which was the time Emily headed home."

"Then she lied to her mother," Marino said.

"It would appear so. But why?"

"Maybe because Emily was up to something."

"Such as?"

"I don't know. You got any Scotch in the room? I mean, there's no point in asking if you got bourbon."

"You're right," I said. "I don't have bourbon."

I found five messages awaiting me when I returned to the Travel-Eze. Three were from Benton Wesley. The Bureau was sending the helicopter to pick me up at dawn.

When I got hold of Wesley he cryptically said, "Among other things, we've got rather a crisis situation with your niece. We're bringing you straight back to Quantico."

"What's happened?" I asked as my stomach closed like a fist. "Is Lucy all right?"

"Kay, this is not a secured line."

"But is she all right?"

"Physically," he said, "she's fine."

10

The next morning I woke up to mist and could not see the mountains. My return north was postponed until afternoon, and I went out for a run in the brisk, moist air.

I wended my way through neighborhoods of cozy homes and modest cars, smiling as a miniature collie behind a chain link fence raced from one border of the yard to another, barking frantically at falling leaves. The owner emerged from the house as I went past.

"Now, Shooter, hush up!"

The woman wore a quilted robe, fuzzy slippers, and curlers, and didn't seem to mind a bit walking outside like that. She picked up the newspaper and smacked it against her palm as she yelled some more. I imagined that prior to Emily Steiner's death, the only crime anyone worried about in this part of the world was a neighbor stealing your newspaper or stringing toilet paper through your trees.

Cicadas were sawing the same scratchy tune they had

159

played last night, and locust, sweet peas, and morning
glories were wet with dew. By eleven, a cold rain had
begun to fall, and I felt as if I were at sea surrounded
by brooding waters. I imagined the sun was a porthole,
and if I could look through it to the other side I might
find an end to this gray day.

It was half past two before the weather improved
enough for me to leave. I was instructed that the
helicopter could not land at the high school because
the Warhorses and majorettes would be in the midst
of practice. Instead, Whit and I were to meet at a
grassy field inside the rugged stone double-arched
gate of a tiny town called Montreat, which was as
Presbyterian as predestination and but a few miles
from the Travel-Eze.

The Black Mountain Police arrived with me before
Whit appeared, and I sat in a cruiser parked on a
dirt road, watching children play flag football. Boys
ran after girls and girls ran after boys as everybody
pursued the small glory of snatching a red rag from
an opposing player's waistband. Young voices carried
on a wind that sometimes caught the ball and passed
it through the fingers of trees huddled at borders, and
whenever it spiraled out of bounds into briars or the
street, everybody paused. Equality was sent to the
bench as girls waited for boys. When the ball was
retrieved, play went on as usual.

I was sorry to interrupt this innocent frolicking when
the distinctive chopping noise became audible. The
children froze into a tableau of wonderment as the
Bell JetRanger lowered itself with a roaring wind to

the center of the field. I boarded and waved good-bye as we rose above trees.

The sun settled into the horizon like Apollo lying down to sleep, and then the sky was as thick as octopus ink. I saw no stars when we arrived at the Academy. Benton Wesley, who had been kept informed of our progress by radio, was waiting when we landed. The instant I climbed out of the helicopter, he had my arm and was leading me away.

"Come on," he said. "It's good to see you, Kay," he added under his breath, and the pressure of his fingers on my arm unsettled me more.

"The fingerprint recovered from Ferguson's panties was left by Denesa Steiner."

"What?"

He propelled me swiftly through the dark. "And the ABO grouping of the tissue we found in his freezer is O-positive. Emily Steiner was O-positive. We're still waiting for DNA, but it appears Ferguson stole the lingerie from the Steiner home when he broke in to abduct Emily."

"You mean, when *someone* broke in and abducted Emily."

"That's right. Gault could be playing games."

"Benton, for God's sake, what crisis? Where's Lucy?"

"I imagine she's in her dorm room," he replied as we walked into the lobby of Jefferson.

I squinted in the light and was not cheered by a digital sign behind the information desk announcing WELCOME TO THE FBI ACADEMY. I did not feel welcome this night.

"What did she do?" I persisted as he used a magnetized card to unlock a set of glass doors with Department of Justice and National Academy seals.

"Wait until we get downstairs," he said.

"How's your hand? And your knee?" I remembered.

"Much better since I went to a doctor."

"Thanks," I said dryly.

"I'm referring to you. You're the only doctor I've been to recently."

"I might as well clean your stitches while I'm here."

"That won't be necessary."

"I need hydrogen peroxide and cotton swabs. Don't worry." I smelled Hoppes as we walked through the gun-cleaning room. "It shouldn't hurt very much."

We took the elevator to the lower level, where the Investigative Support Unit was the fire in the belly of the FBI. Wesley reigned over eleven other profilers, and at this hour, every one of them had left for the day. I had always liked the space where Wesley worked, for he was a man of sentiment and understatement, and one could not possibly know this without knowing him.

While most people in law enforcement filled walls and shelves with commendations and souvenirs from their war against base human nature, Wesley chose paintings, and he had several very fine ones. My favorite was an expansive landscape by Valoy Eaton, who I believed was as good as Remington and one day would cost as much. I had several Eaton oil paintings in my home, and what was odd was that Wesley and I had discovered the Utahan artist independent of each other.

This is not to say that Wesley did not have his occasional exotic trophy, but he displayed only those that held meaning. The Viennese white police cap, the bearskin cap from a Cold Stream Guard, and silver gaucho spurs from Argentina, for example, had nothing to do with serial killers or any other atrocity Wesley worked as a matter of course. They were gifts from well-traveled friends like me. In fact, Wesley had many mementos of our relationship because when words failed I spoke in symbols. So he had an Italian scabbard, a pistol with scrimshawed ivory grips, and a Mont Blanc pen that he kept in a pocket over his heart.

"Talk to me," I said, taking a chair. "What else is going on? You look awful."

"I feel awful." He loosened his tie and ran his fingers through his hair. "Kay"—he looked at me—"I don't know how to tell you this. Christ!"

"Just say it," I said very quietly as my blood went cold.

"It appears that Lucy broke into ERF, that she violated security."

"How could she break in?" I asked incredulously. "She has clearance to be there, Benton."

"She does not have clearance to be there at three o'clock in the morning, which was when her thumb-print was scanned into the biometric lock system."

I stared at him in disbelief.

"And your niece certainly does not have clearance to go into classified files pertaining to classified projects being worked on over there."

163

"What projects?" I dared to ask.

"It appears she went into files pertaining to electro-optics, thermal imaging, video and audio enhancement. And she apparently printed programs from the electronic version of case management that she's been working on for us."

"You mean from CAIN?"

"Yes, that's right."

"What *wasn't* gotten into?" I asked, stunned.

"Well, that's really the point. She got into virtually everything, meaning it's difficult for us to know what she was really after and for whom."

"Are the devices the engineers are working on really so secret?"

"Some of them are, and all of the techniques are, from a security standpoint. We don't want it known that we use this device in this situation and use something else in another."

"She couldn't have," I said.

"We know she did. The question is why."

"All right, then, why?" I blinked back tears.

"Money. That would be my guess."

"That's ridiculous. If she needs money she knows she can come to me."

"Kay"—Wesley leaned forward and folded his hands on top of his desk—"do you have any idea how valuable some of this information is?"

I did not reply.

"Imagine, for example, if ERF developed a surveillance device that could filter out background noise so we could be privy to virtually any conversation of interest to us anywhere in the world. Imagine who out there would love to know the details of our rapid prototyping or tactical satellite systems, or for that matter, the artificial intelligence software Lucy is developing. . . ."

I held up my hand to stop him. "Enough," I said as I took a deep, shaky breath.

"Then you tell me why," Wesley said. "You know Lucy better than I do."

"I'm no longer so sure I know her at all. And I don't know how she could do such a thing, Benton."

He paused, staring off for a moment before meeting my eyes again. "You've indicated to me that you're worried about her drinking. Can you elaborate on that?"

"My guess is she drinks like she does everything else—in extreme. Lucy is either very good or very bad, and alcohol is just one example." I knew even as I said the words I was darkening Wesley's suspicions.

"I see," he said. "Is there alcoholism in her family?"

"I'm beginning to think there's alcoholism in everybody's family," I said bitterly. "But yes. Her father was an alcoholic."

"This would be your brother-in-law?"

"He was very briefly. As you know, Dorothy's been married four times."

"Are you aware that there have been nights when Lucy didn't return to her dormitory room?"

"I know nothing about that. Was she in her bed

the night of the break-in? She has suitemates and a roommate."

"She could have snuck out when everyone was asleep. So we don't know. Are you and your niece getting along well?" he then asked.

"Not especially."

"Kay, could she have done something like this to punish you?"

"No," I said, and I was getting angry with him. "And what I'm not interested in at the moment is your using me to *profile* my niece."

"Kay"—his voice softened—"I don't want this to be true any more than you do. I'm the one who recommended her to ERF. I'm the one who's been working on our hiring her after she graduates from UVA. Do you think I'm feeling very good?"

"There must be some other way this could have happened."

He slowly shook his head. "Even if someone had discovered Lucy's PIN, they still couldn't have gotten in because the biometric system would also require a scan of her actual finger."

"Then she wanted to be caught," I replied. "Lucy more than anyone would know that if she went into classified automated files, she would leave log-in and log-out times, activity logs, and other tracks."

"I agree. She would know this better than anyone. And that's why I'm more interested in possible motive. In other words, what was she trying to prove? Who was she trying to hurt?"

"Benton," I said. "What will happen?"

"OPR will conduct an official investigation," he answered, referring to the Bureau's Office of Professional Responsibility, which was the equivalent of a police department's Internal Affairs.

"If she's guilty?"

"It depends on whether we can prove she stole anything. If she did, she's committed a felony."

"And if she didn't?"

"Again, it depends on what OPR finds. But I think it's safe to say that at the very least Lucy has violated our security codes and no longer has a future with the FBI," he said.

My mouth was so dry I almost couldn't talk. "She will be devastated."

Wesley's eyes were shadowed by fatigue and disappointment. I knew how much he liked my niece.

"In the meantime," he went on in the same flat tone he used when reviewing cases, "she can't stay at Quantico. She's already been told to pack her things. Maybe she can stay in Richmond with you until our investigation is concluded."

"Of course, but you know I won't be there all the time."

"We're not placing her under house arrest, Kay," he said, and his eyes got warmer for an instant. Very briefly I caught a glimpse of what stirred silently in his cool, dark waters.

He got up.

"I'll drive her to Richmond tonight." I got up, too.

"I hope you're all right," he said, and I knew what he meant, and I knew I could not think about that now.

"Thank you," I replied, and impulses fired crazily between neurons, as if a fierce battle were being fought in my mind.

Lucy was stripping her bed when I found her in her room not much later, and she turned her back to me when I walked in.

"What can I help you with?" I asked.

She stuffed sheets into a pillowcase. "Nothing," she said. "I've got it under control."

Her quarters were plainly furnished with institutional twin beds, desks, and chairs of oak veneer. By Yuppie apartment standards, the rooms in Washington dormitory were dreary, but if viewed as barracks they weren't half bad. I wondered where Lucy's suitemates and roommate were and if they had any idea what had happened.

"If you'll just check the wardrobe to make sure I've gotten everything," Lucy said. "It's the one on the right. And check the drawers."

"Everything is empty unless the coat hangers are yours. These nice padded ones."

"They're Mother's."

"Then I assume you want them."

"Nope. Leave them for the next idiot who ends up in this pit."

"Lucy," I said, "it's not the Bureau's fault."

"It's not fair." She knelt on her suitcase to fasten the clasps. "Whatever happened to innocent until proven guilty?"

"Legally, you are innocent until proven guilty. But

until this breach of security is sorted out, you can't blame the Academy for not wanting you to continue working in classified areas. Besides, you haven't been arrested. You've simply been asked to go on leave for a while."

She turned to face me, her eyes exhausted and red. "For a while means forever."

As I questioned her closely in the car, she vacillated from pitiful tears to volatile flares that scorched everything within reach. Then she fell asleep, and I knew nothing more than I had before. As a cold rain began to fall, I turned on fog lamps and followed the trail of bright red taillights streaking the blacktop ahead. At unwelcome intervals rain and clouds gathered densely in dips and turns, making it almost impossible to see. But instead of pulling over and waiting for the weather to pass, I shifted to a lower gear and drove on in my machine of burled walnut, soft leather, and steel.

I still wasn't certain why I had bought my charcoal Mercedes 500E, except that after Mark died, it had seemed important to drive something new. It might have been the memories, for we had loved and fought with each other desperately in my previous car. Or perhaps it was simply that life got harder as I got older and I needed more power to get by.

I heard Lucy stir as I turned into Windsor Farms, the old Richmond neighborhood where I lived amid stately Georgian and Tudor homes not far from the banks of the James. My headlights caught tiny reflectors on ankles of an unfamiliar boy riding a bicycle just ahead, and I passed a couple I did not recognize who were holding hands and walking their dog. Gum trees had dropped another load of prickly seeds over my yard, several rolled newspapers were on the porch, and the supercans were still parked by the street. It did not require long absences for me to feel like an outsider and for my house to look like no one was home.

While Lucy carried in luggage, I started the gas logs in the living room and put on a pot of Darjeeling tea. For a while I sat alone in front of the fire, listening to the sounds of my niece as she got settled, took a shower, and in general took her time. We were about to have a discussion that filled both of us with dread.

"Are you hungry?" I asked when I heard her walk in.

"No. Do you have any beer?"

I hesitated, then replied, "In the refrigerator in the bar."

I listened a little longer without turning around, because when I looked at Lucy I saw her the way I wanted her to be. Sipping tea, I mustered up the strength to face this frighteningly beautiful and brilliant woman with whom I shared snippets of genetic code. After all these years, it was time we met.

She came to the fire and sat on the floor, leaning against the stone hearth as she drank Icehouse beer out of the bottle. She had helped herself to a boldly colorful warm-up suit I wore on the infrequent occasions when I played tennis these days, and her feet were bare, her wet hair combed back. I realized that if I didn't know her and she walked past, I would turn to look again, and this wasn't solely due to her fine figure and face.

One sensed the facility with which Lucy spoke, walked, and in the smallest ways guided her body and her eyes. She made everything seem easy, which was partially why she did not have many friends.

"Lucy," I began, "help me understand."

"I've been fucked," she said, taking a swallow of beer.

"If that's true, then how?"

"What do you mean 'if'?" She stared hard at me, her eyes filling with tears. "How can you think for even a minute . . . Oh, shit. What's the point?" She looked away.

"I can't help you if you don't tell me the truth," I said, getting up as I decided that I wasn't hungry, either. I went to the bar and poured Scotch over crushed ice.

"Let's start with the facts," I suggested as I returned to my chair. "We know someone entered ERF at around three A.M. on this past Tuesday. We know your PIN was used and your thumb was scanned. It is further documented by the system that this person—again, who has your PIN and print—went into numerous files. The log-out time was at precisely four thirty-eight A.M."

"I've been set up and sabotaged," Lucy said.

"Where were you while all this was going on?"

"I was asleep." She angrily gulped down the rest of her beer and got up for another one.

I sipped my Scotch slowly because it was not possible to drink a Dewar's Mist fast. "It has been alleged that there have been nights when your bed was empty," I quietly said.

"And you know what? It's nobody's business."

"Well, it is, and you know that. Were you in your bed the night of the break-in?"

"It's my business what *bed* I'm in, when, and where, and nobody else's," she said.

We were silent as I thought of Lucy sitting on top of the picnic table in the dark, her face illuminated by the match cupped in another woman's hands. I heard her speaking to her friend and understood the emotions carrying her words, for I knew the language of intimacy well. I knew when love was in someone's voice, and I knew when it was not.

"Exactly where were you when ERF was broken into?" I asked her again. "Or should I ask you instead who you were with?"

"I don't ask you who you're with."

"You would if it might save me from being in a lot of trouble."

"My private life is irrelevant," she went on.

"No, I think it is rejection you fear," I said.

"I don't know what you're talking about."

"I saw you in the picnic area the other night. You were with a friend."

She looked away. "So now you're spying on me, too." Her voice trembled. "Well, don't waste any sermons on me, and you can forget Catholic guilt because I don't believe in Catholic guilt."

"Lucy, I'm not judging you," I said, but in a way I was. "Help me understand."

"You imply I'm unnatural or abnormal, otherwise

I would not need understanding. I would simply be accepted without a second thought."

"Can your friend vouch for your whereabouts at three o'clock Tuesday morning?" I asked.

"No," she answered.

"I see" was all I said, and my acceptance of her position was a concession that the girl I knew was gone. I did not know this Lucy, and I wondered what I had done wrong.

"What are you going to do now?" she asked me as the evening tensely wore on.

"I've got this case in North Carolina. I have a feeling I'm going to be there a lot for a while," I said.

"What about your office here?"

"Fielding's holding down the fort. I do have court in the morning, I think. In fact, I need to call Rose to verify the time."

"What kind of case?"

"A homicide."

"I figured that much. Can I come with you?"

"If you'd like."

"Well, maybe I'll just go back to Charlottesville."

"And do what?" I asked.

Lucy looked frightened. "I don't know. I don't know how I'd get there, either."

"You're welcome to my car when I'm not using it. Or you could go to Miami until the semester's over, then back to UVA."

She downed the last mouthful of beer and got up, her eyes bright with tears again. "Go ahead and admit it, Aunt Kay. You think I did it, don't you?"

"Lucy," I said honestly, "I don't know what to think. You and the evidence are saying two different things."

"I have never doubted you." She looked at me as if I had broken her heart.

"You're welcome to stay here through Christmas," I said.

11

The member of the North Richmond Gang on trial the next morning wore a double-breasted navy suit and an Italian silk tie with a perfect Windsor knot. His white shirt looked crisp; he was cleanly shaven and minus his earring.

Trial lawyer Tod Coldwell had dressed his client well because he knew that jurors have an exceedingly difficult time resisting the notion that what you see is what you get. Of course, I believed that axiom, too, which was why I introduced into evidence as many color photographs from the victim's autopsy as possible. It was safe to say that Coldwell, who drove a red Ferrari, did not like me much.

"Isn't it true, Mrs. Scarpetta," Coldwell pontificated in court this cool autumn day, "that people under the influence of cocaine can become very violent and even demonstrate superhuman strength?"

"Certainly cocaine can cause the user to become delusional and excited," I continued directing my answers to the jury. "Superhuman strength, as you call it, is often associated with cocaine or PCP—which is a horse tranquilizer."

"And the victim had both cocaine and benzoylecgonine in his blood," Coldwell went on as if I had just agreed with him.

"Yes, he did."

"Mrs. Scarpetta, I wonder if you would explain to the jury what that means?"

"I would first like to explain to the jury that I am a medical doctor with a law degree. I have a specialty in pathology and a subspecialty in forensic pathology, as you've already stipulated, Mr. Coldwell. Therefore, I would appreciate being addressed as Dr. Scarpetta instead of Mrs. Scarpetta."

"Yes, ma'am."

"Would you please repeat the question?"

"Would you explain to the jury what it means if someone has cocaine"—he glanced at his notes—"and benzoylecgonine in his blood?"

"Benzoylecgonine is the metabolite of cocaine. To say that someone had both on board means some of the cocaine the victim had taken had already metabolized and some had not," I replied, aware of Lucy in a back corner, her face partially hidden by a column. She looked miserable.

"Which would indicate he was a chronic abuser, especially since he had many old needle tracks. And this may also suggest that when my client was confronted by him on the night of July third, my client had a very excited, agitated, and violent person on

his hands, and had no choice but to defend himself."
Coldwell was pacing, his dapper client watching me
like a twitchy cat.

"Mr. Coldwell," I said, "the victim—Jonah Jones—was
shot sixteen times with a Tec-Nine nine-millimeter gun
that holds thirty-six rounds. Seven of those shots were
to his back, and three of them were close or contact
shots to the back of Mr. Jones's head.

"In my opinion, this is inconsistent with a shooting
in which the shooter was defending himself, especially since Mr. Jones had a blood alcohol of point
two-nine, which is almost three times the legal limit in
Virginia. In other words, the victim's motor skills and
judgment were substantially impaired when he was
assaulted. Frankly, I'm amazed that Mr. Jones could
even stand up."

Coldwell swung around to face Judge Poe, who had
been nicknamed "the Raven" for as long as I had been
in Richmond. He was weary to his ancient soul of drug
dealers killing each other, of children carrying guns to
school and shooting each other on the bus.

"Your Honor," Coldwell said dramatically, "I would
ask that Mrs. Scarpetta's last statement be struck from
the record since it is both speculative and inflammatory,
and without a doubt beyond her area of expertise."

"Well, now, I don't know that what the doctor has
to say is beyond her expertise, Mr. Coldwell, and she's
already asked you politely to refer to her properly as *Dr.*
Scarpetta, and I'm losing patience with your antics and
ploys. . . ."

"But, Your Honor—"

"The fact is that I've had Dr. Scarpetta in my court-room on many occasions and I'm well aware of her level of expertise," the judge went on in his Southern way of speaking that reminded me of pulling warm taffy.

"Your Honor . . . ?"

"Seems to me she deals with this sort of thing every day. . . ."

"Your Honor?"

"Mr. Coldwell," the Raven thundered, his balding pate turning red, "if you interrupt me one more goddam time I'm going to hold you in contempt of court and let you spend a few nights in the goddam city jail! Are we clear?"

"Yes, sir."

Lucy was craning her neck to see, and every juror was alert.

"I'm going to allow the record to reflect exactly what Dr. Scarpetta said," the judge went on.

"No further questions," Coldwell said tersely.

Judge Poe concluded with a violent bang of the gavel that woke up an old woman toward the back who had been fast asleep beneath a black straw hat for most of the morning. Startled, she sat straight up and blurted, "Who is it?" Then she remembered where she was and began to cry.

"It's all right, Mama," I heard another woman say as we adjourned for lunch.

Before leaving downtown, I stopped by the Health Department's Division of Vital Records, where an old friend and colleague of mine was the state registrar. In Virginia, one could not legally be born or buried without Gloria Loving's signature, and though she was as local as shad roe, she knew her counterpart in every state in the union. Over the years, I had relied on Gloria many times to verify that people had been on this planet or had not, that they had been married, divorced, or were adopted.

I was told she was on her lunch break in the Madison Building cafeteria. At quarter past one, I found Gloria alone at a table, eating vanilla yogurt and canned fruit cocktail. Mostly, she was reading a thick paperback thriller that was a *New York Times* bestseller, according to the cover.

"If I had to eat lunches like yours, I wouldn't bother," I said, pulling out a chair.

She looked up at me, her blank expression followed by joy. "Goodness gracious! Why, my Lord. What on earth are you doing here, Kay?"

"I work across the street, in case you've forgotten."

Delighted, she laughed. "Can I get you a coffee? Honey, you look tired."

Gloria Loving's name had defined her at birth, and she had grown up true to her calling. She was a big, generous woman of some fifty years who deeply cared about every certificate that crossed her desk. Records were more than paper and nosology codes to her, and she would hire, fire, or blast General Assembly in the name of one. It did not matter whose.

"No coffee, thanks," I said.

"Well, I heard you didn't work across the street anymore."

"I love the way people resign me when I've not been

here for a couple of weeks. I'm a consultant with the FBI now. I'm in and out a lot."

"In and out of North Carolina, I guess, based on what I've been following in the news. Even Dan Rather was talking about the Steiner girl's case the other night. It was on CNN, too. Lord, it's cold in here."

I looked around at the bleak state government cafeteria where few people seemed thrilled with their lives. Many were huddled over trays, jackets and sweaters buttoned to their chins.

"They've got all the thermostats reset to sixty degrees to conserve energy, if that isn't the joke of all time," Gloria went on. "We have *steam heat* that comes out of the Medical College of Virginia, so cutting the thermostats doesn't save one watt of electricity."

"It feels colder in here than sixty degrees," I commented.

"That's because it's fifty-three, which is about what it is outside."

"You're welcome to come across the street and use my office," I said with a sly smile.

"Well, now, that's got to be the warmest spot in town. What can I do to help you, Kay?"

"I need to track down a SIDS that allegedly occurred in California around twelve years ago. The infant's name is Mary Jo Steiner, the parents' names Denesa and Charles."

She made the connection immediately but was too professional to probe. "Do you know Denesa Steiner's maiden name?"

"No."

"Where in California?"

"I don't know that, either," I said.

"Any possibility you can find out? The more information, the better."

"I'd rather you try running what I've got. If that fails, I'll see what else I can find out."

"You said an *alleged* SIDS. There's some suspicion that maybe it wasn't a SIDS? I need to know in case it might have been coded another way."

"Supposedly, the child was a year old when she died. And that bothers me considerably. As you know, the peak age for SIDS is three to four months old. Over six months old, and SIDS is unlikely. After a year, you're almost always talking about some other subtle form of sudden death. So yes, the death could have been coded a different way."

She played with her tea bag. "If this was Idaho, I'd just call Jane and she could run the nosology code for SIDS and have an answer for me in ninety seconds. But California's got thirty-two million people. It's one of the hardest states. It might take a special run. Come on, I'll walk you out. That will be my exercise for the day."

"Is the registrar in Sacramento?" We followed a depressing corridor busy with desperate citizens in need of social services.

"Yes. I'm going to call him as soon as I go back upstairs."

"I assume you know him, then."

"Oh, sure." She laughed. "There are only fifty of us. We have no one to talk to but each other."

That night I took Lucy to La Petite France, where I

surrendered to Chef Paul, who sentenced us to languid hours of fruit-marinated lamb kabobs and a bottle of 1986 Château Gruaud Larose. I promised her *crema di cioccolata eletta* when we got home, a lovely chocolate mousse with pistachio and marsala that I kept in the freezer for culinary emergencies.

But before that we drove to Shocko Bottom and walked along cobblestones beneath lamplight in a part of the city that not so long ago I would not have ventured near. We were close to the river, and the sky was midnight blue with stars flung wide. I thought of Benton and then I thought of Marino for very different reasons.

"Aunt Kay," Lucy said as we entered Chetti's for cappuccino, "can I get a lawyer?"

"For what purpose?" I asked, although I knew.

"Even if the FBI can't prove what they're saying I did, they'll still slam me for the rest of my life." Pain could not hide behind her steady voice.

"Tell me what you want."

"A big gun."

"I'll find you one," I said.

I did not return to North Carolina on Monday as I had planned but flew to Washington instead. There were rounds to make at FBI headquarters, but more than anything I needed to see an old friend.

Senator Frank Lord and I had attended the same Catholic high school in Miami, although not at the same time. He was quite a lot older than I, and our friendship did not begin until I was working for the

182

Dade County Medical Examiner's Office and he was the district attorney. When he became governor, then senator, I was long gone from the southern city of my birth. He and I did not become reconnected until he was appointed chairman of the Senate Judiciary Committee.

Lord had asked me to be an adviser as he fought to pass the most formidable crime bill in the history of the nation, and I had solicited his help, too. Unbeknownst to Lucy, he had been her patron saint, for without his intervention, she probably would not have been granted either permission or academic credit for her internship this fall. I wasn't certain how to tell him the news.

At almost noon, I waited for him on a polished cotton couch in a parlor with rich red walls and Persian rugs and a splendid crystal chandelier. Outside, voices carried along the marble corridor, and an occasional tourist peeked through the doorway in hopes of catching a glimpse of a politician or some other important person inside the Senate dining room. Lord arrived on time and full of energy, and gave me a quick, stiff hug. He was a kind, unassuming man shy about showing affection.

"I got lipstick on your face." I wiped a smudge off his jaw.

"Oh, you should leave it so my colleagues have something to talk about."

"I suspect they have plenty to talk about anyway."

"Kay, it's wonderful to see you," he said, escorting me into the dining room.

"You may not think it's so wonderful," I said.

"Of course I will."

We picked a table before a stained-glass window of George Washington on a horse, and I did not look at the menu because it never changed. Senator Lord was a distinguished man with thick gray hair and deep blue eyes. He was quite tall and lean, and had a penchant for elegant silk ties and old-fashioned finery such as vests, cuff links, pocket watches and stickpins.

"What brings you to D.C.?" he asked, placing his linen napkin in his lap.

"I have evidence to discuss at the FBI labs," I said.

He nodded. "You're working on that awful case in North Carolina."

"Yes."

"That psycho must be stopped. Do you think he's there?"

"I don't know."

"Because I'm just wondering why he would be," Lord went on. "It would seem he would have moved on to another place where he could lay low for a while. Well, I suppose logic has little to do with the decisions these evil people make."

"Frank," I said, "Lucy's in a lot of trouble."

"I can tell something's wrong," he said matter-of-factly. "I see it in your face."

He listened to me for half an hour as I told him everything, and I was so grateful for his patience. I knew he had to vote several times that day and that many people wanted slivers of his time.

"You're a good man," I said with feeling. "And I

184

have let you down. I asked you for a favor, which is something I almost never do, and the situation has ended in disgrace."

"Did she do it?" he asked, and he had scarcely touched his grilled vegetables.

"I don't know," I replied. "The evidence is incriminating." I cleared my throat. "She says she didn't do it."

"Has she always told you the truth?"

"I thought so. But I've also been discovering of late that there are many important facets to her that she has not told me."

"Have you asked?"

"She's made it clear that some things aren't my business. And I shouldn't judge."

"If you're afraid of being judgmental, Kay, then you probably already are. And Lucy would sense this no matter what you say or don't say."

"I've never enjoyed being the one who criticizes and corrects her," I said, depressed. "But her mother, Dorothy, who is my only sibling, is too male dependent and self-centered to deal with the reality of a daughter."

"And now Lucy is in trouble, and you are wondering how much of it is your fault."

"I'm not conscious of wondering that."

"We rarely are conscious of those primitive anxieties that creep out from under reason. And the only way to banish them is to turn on all the lights. Do you think you're strong enough to do that?"

"Yes."

"Let me remind you that if you ask, you also must be able to live with the answers."

"I know."

"Let's just suppose for a moment that Lucy's innocent," said Senator Lord.

"Then what?" I asked.

"If Lucy didn't violate security, obviously someone else did. My question is why?"

"My question is *how*," I said.

He gestured for the waitress to bring coffee. "What we really must determine is motive. And what would Lucy's motive be? What would anybody's motive be?"

Money was the easy answer, but I did not think that was it and told him so.

"Money is power, Kay, and everything is about power. We fallen creatures can never get enough of it."

"Yes, the forbidden fruit."

"Of course. All crime stems from it," he said.

"Every day that tragic truth is carried in on a stretcher," I agreed.

"Which tells you what about the problem at hand?" He stirred sugar into his coffee.

"It tells me motive."

"Well, of course. Power, that's it. Please, what would you like me to do?" my old friend asked.

"Lucy will not be charged with any crime unless it is proven that she stole from ERF. But as we speak, her future is ruined—at least in terms of a career in law enforcement or any other one that might involve a background investigation."

"Have they proven that she was the one who got in at three in the morning?"

"They have as much proof as they need, Frank. And that's the problem. I'm not certain how hard they'll work to clear her name, if she is innocent."

"If?"

"I'm trying to keep an open mind." I reached for my coffee and decided that the last thing I needed was more physical stimulation. My heart was racing and I could not keep my hands still.

"I can talk to the director," Lord said.

"All I want is someone behind the scenes making sure this thing is thoroughly investigated. With Lucy gone, they may not think it matters, especially since there is so much else to cope with. And she's just a college student, for God's sake. So why should they care?"

"I would hope the Bureau would care more than that," he said, his mouth grim.

"I understand bureaucracies. I've worked in them all my life."

"As have I."

"Then you must be clear on what I'm saying."

"I am."

"They want her in Richmond with me until next semester," I said.

"Then that is their verdict." He reached for his coffee again.

"Exactly. And that's easy for them, but what about my niece? She's only twenty-one years old. Her dream has just blown up midflight. What is she supposed to do? Go back to UVA after Christmas and pretend nothing went wrong?"

"Listen." He touched my arm with a tenderness that always made me wish he were my father. "I will do what I can without the impropriety of meddling with an administrative problem. Trust me on that front?"

"I do."

"In the meantime, if you don't mind a little personal advice?" He motioned for the waitress as he glanced at his watch. "Well, I'm late." He looked back at me. "Your biggest problem is a domestic one."

"I disagree," I said with feeling.

"You can disagree all you like." He smiled at the waitress as she gave him the check. "You're the closest thing to a mother Lucy has ever had. How are you going to help her through this?"

"I thought I was doing that today."

"And I thought you were doing this because you wanted to see me. Excuse me?" He motioned for the waitress. "I don't think this is our check. We didn't have four entrées."

"Let me see. Oh, my. Oh, I sure am sorry, Senator Lord. It's the table there."

"In that case, make Senator Kennedy pay both tabs. His and mine." He handed her both bills. "He won't object. He believes in tax and spend."

The waitress was a big woman in a black dress and white apron, and hair stiffened into a black pageboy. She smiled and suddenly felt fine about her mistake. "Yes, sir! I sure will tell the senator that."

"And you tell him to add on a generous tip,

188

Missouri," he said as she walked off. "You tell him I said so."

Missouri Rivers wasn't a day younger than seventy, and since she'd left Raleigh decades ago on a northbound train, she had seen senators feast and fast, resign and get reelected, fall in love and fall from glory. She knew when to interrupt and get on with the business of serving food, and when to refill tea or simply disappear. She knew the secrets of the heart hidden so well in this lovely room, for the true measure of a human being is the way he treated people like her when no one was observing. She loved Senator Lord. I knew that from the soft light in her eyes when she looked at him or heard his name.

"I'm just encouraging you to spend some time with Lucy," he continued. "And don't get caught up in slaying other people's dragons, especially her dragons."

"I don't believe she can slay this dragon alone."

"My point is that Lucy doesn't need to know from you we had this conversation today. She doesn't need to know from you that I will pick up the phone on her behalf as soon as I return to my office. If anybody tells her anything, let it be me."

"Agreed," I said.

A little later I caught a taxi outside the Russell Building and found Benton Wesley where he said he would be at precisely two-fifteen. He was sitting on a bench in the amphitheater outside FBI headquarters, and though he seemed engrossed in a novel, he sensed me long before I was about to call his name. A group taking a tour paid no attention to us as they walked past, and Wesley closed his book and slipped it into the pocket of his coat as he got up.

"How was your trip?" he asked.

"By the time I get to and from National, it takes as long to fly as it does to drive."

"You flew?" He held the door to the lobby for me.

"I'm letting Lucy use my car."

He slipped off his sunglasses and got each of us a visitor's pass. "You know the director of the crime labs, Jack Cartwright?"

"We've met."

"We're going to his office for a quick and dirty briefing," he said. "Then there's a place I want to take you."

"Where might that be?"

"A place that's difficult to go to."

"Benton, if you're going to be cryptic, then I'll have no choice but to retaliate by speaking Latin."

"And you know how much I hate it when you do that."

We inserted our visitor's passes into a turnstile and followed a long corridor to an elevator. Every time I came to headquarters I was reminded of how much I did not like the place. People rarely gave me eye contact or smiled, and it seemed everything and everyone hid behind various shades of white and gray. Endless corridors connected a labyrinth of laboratories that I could never find when left to my own devices, and worse, people who worked here did not seem to know how to get anywhere, either.

Jack Cartwright had an office with a view, and

sunlight filled his windows, reminding me of the splendid days I missed when I was working hard and worried.

"Benton, Kay, good afternoon." Cartwright shook our hands. "Please have a seat. And this is George Kilby and Seth Richards from the labs. Have you met?"

"No. How do you do?" I said to Kilby and Richards, who were young, serious, and soberly attired.

"Would anybody like coffee?"

Nobody did, and Cartwright seemed eager to get on with our business. He was an attractive man whose formidable desk bore testimony to the way he got things done. Every document, envelope, and telephone message was in its proper place, and on top of a legal pad was an old silver Parker fountain pen that only a purist would use. I noticed he had plants in his windows and photographs of his wife and daughters on the sills. Outside sunlight winked on windshields as cars moved in congested herds, and vendors hawked T-shirts, ice cream, and drinks.

"We've been working on the Steiner case," Cartwright began, "and there are a number of interesting developments so far. I will start with what is probably most important, and that's the typing of the skin found in the freezer.

"Although our DNA analysis is not finished, we can tell you with certainty that the tissue is human and the ABO grouping is O-positive. As I'm sure you know, the victim, Emily Steiner, was also O-positive. And the size and shape of the tissue are consistent with her wounds."

"I'm wondering if you've been able to determine what sort of cutting instrument was used to excise the tissue," I said, taking notes.

"A sharp cutting instrument with a single edge."

"Which could be just about any type of knife," Wesley said.

Cartwright went on. "You can see where the point penetrated the flesh first as the assailant began to cut. So we're talking about a knife with a point and a single edge. That's as much as we can narrow it down. And by the way"—he looked at Wesley—"we've found no human blood on any of the knives you had sent in. Uh, the things from the Ferguson house."

Wesley nodded, his face impervious as he listened.

"Okay, trace evidence," Cartwright resumed. "And this is where it begins to get interesting. We have some unusual microscopic material that came from Emily Steiner's body and hair, and also from the bottoms of her shoes. We've got several blue acrylic fibers consistent with the blanket from her bed, plus green cotton fibers consistent with the green corduroy coat she wore to the youth group meeting at her church.

"There are some other wool fibers that we don't know the origin of. Plus we found dust mites, which could have come from anywhere. But what couldn't have come from anywhere is this."

Cartwright swiveled around in his chair and turned on a video display on the credenza behind him. The screen was filled with four different sections of some sort of cellular material that brought to mind honeycomb, only this had peculiar areas stained amber.

"What you're looking at," Cartwright told us, "are sections of a plant called *Sambucus simpsonii*, which is simply a woody shrub indigenous to the coastal plains and lagoons of southern Florida. What's fascinating are these dark spots right here." He pointed to the stained areas. "George"—he looked at one of the young scientists—"this is your bailiwick."

"Those are tannin sacs." George Kilby moved closer to us, joining the discussion. "You can see them especially well here on this radial section."

"What exactly is a tannin sac?" Wesley wanted to know.

"It's a vessel that transports material up and down the plant's stem."

"What sort of material?"

"Generally waste products that result from cellular activities. And just so you know, what you're looking at here is the pith. That's the part of the plant that has these tannin sacs."

"Then you're saying that the trace evidence in this case is pith?" I asked.

Special Agent George Kilby nodded. "That's right. The commercial name is pithwood, even though technically there really is no such thing."

"What is pithwood used for?" Wesley asked.

It was Cartwright who answered, "It's often used to hold small mechanical parts or pieces of jewelry. For example, a jeweler might stick a small earring or watch gear into a pith button so it doesn't roll off the table or get brushed off by his sleeve. These days, most people just use Styrofoam."

"Was there much of this pithwood trace on her body?" I asked.

"There was a fair amount of it, mostly in the bloody areas, which was where most of her trace was."

"If someone wanted pithwood," Wesley said, "where would he get it?"

"The Everglades, if you wanted to cut down the shrub yourself," Kilby replied. "Otherwise you'd order it."

"From where?"

"I know there's a company in Silver Spring, Maryland."

Wesley looked at me. "Guess we need to find out who repairs jewelry in Black Mountain."

I said to him, "I'd be surprised if they even have a jeweler in Black Mountain."

Cartwright spoke again. "In addition to the trace evidence already mentioned, we found microscopic pieces of insects. Beetles, crickets, and roaches—nothing peculiar, really. And there were flecks of white and black paint, neither of them automotive. Plus, she had sawdust in her hair."

"From what kind of wood?" I asked.

"Mostly walnut, but we did also identify mahogany." Cartwright looked at Wesley, who was looking out the window. "The skin you found in the freezer didn't have any of this same material on it, but her wounds did."

"Meaning those injuries were inflicted before her body came in contact with wherever it was that it picked up this trace?" Wesley said.

"You could assume that," I said. "But whoever

excised the skin and saved it may have rinsed it off. It would have been bloody."

"What about the inside of a vehicle?" Wesley went on. "Such as a trunk?"

"It's a possibility," Kilby said.

I knew the direction Wesley's thoughts were heading. Gault had murdered thirteen-year-old Eddie Heath inside a beat-up used van that had been rife with a baffling variety of trace evidence. Succinctly put, Mr. Gault, the psychopathic son of a wealthy pecan plantation owner in Georgia, derived intense pleasure from leaving evidence that seemed to make no sense.

"About the blaze orange duct tape," Cartwright said, finally getting around to that subject. "Am I correct in saying a roll of it has yet to show up?"

"We haven't found anything like that," Wesley replied.

Special Agent Richards looked through pages of notes as Cartwright said to him, "Well, let's get on with that, because I personally think it's going to be the most important thing we've got in this case."

Richards began talking in earnest, for like every devout forensic scientist I had met, he had a passion for his specialty. The FBI's reference library of duct tapes contained more than a hundred types for the purpose of identification when duct tape was involved in the commission of a crime. In fact, malevolent use of the silvery stuff was so common that I honestly could not pass by a roll of it in hardware or grocery stores without household thoughts turning into remembered horrors.

I had collected body parts of people blown up by bombs made with duct tape. I had removed it from the bound victims of sadistic killers and from bodies weighted with cinder blocks and dumped into rivers and lakes. I could not count the times I had peeled it from the mouths of people who were not allowed to scream until they were wheeled into my morgue. For it was only there the body could speak freely. It was only there someone cared about every awful thing that had been done.

"I've never seen duct tape like this before," Richards was saying. "And due to its high yarn count I can also say with confidence that whoever bought the tape did not get it from a store."

"How can you be so sure of that?" Wesley asked.

"This is industrial grade, with a yarn count of sixty-two warp and a fifty-six woof, versus your typical economy grade of twenty/ten that you might pick up at Walmart or Safeway for a couple of bucks. The industrial grade can cost as much as ten bucks a roll."

"Do you know where the tape was manufactured?" I asked.

"Shuford Mills of Hickory, North Carolina. They're one of the biggest duct tape manufacturers in the country. Their best-known brand is Shurtape."

"Hickory is only sixty miles or so east of Black Mountain," I said.

"Have you talked to anyone at Shuford Mills?" Wesley asked Richards.

"Yes. They're still trying to track down information

for me. But this much we already know. The blaze orange tape was a specialty item that Shuford Mills manufactured solely for a private label customer in the late eighties."

"What is a private label customer?" I asked.

"Someone who wants a special tape and orders maybe a minimum of five hundred cases of it. So there could be hundreds of tapes out there we're never going to see, unless it turns up like this blaze orange tape did."

"Can you give me an example of what sort of person might design his own duct tape?" I inquired further.

"I know some stock car racers do," Richards replied. "For example, the duct tape Richard Petty has made for his pit crew is red and blue, while Daryl Waltrip's is yellow. Shuford Mills also had a contractor some years back who was sick of his workers walking off the job with his expensive tape. So he had his own bright purple tape made. You know, you got purple tape repairing your ductwork at home or fixing the leak in your kid's wading pool, and it's pretty obvious you stole it."

"Could that be the purpose of the blaze orange tape? To prevent workers from stealing it?" I asked.

"Possibly," said Richards. "And by the way, it's also flame retardant."

"Is that unusual?" Wesley asked.

"Very much so," Richards replied. "I associate flame-retardant duct tapes with aircraft and submarines, neither of which would have any need of a tape that's blaze orange, or at least I wouldn't think so."

"Why would anyone need a tape that is blaze orange?" I asked.

"The million-dollar question," Cartright said. "When I think of blaze orange, I think of hunting and traffic cones."

"Let's get back to the killer taping up Mrs. Steiner and her daughter," Wesley suggested. "What else can you tell us about the mechanics of that?"

"We found traces of what appears to be furniture varnish on some of the tape ends," Richards said. "Also, the sequence the tape was torn from the roll is inconsistent with the sequence it was applied to the mother's wrists and ankles. All this means is that the assailant tore off as many segments of tape as he thought he would need, and probably stuck them to the edge of a piece of furniture. When he began binding Mrs. Steiner, the tape was ready and waiting for him to use, one piece at a time."

"Only he got them out of order," Wesley said.

"Yes," said Richards. "I have them numbered according to the sequence they were used to bind the mother and her daughter. Would you like to look?"

We said that we would.

Wesley and I spent the rest of the afternoon in the Materials Analysis Unit, with its gas chromatographs, mass spectrometers, differential scanning calorimeters, and other intimidating instruments for determining materials and melting points. I parked myself near a portable explosive detector while Richards went on about the weird duct tape used to bind Emily and her mother.

He explained that when he had used hot blowing air to open the tape receipted to him by the Black Mountain police, he counted seventeen pieces ranging from eight to nineteen inches in length. Mounting them on sheets of thick transparent vinyl, he had numbered the segments two different ways—to show the sequence the tape had been torn from the roll and the sequence the assailant had used when he taped his victims.

"The sequence of the tape used on the mother is completely out of whack," he was saying. "This piece here should have been first. Instead, it was last. And since this one was torn from the roll second, it should have been used second instead of fifth.

"The little girl, on the other hand, was taped in sequence. Seven pieces were used, and they went around her wrists in the order they were torn from the roll."

"She would have been easier to control," Wesley remarked.

"One would think so," I said, and then I asked Richards, "Did you find any of the varnish-type residue on the tape recovered from her body?"

"No," he replied.

"That's interesting," I said, and the detail bothered me.

We saved the dirty streaks on the tape for last. They had been identified as hydrocarbons, which is just a highbrow name for grease. So this didn't guide us a bit one way or another because unfortunately grease is grease. The grease on the tape could have come from a car. It could have come from a Mack truck in Arizona.

12

Wesley and I went on to the Red Sage at half past four, which was early for drinks. But neither of us felt very good.

It was hard for me to meet his eyes now that we were alone again, and I wanted him to bring up what had happened between us the other night. I did not want to believe I was the only one who thought it mattered.

"They have microbrewery beer on tap," Wesley said as I studied the menu. "It's quite good, if you're a beer drinker."

"Not unless I've worked out for two hours in the middle of summer and am very thirsty and craving pizza," I said, a little stung that he didn't seem to know this detail about me. "In fact, I really don't like beer and never have. I only drink it when there's absolutely nothing else, and even then I can't say it tastes good."

"Well, there's no point in getting angry about it."

"I'm certainly not angry."

"You sound angry. And you won't look at me."

"I'm fine."

"I study people for a living and I'm telling you that you're not fine."

"You study psychopaths for a living," I said. "You don't study female chief medical examiners who reside on the right side of the law and simply want to relax after an intense, long day of thinking about murdered children."

"It's very hard to get into this restaurant."

"I can see why. Thank you for going to a lot of trouble."

"I had to use my influence."

"I'm sure you did."

"We'll have wine with dinner. I'm surprised they have Opus One. Maybe that will make you feel better."

"It's overpriced and styled after a Bordeaux, which is a little heavy for sipping, and I wasn't aware we were dining here. I've got a plane to catch in less than two hours. I think I'll just have a glass of Cabernet."

"Whatever you'd like."

I did not know what I liked or wanted at the moment.

"I'm heading back to Asheville tomorrow," Wesley went on. "If you want to stay over tonight, we could go together."

"Why are you going back there?"

"Our assistance was requested before Ferguson ended up dead and Mote had a heart attack. Trust me, the Black Mountain police are sincere in their appreciation and panic. I've made it clear to them that we will do what we can to help. If it turns out that I need to bring in other agents, I will."

Wesley had a habit of always getting the waiter's name and addressing him by it throughout the meal. Our waiter's name was Stan, and it was Stan this and Stan that as Wesley and he discussed wines and specials. It was really the only dopey thing Wesley did, his sole quirky mannerism, and as I witnessed it this evening it irritated the hell out of me.

"You know, it doesn't make the waiter feel he has a relationship with you, Benton. In fact, it seems just a little patronizing, like the sort of thing a radio personality would do."

"What does?" He was without a clue.

"Calling him by name. Repeatedly doing it, I mean."

He stared at me.

"Well, I'm not trying to be critical," I went on, making matters worse. "I'm just mentioning it as a friend because no one else would, and you should know. A friend would be that honest, I'm saying. A *true* one would."

"Are you quite finished?" he asked.

"Quite." I forced a little smile.

"Now, then, do you want to tell me what's really bothering you, or should I just bravely hazard a guess?"

"There is absolutely nothing bothering me," I said as I began to cry.

"My God, Kay." He offered me his napkin.

"I have my own." I wiped my eyes.

"This is about the other night, isn't it?"

"Maybe you should tell me which other night you mean. Maybe you have *other nights* on a regular basis."

Wesley tried to suppress his laughter, but he could not. For several minutes neither of us could talk because he was laughing and I was caught between crying and laughing.

Stan the waiter returned with drinks, and I took several swallows of mine before speaking again.

"Listen," I finally said. "I'm sorry. But I'm tired, this case is horrible to deal with, Marino and I aren't getting along, and Lucy's in trouble."

"That's enough to push anyone to tears," Wesley said, and I could tell it bothered him that I hadn't added him to my list of things wrong. It perversely pleased me that it bothered him.

"And yes, I'm concerned about what happened in North Carolina," I added.

"Do you regret it?"

"What good does it do to say that I do or I don't?"

"It would do me good for you to say that you don't."

"I can't say that," I said.

"Then you do regret it."

"No, I don't."

"Then you don't regret it."

"Dammit, Benton, leave it be."

"I'm not going to," he said. "I was there, too."

"Excuse me?" I puzzled.

"The night it happened? Remember? Actually it was

203

very early in the morning. What we did took two. I was there. You weren't the only person there who had to think about it for days. Why don't you ask me whether I regret it?"

"No," I said. "You're the one who's married."

"If I committed adultery, so did you. *It takes two*," he said again.

"My plane leaves in an hour. I've got to go."

"You should have thought about that before starting this conversation. You can't just walk out in the middle of something like this."

"Certainly I can."

"Kay?" He looked into my eyes and lowered his voice. He reached across the table and took my hand.

I got a room in the Willard that night. Wesley and I talked a very long time and resolved matters sufficiently for us to rationalize our repeating the same sin. When we got off the elevator in the lobby early the next morning, we were very low key and polite with one another, as if we had only just met but had a lot in common. We shared a taxi to National Airport and got a flight to Charlotte, where I spent an hour with Lucy on the phone. "Yes," I said. "I am finding someone and have in fact already started on that," I told her in the USAir Club.

"I need to do something now," she said again.

"Please try to be patient."

"No. I know who's doing this to me and I'm going to do something about it."

"Who?" I asked, alarmed.

204

"When it's time, it will be known."

"Lucy, who did what to you? Please tell me what you're talking about."

"I can't right now. There's something I must do first. When are you coming home?"

"I don't know. I'll call you from Asheville as soon as I get a feel for what's going on."

"So it's okay for me to use your car?"

"Of course."

"You won't be using it for at least a couple days, right?"

"I don't think so. But what is it you're contemplating?" I was getting increasingly unsettled.

"I might need to go up to Quantico, and if I do and spend the night I wanted to make sure you wouldn't mind."

"No, I don't mind," I said. "As long as you're careful, Lucy, that's what matters to me."

Wesley and I boarded a prop plane that made too much noise for us to talk in the air. So he slept while I sat quietly with my eyes shut as sunlight filled the window and turned the inside of my eyelids red. I let my thoughts wander wherever they would, and many images came to me from corners I had forgotten. I saw my father and the white gold ring he wore on his left hand where a wedding band would have been, but he had lost his at the beach and could not afford another one.

My father had never been to college, and I remembered his high school ring was set with a red stone that I wished were a ruby because we were so poor. I thought we could sell it and have a better life, and I remembered my disappointment when my father finally told me that his ring wasn't worth the gasoline it would take to drive to South Miami. There was something about the way he said this that made me know he had never really lost his wedding ring.

He had sold it when he did not know what else to do, but to tell Mother was to destroy her. It had been many years since I had thought about this, and I supposed my mother still had his ring somewhere, unless she had buried it with him, and maybe she had. I could not recall, since I was only twelve when he had died.

As I drifted in and out of places, I saw silent scenes of people who simply appeared without invitation. It was very odd. I did not know why it mattered, for example, that Sister Martha, my third-grade teacher, was suddenly writing with chalk on the board or a girl named Jennifer was walking out a door as hail bounced on the churchyard like a million small white marbles.

These people from my past slipped in and vanished as I almost slept, and a sorrow welled up that made me aware of Wesley's arm. We were touching slightly. When I focused on the exact point of contact between us, I could smell the wool of his jacket warming in the sun and imagine long fingers of elegant hands that brought to mind pianos and fountain pens and brandy snifters by the fire.

I think it was precisely then I knew I was in love with Benton Wesley. Because I had lost every man I had loved before him, I did not open my eyes until the flight attendant asked us to put our seats in the upright position because we were about to land.

"Is someone meeting us?" I asked him as if this were all that had been on my mind during our hour in the air.

He looked at me for a long moment. His eyes were the color of bottled beer when light hit them a certain way. Then the shadow of deep preoccupations returned them to hazel flecked with gold, and when his thoughts were more than even he could bear, he simply looked away.

"I suppose we're returning to the Travel-Eze," I next asked as he collected his briefcase and unbuckled his seat belt before we had been signaled that we could. The flight attendant pretended not to notice, because Wesley sent out his own signals that made most people slightly afraid.

"You talked to Lucy a long time in Charlotte," he said.

"Yes." We rolled past a wind sock having a deflated day.

"Well?" His eyes filled with light again as he turned toward the sun.

"Well, she thinks she knows who's behind what's happened to her."

"What do you mean, *who's behind* it?" He frowned.

"I think the meaning's apparent," I said. "It's not apparent only if you assume nobody is behind anything because Lucy is guilty."

"Her thumb was scanned at three in the morning, Kay."

"That much is clear."

"And what is also clear is that her thumb couldn't have been scanned without her thumb being physically present, without her hand, arm, and the rest of her being physically present at the time the computer says she was."

"I'm very aware of how it looks," I said.

He put on sunglasses and we got up. "And I'm reminding you of how it looks," he said in my ear as he followed me down the aisle.

We could have moved out of the Travel-Eze for more luxurious quarters in Asheville. But where we stayed did not seem important to anyone by the time we met Marino at the Coach House restaurant, which was famous for reasons that were not exactly clear.

I got a peculiar feeling immediately when the Black Mountain officer who had collected us at the airport let us off in the restaurant parking lot and silently drove away. Marino's state-of-the-art Chevrolet was near the door, and he was inside alone at a corner table, facing the cash register, as everyone tries to do if he's ever been touched by the law.

He did not get up when we walked in, but watched us dispassionately as he stirred a tall glass of iced tea. I had the uncanny sensation that he, the Marino I had worked with for years, the well-meaning, street-smart hater of potentates and protocol, was granting us an audience. Wesley's cool caution told me that he knew something was very off center, too. For one thing, Marino had on a dark suit that clearly was new.

"Pete," Wesley said, taking a chair.

"Hello," I said, taking another chair.

"They got really good chicken fried steak here," Marino said, not looking at either of us. "They got chef salads, if you don't want nothing that heavy," he added, apparently for my benefit.

The waitress was pouring water, handing out menus, and rattling off specials before anyone had a chance to say another word. By the time she went on her way with our apathetic orders, the tension at our table was almost unbearable.

"We have quite a lot of forensic information that I think you'll find interesting," Wesley began. "But first, why don't you fill us in?"

Marino, who looked the unhappiest I'd ever seen him, reached for his iced tea and then set it back down without taking a sip. He patted his pocket for his cigarettes before picking them up from the table. He did not talk until he was smoking, and it frightened me that he would not give us his eyes. He was so distant it was as if we had never known him, and whenever I had seen this in the past with someone I had worked with, I knew what it meant. Marino was in trouble. He had slammed shut the windows leading into his soul because he did not want us to see what was there.

"The big thing going down right now," Marino began as he exhaled smoke and nervously tapped an ash, "is the janitor at Emily Steiner's school. Uh, the subject's name is Creed Lindsey, white male, thirty-four, works as a janitor at the elementary school, has for the past two years.

"Prior to that he was a janitor at the Black Mountain public library, and before that did the same damn thing for an elementary school in Weaverville. And I might add that at the school in Weaverville during the time the subject was there, they had a hit-and-run of a ten-year-old boy. There was suspicion that Lindsey was involved. . . ."

"Hold on," Wesley said.

"A hit-and-run?" I asked. "What do you mean he was involved?"

"Wait," Wesley said. "Wait, wait, wait. Have you talked to Creed Lindsey?" He looked at Marino, who met his gaze but fleetingly.

"That's what I'm leading to. The drone's disappeared. The minute he got the word we wanted to talk to him—and I'll be damned if I know who opened his fat mouth, but someone did—he split. He ain't showed up at work and he ain't been back to his crib."

He lit another cigarette. When the waitress was suddenly at his elbow with more tea, he nodded her way as if he'd been here many times before and always tipped well.

"Tell me about the hit-and-run," I said.

"Four years ago this November, a ten-year-old kid's riding his bike and gets slammed by some asshole who's over the center line coming around a curve. The kid's DOA, and all the cops ever get is there's a white pickup truck driving at a high rate of speed in the area around the time the accident occurred. And they get white paint off the kid's jeans.

"Meanwhile, Creed Lindsey's got an old white

pickup, a Ford. He's known to drive the same road where the accident occurred, and he's known to hit the package store on payday, which coincidentally was exactly when the kid got hit."

Marino's eyes never stopped moving as he talked on and on. Wesley and I were getting increasingly restless.

"So when the cops want to question him, boom, he's gone," Marino continued. "Don't come back to the area for five damn weeks—says he was visiting a sick relative or some bullshit like that. By then, the friggin' truck's as blue as a robin's egg. Everybody knows the son of a bitch did it, but they got no proof."

"Okay." Wesley's voice commanded that Marino stop. "That's very interesting, and maybe this janitor was involved in the hit-and-run. But where are you going with this?"

"Seems like that ought to be pretty obvious."

"Well, it's not, Pete. Help me out here."

"Lindsey likes kids, plain and simple. He takes jobs that put him in contact with kids."

"It sounds to me like he takes the jobs he has because he's unskilled at anything but sweeping floors."

"Shit. He could do that at the grocery store, the old folks' home, or something. Every place he's worked is full of kids."

"Okay. Let's just go with that. So he sweeps floors in places where children are. Then what?" Wesley studied Marino, who clearly had a theory he was not to be dissuaded from.

"Then he kills his first kid four years ago, and I'm sure

as hell not saying he meant to do it. But he does, and he lies, and he's guilty as hell and gets totally screwed up because of this terrible secret he carries. That's how other things get started in people."

"Other things?" Wesley asked very smoothly. "What other things, Pete?"

"He's feeling guilty about kids. He's looking at 'em every goddam day and wanting to reach out, be forgiven, get close, undo it, shit. I don't know.

"But next thing his emotions get carried away and now he's watching this little girl. He gets sweet on her, wants to reach out. Maybe he spots her the night she's walking home from the church. Maybe he even talks to her. But hell, ain't no problem to figure out where she lives. It's a friggin' small town. He's into it now."

He took a swallow of tea and lit another cigarette as he talked on.

"He snatches her because if he can keep her with him for a while, he can make her understand that he never meant to hurt no one, that he's good. He wants her to be his friend. He wants to be loved because if she'll love him, she'll undo the terrible thing he did back then. But it don't go down like that. See, she's not cooperating. She's terrified. And bottom line is when what goes down don't fit the fantasy, he freaks and kills her. And now, goddam it, he's done it again. Two kids killed."

Wesley started to speak, but our food was arriving on a big brown tray.

The waitress, an older woman with thick, tired legs, was slow serving us. She wanted everything to please

212

the important man from out of town who was wearing a new navy blue suit.

The waitress said many yes sirs and seemed very pleased when I thanked her for my salad, which I did not plan to eat. I had lost any appetite I might have had before we arrived at the Coach House, which was famous for something, I felt quite sure. But I could not look at julienne strips of ham, turkey, and cheddar cheese, and especially not sliced boiled eggs. In fact, I felt sick.

"Would there be anything else?"

"No, thank you."

"This looks real good, Dot. You mind bringing a little more butter?"

"Yes, sir, it will be coming right up. And what about you, ma'am? Can I get you some more dressing maybe?"

"Oh, no, thank you. This is perfect the way it is."

"Why, thank you. You folks are mighty nice, and we sure appreciate your visiting. You know, we have a buffet every Sunday after church."

"We'll remember that." Wesley smiled at her.

I knew I was going to leave her at least five dollars, if only she would forgive me for not touching my food.

Wesley was trying to think what to say to Marino, and I had never before been witness to anything between them quite like this.

"I guess I'm wondering if you've completely abandoned your original theory," Wesley said.

"Which theory?" Marino tried to cut into his fried

steak with a fork, and when that didn't work, he reached for the pepper and A.1. sauce.

"Temple Gault," Wesley said. "It would appear that you aren't looking for him anymore."

"I didn't say nothing like that."

"Marino," I said, "what about this hit-and-run business?"

He raised his hand and motioned for the waitress. "Dot, I guess I'm going to need a sharp knife. The hit-and-run is important because this guy's got a history of violence. The local people are real antsy about him because of that and also because he paid a lot of attention to Emily Steiner. So I'm just letting you know that's what's going down."

"How would that theory explain the human skin in Ferguson's freezer?" I asked. "And by the way, the blood type is the same as Emily's. We're still waiting on DNA."

"Wouldn't explain it worth a damn."

Dot returned with a serrated knife, and Marino thanked her. He sawed into his fried steak. Wesley nibbled broiled flounder, staring down at his plate for long intervals while his VICAP partner talked.

"Listen, for all we know, Ferguson did the kid. And sure, we can't rule out the possibility Gault's in town, and I'm not saying we should."

"What more do we know about Ferguson?" Wesley asked. "And are you aware that the print lifted from the panties he was wearing comes back to Denesa Steiner?"

"That's because the panties was stolen from her

214

house the night the squirrel busted in and snatched her kid. Remember? She said while she was in the closet she thought she heard him going through her drawers, and later was suspicious he took some of her clothing."

"That and the skin in his freezer certainly cause me to want to look very hard at this guy," Wesley said. "Is there any possibility he'd had contact with Emily in the past?"

I interjected, "Because of his profession, he certainly would have had reason to know about the cases in Virginia, about Eddie Heath. He could have tried to make the Steiner murder mimic something else. Or maybe he got the idea from what happened in Virginia."

"Ferguson was squirrelly," Marino said, sawing off another piece of meat. "That much I can tell you, but nobody around here seemed to know a whole hell of a lot."

"How long did he work for the SBI?" I asked.

"Going on ten years. Before that he was a state trooper, and before that he was in the army."

"He was divorced?" Wesley asked.

"You mean there's somebody who ain't?"

Wesley was quiet.

"Divorced twice. Got an ex-wife in Tennessee and one in Enka. Four kids all grown and living the hell all over the place."

"What does his family have to say about him?" I asked.

"You know, it's not like I've been here for six

months." Marino reached for the A.1. sauce again. "I can only talk to so many people in one day, and that's only if I'm lucky enough to get them the first or second time I call. And seeing's how you two haven't been here and all of this has been dumped in my lap, I hope you won't take it personal if I say that there's only so much goddam time in a day."

"Pete, we understand that," Wesley said in his most reasonable tone. "And that's why we're here. We are well aware there is a lot of investigating to do. Maybe even more than I originally thought, because nothing's fitting together right. It seems this case is going in at least three different directions and I'm not seeing many connections, except that I really want to look hard at Ferguson. We do have forensic evidence that points at him. The skin in his freezer. Denesa Steiner's lingerie."

"They got good cherry cobbler here," Marino said, looking for the waitress. She was standing just outside the kitchen door watching him, waiting for his slightest signal.

"How many times have you eaten here?" I asked him.

"I got to eat somewhere, isn't that right, Dot?" He raised his voice as our ever-vigilant waitress appeared.

Wesley and I ordered coffee.

"Why, honey, wasn't your salad all right?" She was sincerely distressed.

"It was fine," I assured her. "I'm just not as hungry as I thought."

"You want me to wrap that up for you?"

"No, thank you."

When she moved on, Wesley got around to telling Marino what we knew about the forensic evidence. We talked for a while about the pithwood and the duct tape, and by the time Marino's cobbler had been served and eaten and he had started smoking again, we had pretty much exhausted the conversation. Marino had no more idea what the blaze orange flame-retardant duct tape or pithwood meant than we did.

"Damn," he said again. "That's just strange as shit. I haven't come across a thing that would fit with any of that."

"Well," said Wesley, whose attention was beginning to drift, "the tape is so unusual that someone around here has to have seen it before. If it's from around here. And if it isn't, I'm confident we'll track it down." He pushed back his chair.

"I'll take care of this." I picked up the bill.

"They don't take American Express here," Marino said.

"It's one-fifty now." Wesley got up. "Let's meet back at the hotel at six and work out a plan."

"I hate to remind you," I said to him. "But it's a motel, not a hotel, and at the moment you and I don't have a car."

"I'll drop you at the Travel-Eze. Your car should already be there waiting. And Benton, we can find you one, too, if you think you're gonna need it," Marino said as if he were Black Mountain's new chief of police, or perhaps the mayor.

"I don't know what I'm going to need right now," he said.

13

Detective Mote had been moved to a private room and was in stable but guarded condition when I went to see him later that day. Not knowing my way around town very well, I'd resorted to the hospital gift shop, where they had but a very small selection of flower arrangements to choose from behind refrigerated glass.

"Detective Mote?" I hesitated in his doorway.

He was propped up in bed dozing, the TV on loud.

"Hi," I said a little louder.

He opened his eyes and for an instant had no idea who I was. Then he remembered and smiled as if he'd been dreaming of me for days.

"Well, Lord have mercy, Dr. Scarpetta. Now I never would've thought you'd still be hanging 'round here."

"I'm sorry about the flowers. They didn't have much to choose from downstairs." I carried in a pitiful bunch of mums and daisies in a thick green vase. "How about if I just put them right here?"

I set the arrangement on the dresser, and felt sad that his only other flowers were more pathetic than mine.

"There's a chair right there if you can sit for a minute."

"How are you feeling?" I asked.

He was pale and thinner, and his eyes looked weak as he stared out the window at a lovely fall day.

"Well, I'm just trying to go with the flow, like they say," he said. "It's hard to know what's around the corner, but I'm thinking about fishing and the woodworking I like to do. You know, I've been wanting for years to build a little cabin someplace. And I like to whittle walking sticks from basswood."

"Detective Mote," I said hesitantly, for I did not want to upset him, "has anyone from your department come to visit?"

"Why sure," he answered as he continued staring out at a stunning blue sky. "A couple fellas have dropped by or else called."

"How do you feel about what's going on in the Steiner investigation?"

"Not too good."

"Why?"

"Well, I'm not there, for one thing. For another, it seems like everybody's riding off in his own direction. I'm worried about it some."

"You've been involved in the case from the start," I said. "You must have known Max Ferguson pretty well."

"I guess not as well as I thought."

"Are you aware that he's a suspect?"

"I know it. I know all about it."

The sun through the window made his eyes so pale they seemed made of water. He blinked several times and dabbed tears caused by bright light or emotion.

He talked some more. "I also know they're looking hard at Creed Lindsey, and you know it's sort of a shame for either of 'em."

"In what way?" I asked.

"Well, now, Dr. Scarpetta, Max ain't exactly here to defend himself."

"No, he isn't," I agreed.

"And Creed couldn't begin to know how to defend himself, even if he was here."

"Where is he?"

"I hear he's run off someplace, not that it's the first time. He done the same thing when that little boy was run over and killed. Everybody thought Creed was guiltier than sin. So he disappeared and turned up again like a bad penny. Now and again he just goes off to what they used to call Colored Town and drinks himself into a hole."

"Where does he live?"

"Off Montreat Road, up there in Rainbow Mountain."

"I'm afraid I'm not familiar with where that is."

"When you get to the Montreat gate, it's the road going up the mountain to the right. Used to be only mountain folk up there, what you'd probably call hillbillies. But during the last twenty years a lot of them has gone on to other places or passed on and folk like Creed's moved in."

He paused for a minute, his expression distant and thoughtful. "You can see his place from down below on the road. He's got an old washing machine on the porch and pitches most his trash out the back door into the woods." He sighed. "The plain fact is, Creed wasn't gifted with smarts."

"Meaning?"

"Meaning he's scared of what he don't understand, and he can't understand something like what's going on around here."

"Meaning you also don't think he's involved in the Steiner girl's death," I said.

Detective Mote closed his eyes as the monitor over his bed registered a steady pulse of 66. He looked very tired. "No ma'am, I don't for a minute. But there's a reason he's running, you ask me, and I can't get that out of my mind."

"You said he was scared. That seems reason enough."

"I just have this feeling there's something else. But I guess there's no point in my stewing over it. Not a darn thing I can do. Not unless all of 'em want to line up outside my door and let me ask 'em whatever I want, and that sure isn't likely to happen."

I did not want to ask him about Marino, but I felt I must. "What about Captain Marino? Have you heard much from him?"

Mote looked straight at me. "He came on in the other day with a fifth of Wild Turkey. It's in my closet over there." He raised an arm off the covers and pointed.

We both sat silently for a moment.

221

"I know I'm not supposed to be drinking," he added.

"I want you to listen to your doctors, Lieutenant Mote. You've got to live with this, and that means not doing any of those things that got you into trouble."

"I know I got to quit smoking."

"It can be done. I never thought I could."

"You still miss it?"

"I don't miss the way it made me feel."

"I don't like the way any bad habit makes me feel, but that's got nothing to do with it."

I smiled. "Yes, I miss it. But it does get easier."

"I told Pete I don't want to see him ending up in here like me, Dr. Scarpetta. But he's a hardhead."

I was unsettled by the memory of Mote turning blue on the floor as I tried to save his life, and I believed it was simply a matter of time before Marino suffered a similar experience. I thought of the fried steak lunch, his new clothes and car and strange behavior. It almost seemed he had decided he did not want to know me anymore, and the only way to bring that about was to change into someone I did not recognize.

"Certainly Marino has gotten very involved. The case is terribly consuming," I lamely said.

"Mrs. Steiner can't think of much else, not that I blame her a bit. If it was me, I reckon I'd put everything I got into it, too."

"What has she put into it?" I said.

"She's got a lot of money," Mote said.

"I wondered about that." I thought of her car.

"She's done a lot to help in this investigation."

"Help?" I asked. "In what way, exactly?"

"Cars. Like the one Pete's driving, for example. Someone's got to pay for all that."

"I thought those things were donated by area merchants."

"Now, I will have to say that what Mrs. Steiner's done has inspired others to pitch in. She's got this whole area thinking about this case and feeling for her, and not a soul wants someone else's child to suffer the same thing.

"It's really like nothing I've ever seen in my twenty-two years of police work. But then, I have to say I've never seen a case like this to begin with."

"Did she actually pay for the car I'm driving?" It required great restraint on my part not to raise my voice or seem anything but calm.

"She donated both cars and some other business-people have kicked in the other things. Lights, radios, scanners."

"Detective Mote," I said, "how much money has Mrs. Steiner given to your department?"

"I reckon close to fifty."

"Fifty?" I looked at him in disbelief. "Fifty thousand dollars?"

"That's right."

"And no one has a problem with that?"

"Far as I'm concerned, it's no different than the power company donating a car to us some years back because there's a transformer they want us to keep an eye on. And the Quick Stops and 7-Elevens give us coffee so we'll come in all hours. It's all about

223

people helping us to help them. It works fine as long as nobody tries to take advantage."

His eyes were steady on me, his hands still on top of the covers. "I guess in a big city like Richmond you got more rules."

"Any gift to the Richmond Police Department that is over twenty-five hundred dollars has to be approved by an O and R," I said.

"I don't know what that is."

"An Ordinance and Resolution, which has to be brought before the city council."

"Sounds mighty complicated."

"And it should be, for obvious reasons."

"Well, sure," Mote said, and mainly he just sounded weary and worn down by the revelation that his body was not to be trusted anymore.

"Can you tell me just what this fifty thousand dollars is to be used for, besides acquiring several additional cars?" I asked.

"We need a chief of police. I was pretty much the whole enchilada, and it don't look too good for me at this point, to be honest. And even if I can go back to some sort of light duty, it's time the town has someone with experience in charge. Things aren't the way they used to be."

"I see," I commented, and the reality of what was happening was clarifying in a very disturbing way. "I should let you get some rest."

"I'm mighty glad you came by."

He squeezed my hand so hard I was in pain, and I sensed a deep despair he probably could not have explained were he completely conscious of it. To almost die is to know that one day you will, and to never again feel the same about anything.

Before I returned to the Travel-Eze, I drove to the Montreat gate, went through it, and turned around. I went back out the other side as I tried to think what to do. There was very little traffic, and when I pulled off on the shoulder and stopped for a bit, people passing me probably assumed I was but one more tourist who was lost or looking for Billy Graham's house. From where I was parked, I had a perfect view of Creed Lindsey's neighborhood. In fact, I could see his house and its old boxy white washing machine on the porch.

Rainbow Mountain must have been named on an October afternoon like this one. Leaves were varying intensities of red, orange, and yellow that were fiery in the sun and rich in the shade, and shadows crept deeper into clefts and valleys as the sun settled lower. In another hour light would be gone. I might not have decided to drive up that dirt road had I not detected wisps of smoke drifting from Creed's leaning stone chimney.

Pulling back out on the pavement, I crossed to the other side and turned onto a dirt road that was narrow and rutted. Red dust boiled up from the rear of my car as I climbed closer to a neighborhood that was about as unwelcoming as any I had ever seen. It appeared that the road went to the top of the mountain and quit. Scattered along it were a series of old humpbacked trailers and dilapidated homes built of unpainted boards or logs. Some had tar paper roofs while others were tin, and the few vehicles I saw were old pickup trucks and a station wagon painted a strange crème de menthe green.

Creed Lindsey's place had an empty patch of dirt beneath trees where I could tell he usually parked, and I pulled in and cut the engine. For a time, I sat looking at his shack and its dilapidated, slanting porch. It seemed a light might have been on inside, or it could have been the way the window caught the low sun. As I thought about this man who sold red-hot toothpicks to children and had picked wildflowers for Emily as he swept floors and emptied trash at their school, I debated the wisdom of what I was doing.

My original intention, after all, had been to see where Creed Lindsey lived in relation to the Presbyterian church and Lake Tomahawk. Now that certain questions were answered, I had other ones. I could not just drive away from a fire on a hearth in a home where no one was supposed to be. I could not stop thinking about what Mote had said, and of course there were the Fireballs I had found. They really were the main reason I had to talk to this man called Creed.

I knocked on the door for a long time, thinking I heard someone move around inside, and feeling watched. But no one came to let me in, and my verbal salutations went unanswered. The window to my left was dusty and had no screen. On the other side I could see a margin of dark wood flooring and part of a wooden chair illuminated by a small lamp on a table.

Though I reasoned that a lamp on did not mean

anyone was home, I smelled wood smoke and thought the stack of kindling on the porch was piled high and freshly split. I knocked again and the wooden door felt loose beneath my knuckles, as if it wouldn't take much to kick it in.

"Hello?" I called. "Is anybody home?"

I was answered by the sound of trees shaken by gusts of wind. The air was chilled in the shade and I detected the faint odor of things rotting, mildewing, and falling apart. In the woods on either side of this one- or two-room shack with its rusting roof and bent TV antenna was the trash of many years blessedly covered in part by leaves. Mostly I saw disintegrating paper, plastic milk jugs, and cola bottles that had been lying out there long enough for labels to be bleached.

So I concluded that the lord of the manor had forsaken his unseemly way of pitching garbage out the door, since none of it looked recent. As I was momentarily lost in this observation, I became aware of a presence behind me. I felt eyes on my back so palpably that hair raised on my arms as I slowly turned around.

The girl was a strange apparition on the road near the rear bumper of my car. She stood as motionless as a deer staring at me in the gathering dusk, dull brown hair limp around her narrow pale face, eyes slightly crossed. She held herself very still. I sensed in her long, lanky limbs that she would bound out of sight if I made any movement or sound the least bit startling. For the longest time, she continued to stare and I looked right back as if I accepted the necessity of this strange encounter. When she shifted her stance a little and seemed to breathe and blink again, I dared to speak.

"I wonder if you can help me," I said gently without fear.

She slipped bare hands in the pockets of a dark wool coat that was several sizes too small. She wore wrinkled khaki pants rolled up at the ankles, and scuffed tan leather boots. I thought she was in her early teens, but it was hard to say.

"I'm from out of town," I tried again, "and it's very important that I locate Creed Lindsey. The man who lives here, or at least I think he lives in this house. Can you help me?"

"Whadyou want thar fer?" Her voice was high-pitched and reminded me of banjo strings. I knew I would have a hard time understanding a word of what she might have to say.

"I need him to help me," I said very slowly.

She moved several steps closer, her eyes never leaving mine. They were pale and crossed like a Siamese cat's.

"I know he thinks there are people looking for him," I went on with deadly calm. "But I'm not one of them. I'm not one of them at all. I'm not here to cause him harm in any way."

"What's thar name?"

"My name is Dr. Kay Scarpetta," I answered her.

She stared harder at me as if I had just told her the most curious secret. It occurred to me that if she knew what a doctor was, she might never have encountered one who was a woman.

"Do you know what a medical doctor is?" I asked her.

She stared at my car as if it contradicted what I had just said.

"There are some doctors who help the police when people get hurt. That's what I do," I said. "I'm helping the police here. That's why I have a car like this. The police are letting me drive it while I'm here because I'm not from these parts. I'm from Richmond, Virginia."

My voice trailed off as she looked silently at my car, and I had the disheartening feeling that I had said too much and all was lost. I would never find Creed Lindsey. It had been incredibly foolish to imagine for even a moment that I could communicate with a people I did not know and could not begin to understand.

I was about to decide to return to my car and drive away when the girl suddenly approached. I was startled when she took my hand and without a word tugged me toward my car. She pointed through the window at my black medical bag on the passenger's seat.

"That's my medical bag," I said. "Do you want me to get it?"

"Yes, get thar," she said.

Opening the door, I did. I wondered if she was merely curious, but then she was pulling me out onto the unpaved street where I had first seen her. Wordlessly, she led me up the hill, her hand rough and dry like corn husks as it continued to grasp mine firmly and with purpose.

"Would you tell me your name?" I asked as we climbed at a brisk pace.

"Deborah."

Her teeth were bad, and she was gaunt and old before her time, typical in the cases of chronic malnutrition that I often saw in a society where food was not always the answer. I expected that Deborah's family, like many I encountered in inner cities, subsisted on all the high empty calories that food stamps could buy.

"Deborah what?" I asked as we neared a tiny slab house. It appeared to have been built of trimmings from a sawmill and covered with tar paper, portions of which were supposed to look like brick.

"Deborah Washburn."

I followed her up rickety wooden steps leading to a weathered porch with nothing on it but firewood and a faded turquoise glider. She opened a door that hadn't seen paint in too long to remember its color, and pulled me inside, where the reason for this mission became instantly clear.

Two tiny faces too old for their very young years looked up from a bare mattress on the floor where a man sat bleeding into rags in his lap as he tried to sew up a cut on his right thumb. On the floor nearby was a glass jar half filled with a clear liquid that I doubted was water, and he had managed to get a stitch or two in with a regular needle and thread. For a moment, we regarded each other in the glare of an overhead bare light bulb.

"Thar's a doctor," Deborah said to him.

He stared at me some more as blood dripped from his thumb, and I guessed he was in his late twenties or early thirties. His hair was long and black and in his eyes, his skin sickly pale, as if it had never seen the sun. Tall and thick through the middle, he stunk of old grease, sweat, and alcohol.

"Where'd you get her from?" the man asked the child.

The other children stared vacantly at the TV, which as best I could see was the only electrical object in the house besides the one light bulb.

"Thar was looking for thar," Deborah said to him, and I realized with amazement that she used *thar* for every pronoun, and that the man must be Creed Lindsey.

"Why'd you bring her?" He didn't seem particularly upset or afraid.

"Thar hurt."

"How did you cut yourself?" I asked him as I opened my bag.

"On my knife."

I looked closely. He had raised a substantial flap of skin.

"Stitching's not going to be the best thing to do here," I said, and I got out topical antiseptic, Steristrips and Benzoin-glue. "When did you do this?"

"This afternoon. I come in and tried to pry the lid off a can."

"Do you remember the last time you had a tetanus shot?"

"Naw."

"You should go get one tomorrow. I'd do it but I don't have anything like that with me."

He watched me as I looked around for paper towels. The kitchen was nothing but a woodstove, and water came from a pump in the sink. Rinsing my hands and shaking them dry as best I could, I knelt by him on the mattress and took hold of his hand. It was callused and muscular, with dirty, torn nails.

"This is going to hurt a little," I said. "And I don't have anything to help with pain, so if you've got something, go ahead." I looked at the jar of clear fluid.

He looked down at it, too, then reached for it with his good hand. He took a swallow and the white lightning or corn liquor or whatever the hell it was brought tears to his eyes. I waited until he took another swallow before cleaning his wound and holding the flap in place with glue and paper tapes. When I was finished he was relaxed. I wrapped his thumb with gauze and wished I had an Ace bandage.

"Where's your mother?" I said to Deborah as I put wrappers and the needle inside my bag, since I didn't see a trash can.

"Thar's at thar Burger Hut."

"Is that where she works?"

She nodded as one of her siblings got up to change channels.

"Are you Creed Lindsey?" I matter-of-factly asked my patient.

"Why're you asking?" He spoke with the same twang, and I did not think he was as mentally slow as Lieutenant Mote had indicated.

232

"I need to speak to him."

"What for?"

"Because I don't think he had anything to do with what happened to Emily Steiner. But I think he knows something that might help us find who did."

He reached for the jar of liquor. "What would he know?"

"I guess I'd like to ask him that," I said. "I suspect he liked Emily and feels real upset about what happened. And I also suspect that when he feels upset he gets away from people like he's doing now, especially if he thinks he might be in any sort of trouble."

He stared down at the jar, slowly swirling its contents.

"He never did nothing to her that night."

"That night?" I asked. "Do you mean the night she disappeared?"

"He saw her walking with her guitar and slowed his truck to say hi. But he didn't do nothing. He didn't give her a ride or nothing."

"Did he ask to give her a ride?"

"He wouldn't have 'cause he'd know she wouldn't have a-taken it."

"Why wouldn't she have?"

"She don't like him. She don't like Creed even though he gives her presents." His lower lip trembled.

"I hear he was very nice to her. I hear he gave her flowers at school. And candy."

"He never gave her no candy 'cause she wouldn't have a-taken it."

"She wouldn't take it?"

233

"She wouldn't. Not even the kind she liked. I seen her take it from others."

"Fireballs?"

"Wren Maxwell trades 'em to me for the toothpicks and I seen him give the candy to her."

"Was she by herself when she was walking home that night with her guitar?"

"She was."

"Where?"

"On the road. About a mile from the church."

"Then she wasn't walking on the path that goes around the lake?"

"She was on the road. It was dark."

"Where were the other children from her youth group?"

"They was way behind her, the ones I saw. I didn't see but three or four. She was walking fast and crying. I slowed down when I seen she was crying. But she kept walking and I went on. I kept her in sight for a while 'cause I was afeared something was wrong."

"Why did you think that?"

"She was crying."

"Did you watch her until she got to her house?"

"Yeah."

"You know where her house is?"

"I know where."

"Then what happened?" I asked, and I knew very well why the police were looking for him. I could understand their suspicions and knew they would grow only darker if they heard what he was telling me.

"I seen her go in the house."

"Did she see you?"

"Naw. Some of the time I didn't have my headlights on."

Dear God, I thought. "Creed, do you understand why the police are concerned?"

He swirled the liquor some more, and his eyes turned in a little and were an unusual mixture of brown and green.

"I didn't do nothing to her," he said, and I believed him.

"You were just keeping your eye on her because you saw she was upset," I said. "And you liked her."

"I saw she was upset, I did." He took a sip from the jar.

"Do you know where she was found? Where the fisherman found her?"

"I know of it."

"You've been to the spot."

He did not answer.

"You visited the spot and left her candy. After she was dead."

"A lot of folks has been there. They go to look. But her kin don't go."

"Her kin? Do you mean her mother?"

"She don't go."

"Has anyone seen you go there?"

"Naw."

"You left candy in that place. A present for her."

His lip was trembling again and his eyes watered. "I left her Fireballs." When he said "fire" it sounded like "far."

"Why in that place? Why not on her grave?"

"I didn't want no one to see me."

"Why?"

He stared at the jar and did not need to say it. I knew why. I could imagine the names the schoolchildren called him as he pushed his broom up and down halls. I could imagine the smirks and laughter, the terrible teasing that ensued if it seemed Creed Lindsey got sweet on anyone. And he had been sweet on Emily Steiner and she had been sweet on Wren.

It was very dark when I went out, and Deborah followed me like a silent cat as I returned to my car. My heart physically ached, as if I had pulled muscles in my chest. I wanted to give her money but I knew I should not.

"You make him be careful with that hand and keep it clean," I said to her as I opened the door to my Chevrolet. "And you need to get him to a doctor. Do you have a doctor here?"

She shook her head.

"You get your mother to find him one. Someone at the Burger Hut can tell her. Will you do that?"

She looked at me and took my hand.

"Deborah, you can call me at the Travel-Eze. I don't have the number, but it's in the phone book. Here's my card so you can remember my name."

"Thar don't have a phone," she said, watching me intently as she held on to my hand.

"I know you don't. But if you needed to call, you could find a pay phone, couldn't you?"

She nodded.

A car was coming up the hill.

"Thar's thar mother."

"How old are you, Deborah?"

"Eleven."

"Do you go to the public school here in Black Mountain?" I asked, shocked to think she was Emily's age.

She nodded again.

"Did you know Emily Steiner?"

"Thar was ahead of thar."

"You weren't in the same grade?"

"No." She let go of my hand.

The car, an ancient heap of a Ford with a headlight out, rumbled past, and I caught a glimpse of the woman looking our way. I would never forget the weariness of that flaccid face with its sunken mouth and hair in a net. Deborah loped after her mother, and I shut my door.

I took a long hot bath when I got back to the motel and thought about getting something to eat. But when I looked at the room service menu I found myself staring mindlessly and decided instead to read for a while. The telephone startled me awake at half past ten.

"Yes?"

"Kay?" It was Wesley. "I need to talk to you. It's very important."

"I'll come to your room."

I went straight there and knocked on the door. "It's Kay," I said.

"Hold on." His voice sounded from the other side.

A pause, and the door opened. His face confirmed that something was terribly wrong.

"What is it?" I walked in.

"It's Lucy."

He shut the door, and I judged by the desk that he had spent most of the afternoon on the phone. Notes were scattered everywhere. His tie was on the bed, his shirt untucked.

"She's been in an accident," he said.

"What?" My blood went cold.

He shut the door and was very distracted.

"Is she all right?" I could not think.

"It happened earlier this evening on Ninety-five just north of Richmond. She'd apparently been at Quantico and went out to eat and then drove back. She ate at the Outback. You know, the Australian steakhouse in northern Virginia? We know she stopped in Hanover at the gun store—at Green Top—and it was after she left there that she had the accident." He paced as he talked.

"Benton, *is she all right*?" I could not move.

"She's at MCV. It was pretty bad, Kay."

"Oh my God."

"Apparently she ran off the road at the Atlee/Elmont exit and overcorrected. When the tags came back to you, the state police called your office from the scene and the service got Fielding to track you down. He called me because he didn't want you to get the news over the phone. Well, the point is, since he's a medical examiner he was afraid of what your first reaction would be if he started to tell you that Lucy had just been in an accident—"

"Benton!"

"I'm sorry." He put his hands on my shoulders. "Jesus. I'm not good at this when it's . . . Well, when it's you. She's got some cuts and a concussion. It's a damn miracle she's alive. The car flipped several times. Your car. It's totaled. They had to cut her out of it and Medflight her in. To be honest, they thought by the look of the wreck that it wasn't survivable. It's just unbelievable she's okay."

I closed my eyes and sat on the edge of the bed. "Was she drinking?" I asked.

"Yes."

"Tell me the rest of it."

"She's been charged with driving under the influence. They took her blood alcohol at the hospital and it's high. I'm not sure how high."

"And no one else was hurt?"

"No other car was involved."

"Thank God."

He sat next to me and rubbed my neck. "It's a wonder she made it as far as she did without incident. She'd had a lot to drink when she was out to dinner, I guess." He put his arm around me and pulled me close. "I've already booked a flight for you."

"What was she doing at Green Top?"

"She purchased a gun. A Sig Sauer P230. They found it in the car."

"I have to get back to Richmond now."

"There isn't anything until early in the morning, Kay. It can wait until then."

"I'm cold," I said.

He got his suit jacket and put it over my shoulders. I

239

began to shiver. The terror I'd felt when I saw Wesley's face and felt the tension in his tone brought back the night when he had called about Mark.

I had known the instant I'd heard Wesley's voice on the line that his news was very bad, and then he had begun to explain about the bombing in London, about Mark being in the train station walking past at the very moment it happened, and it had nothing to do with him, wasn't directed at him, but he was dead. Grief was like a seizure that shook me like a storm. It left me spent in a way I had never known before, not even when my father had died. I could not react back then, when I was young, when my mother was weeping and everything seemed lost.

"It will be all right," Wesley said, and now he was up pouring me a drink.

"What else do you know about it?"

"Nothing else, Kay. Here, this will help." He handed me a Scotch straight up.

Had there been a cigarette in the room, I would have put it between my lips and lit it. I would have ended my abstinence and forgotten my resolve just like that.

"Do you know who her doctor is? Where are the cuts? Did the air bags deploy?"

He began kneading my neck again and did not answer my questions because he had already made it clear he knew nothing more. I drank the Scotch quickly because I needed to feel it.

"I will go in the morning, then," I said.

His fingers worked their way up into my hair and felt wonderful.

My eyes were shut as I began to talk to him about my afternoon. I told him about my visit in the hospital with Lieutenant Mote. I told him about the people on Rainbow Mountain, about the girl who knew no pronouns and Creed, who knew that Emily Steiner had not taken the shortcut around the lake after her youth group meeting at the church.

"It's so sad, because I could see it as he was telling me," I went on, thinking of her diary. "She was supposed to meet Wren early and of course he did not show. Then he ignored her completely, so she didn't wait until the meeting was over. She ran ahead of everyone else.

"She hurried off because she was hurt and humiliated and didn't want anyone to know. Creed just happened to be out in his truck and saw her, and wanted to make sure she got home okay because he could tell she was upset. He liked her from afar just as she liked Wren from afar. And now she's horribly dead. It seems this is all about people loving people who don't love them back. It's about hurt getting passed on."

"Murder is always about that, really."

"Where's Marino?"

"I don't know."

"What he's doing is all wrong. He knows better than this."

"I think he's gotten involved with Denesa Steiner."

"I know he has."

"I can see how it would happen. He's lonely, had no luck with women, and in fact hasn't even had a clue about women since Doris left. Denesa

241

Steiner's devastated, needy, appeals to his bruised male ego."

"Apparently, she has a lot of money."

"Yes."

"How did that happen? I thought her late husband taught school."

"I understand his family had a lot of money. They made it in oil or something out west. You're going to have to pass on the details of your encounter with Creed Lindsey. It's not going to look good for him."

I knew that.

"I can imagine how you feel about it, Kay. But I'm not even sure I'm comfortable with what you've told me. It bothers me that he followed her in his truck and had his headlights off. It bothers me that he knew where she lived and had been so aware of her at school. It bothers me a great deal that he visited the spot where her body was found and left the candy."

"Why was the skin in Ferguson's freezer? How does Creed Lindsey fit with that?"

"Either Ferguson put the skin in there or someone else did. It's as simple as that. And I don't think Ferguson did it."

"Why not?"

"He doesn't profile right. And you know that, too."

"And Gault?"

Wesley did not answer.

I looked up at him, for I had learned to feel his silence. I could follow it like the cool walls of a cave. "You're not telling me something," I said.

"We've just gotten a call from London. We think he's killed again, this time there."

I shut my eyes. "Dear God, no."

"This time a boy. Fourteen. Killed within the past few days."

"Same MO as Eddie Heath?"

"Eradicated bite marks. Gunshot to the head, body displayed. Close enough."

"That doesn't mean Gault wasn't in Black Mountain," I said as my doubts grew.

"At this moment we can't say it doesn't mean that. Gault could be anywhere. But I don't know about him anymore. There are many similarities between the Eddie Heath and Emily Steiner cases. But there are many differences."

"There are differences because this case is different," I said. "And I don't think Creed Lindsey put the skin in Ferguson's freezer."

"Listen, we don't know why that was there. We don't know that someone didn't leave it on his doorstep and Ferguson found it the minute he got home from the airport. He put it in the freezer like any good investigator would, and didn't live long enough to tell anyone."

"You're suggesting Creed waited until Ferguson got home and then delivered it?"

"I'm suggesting the police are going to consider Creed left it."

"Why would he do that?"

"Remorse."

"Whereas Gault would do it to jerk us around."

"Absolutely."

I was silent for a moment. Then I said, "If Creed did all this, then how do you explain Denesa Steiner's print on the panties Ferguson was wearing?"

"If he had a fetish about wearing women's clothing when he did his autoerotic thing, he could have stolen them. He was in and out of her house while he was working Emily's case. He could have taken lingerie from her very easily. And wearing something of hers while he masturbated added to the fantasy."

"Is that really what you think?"

"I really don't know what I think. I'm throwing these things out at you because I know what's going to happen. I know what Marino will think. Creed Lindsey is a suspect. In fact, what he told you about following Emily Steiner gives us probable cause to search his house and truck. If we find anything, and if Mrs. Steiner thinks he looks or sounds like the man who broke into her house that night, Creed's going to be charged with capital murder."

"What about the forensic evidence?" I said. "Have the labs come back with anything more?"

Wesley got up and tucked his shirttail in as he talked. "We've traced the blaze orange duct tape to Attica Correctional Facility in New York. Apparently, some prison administrator got tired of duct tape walking off and decided to have some specially made that would be less convenient to steal.

"So he picked blaze orange, which was also the color of the clothes the inmates wore. Since the tape was used inside the penitentiary to repair things like mattresses, for example, it was essential that it be flame-retardant.

Shuford Mills made one run of the stuff—I think around eight hundred cases—back in 1986."

"That's very weird."

"As for the trace evidence on the adhesive of the strips used to bind Denesa Steiner, the residue is a varnish that's consistent with the varnish on the dresser in her bedroom. And that's pretty much what you would expect, since he bound her in her bedroom. So that information is relatively useless."

"Gault was never incarcerated at Attica, was he?" I asked.

Wesley was putting on his tie in front of the mirror. "No. But that wouldn't preclude his getting hold of the tape in another way. Someone could have given it to him. He did have a close friendship with the warden when the state pen was in Richmond—the warden he later murdered. I suppose it's worth checking that out, in the event some of the tape somehow ended up there."

"Are we going somewhere?" I asked as he slipped a fresh handkerchief into his back pocket and his pistol into a holster on his belt.

"I'm taking you out to dinner."

"What if I don't want to go?"

"You will."

"You're awfully sure of yourself."

He leaned over and kissed me as he removed his jacket from my shoulders. "I don't want you by yourself right now." He put the jacket on and looked very handsome in his precise, somber way.

We found a big brightly lit truck stop that featured

everything from T-bones to a Chinese buffet. I ate egg drop soup and steamed rice because I did not feel well. Men in denim and boots heaped ribs and pork and shrimp in thick orange sauces on their plates and stared at us as if we were from Oz. My fortune cookie warned of fair-weather friends while Wesley's promised marriage.

Marino was waiting for us at the motel when we got back at shortly after midnight. I told him what I knew and he was not happy about it.

"I wish you hadn't gone up there," he said. We were in Wesley's room. "It's not your place to be interviewing people."

"I am authorized to investigate any violent death fully and to ask any questions I wish. It's ridiculous for you to even say such a thing, Marino. You and I have worked together for years."

"We're a team, Pete," Wesley said. "That's what the unit's all about. It's why we're here. Listen, I don't mean to be a hardass, but I can't let you smoke in my room."

He put his pack and lighter back into his pocket. "Denesa's told me Emily used to complain about Creed."

"She knows the police are looking for him?" Wesley asked.

"She's not in town," he evasively replied.

"Where is she?"

"She's got a sick sister in Maryland and went up there for a few days. My point is, Creed gave Emily the creeps."

I envisioned Creed on the mattress sewing up his thumb. I saw his crooked stare and pasty face, and I was not surprised that he might have frightened a little girl.

"A lot of questions still aren't answered," I said.

"Yeah, well, a lot of questions have been answered," Marino countered.

"To think that Creed Lindsey did this doesn't make sense," I said.

"It's making more sense every day."

"I wonder if he has a television in his house," Wesley said.

I thought for a minute. "Certainly, people don't have much up there, but they seem to have TVs."

"Creed could have learned all about Eddie Heath from television. Several of these true crime and news shows did segments on the case."

"Shit, stuff about that case was all over the friggin' universe," Marino said.

"I'm going to bed," I said.

"Well, don't let me hold you up." Marino glared at both of us as he got up from his chair. "I sure wouldn't want to do that."

"I've about had enough of your insinuations," I said as my anger boiled up.

"I sure as hell ain't insinuating. I'm just calling 'em as I see 'em."

"Let's not get into this," Wesley calmly said.

"Let's do." I was tired and stressed and fueled by Scotch. "Let's just do it right here in this room, the three of us together. Since this is all about the three of us."

"It sure as hell isn't," Marino said. "There's only one relationship in this room, and I'm not part of it. My opinion of it's my own business, and I have a right to it."

"Your opinion is self-righteous and wrongheaded," I said, furious. "You're acting like a thirteen-year-old with a crush."

"If that ain't just the biggest load of bullshit I ever heard." Marino's face was dark.

"You're so damn possessive and jealous you're making me crazy."

"In your dreams."

"You've got to stop this, Marino. You're destroying our relationship."

"I wasn't aware we had one."

"Of course we do."

"It's late," Wesley warned. "Everybody's under a lot of stress. We're tired. Kay, now is not a good time for this."

"Now is all we've got," I said. "Marino, goddam it, I care about you, but you're pushing me away. You're getting into things here that are scaring me to death. I'm not sure you even see what you're doing."

"Well, let me tell you something." Marino looked as if he hated me. "I don't think you're in a position to say I'm into anything. In the first place, you don't know shit. And in the second, at least I'm not screwing anybody who's married."

"Pete, that's enough," Wesley snapped.

"You're damn right it is." Marino stormed out of the

room, slamming the door so hard I was certain it could be heard throughout the entire motel.

"Dear God," I said. "This is just awful."

"Kay, you spurned him, and that's why he's out of his mind."

"I did not spurn him."

Wesley was walking around, agitated. "I knew he was attached to you. All these years I've known he really cares about you. I just had no idea it went this deep. *I had absolutely no idea.*"

I did not know what to say.

"The guy's not stupid. I suppose it was just a matter of time before he figured some things out. But I had no way of knowing it would affect him this way."

"I'm going to bed," I said again.

I slept for a while, and then I was wide awake. I stared into the dark, thinking about Marino and what I was doing. I was having an affair and did not feel concerned about it, and I did not understand that. Marino knew I was having an affair, and he was jealous beyond reason. I could never be romantically interested in him. I would have to tell him, but I could not imagine the occasion when such a conversation might occur.

I got up at four and sat out on the porch in the cold, looking at the stars. The Big Dipper was almost directly overhead, and I remembered Lucy as a toddler worrying that it would pour water on her if she stood under it very long. I remembered her perfect bones and skin, and incredible green eyes. I remembered the way she had looked at Carrie Grethen and believed that was part of what went wrong.

14

Lucy was not in a private room, and I walked right past her at first because she did not look like anyone I knew. Her hair, stiff with blood, was dark red and standing up, her eyes black-and-blue. She was propped up in bed in a drug-induced stage that was neither here nor there. I got close to her and took her hand.

"Lucy?"

She barely opened her eyes. "Hi," she said groggily.

"How are you feeling?"

"Not too bad. I'm sorry, Aunt Kay. How did you get here?"

"I rented a car."

"What kind?"

"A Lincoln."

"Bet you got one with air bags on both sides." She smiled wanly.

"Lucy, what happened?"

"All I remember is going to the restaurant. Then

250

someone was sewing up my head in the emergency room."

"You have a concussion."

"They think I hit the top of my head on the roof when the car was flipping. I feel so bad about your car." Her eyes filled with tears.

"Don't worry about the car. That's not important. Do you remember anything at all about the accident?"

She shook her head and reached for a tissue.

"Do you remember anything about dinner at the Outback or your visit to Green Top?"

"How did you know? Oh, well." She drifted for a moment, eyelids heavy. "I went to the restaurant about four."

"Who did you meet?"

"Just a friend. I left at seven to come back here."

"You had a lot to drink," I said.

"I didn't think I had that much. I don't know why I ran off the road, but I think something happened."

"What do you mean?"

"I don't know. I can't remember, but it seems like something happened."

"What about the gun store? Do you remember stopping there?"

"I don't remember leaving."

"You bought a .380 semiautomatic pistol, Lucy. Do you remember that?"

"I know that's why I went there."

"So you go to a gun shop when you've been drinking. Can you tell me what was in your mind?"

"I didn't want to be staying at your house without protection. Pete recommended the gun."

"Marino did?" I asked, shocked.

"I called him the other day. He said to get a Sig and said he always uses Green Top in Hanover."

"He's in North Carolina," I said.

"I don't know where he was. I called his pager and he called me back."

"I have guns. Why didn't you ask me?"

"I want my own and I'm old enough now." She could not keep her eyes open much longer.

I found her doctor on the floor and caught up with him for a moment before I left. He was very young and talked to me as if I were a worried aunt or mother who did not know the difference between a kidney and a spleen. When he rather abruptly explained to me that a concussion was basically a bruised brain resulting from a severe blow, I did not say a word or change the expression on my face. He blushed when a medical student, who happened to be one of my advisees, passed us in the hall and greeted me by name.

I left the hospital and went to my office, where I had not been for more than a week. My desk looked rather much as I feared it would, and I spent the next few hours trying to clear it while I tried to track down the state police officer who worked Lucy's accident. I left a message, then called Gloria Loving at Vital Records.

"Any luck?" I asked.

"I can't believe I'm getting to talk to you twice in one week. Are you across the street again?"

"I am." I couldn't help but smile.

"No luck so far, Kay," she said. "We haven't found any record in California of a Mary Jo Steiner who died of SIDS. We're trying to code the death several other ways. Is it possible you could get a date and place of death?"

"I'll see what I can do," I said.

I thought of calling Denesa Steiner and ended up just staring at the phone. I was about to do it when State Police Officer Reed, whom I had been trying to reach, returned my call.

"I wonder if you could fax me your report," I said to him.

"Actually, Hanover's got a lot of that."

"I thought the accident occurred on Ninety-five," I said, for the interstate was state police jurisdiction, no matter the locale.

"Officer Sinclair rolled up just as I did, so he gave me a hand. When the tags came back to you, I thought it was important to check that out."

Oddly, it had not crossed my mind before this moment that tags coming back to me would have created quite a stir.

"What is Officer Sinclair's first name?" I asked.

"His initials are A. D., I believe."

I was very fortunate that Officer Andrew D. Sinclair was in his office when I called him next. He told me Lucy was involved in a single-car accident that occurred while she was driving at a high rate of speed southbound on Ninety-five just north of the Henrico County line.

"How high a rate of speed?" I asked him.

"Seventy miles per hour."

"What about skid marks?"

"We found one thirty-two feet long where it appears she tapped her brakes and then went off the road."

"Why would she tap her brakes?"

"She was traveling at a high rate of speed and under the influence, ma'am. Could be she drifted off to sleep and suddenly was on somebody's bumper."

"Officer Sinclair, you need a skid mark of three hundred and twenty-nine feet to calculate that someone was driving seventy miles an hour. You have a thirty-two-foot skid mark here. I don't see how you can possibly calculate that she was driving seventy miles an hour."

"The speed limit on that stretch is sixty-five" was all he had to say.

"What was her blood alcohol?"

"Point one-two."

"I wonder if you could fax me your diagrams and report as soon as possible and tell me where my car was towed."

"It's at Covey's Texaco in Hanover. Off Route One. It's totaled, ma'am. If you can give me your fax number, I'll get you those reports right away."

I had them within the hour, and by using an overlay to interpret the codes I determined that Sinclair basically assumed Lucy was drunk and fell asleep at the wheel. When she suddenly awoke and tapped her brakes, she went into a skid, lost control of the car, left the pavement, and overcorrected. This resulted in her jerking back onto the road and flipping across two lanes of traffic before crashing upside down into a tree.

I had serious problems with his assumptions and one important detail. My Mercedes had antilock brakes. When Lucy hit the brakes she should not have gone into the sort of skid Officer Sinclair had described.

I left my office and went downstairs to the morgue. My deputy chief, Fielding, and two young female forensic pathologists I had hired last year had cases on the three stainless steel tables. The sharp noise of steel against steel rose above the background thunder of water drumming into sinks, air blowing, and generators humming. The huge stainless steel refrigerator door opened with a loud suck as one of the morgue assistants rolled out another body.

"Dr. Scarpetta, can you look at this?" Dr. Wheat was a woman from Topeka. Her intelligent gray eyes peered out at me from behind a plastic face shield speckled with blood.

I went to her table.

"Does this look like soot in the wound?" She pointed a bloody gloved finger at a bullet wound to the back of the neck.

I bent close. "It's got burned edges, so maybe it's searing. Was there clothing?"

"He didn't have a shirt on. It happened in his residence."

"Well, this is an ambiguous one. We need to get a microscopic."

"Entrance or exit?" Fielding asked as he studied a

wound from his own case. "Let me get your vote while you're here."

"Entrance," I said.

"Me, too. Are you going to be around?"

"In and out."

"In and out of town or in and out of here?"

"Both. I've got my Skypager."

"It's going all right?" he asked, his formidable biceps bunching as he cut through ribs.

"It's a nightmare, really," I said.

It took half an hour to get to the Texaco gas station with the twenty-four-hour towing service that had taken care of my car. I spotted my Mercedes in a corner near a chain link fence, and the sight of its destruction tightened my stomach. I got weak in the knees.

The front end was crumpled up against the windshield, the driver's side gaping like a toothless mouth. Hydraulic tools had forced open the doors, which had been removed along with the center post. My heart beat hard as I got close, and I jumped when a deep drawl sounded behind me.

"May I help ya?"

I turned to face a grizzled old man wearing a faded red cap with PURINA over the bill.

"This is my car," I told him.

"I sure as hell hope you wasn't the one driving it."

I noticed the tires were not flat and both air bags had deployed.

"It sure is a shame." He shook his head as he stared at my hideously mangled Mercedes-Benz. "Believe this

256

is the first one of these I've seen. A 500E. Now, one of the boys here knows Mercedes and tells me Porsche helped design the engine in this one and there aren't but so many around. What is it? A '93? I don't reckon your husband got it around here."

I noticed that the left taillight was shattered, and near it was a scrape that was smudged with what appeared to be greenish paint. I bent over to get a closer look as my nerves began to tensely hum.

The man talked on. "Course, with as few miles as you had on it, it's more'n likely a '94. If you don't mind my asking, about how much would one like this cost? About fifty?"

"Did you tow this in?" I straightened up, my eyes darting over details that were sending off alarms, one right after another.

"Toby brought it in last night. I don't guess you'd know the horsepower."

"Was it *exactly* like this at the scene?"

The man looked slightly befuddled.

"For example," I went on, "the phone's off the hook."

"I guess so when a car's been flipping and slams into a tree."

"And the sunscreen's up."

He leaned over and peered in at the back windshield. He scratched his neck. "I just figured it was dark because the glass is tinted. I didn't notice the screen was up. You wouldn't think someone'd put it up at night."

I carefully leaned inside to look at the rearview

257

mirror. It had been flipped up to reduce the glare of headlights from the rear. I got keys out of my pocketbook and sat sidesaddle on the driver's seat.

"Now I wouldn't be doing that if I was you. That metal's like bunches of knives in there. And there's an awful lot of blood on the seats and ever'where."

I hung up the car phone and turned on the ignition. The phone sounded its tone to tell me it was working, and red lights went on warning me not to run down the battery. The radio and the CD player were off. Headlights and fog lamps were on. I picked up the phone and hit redial. It began to ring and a woman's voice answered.

"Nine-one-one."

I hung up, my pulse pounding in my neck as chills raced up to the roots of my hair. I looked around at red spatters on the dark gray leather, on the dash and console, and all over the inside of the roof. They were too red and thick. Here and there bits of angel hair pasta were cemented to the interior of my car.

I got out a metal fingernail file and scraped off greenish paint from the damage to the rear. Folding the paint flecks into a tissue, next I tried to pry off the damaged taillight unit. When I couldn't, I got the man to fetch a screwdriver.

"It's a '92," I said as I rapidly walked away, leaving him staring after me with an open mouth. "Three hundred and fifteen horsepower. It cost eighty thousand dollars. There are only six hundred in this country—*were*. I bought it at McGeorge in Richmond. I don't have a husband." I was breathing hard as I got in the Lincoln. "It's not blood inside it, goddam it. Goddam it. Goddam it!" I muttered on as I slammed the door shut and started the engine.

Tires squealed as I shot out into the highway and raced back to 95 South. Just past the Atlee/Elmont exit I slowed down and pulled off the road. I kept as far off the pavement as I could, and when cars and trucks roared past I was hit by walls of wind.

Sinclair's report stated that my Mercedes had left the pavement approximately eighty feet north of the eighty-six-mile marker. I was at least two hundred feet north of that when I spotted a yaw mark not far from broken taillight glass in the right lane. The mark, which was a sideways scuff about two feet long, was about ten feet from a set of straight skid marks that were approximately thirty feet long. I darted in and out of traffic, collecting glass.

I started walking again, and it was approximately another hundred feet before I got to marks on pavement that Sinclair had diagrammed in his report. My heart skipped another beat as I stared, stunned, at black rubber streaks left by my Pirelli tires the night before last. They were not skids at all, but acceleration marks made when tires spin abruptly straight ahead, as I had done when leaving the Texaco station moments earlier.

It was just after she had made these marks that Lucy had lost control and had gone off the road. I saw her tire impressions in the dirt, the smear of rubber when she overcorrected and a tire caught the pavement's edge. I surveyed deep gashes in the road made when the car flipped, the gouge in the tree in the median, and bits of metal and plastic scattered everywhere.

I drove back to Richmond not sure what to do or whom to call. Then I thought of Investigator McKee with the state police. We had worked many traffic fatality scenes together and spent many hours in my office moving Matchbox cars on my desk until we believed we had reconstructed what had led to a crash. I left a message with his office, and he returned my call shortly after I got home.

"I didn't ask Sinclair if he got casts of the tire impressions where she left the road, but I can't imagine he would have," I said, after explaining a little of what was going on.

"No, he wouldn't have," McKee concurred. "I heard a lot about it, Dr. Scarpetta. There was a lot of talk. And the thing was, what Reed first noticed when he responded to the scene was your low number tag."

"I talked to Reed briefly. He wasn't very involved."

"Right. Under ordinary circumstances, when the Hanover officer . . . uh, Sinclair, rolled up, Reed would have told him things were under control and done all the diagrams and measurements himself. But he sees this low three-digit tag and bells go off. He knows the car belongs to somebody important in government.

"Sinclair gets to do his thing while Reed gets on the radio and the phone, calls for a supervisor, runs the tag ASAP. Bingo. The car comes back to you, and now his first thought is it's you inside. So you can imagine how it was out there."

"A circus."

"You got it. Turns out Sinclair just got out of the academy. Your wreck was his second."

"Even if it was his twentieth, I can see how he might have made a mistake. There was no reason for him to look for skid marks two hundred feet up from where Lucy went off the road."

"And you're certain it was a yaw mark you saw?"

"Absolutely. You make those casts, and you're going to find the impression on the shoulder's going to match the impression back there on the road. The only way that yaw mark or scuff could have been left was if an outside force caused the car to suddenly change direction."

"And then acceleration marks two hundred or so feet later," he thought out loud. "Lucy gets hit from the rear, taps her brakes, and keeps on going. Seconds later she suddenly accelerates and loses control."

"Probably about the same time she dialed Nine-one-one," I said.

"I'll check with the cellular phone company and get the exact time of that call. Then we'll find it on the tape."

"Someone was on her bumper with their high beams on, and she flipped on the night mirror, and finally resorted to putting up the rear sunscreen to block out the glare. She didn't have the radio or CD player on because she was concentrating hard. She was wide awake and scared because someone's on top of her.

"This person finally hits her from the rear and Lucy applies the brakes," I continued to reconstruct what I believed had happened. "She drives on, and realizes the person is gaining on her again. Panicking, Lucy floors it and loses control. All of this would have taken place in seconds."

"If what you found out there is right, it sure could have happened exactly like that."

"Will you look into it?"

"You bet. What about the paint?"

"I'll turn it, the taillight unit, and everything else in to the labs and ask them to put a rush on it."

"Put my name on the paperwork. Have them call me with the results right away."

It was five o'clock and dark out when I got off the phone in my upstairs office. I looked around dazed, and felt like a stranger in my house. Hunger gnawing my stomach was followed by nausea, and I drank Mylanta from the bottle and rummaged in the medicine cabinet for Zantac. My ulcer had vanished during the summer, but unlike former lovers, it always came back.

Both phone lines rang and were answered by voice mail. I heard the fax machine as I soaked in the tub and sipped wine on top of medicine. I had so much to do. I knew my sister, Dorothy, would want to come immediately. She always rose to crisis occasions because it fed her need for drama. She would use it for research. No doubt, in her next children's book, one of her characters would deal with an auto wreck. Critics again would rave about the sensitivity and wisdom of Dorothy, who mothered people she imagined much better than she did her only daughter.

The fax, I found, was Dorothy's flight schedule. She

was arriving late tomorrow afternoon and would stay with Lucy in my home.

"She won't be in the hospital long, will she?" she asked, when I called her minutes later.

"I imagine I'll be bringing her here in the afternoon," I said.

"She must look terrible."

"Most people do after automobile accidents."

"But is any of it *permanent*?" She almost whispered. "She won't be disfigured, will she?"

"No, Dorothy. She won't be disfigured. How aware have you been of her drinking?"

"Now how would I know anything about that? She's up there near you in school and never seems to want to come home. And when she does she certainly doesn't confide in me or her grandmother. I would think if anyone were aware, you should have been."

"If she's convicted of DUI, the courts could order her into treatment," I said as patiently as possible.

Silence.

Then, "My God."

I went on, "Even if they don't, it would be a good idea for two reasons. The most obvious is that she needs to deal with the problem. Second, the judge may look upon her case with more sympathy if she volunteers to get some help."

"Well, I'm just going to leave all that up to you. You're the doctor-lawyer in the family. But I know my little girl. She's not going to want to do it. I can't imagine her going off to some mental ward where they don't have computers. She'd never be able to face anyone again."

"She will not be going off to a *mental ward*, and there is nothing the least bit shameful about being treated for alcohol or drug abuse. What's shameful is to let it go on to ruin your life."

"I've always stopped at three glasses of wine."

"There are many types of addictions," I said. "Yours happens to be to men."

"*Oh, Kay.*" She laughed. "That's quite something coming from you. By the way, are you seeing anyone?"

15

Senator Frank Lord heard a rumor that I had been in a wreck and called me before the sun was up the next morning.

"No," I told him as I sat half dressed on the edge of my bed. "Lucy was driving my car."

"Oh, dear!"

"She's doing fine, Frank. I'll be bringing her home this afternoon."

"Apparently one of the papers up here printed that it was you who had wrecked and there was a suspicion alcohol was a factor."

"Lucy was trapped in the car for a while. No doubt some policeman made an assumption when the tags came back to me, and this ended up being relayed to a reporter on deadline." I thought of Officer Sinclair. He would get my vote for such a blunder.

"Kay, can I do anything to help?"

"Do you have any further clues as to what might have happened at ERF?"

"There are some interesting developments. Have you heard Lucy mention someone named Carrie Grethen?"

"They're co-workers. I've met her."

"Apparently she's connected to a spy shop, one of these places that sells high-tech surveillance devices."

"You aren't serious."

"Afraid so."

"Well, I can certainly see why she would have been interested in getting a job at ERF, and it stuns me that the Bureau would have hired her with that in her background."

"No one knew. Apparently, it's her boyfriend who owns the shop. The only reason we know she's a frequent visitor is she's been under surveillance."

"She dates a man?"

"Excuse me?"

"The owner of the spy shop is a man?"

"Yes."

"Who says it is her boyfriend?"

"Apparently she did when questioned after being seen in the shop."

"Can you tell me more about both of them?"

"Not much at present, but I have the shop's address, if you want to hold on a minute. Let me dig it out."

"What about her home address or the boyfriend's home address?"

"I'm afraid I don't have those."

"Whatever information you can give me, then."

I looked around for a pencil and wrote as my mind raced. The name of the shop was Eye Spy, and it was in the Springfield Mall, just off I-95. If I left now, I could be there by mid-morning and back in time to bring Lucy home from the hospital.

"Just so you know," Senator Lord was saying, "Miss Grethen has been dismissed from ERF because of the spy shop connection, which she obviously omitted divulging during her application process. But at this point, there's no evidence whatsover she was involved in the break-in."

"She certainly had motive," I said, holding my anger in check. "ERF is a Santa's workshop for someone who sells espionage equipment." I paused, thinking. "Do you know when she was hired by the Bureau, and did she apply for the job or did ERF recruit her?"

"Let's see. It's in my notes here. It just says here that she submitted an application last April and started mid-August."

"Mid-August was about the same time Lucy started. What did Carrie do before that?"

"It seems her entire career has been in computers. Hardware, software, programming. And engineering, which was partly why the Bureau was interested in her. She's very creative and ambitious, and unfortunately, dishonest. Several people recently interviewed have begun to paint a portrait of a woman who has been lying and cheating her way to the top for years."

"Frank, she applied for the job at ERF so she could spy for the spy shop," I said. "She may also be one of these people who hates the FBI."

"Both scenarios are possible," he agreed. "It's a matter of finding proof. Even if we can, unless there is evidence she took something, she can't be prosecuted."

"Lucy mentioned to me before all this happened that she was involved in some research pertaining to the biometric lock system at ERF. Do you know anything about that?"

"I'm not aware of any research projects of that nature."

"But would you necessarily know if there was one?"

"There's a good chance I would. I've been given quite a lot of detailed information pertaining to ongoing classified projects at Quantico—because of the crime bill, the money I've been trying to appropriate for the Bureau."

"Well, it's strange that Lucy would say she was involved in a project that doesn't seem to exist," I said.

"Sadly, that detail might only make her situation look more incriminating."

I knew he was right. As suspicious as Carrie Grethen appeared, the case against Lucy was still stronger.

"Frank," I went on, "do you happen to know what types of cars Carrie Grethen and her boyfriend drive?"

"Certainly, we can get that information. Why are you interested?"

"I have reason to believe Lucy's wreck was no accident and she may still be in serious danger."

He paused. "Would it be a good idea to keep her on the Academy's security floor for a while?"

"Ordinarily, that would be the perfect place," I said. "But I don't think she needs to be anywhere near the Academy right now."

"I see. Well, that makes sense. There are other places if you need me to intervene."

"I think I have a place."

"I'm off to Florida tomorrow, but you've got my numbers there."

"More fund-raisers?" I knew he was exhausted, for the election was little more than a week away.

"That, too. And the usual brush fires. NOW's picketing, and my opponent remains very busy painting me as the woman hater with horns and a pointed tail."

"You've done more for women than anyone I know," I said. "Especially this one right here."

I finished getting dressed and by seven-thirty was drinking my first cup of coffee on the road in my rental car. The weather was gloomy and cold, and I noticed very little of what I passed as I drove north.

A biometric lock system, like any lock system, would have to be *picked* were someone to bypass it. Some locks truly did require nothing more than a credit card, while others could be dismantled or released with various tools, such as Slim Jims. But a lock system that scanned fingerprints could not be violated by such simple mechanical means. As I contemplated the break-in at ERF and how someone might have accomplished this, several thoughts drifted through my mind.

Lucy's print had been scanned into the system at approximately three o'clock in the morning, and that was only possible if her finger had been present—or a facsimile of her finger had been present. I recalled from International Association of Identification meetings I had attended over the years that many notorious criminals had made many creative attempts at altering their fingerprints.

The ruthless gangster John Dillinger had dropped acid on his cores and deltas, while the lesser-known Roscoe Pitts had surgically removed his prints from the first knuckle up. These methods and others had failed, and the gentlemen would have been better served had they stayed painlessly with the prints God had given them. Their altered latents simply went into the FBI's Mutilated File, which, frankly, was far easier to search. Not to mention, burned and mangled fingers look a little fishy if you happen to be a suspect.

But what came to mind most vividly was a case years ago of an especially resourceful burglar whose brother worked in a funeral home. The burglar, who had been imprisoned many times, attempted to give himself a pair of gloves that would leave someone else's prints. This he accomplished by repeatedly dipping a dead man's hands into liquid rubber, forming layer after layer until the "gloves" could be pulled off.

The plan did not work well for at least two reasons. The burglar had neglected to knock air bubbles out with each layer of rubber, and this made for rather odd latent prints recovered at the next mansion he hit. He also had not bothered to research the individual whose prints he stole. Had he done so, he would have learned that the decedent was a convicted felon who had died peacefully while out on parole.

I thought of my visit to ERF on a sunny afternoon that now seemed years ago. I had sensed
that Carrie Grethen was not pleased to find Wesley
and me in her office when she walked in stirring a
viscous substance, which, in retrospect, could have
been liquid silicone or rubber. It was during this
visit that Lucy mentioned the biometric lock research
she was "in the middle of." Maybe what she had
said was literally true. Maybe Carrie had intended
at that moment to make a rubber cast of Lucy's
thumb.

If my theory about what Carrie had done was accu-
rate, I knew it could be proven. I wondered why none
of us had thought before to ask a very simple question.
Did the print scanned into the biometric lock system
physically match Lucy's, or were we simply taking the
computer's word for it?"

"Well, I would assume so," Benton Wesley said to
me when I got him on the car phone.

"Of course you would assume it. Everyone would
assume it. But if someone made a cast of Lucy's thumb
and scanned it into the system, the print should be
a *reversal* of the corresponding one on her ten-print
card on file with the Bureau. A mirror image, in other
words."

Wesley paused, then sounded surprised. "Damn.
But wouldn't the scanner have detected the print was
backward and rejected it?"

"Very few scanners could distinguish between a print
and an inversion of that same print. But a fingerprint
examiner could," I said. "The print scanned into the

biometric lock system should still be digitally stored in the data base."

"If Carrie Grethen did this, don't you think she would have eradicated the print from the data base?"

"I doubt it," I replied. "She's not a fingerprint examiner. It's unlikely she would realize that every time a latent print is left, it's reversed. And it matches a ten-print card only because those prints are reversed as well. Now if you made a cast of a digit and left a latent print with it, you would actually have a reversal of a reversal."

"So a latent made with this rubber thumb would be a reversal of the same latent made with the person's actual thumb."

"Precisely."

"Christ, I'm not good with things like this."

"Don't worry about it, Benton. I know it's confusing, but take my word for it."

"I always do, and it sounds like we need to get a hard copy of the print in question."

"Absolutely, and right away. There's something else I want to ask you. Were you aware of a research project pertaining to ERF's biometric lock system?"

"A research project conducted by the Bureau?"

"Yes."

"No. I'm not aware of any project like that."

"That's what I thought. Thank you, Benton."

Both of us paused, waiting for a personal word from the other. But I did not know what else to say. So much was inside me.

"Be careful," he told me, and we said good-bye.

I found the spy shop not more than a half hour later in a huge shopping mall teaming with cars and people. Eye Spy was inside near Ralph Lauren and Crabtree & Evelyn. It was a small shop with a window display of the finest that legal espionage had to offer. I hesitated a safe distance away until a customer at the register moved, allowing me to see who was working at the counter. An older, overweight man was ringing up an order, and I could not believe he could be Carrie Grethen's lover. No doubt this detail was yet one more of her lies.

When the customer left, there was only one other, a young man in a leather jacket perusing a showcase of voice-activated tape recorders and portable voice stress analyzers. The fat man behind the counter wore thick glasses and gold chains, and looked like he always had a deal for someone.

"Excuse me," I said as quietly as possible. "I'm looking for Carrie Grethen."

"She went out for coffee, should be back in a minute." He studied my face. "Can I help you with something?"

"I'll look around until she returns," I said.

"Sure."

I had just gotten interested in a special attaché case that included a hidden tape recorder, wire tap alerts, telephone descrambler, and night vision devices, when Carrie Grethen walked in. She stopped when she saw me, and for an unnerving instant I thought she might fling her cup of coffee in my face. Her eyes drove through mine like two steel nails.

"I need a word with you," I said.

"I'm afraid this is not a good time." She tried to smile, to sound civil, because now there were four customers in this very small store.

"Of course it's a good time," I said, holding her gaze.

"Jerry?" She looked at the fat man. "Can you handle things for a few minutes?"

He stared hard at me like a dog ready to lunge.

"I promise I won't be long," she reassured him.

"Yeah, sure," he said with the distrust of the dishonest.

I followed her out of the store and we found an empty bench near a fountain.

"I heard about Lucy's accident and I'm sorry about that. I hope she's all right," Carrie said coldly as she sipped her coffee.

"You don't care in the least how Lucy is," I said. "And there's no point in wasting any of your charm on me because I have you figured out. I *know* what you did."

"You don't know anything." She smiled her frosty smile, and the air was filled with the sounds of water.

"I know you made a cast of Lucy's thumb in rubber, and figuring out her Personal Identification Number was simple since you were with each other so much. All you had to do was be observant and note the code she punched in. This was how you accessed the biometric lock system the early morning you violated ERF."

"My, don't you have an active imagination?" She laughed and her eyes got harder. "And I might

274

advise you to be very careful making accusations like that."

"I'm not interested in your advice, Miss Grethen. I'm interested only in giving you a warning. It will soon be proven that Lucy did not break into ERF. You were smart but not smart enough, and you made one fatal oversight."

She was silent, but I could see her mind racing behind her icy façade. Her curiosity was desperate.

"I don't know what you're talking about," she said with self-confidence that was beginning to waver.

"You may be good with computers, but you are not a forensic scientist. The case against you is very simple." I put forth my theory with the certitude of any good lawyer who knows how to play the game. "You asked Lucy to assist you in a so-called research project involving the biometric lock system at ERF."

"Research project? There is no research project," she said hatefully.

"And that's the point, Miss Grethen. There is no research project. You lied to her so you could get her to let you make a cast of her thumb in liquid rubber."

She laughed shortly. "My goodness. You've been watching too much James Bond. You don't really think anyone would believe—"

I cut her off. "This rubber thumb you made was then used to get into the lock system so you and whoever else could commit what amounts to industrial espionage. But you made *one mistake*."

Her face was livid.

"Would you like to hear what that mistake was?"

Still, she said nothing, but she wanted to know. I could feel her paranoia radiating like heat.

"You see, Miss Grethen," I went on in the same reasonable tone. "When you make a cast of a finger, the print impression on it is actually a reversal or mirror image of the original one. So the print of your rubber thumb was an inversion of Lucy's print. *In other words, it was backward.* And an examination of the print that was scanned into the system at three in the morning will show this quite clearly."

She swallowed hard, and what she said next validated all that I conjectured. "You can't prove it was me who did that."

"Oh, we will prove it. But there's a more important bit of information for you to go away with this day." I leaned closer. I could smell her coffee breath. "You took advantage of my niece's feelings for you. You took advantage of her youth and naïveté and decency."

I leaned so close I was in her face. "Don't you ever come near Lucy again. Don't you ever speak to her. Don't you ever call her again. Don't you ever *think* about her."

My hand in my coat pocket gripped my .38. I almost wanted her to make me use it.

"And if I find out you were the one who ran her off the road," I went on in a quiet voice that rang like cold surgical steel, "I will personally track you down. You will be haunted by me the rest of your wretched life. I will always be there when you come up for parole. I will tell parole board after parole board and governor after governor that you are a character disorder who is a menace to society. Do you understand?"

"Go to hell," she said.

"I will never go to hell," I said. "But you are already there."

She abruptly got up, and her angry strides carried her back into the spy shop. I watched a man follow her in and begin to speak to her as I sat on the bench, my heart beating hard. I did not know why he made me pause. There was something about the sharpness of his profile at a glance, the V-shape of his lean, strong back, and the unnatural blackness of his slicked hair. Dressed in a splendid midnight-blue silk suit, he carried what looked like an alligator skin briefcase. I was about to walk away when he turned toward me, and for an electric instance our eyes met. His were piercing blue.

I did not run. I was like a squirrel in the middle of a road that starts to dash this way and that only to end up where it began. I began walking as fast as I could, then began to run, and the sound of water falling was like feet falling as I imagined him in pursuit. I did not go to a pay phone because I was afraid to stop. I thought my heart would burst as it hammered harder and harder.

I sprinted through the parking lot, my hands shaking as I unlocked my car. I did not reach for the phone until I was moving fast and did not see him.

"Benton! Oh my God!"

"Kay? Jesus, what is it?" His alarmed voice crackled horribly over the phone, for northern Virginia is notorious for too much cellular traffic.

277

"Gault!" I breathlessly exclaimed as I slammed on my brakes just before rear-ending a Toyota. "I saw Gault!"

"You saw Gault? Where?"

"In Eye Spy."

"In what? What did you say?"

"The shop Carrie Grethen works in. The one she's been connected to. He was there, Benton! I saw him walk in as I was leaving, and he started talking to her, and then he saw me and I ran."

"Slow down, Kay!" Wesley's voice was tense. I couldn't recall him ever sounding this tense. "Where are you now?"

"I'm on I-95 South. I'm fine."

"Just keep driving, for God's sake. Don't stop for anything. Do you think he saw you get into your car?"

"I don't think so. Shit, I don't know!"

"Kay," he said with authority. "Calm down." He spoke slowly. "I want you to calm down. I don't want you getting into an accident. I'm going to make calls. We'll find him."

But I knew we wouldn't. I knew by the time the first agent or cop got the first call, Gault would be gone. He had recognized me. I had seen it in his cold blue stare. He would know exactly what I would do the minute I could, and he would disappear again.

"I thought you said he was in England," I stupidly said.

"I said we believe he was," Wesley said.

"Don't you see, Benton?" I went on because my mind would not stop. Connections were being made left and right. "He's involved in this. He's involved in what happened at ERF. *It may be he's the one who sent Carrie Grethen, who got her to do what she did. His spy.*"

Wesley was silent as this sank in. It was a thought so terrible that he did not want to think it.

His voice began to break up. I knew he was getting frantic, too, because conversations like this one should not be conducted over a car phone. "To get what?" he crackled. "What would he want to get into there?"

I knew. I knew exactly what. "CAIN," I said as the line went dead.

16

I got back to Richmond and did not sense Gault's malignant shadow at my heels. He had other agendas and demons to fight, and had not chosen to come after me, I believed. Even so, I reset the alarm the moment I entered my house. I went nowhere, not even to the bathroom, without my gun.

At shortly after two P.M., I drove to MCV, and Lucy traveled by wheelchair to my car. She insisted on wheeling herself despite my insistence that I propel her prudently, as a loving aunt would. She would have none of my help. But as soon as we got home she succumbed to my attentions and I tucked her in bed, where she sat up dozing.

I put on a pot of Zuppa di Aglio Fresco, a fresh garlic soup popular in the hills of Brisighella, where it has been fed to babies and the elderly for many years. That and ravioli filled with sweet squash and chestnuts would do the trick, and it lifted my mood when a fire was blazing in the living room and wonderful aromas filled the air. It was true that when I went long periods without cooking, it felt as if no one lived in my lovely home or cared. It almost seemed my house got sad.

Later, beneath a sky threatening rain, I drove to the airport to meet my sister's plane. I had not seen her for a while, and she was not the same. She never was from visit to visit, for Dorothy was acutely insecure, which was why she could be so mean, and she had a habit of changing her hair and dress regularly.

This late afternoon as I stood at the USAir gate, I scanned faces of passengers coming off the jetway, leaving myself open for anything familiar. I recognized her by her nose and the dimple in her chin, since neither was easily altered. She wore her hair black and close to her head like a leather helmet, her eyes behind large glasses, a bright red scarf thrown around her neck. Fashionably thin in jodhpurs and lace-up boots, she strode straight to me and kissed my cheek.

"Kay, it's so wonderful to see you. *You look tired.*"

"How's Mother?"

"Her hip, you know. What are you driving?"

"A rental car."

"Well, the first thing that went through my mind was your being without your Mercedes. I couldn't possibly imagine being without mine."

Dorothy had a 190E that she had gotten while dating a Miami cop. The car had been confiscated from a drug dealer and was sold at auction for a pittance. It was dark blue with spoilers and custom pinstripes.

"Do you have luggage?" I asked.

"Just this. How fast was she driving?"

"Lucy doesn't remember anything."

"You can't imagine how I felt when the phone rang. My God. My heart literally stopped."

It was raining and I had not brought an umbrella.

"No one can relate unless they've experienced the same thing. That moment. That simply awful moment when you don't know exactly what's happened, but you can tell the news is bad about someone you love. I hope you're not parked too far from here. Maybe it's best if I just wait."

"I'll have to leave the lot, pay, then come back around." I could see my car from where we stood on the sidewalk. "It will take ten or fifteen minutes."

"That's perfectly all right. Don't you worry about me. I'll just stand inside and watch for you. I need to use the ladies' room. It must be so nice not to have to worry about some things anymore."

She did not elaborate until she was in the car and we were on our way.

"Do you take hormones?"

"For what?" It was raining very hard, large drops hammering the roof like a stampeding herd of small animals.

"The change." Dorothy pulled a plastic bag out of her purse and began nibbling on a gingersnap.

"What change?"

"You know. Hot flashes, moods. I know a woman who started getting them the minute she turned forty. The mind's a powerful thing."

I turned on the radio.

"We were offered some dreadful snack, and you

know how I get when I don't eat." She ate another gingersnap. "Only twenty-five calories and I allow myself eight a day, so we'll need to stop and get some. And apples, of course. You're so lucky. You don't seem to have to worry about your weight at all, but then I imagine if I did what you do I probably wouldn't have much of an appetite, either."

"Dorothy, there's a treatment center in Rhode Island that I want to talk to you about."

She sighed. "I'm worried sick about Lucy."

"It's a four-week program."

"I just don't know if I could stand the thought of her being all the way up there, locked up like that." She ate another cookie.

"Well, you're going to have to stand it, Dorothy. This is very serious."

"I doubt she'll go. You know how stubborn she can be." She thought for a minute. "Well, maybe it would be a good thing." She sighed again. "Maybe while she's there they can fix a few other things."

"What other things, Dorothy?"

"I might as well tell you that I don't know what to do about her. I just don't understand what went wrong, Kay." She began to cry. "With all due respect, you can't imagine what it's like to have a child turn out this way. Bent like a twig. I don't know what happened. Certainly, it's not from any example set at home. I'll take the blame for some things, but not for this."

I turned the radio off and looked over at her. "What *are* you talking about?" I was struck again by how much I disliked my sister. It made no sense to me that she was my sister, for I failed to find anything in common between us except our mother and memories of once living in the same house.

"I can't believe you haven't wondered about it, or maybe to you it somehow seems normal." Her emotions gathered momentum as our encounter tumbled farther downhill. "And I'd be less than honest if I didn't tell you I've worried about your influence in that department, Kay, not that I'm judging because certainly your personal life is your own business and some things you can't help." She blew her nose as tears flowed and rain fell hard. "Damn! This is so difficult."

"Dorothy, for God's sake. *What on earth are you talking about?*"

"She watches every goddam thing you do. If you brush your teeth a certain way, you can rest assured she's going to do the same thing. And for the record I've been very understanding when not everybody would. Aunt Kay this and Aunt Kay that. All these years."

"Dorothy . . ."

"Not once have I complained or tried to pry her away from your bosom, so to speak. I've always just wanted what's best for her, and so I indulged her little case of hero worship."

"Dorothy . . ."

"You have no idea of the sacrifice." She blew her nose loudly. "It wasn't like it wasn't bad enough that I was always being compared to you in school, and putting up with Mother's comments because you were always so fucking *perfect* at everything.

"I mean, goddam. Cooking, fixing things, taking care of the car, paying the bills. You were just a regular man of the house when we were growing up. And then you became my daughter's *father*—if that doesn't take the cake."

"Dorothy!"

But she would not stop.

"And I can't compete with that. I certainly can't be her *father*. I will concede that you're more of a man than I am. Oh yes. You win the hell out of that one hands down, *Dr. Scarpetta, Esquire*. I mean, shit. It's so unfair, and then you get the tits in the family to boot. *The man in the family gets the big tits!*"

"Dorothy, shut up."

"No, I won't and you can't make me," she whispered furiously.

We were back in our small room with the small bed we shared, where we learned to hate each other quietly while Father was dying. We were at the kitchen table silently eating macaroni again while he dominated our lives from his sickbed down the hall. Now we were about to walk into my house where Lucy was hurt, and I marveled that Dorothy did not recognize a script that was as old and predictable as we were.

"Just what exactly are you trying to blame me for?" I said as I opened the garage door.

"Let's put it this way. Lucy's not dating is not something she got from me. That's for damn sure."

I switched off the engine and looked at her.

"Nobody appreciates and enjoys men more than I do, and next time you start to criticize me as a mother, you ought to take a hard look at your contributions to Lucy's development. I mean, who the hell's she like?"

"Lucy's not like anyone I know," I said.

"Bullshit. She's your spitting image. And now she's a drunk, and I think she's queer." She burst into tears again.

"Are you suggesting I'm a lesbian?" I was beyond anger.

"Well, she got it from someone."

"I think you should go inside now."

She opened her door and looked surprised when I made no move to get out of the car. "Aren't you coming in?"

I gave her the key and the alarm code. "I'm going to the grocery store," I said.

At Ukrop's I bought gingersnaps and apples, and wandered the aisles for a while because I did not want to go home. In truth, I never enjoyed Lucy when her mother was around, and this visit certainly had started worse than usual. I understood some of what Dorothy felt, and her insults and jealousies came as no great surprise because they were not new.

It was not her behavior that had me feeling so bad but, rather, the reminder that I was alone. As I passed cookies, candies, dips, and spreadable cheeses, I wished what I had could be cured by an eating binge. Or if filling up with Scotch could have filled up the empty spaces, I might have done that. Instead, I went home with one small bag and served dinner to my pitifully small family.

Afterward, Dorothy retired to a chair before the fire. She read and sipped Rumple Minze while I got Lucy ready for bed.

"Are you hurting?" I asked.

"Not too much. But I can't stay awake. All of a sudden my eyes cross."

"Sleep is exactly what you need."

"I have these awful dreams."

"Do you want to tell me about them?"

"Someone's coming after me, chasing me, usually in a car. And I hear noises from the wreck that wake me up."

"What sort of noises?"

"Metal clanging. The air bag going off. Sirens. Sometimes it's like I'm asleep but not asleep and all these images dance behind my eyes. I see lights throbbing red on the pavement and men in yellow slickers. I thrash around and sweat."

"It's normal for you to experience posttraumatic stress, and it may go on for a while."

"Aunt Kay, am I going to be arrested?" Her frightened eyes stared out from bruises that broke my heart.

"You're going to be fine, but there's something I want to suggest that you probably won't like."

I told her about the private treatment center in Newport, Rhode Island, and she began to cry.

"Lucy, with a DUI conviction you're likely to have to do this anyway as part of your sentencing. Wouldn't it be better to decide on your own and get it over with?"

She gingerly dabbed her eyes. "I can't believe this is happening to me. Everything I've ever dreamed of is gone."

"That couldn't be further from the truth. You are alive. No one else was hurt. Your problems can be fixed, and I want to help you do that. But you need to trust me and listen."

She stared down at her hands on top of the covers, tears flowing.

"And I need for you to be honest with me, too."

She did not look at me.

"Lucy, you didn't eat at the Outback—not unless they've suddenly added spaghetti to their menu. There was spaghetti all over the inside of the car that I assume is from your carrying out leftovers. Where did you go that night?"

She looked me in the eye. "Antonio's."

"In Stafford?"

She nodded.

"Why did you lie?"

"Because I don't want to talk about it. It's nobody's business where I went."

"Who were you with?"

She shook her head. "It's not germane."

"It was Carrie Grethen, wasn't it? And some weeks ago she had convinced you to participate in a little research project, which is why you got in so much trouble. In fact, she was stirring the liquid rubber when I came to see you at ERF."

My niece looked away.

"Why won't you tell me the truth?"

A tear slid down her cheek. To discuss Carrie with her was hopeless, and taking a deep breath, I went on, "Lucy, I think somebody tried to run you off the road."

Her eyes widened.

"I've looked at the car and where it happened, and there are many details that disturb me a great deal. Do you remember dialing Nine-one-one?"

"No. Did I?" She looked bewildered.

"Whoever used the phone last did, and I'll assume that was you. A state police investigator is tracking down the tape, and we'll see exactly when the call was made and what you said."

"My God."

"Plus, there are indications that someone may have been on your rear with lights on high. You had the night mirror flipped on and the sunscreen up. And the only reason I can imagine you might have the sunscreen up on a dark highway was that light was coming in the back windshield making it difficult to see." I paused, studying her shocked face. "You don't remember any of this?"

"No."

"Do you remember anything about a car that may have been green? Perhaps a pale green?"

"No."

"Do you know anybody who has a car that color?"

"I'll have to think."

"Does Carrie?"

She shook her head. "She has a BMW convertible. It's red."

"What about a man she works with? Has she ever mentioned someone named Jerry to you?"

"No."

"Well, a vehicle left greenish paint on a damaged area on the rear of my car and took out the taillight, too. The long and short of it is that after you left Green Top, somebody followed you and hit you from the rear.

"Then several hundred feet later you suddenly accelerated, lost control of the car, and went off the road. My conjecture is that you accelerated about the same time you dialed Nine-one-one. You were frightened, and it may be that the person who struck you was on your tail again."

Lucy pulled the covers up around her chin. She was pale. "Someone tried to kill me."

"It looks to me like someone almost did kill you, Lucy. Which is why I've asked what seem very personal questions. Someone's going to ask them. Wouldn't you rather tell me?"

"You know enough."

"Do you see a relation between what's happened to you at ERF and this?"

"Of course I do," she said with feeling. "I was set up, Aunt Kay. I never went inside the building at three A.M. I never stole any secrets!"

"We must prove that."

She stared hard at me. "I'm not sure you believe me."

I did, but I could not tell her that. I could not tell her about my meeting with Carrie. I had to muster all the discipline I could to be lawyerly with my

290

niece right then because I knew it would be wrong to lead her.

"I can't really help if you don't talk freely to me," I said. "I'm doing my best to keep an open mind and clear head so I can do the right thing. But frankly, I don't know what to think."

"I can't believe you would . . . Well, fuck it. Think what you want." Her eyes filled with tears.

"Please don't be angry with me. This is a very serious matter we're dealing with, and how we handle it will affect the rest of your life. There are two priorities.

"The first is your safety, and after hearing what I've just told you about your accident, maybe you have a better idea why I want you in the treatment center. No one will know where you are. You will be perfectly safe. The other priority is to get you out of these snarls so your future isn't jeopardized."

"I'll never be an FBI agent. It's too late."

"Not if we clear your name at Quantico and get a judge to reduce the DUI charge."

"How?"

"You asked for a big gun. Maybe you've got one."

"Who?"

"Right now all you need to know is your chances are good if you listen to me and do what I say."

"I'll feel like I'm being sent to a detention center."

"The therapy will be good for you for a lot of reasons."

"I'd rather stay here with you. I don't want to be labeled an alcoholic the rest of my life. Besides, I don't think I am one."

"Maybe you aren't. But you need to gain some insight into why you've been abusing alcohol."

"Maybe I just like the way it feels when I'm not here. Nobody's ever wanted me here anyway. So maybe it makes sense," she said bitterly.

We talked a while longer, then I spent time on the phone with airlines, hospital personnel, and a local psychiatrist who was a good friend. Edgehill, a well-respected treatment center in Newport, could admit her as early as the next afternoon. I wanted to take her, but Dorothy would not hear of it. This was a time when a mother should be with her daughter, she said, and my presence was neither necessary nor appropriate. I was feeling very out of sorts when the phone rang at midnight.

"I hope I didn't wake you," Wesley said.

"I'm glad you called."

"You were right about the print. It's a reversal. Lucy couldn't have left it unless she made the cast herself."

"Of course she didn't make it herself. My God," I said impatiently. "I was hoping this would be over, Benton."

"Not quite yet."

"What about Gault?"

"No sign of him. And the asshole at Eye Spy denies Gault was ever there." He paused. "You're sure you saw him?"

"I would swear to it in court."

I would have recognized Temple Gault anywhere. Sometimes I saw his eyes in my sleep, saw them bright

292

like blue glass staring through a barely opened door leading into a strange, dark room filled with a putrid smell. I would envision Helen the prison guard in her uniform and decapitated. She was propped up in the chair where Gault had left her, and I wondered about the poor farmer who had made the mistake of opening the bowling bag he had found on his land.

"I'm sorry, too," Wesley was saying. "You can't imagine how sorry I am."

Then I told him I was sending Lucy to Rhode Island. I told him everything I could think of that I had not already told him, and when it was his turn to fill me in I switched the lamp off on the table by my bed and listened to him in the dark.

"It's not going well here. As I've said, Gault's vanished again. He's screwing with our minds. We don't know what he's involved in and what he isn't. We have this case in North Carolina and now one in England, and suddenly he shows up in Springfield and appears to be involved in the espionage that's gone on at ERF."

"There's no *appears to be* about it, Benton. He's been inside the Bureau's brain. The question is, what are you going to do about it?"

"At present, ERF's changing codes, passwords, that sort of thing. We're hoping he's not been in too deep."

"Hope on."

"Kay, Black Mountain's got a search warrant for Creed Lindsey's house and truck."

"Have they found him?"

"No."

"What does Marino have to say?" I asked.

"Who the hell knows?"

"You haven't seen him?"

"Not much. I think he's spending a lot of time with Denesa Steiner."

"I thought she was out of town."

"She's back."

"How serious is this with them, Benton?"

"Pete's obsessed. I've never seen him like this. I don't believe we're going to be able to pull him out of here."

"And you?"

"I'll probably be in and out for a while, but it's hard to say." He sounded discouraged. "All I can do is give my advice, Kay. But the cops are listening to Pete, and Pete's not listening to anybody."

"What does Mrs. Steiner have to say about Lindsey?"

"She says it could have been him in her house that night. But she really didn't get much of a look."

"His speech is distinctive."

"That's been mentioned to her. She says she doesn't remember much about the intruder's voice except that he sounded white."

"He also has a strong body odor."

"We don't know if he would have that night."

"I doubt his hygiene is good on any night."

"The point is, her not being sure only makes the case against him stronger. And the cops are getting all kinds of calls about him. He was spotted here and there doing suspicious things like staring at some kid he drove past. Or a truck like his was seen near Lake Tomahawk shortly after Emily disappeared. You know what happens when people make up their minds about something."

"What have you made up your mind about?" Darkness clung to me like a soft, comforting cover, and I was aware of the timbre of the tones in the sounds he made. He had a lean, muscular voice. Like his physique, it was very subtle in its beauty and power.

"This guy, Creed, doesn't fit, and I'm still disturbed about Ferguson. By the way, we got the DNA results and the skin was hers."

"No big surprise."

"Something just doesn't feel right about Ferguson."

"Do you know anything more about him?"

"I'm running down some things."

"And Gault?"

"We still have to consider him. That he did her." He paused. "I want to see you."

My eyelids were heavy and my voice sounded dreamy to me as I lay against my pillows in the dark. "Well, I've got to go to Knoxville. That's not very far from you."

"You're seeing Katz?"

"He and Dr. Shade are running my experiment. They should be about finished."

"The Farm is one place I have no desire to visit."

"I guess you're saying you won't meet me there."

"That's not why I won't."

"You'll go home for the weekend," I said.

"In the morning."

"Is everything all right?" It was awkward to ask about his family, and rarely did either of us mention his wife.

"Well, the kids are too old for Halloween, so at least there are no parties or costume making to worry about."

"No one's ever too old for Halloween."

"You know, trick-or-treating used to be a big production in my house. I had to drive the kids around and all that."

"You probably carried a gun and X-rayed their candy."

"You're one to talk," he said.

17

In the early hours of Saturday morning I packed for Knoxville and helped Dorothy put together the appropriate accoutrements for someone going where Lucy was. It was not easy to make my sister understand that Lucy would need no clothing that was expensive or required dry cleaning or ironing. When I emphasized that nothing valuable should be taken, Dorothy got quite upset.

"Oh my God. It's like she's going off to a penitentiary!"

We were working in the bedroom where she was staying so we would not wake Lucy.

I tucked a folded sweatshirt into the suitcase open on the bed. "Listen, I don't even recommend taking expensive jewelry when you're staying in a fine hotel."

"I have a lot of expensive jewelry and stay in fine hotels all the time. The difference is I don't have to worry about drug addicts being down the hall."

"Dorothy, there are drug addicts everywhere. You don't have to go to Edgehill to find them."

"She's going to pitch a fit when she finds out she can't have her laptop."

"I'll explain to her that it's not allowed, and I am confident she'll understand."

"I think it's very rigid on their part."

"The point of Lucy's being there is to work on herself, not on computer programs."

I picked up Lucy's Nikes and thought of the locker room at Quantico, of her being muddy from head to toe and bleeding and burned from running the Yellow Brick Road. She had seemed so happy then, and yet she could not have been. I felt sick that I had not known of her difficulties earlier. If only I had spent more time with her, maybe none of this would have happened.

"I still think it's ridiculous. If I had to go to a place like that, they certainly couldn't stop me from doing my writing. It's my best therapy. It's just a shame Lucy doesn't have something like that because if she did I'm convinced she wouldn't have so many problems. Why didn't you pick the Betty Ford Clinic?"

"I see no reason to send Lucy to the West Coast, and it takes longer to get in."

"I suppose they would have quite a waiting list." Dorothy looked thoughtful as she folded a pair of faded jeans. "Imagine, you might end up spending a month with movie stars. Why, you might end up in love with one of them and next thing you know you're living in Malibu."

"Meeting movie stars is not what Lucy needs right now," I said irritably.

"Well, I just hope you know that she's not the only one who has to worry about how this looks."

I stopped what I was doing and stared at her. "Sometimes I'd like to slap the hell out of you."

Dorothy looked surprised and slightly frightened. I had never shown her the full range of my rage. I had never held up a mirror to her narcissistic, niggling life so she could see herself as I did. Not that she would have, and that, of course, was the problem.

"You're not the one who has a book about to come out. We're talking days, and then I'm on tour again. And what am I supposed to say when some interviewer asks about my daughter? How do you think my publisher is going to feel about this?"

I glanced around to see what else needed to go into the suitcase. "I really don't give a damn how your publisher feels about this. Frankly, Dorothy, I don't give a damn how your publisher feels about anything."

"This could actually discredit my work," she went on as if she had not heard me. "And I *will* have to tell my publicist so we can figure out the best strategy."

"You will not breathe a word about Lucy to your publicist."

"You are getting very violent, Kay."

"Maybe I am."

"I suppose that's an occupational hazard when you cut people up all the livelong day," she snapped.

Lucy would need her own soap because they

wouldn't have what she liked. I went into the bathroom and got her bars of Lazlo mud soap and Chanel as Dorothy's voice followed me. I went into the bedroom where Lucy was and found her sitting up.

"I didn't know you were awake." I kissed her. "I'm heading out in a few minutes. A car will be coming a little later to get you and your mother."

"What about the stitches in my head?"

"They can come out in a few more days and someone in the infirmary will take care of it. I've already discussed these things with them. They're very aware of your situation."

"My hair hurts." She made a face as she touched the top of her head.

"You've got a little nerve damage. It will go away eventually."

I drove to the airport through another dreary rain. Leaves covered pavement like soggy cereal, and the temperature had dropped to a raw fifty-two degrees.

I flew to Charlotte first, for it did not seem possible to go anywhere from Richmond without stopping in another city that wasn't always on the way. When I arrived in Knoxville many hours later, the weather was the same but colder, and it had gotten dark.

I got a taxi, and the driver, who was local and called himself Cowboy, told me he wrote songs and played piano when he wasn't in a cab. By the time he got me to the Hyatt, I knew he went to Chicago once a year to please his wife, and that he regularly drove ladies from Johnson City who came here to shop in the malls.

I was reminded of the innocence people like me had lost, and I gave Cowboy an especially generous tip. He waited while I checked into my room, then took me to Calhoun's, which overlooked the Tennessee River and promised the best ribs in the USA.

The restaurant was extremely busy, and I had to wait at the bar. It was the University of Tennessee's homecoming weekend, I discovered, and everywhere I looked I found jackets and sweaters in flaming orange, and alumni of all ages drinking and laughing and obsessing about this afternoon's game. Their raucous instant replays rose from every corner, and if I did not focus on any one conversation, what I heard was a constant roar.

The Vols had beat the Gamecocks, and it had been a battle as serious as any fought in the history of the world. When men in UT hats on either side occasionally turned my way for agreement, I was very sincere in my nods and affirmations, for to admit in that room that I had not *been there* would surely come across as treason. I was not taken to my table until close to ten P.M., by which time my anxiety level was quite high.

I ate nothing Italian or sensible this night, for I had not eaten well in days and finally I was starving. I ordered baby back ribs, biscuits, and salad, and when the bottle of Tennessee Sunshine Hot Pepper Sauce said "Try Me," I did. Then I tried the Jack Daniel's pie. The meal was wonderful. Throughout it I sat beneath Tiffany lamps in a quiet corner looking out at the river. It was alive with lights reflected from the bridge in varying lengths and intensities, as if

the water were measuring electronic levels for music
I could not hear.

I tried not to think about crime. But blaze orange
burned like small fires around me, and then I would
see the tape around Emily's little wrists. I saw it over
her mouth. I thought of the horrible creatures housed
in Attica and of Gault and people like him. By the time
I asked the waiter to call for my cab, Knoxville seemed
as scary as any city I had ever been in.

My unease grew only worse when I found myself
waiting outside on the porch for fifteen minutes, then
half an hour, waiting for Cowboy to come. But it
seemed he had ridden off to other horizons, and by
midnight I was stranded and alone watching waiters
and cooks go home.

I went back into the restaurant one last time.

"I've been waiting for the taxi you called for more
than an hour now," I said to a young man cleaning
up the bar.

"It's homecoming weekend, ma'am. That's the
problem."

"I understand, but I must get back to my hotel."

"Where are you staying?"

"The Hyatt."

"They have a shuttle. Want me to try it for ya?"

"Please."

The shuttle was a van, and the chatty young driver
asked all about a football game I never saw as I thought
how easy it would be to find yourself helped by a
stranger who was a Bundy or a Gault. That was how
Eddie Heath had died. His mother sent him to a nearby

convenience store for a can of soup, and hours later he was naked and maimed with a bullet in his head. Tape was used in his case, too. It could have been any color because we never saw it.

Gault's weird little game had included taping Eddie's wrists after he was shot, and then removing the tape before dumping the body. We were never clear on why he had done this. Rarely were we clear on so many things that were manifestations of aberrant fantasies. Why a hangman's noose versus a simple, safer slip knot? Why a duct tape that was blaze orange? I wondered if that bright orange tape was something Gault would use, and felt it was. He certainly was flamboyant. He certainly loved bondage.

Killing Ferguson and placing Emily's skin in the freezer also sounded like him. But sexually molesting her did not, and that had continued to nag at me. Gault had killed two women and had shown no sexual interest in them. It was the boy he had stripped and bitten. It was Eddie he had impulsively snatched so he could have his perverted fun. It was another boy in England, or so it seemed now.

Back at the hotel, the bar was jammed and there were many lively people in the lobby. I heard much laughter on my floor as I quietly returned to my room, and I was contemplating turning on a movie when my pager began to vibrate on the dresser. I thought Dorothy was trying to get hold of me, or perhaps Wesley was. But the number displayed began with 704, which was the area code for western North Carolina. Marino, I thought, and I was both startled and thrilled. I sat on the bed and returned the call.

"Hello?" a woman's soft voice asked.

For a moment, I was too confused to speak.

"Hello?"

"I'm returning a page," I said. "Uh, this number was on my pager."

"Oh. Is this Dr. Scarpetta?"

"Who is this?" I demanded, but I already knew. I had heard the voice before in Judge Begley's chambers and in Denesa Steiner's house.

"This is Denesa Steiner," she said. "I apologize for calling so late. But I'm just so glad I got you."

"How did you get my pager number?" I did not have it on my business card because I would be bothered all the time. In fact, I did not let many people have it.

"I got it from Pete. From Captain Marino. I've been having just such a hard time and I told him I thought it would help if I could talk to you. I'm so sorry to bother you."

I was shocked that Marino would have done such a thing, and it was just one more example of how much he had changed. I wondered if he was with her now. I wondered what could be so important that she would page me at this hour.

"Mrs. Steiner, what can I help you with?" I asked, for I could not be ungracious to this woman who had lost so much.

"Well, I heard about your car wreck."

"Excuse me?"

"I'm just so grateful you're all right."

"I wasn't the person in the accident," I said, perplexed and unsettled. "Someone else was driving my car."

"I'm so glad. The Lord is looking after you. But I had a thought that I wanted to pass on—"

"Mrs. Steiner," I interrupted her, "how did you know about the accident?"

"There was a mention of it in the paper here and my neighbors were talking about it. People know you've been here helping Pete. You and that man from the FBI, Mr. Wesley."

"What exactly did the article say?"

Mrs. Steiner hesitated as if embarrassed. "Well, I'm afraid it indicated that you were arrested for being under the influence, and that you'd run off the road."

"This was in the Asheville paper?"

"And then it ended up in the *Black Mountain News* and someone heard it on the radio, too. But I'm just so relieved you're okay. You know, accidents are terribly traumatic, and unless you've been in one yourself, you can't imagine how it feels. I was in a very bad one when I lived in California, and I still have nightmares about it."

"I'm sorry to hear that," I told her, because I did not know what else to say. I was finding this entire conversation bizarre.

"It was at night and this man changed lanes and I guess I was in his blind spot. He hit me from behind and I lost control of the car. I ended up cutting across the other lanes and hitting another car. That person was killed instantly. A poor old woman in a Volkswagen. I've never gotten over it. Memories like that certainly can scar you."

"Yes," I said. "They can."

"And when I think about what happened to Socks. I suppose that's really why I called."

"Socks?"

"You remember. The kitten he killed."

I was silent.

"You see, he did that to me and as you know I've gotten phone calls."

"Are you still getting them, Mrs. Steiner?"

"I've gotten a few. Pete wants me to get Caller I.D."

"Maybe you should."

"What I'm trying to say is these things have been happening to me, and then to Detective Ferguson, and Socks, and then you have the accident. So I'm worried it's all connected. I've certainly been telling Pete to look over his shoulder, too, especially after he tripped yesterday. I'd just mopped the kitchen floor and his feet went right out from under him. It's like some kind of curse straight out of the Old Testament."

"Is Marino all right?"

"He's a little bruised. But it could have been bad since he usually has that big gun stuck in the back of his pants. He's such a fine man. I don't know what I'd do without him these days."

"Where is he?"

"I imagine he's asleep," she said, and I was beginning to see how skillful she was at evading questions. "I'll

306

be glad to tell him to call you if you'll tell me where he can reach you."

"He has my pager number," I said, and I sensed in her pause that she knew I did not trust her.

"Well, that's right. Of course he does."

I did not sleep well after that conversation, and finally called Marino's pager. My phone rang minutes later and immediately stopped before I could pick it up. I dialed the front desk.

"Did you just try to put a call through for me?"

"Yes, ma'am. I guess the person hung up."

"Do you know who it was?"

"No, ma'am. I'm sorry, but I wouldn't have any idea."

"Was it a man or a woman?"

"It was a woman who asked for you."

"Thank you."

Fright jolted me wide awake as I realized what had happened. I thought of Marino asleep in her bed with the pager on a table, and the hand I saw reach for it in the dark was hers. She had read the number displayed and gone into another room to call it.

When she had discovered it was for the Hyatt in Knoxville, she asked for me to see if I were a guest. Then she hung up as the desk rang my room, because she did not want to talk to me. She simply wanted to know where I was, and now she did. Damn! Knoxville was a two-hour drive from Black Mountain. Well, she wouldn't come here, I reasoned. But I could not shake how unsettled I felt, and I was afraid to follow my thoughts into the dark places they were trying to creep.

I started making calls as soon as the sun rose. The first was to Investigator McKee with the Virginia State Police, and I could tell by his voice that I had awakened him from a deep sleep.

"It's Dr. Scarpetta. I'm sorry to call so early," I said.

"Oh. Hold on a minute." He cleared his throat. "Good morning. Listen, it's a good thing you called. I've got some information for you."

"That's wonderful," I said, enormously relieved. "I was hoping you would."

"Okay. The taillight is made out of methylacrylate like most of them are these days, but we were able to fracture-match pieces back to the single unit you removed from your Mercedes. Plus there was a logo on one of these pieces that identified it as being from a Mercedes."

"Good," I said. "That's what we suspected. What about the headlight glass?"

"It's a little trickier, but we got lucky. They analyzed the headlight glass you recovered, and based on its refraction index, density, design, logo, and so on, we know it came from an Infiniti J30. And that helped us narrow down possibilities for the origin of the paint. When we started looking at Infiniti J30s, there's a model painted a pale green called Bamboo Mist. To make a long story short, Dr. Scarpetta, you got hit by a '93 Infiniti J30 painted Bamboo Mist green."

I was shocked and confused. "My God," I muttered as chills swept up my body.

"Is that familiar?" He sounded surprised.

"This can't be right." I had blamed Carrie Grethen and had threatened her. I had been so sure.

"You know someone who has a car like that?" he asked.

"Yes."

"Who?"

"The mother of the eleven-year-old girl who was murdered in western North Carolina," I answered. "I'm involved in that case and have had several contacts with the woman."

McKee did not respond. I knew what I was saying sounded crazy.

"She also was not in Black Mountain when the accident occurred," I went on. "She supposedly had headed north to visit a sick sister."

"Her car should be damaged," he said. "And if she's the one who did this, you can bet she's already getting it fixed. In fact, it may already be fixed."

"Even if it is, the paint left on my car could be matched back to it," I said.

"We'll hope so."

"You sound doubtful."

"If the paint job on her car is original and has never been touched up since it came off the assembly line, we could have a problem. Paint technology's changed. Most car manufacturers have gone to a clear base coat, which is a polyurethane enamel. Even though it's cheaper, it looks really rich. But it's not as many layers, and what's unique in vehicle paint identification is the layer sequence."

"So if ten thousand Bamboo Mist Infinitis came off the assembly line at the same time, we're screwed."

"Big-time screwed. A defense attorney will say you can't prove the paint came from her car, especially since the accident occurred on an interstate that's used by people from all over the country. So it won't even do any good to try to find out how many Infinitis painted that color were shipped to certain regions. And she's not from the area where the accident occurred, anyway."

"What about the Nine-one-one tape?" I asked.

"I've listened to it. The call was made at eight forty-seven P.M., and your niece said, "This is an emergency." That's as much as she got out before she was cut off by a lot of noise and static. She sounded like she was in a panic."

The story was awful, and I felt no better when I called Wesley at home and his wife answered.

"Hold on, and I'll get him to the phone." She was as friendly and gracious as she had always been.

I had weird thoughts while I waited. I wondered if they slept in separate bedrooms, or if she simply had gotten up earlier than he had and this was why she had to go someplace to tell him I was on the phone.

Of course, she might be in their bed and he was in the bathroom. My mind spun on, and I was unnerved by what I was feeling. I liked Wesley's wife, and yet I did not want her to be his wife. I did not want anyone to be his wife. When he got on the phone, I tried to talk calmly but did not succeed.

"Kay, wait a minute," he said, and he sounded as

if I had awakened him, too. "Have you been up all night?"

"More or less. You've got to get back out there. We can't rely on Marino. If we even try to contact him, she'll know."

"You can't be certain it was her who called your pager."

"Who else could it have been? No one knows I'm here, and I'd just left the hotel number on Marino's pager. It was only minutes before I got called back."

"Maybe it was Marino who called."

"The clerk said it was a woman's voice."

"Dammit," Wesley said. "Today is Michele's birthday."

"I'm sorry." I was about to cry and didn't know why. "We've got to find out if Denesa Steiner's car has been damaged. Someone's got to go look. I've got to know why she was after Lucy."

"Why would she go after Lucy? How could she have known where Lucy was going to be that night and what kind of car she would be in?"

I recalled Lucy telling me that Marino had advised her on her gun purchase. It may have been that Mrs. Steiner overheard their telephone conversation, and I voiced this theory to Wesley.

"Did Lucy have a time when she was going to be there, or did she impulsively stop there on her way back from Quantico?" he asked.

"I don't know, but I'll find out." I began to shake with rage. "The bitch. Lucy could have been killed."

"Christ, *you* could have been killed."

PATRICIA CORNWELL

"The goddam bitch."

"Kay, be still and listen to me." He said the words slowly and in a way that was meant to soothe. "I will get back down to North Carolina and see what the hell's going on. We'll get to the bottom of this. I promise. But I want you to get out of that hotel as soon as you can. How long are you supposed to be in Knoxville?"

"I can leave after I meet Katz and Dr. Shade at the Farm. Katz is picking me up at eight. God, I hope it isn't still raining. I haven't even looked out the window yet."

"It's sunny here," he said as if that meant it had to be sunny in Knoxville. "If something comes up and you decide not to leave, then change hotels."

"I will."

"Then go back to Richmond."

"No," I said. "I can't do anything about this in Richmond. And Lucy's not there. At least I know she's safe. If you talk to Marino, don't tell him anything about me. Don't breathe a word about where Lucy is. Just assume he will tell Denesa Steiner. He's out of control, Benton. He's confiding in her now, I know it."

"I don't think it would be wise for you to come to North Carolina right now."

"I've got to."

"Why?"

"I've got to find Emily Steiner's old medical records. I need to go through all of them. I also want you to find out for me every place Denesa Steiner has lived. I want to know about other children or husbands and

312

siblings. There may be other deaths. There may be other exhumations we have to do."

"What are you thinking?"

"For one thing, I'll bet you'll find there is no sick sister who lives in Maryland. Her purpose in driving north was to run my car off the road and hope Lucy died."

Wesley did not say anything. I sensed his equivocation and did not like it. I was afraid to say what was really on my mind, but I could not be silent.

"And so far there's no record of the SIDS. Her first child. Vital Records can't find anything about that in California. I don't think the child ever existed, and that fits the pattern."

"What pattern?"

"Benton," I said, "we don't know that Denesa Steiner didn't kill her own daughter."

He let out a deep breath. "You're right. We don't know that. We don't know much."

"And Mote pointed out in the consultation that Emily was sickly."

"What are you getting at?"

"Munchausen's by proxy."

"Kay, no one will want to believe that. I don't think I want to believe that."

It is an almost unbelievable syndrome in which primary care givers—usually mothers—secretly and cleverly abuse their children to get attention. They cut their flesh and break their bones, poison and smother them almost to death. Then these women rush to doctors' offices and emergency rooms and tell teary tales of how their little one got sick or hurt, and the staff feels so sorry for Mother. She gets so much attention. She becomes a master at manipulating medical professionals and her child may eventually die.

"Imagine the attention Mrs. Steiner has gotten because of her daughter's murder," I said.

"I won't argue that. But how would Munchausen's explain Ferguson's death or what you're alleging happened to Lucy?"

"Any woman who could do what was done to Emily could do anything to anyone. Besides, maybe Mrs. Steiner is running out of relatives to kill. I'll be surprised if her husband really died of a heart attack. She probably killed him in some disguised, subtle manner, too. These women are pathological liars. They are incapable of remorse."

"What you're suggesting goes beyond Munchausen's. We're talking serial killings now."

"Cases aren't always one thing, because people aren't always one thing, Benton. You know that. And women serial killers often murder husbands, relatives, significant others. Their methods are usually different from those of male serial killers. Women psychopaths don't rape and strangle people. They like poisons. They like to smother people who can't defend themselves because they're either too young or too old or incapacitated for some other reason. The fantasies are different because women are different from men."

"No one around her is going to want to believe what you're proposing," Wesley said. "It will be hell to prove, if you're right."

"Cases like this are always hell to prove."

"Are you suggesting I present this possibility to Marino?"

"I hope you won't. I certainly don't want Mrs. Steiner privy to what we're thinking. I need to ask her questions. I need her to cooperate."

"I agree," he said, and I knew it had to be very hard for him when he added, "Truth is, we really can't have Marino working this case any longer. At the very least, he's personally involved with a potential suspect. He may be sleeping with the killer."

"Just like the last investigator was," I reminded him.

He did not respond. Our shared fear for Marino's safety did not need to be said. Max Ferguson had died, and Denesa Steiner's fingerprint was on an article of clothing he was wearing at the time. It would have been so simple to lure him into unusual sex play and then kick the stool out from under him.

"I really hate for you to get more deeply into this, Kay," Wesley said.

"One of the complications of our knowing each other so well," I said. "I hate it, too. I wish you weren't, either."

"It's different. You're a woman and a doctor. If what you're thinking is right, you'll push her buttons. She's going to want to draw you into her game."

"She's already drawn me into it."

"She'll draw you in deeper."

"I hope she does." I felt the rage again.

He whispered, "I want to see you."

"You will," I said. "Soon."

18

The University of Tennessee's Decay Research Facility was simply known as The Body Farm, and had gone by that name for as long as I could remember. People like me intended no irreverence when we called it that, for no one respects the dead more than those of us who work with them and hear their silent stories. The purpose is to help the living.

That was the point when The Body Farm came into being more than twenty years before, when scientists got determined to learn more about time of death. On any given day its several wooded acres held dozens of bodies in varying stages of decomposition. Research projects had brought me here periodically over the years, and though I would never be perfect in determining time of death, I had gotten better.

The Farm was owned and run by the university's Anthropology Department, headed by Dr. Lyall Shade and oddly located in the basement of the football stadium. At 8:15, Katz and I went downstairs, passing the zooarchaeology mollusk and neotropical primates labs, and the tamarin and marmuses collection and strange projects named with roman numerals. Many of the doors were plastered with Far Side cartoons and pithy quotations that made me smile.

We found Dr. Shade at his desk looking over fragments of charred human bone.

"Good morning," I said.

"Good morning, Kay," he said with a distracted smile.

Dr. Shade was well served by his name for more reasons than the apparent ironical one. It was true he communed with the ghosts of people past through their flesh and bones and what they revealed as they lay for months on the ground.

But he was unassuming and introverted, a very gentle spirit much older than his sixty years. His hair was short and gray, his face pleasant and preoccupied. Tall, he was hard bodied and weathered like a farmer, which was yet another irony, for Farmer Shade was one of his nicknames. His mother lived in a nursing home and made skull rings for him from fabric remnants. The ones he had sent to me looked like calico doughnuts, but they functioned very well when I was working with a skull, which is unwieldy and tends to roll no matter whose brain it once held.

"What have we got here?" I moved closer to bits of bone reminiscent of burned wood chips.

"A murdered woman. Her husband tried to burn her after he killed her, and did amazingly well. Better than

317

PATRICIA CORNWELL

any crematorium, really. But it was rather stupid. He built the fire in his own backyard."

"Yes, I would say that was rather stupid. But then so are rapists who drop their wallets as they leave the scene."

"I had a case like that once," said Katz. "Got a fingerprint from her car and was so proud until I was told the guy left his wallet in the backseat. The print wasn't needed much after that."

"How's your contraption doing?" Dr. Shade asked Katz.

"I won't get rich from it."

"He got a great latent from a pair of panties," I said.

"He was a *latent*, all right. Any man who'd dress like that." Katz smiled. He could be corny now and then.

"Your experiment's ready, and I'm eager to take a look." Shade got up from his chair.

"You haven't looked yet?" I asked.

"No, not today. We wanted you here for the final unveiling."

"Of course, you always do that," I said.

"And I always will unless you don't want to be present. Some people don't."

"I will always want to be present. And if I don't, I think I should change careers," I said.

"The weather really cooperated," Katz added.

"It was perfect." Dr. Shade was pleased to announce. "It was exactly what it must have been during the interval between when the girl vanished and her body was found. And we got lucky with the bodies because

318

I needed two and thought that was never going to happen at the last minute. You know how it goes."

I did.

"Sometimes we get more than we can handle. Then we don't get any," Dr. Shade went on.

"The two we got are a sad story," Katz said, and we were going up the stairs now.

"They're all a sad story," I said.

"So true. So true. He had cancer and called to see if he could donate his body to science. We said yes, so he filled out the paperwork. Then he went into the woods and shot himself in the head. The next morning, his wife, who wasn't well, either, took a bottle of Nembutal."

"And they're the ones?" My heart seemed to lose its rhythm for a moment the way it often did when I heard stories like this.

"It happened right after you told me what you wanted to do," Dr. Shade said. "It was interesting timing, because I had no fresh bodies. And then the poor man calls. Well. The two of them have done some real good."

"Yes, they have." I wished I could somehow thank those poor sick people who had wanted to die because life was leaving in a way that was unbearably painful.

Outside we climbed into the big white truck with university seals and camper shell that Katz and Dr. Shade used to pick up donated or unclaimed bodies and bring them to where we were about to go. It was a clear, crisp morning, and had Calhoun's not taught me a lesson about the fierce loyalty of football fans, I would have called the sky Carolina blue.

Foothills rolled into the distant Smoky Mountains, trees around us blazed, and I thought of the shacks I had seen on that unpaved road near the Montreat gate. I thought of Deborah with her crossed eyes. I thought of Creed. At moments I could be overwhelmed by a world that was both so splendid and so horrible. Creed Lindsey would go to prison if I did not stop it from happening soon. I was afraid Marino would die, and I did not want my last vision of him to be like the one of Ferguson.

We chatted as we drove and soon passed farms for the veterinary school, and corn and wheat fields used for agricultural research. I wondered about Lucy at Edgehill and was afraid for her, too. I seemed to be afraid for anyone I loved. Yet I was so reserved, so logical. Perhaps my greatest shame was that I could not show what I should, and I worried no one would ever know how much I cared. Crows picked at the roadside, and sunlight breaking through the windshield made me blind.

"What did you think of the photographs I sent?" I asked.

"I've got them with me," said Dr. Shade. "We put a number of things under his body to see what would happen."

"Nails and an iron drain," said Katz. "A bottle cap. Coins and other metal things."

"Why metal?"

"I'm pretty sure of that."

"Did you have an opinion before your experiments?"

"Yes," said Dr. Shade. "She lay on something that began to oxidize. Her body did. After she was dead."

"Like what? What could have made that mark?"

"I really don't know. We'll know a lot more in a few minutes. But the discoloration that caused the strange mark on the little girl's buttock is from something oxidizing as she lay on top of it. That's what I think."

"I hope the press isn't here," said Katz. "I have a real hard time with that. Especially this time of year."

"Because of Halloween," I said.

"You can imagine. I've had them hung up in the razor wire before and end up in the hospital. Last time it was law school students."

We pulled into a parking lot that in warm months could be quite unpleasant for hospital employees assigned there. A tall unpainted wooden fence topped with coiled razor wire began where pavement ended, and beyond was The Farm. A trace of a foul odor seemed to darken the sun as we got out, and no matter how often I had smelled that smell, I never really got used to it. I had learned to block it without ignoring it, and I never diminished it with cigars, perfume, or Vicks. Odors were as much a part of the language of the dead as scars and tattoos were.

"How many residents today?" I asked as Dr. Shade dialed the combination of a large padlock securing the gate.

PATRICIA CORNWELL

"Forty-four," he said.

"They've all been here for a while, except for yours," Katz added. "We've had the two of them exactly six days."

I followed the men inside their bizarre but necessary kingdom. The smell was not too bad because the air was refrigerator cold and most of the clients had been here long enough to have gone through their worst stages. Even so, the sights were abnormal enough that they always gave me pause. I saw a parked body sled, a gurney, and piles of red clay, and there were plastic-lined pits where bodies tethered to cinder blocks were submerged in water. Old rusting cars held foul surprises in their trunks or behind the wheel. A white Cadillac, for example, was being driven by a man's bare bones.

Of course, there were plenty of people on the ground, and they blended so well with their surroundings that I might have missed some of them were it not for a gold tooth glinting or mandibles gaping. Bones looked like sticks and stones, and words would never hurt anyone here again except for amputated limbs, whose donors, I hoped, were still among the living.

A skull grinned at me from beneath a mulberry tree, and the bullet hole between its orbits looked like a third eye. I saw a perfect case of pink teeth (probably caused by hemolysis, and still argued about at almost every forensic meeting). Walnuts were all around, but I would not have eaten one of them because death saturated the soil and body fluids streaked the hills.

Death was in the water and the wind, and rose to the clouds. It rained death on the Farm, and the insects and animals were fed up with it. They did not always finish what they started, because the supply was too vast.

What Katz and Dr. Shade had done for me was to create two scenes. One was to simulate a body in a basement by monitoring the postmortem changes that take place in dark, refrigerated conditions. The other was to place a body outside in similar conditions for the same length of time.

The basement scene had been staged in the only building on the Farm, which was nothing more than a cinder-block shed. Our helper, the husband with cancer, had been placed on a cement slab inside, and a plyboard box had been built around him to protect him from predators and changes in the weather. Photographs had been taken daily, and Dr. Shade was showing them to me now. The first few days revealed virtually no change to the body. Then I began to note that the eyes and fingers were drying.

"Are you ready to do this?" Dr. Shade asked.

I returned the photographs to their envelope. "Let's take a look."

They lifted off the crate, and I squatted near the body to study it carefully. The husband was a small, thin man who had died with white stubble on his chin and a perfect Popeye tattoo of an anchor on an arm. After six days in his plyboard crypt, his eyes were sunken, his skin doughy, and there was discoloration of his left lower quadrant.

His wife, on the other hand, had not fared nearly so well, even though the weather conditions outside the hut were very similar to those inside. But it had rained once or twice, my colleagues said. At times she had been in the sun, and buzzard feathers nearby helped explain some of the damage I saw. The discoloration of her body was much more marked, the skin slipping badly and not the least bit doughy.

I silently observed her for a while in a wooded area not far from the shed, where she lay on her back, naked, on leaves from surrounding locust, hickory, and ironwood trees. She looked older than her husband and was so stooped and wizened by age that her body had reverted to a childlike androgynous state. Her nails were painted pink, and she had dentures and pierced ears.

"We've got him turned over if you want to look," Katz called out.

I went back to the shed and squatted by the husband again while Dr. Shade directed a flashlight at the marks on the back. The pattern left by an iron drain was easy to recognize, but those left by nails were straight red streaks that looked more like burns. It was the marks left by coins that fascinated us the most, especially one left by a quarter. Upon close scrutiny, I could barely make out the partial outline of an eagle left on the man's skin, and I got out Emily's photographs and made comparisons.

"What I've figured out," Dr. Shade said, "is the

impurities in the metal cause the coin to oxidize unevenly while the body's on top of it. So you get blank spots, an irregular imprint, very much like a shoe print, which usually isn't complete, either, unless the weight is distributed uniformly and you're standing on a perfectly flat surface."

"Have they done image enhancement with the Steiner photographs?" Katz asked.

"The FBI labs are working on it," I said.

"Well, they can really be slow," Katz said. "They're so backed up, and it just gets worse all the time because there are so many more cases."

"And you know how it goes with budgets."

"Ours is already bare bones."

"Thomas, Thomas, that's a terrible pun."

In fact, I had personally paid for the plyboard in this experiment. I had offered to furnish an air conditioner, too, but because of the weather, that had not been needed.

"It's hard as hell to get politicians excited about what we do out here. Or about what you do, Kay."

"The problem is, the dead don't vote," I said.

"I've heard of cases where they did."

We drove back along Neyland Drive, and I followed the river with my eyes. At a bend in it I could see the top of the Farm's back fence peeking above trees, and I thought of the River Styx. I thought of crossing the water and ending up in that place as the husband and wife from our work had done. I thanked them in my mind, for the dead were silent armies I mustered to save us all.

"Too bad you couldn't have gotten here earlier," said Katz, who was always so kind.

"You missed quite a game yesterday," Dr. Shade added.

"I feel like I saw it," I said.

19

I did not follow Wesley's advice but returned to my same room at the Hyatt. I did not want to spend the rest of the day moving into someplace new when I had many calls to make and a plane to catch.

But I was very alert as I walked through the lobby and got on the elevator. I looked at every woman, and then remembered I should pay attention to men, too, for Denesa Steiner was very clever. She had spent most of her life in deceptions and incredible schemes, and I knew how intelligent evil could be.

I saw no one who caught my eye as I walked briskly to my room. But I got my revolver out of the briefcase I had checked in baggage. I had it next to me on the bed as I got on the phone. First, I called Green Top, and Jon, who answered, was very nice. He had waited on me many times, and I did not hesitate to ask pointed questions about my niece.

"I can't tell you how sorry I am," he said again. "I just couldn't believe it when I read the papers."

"She is doing well," I said. "Her guardian angel was with her that night."

"She's a special young lady. You must be proud of her."

It occurred to me that I was no longer sure, and the thought made me feel terrible. "Jon, I need to know several important details. Were you working when she came in that night and bought the Sig?"

"Sure. I'm the one who sold it to her."

"Did she get anything else?"

"An extra magazine, several boxes of hollow points. Uhhhh. I think they were Federal Hydra-Shok. Yup, pretty sure of that. Let's see. I also sold her an Uncle Mike's paddle holster, and the same ankle holster I sold to you last spring. A top-of-the-line Bianchi in leather."

"How did she pay?"

"Cash, and that surprised me a little, to be honest. Her bill was pretty high, as you might imagine."

Lucy had been good about saving money over the years, and I had given her a substantial check when she turned twenty-one. But she had charge cards, so I assumed she didn't use them because she didn't want a record of her purchase, and that didn't necessarily surprise me. She was afraid and very paranoid, as are most people who have been intensely exposed to law enforcement. For people like us, everybody is a suspect. We tend to overreact, look over our shoulders, and cover our tracks when we feel the slightest bit threatened.

"Did Lucy have an appointment with you or did she just stop in?" I asked.

"She had called first and said exactly when she would be here. In fact, she even called again to confirm."

"Did she talk to you both times?"

"No, just the first time. The second time Rick answered the phone."

"Can you tell me exactly what she said to you when she called the first time?"

"Not much. She said she'd been talking to Captain Marino, who had recommended the Sig P230 and he had also recommended that she deal with me. As you may know, the captain and I fish together. Anyway, she asked if I would still be here around eight P.M. on Wednesday."

"Do you remember what day she called?"

"Well, it was just a day or two before she wanted to come in. I think it was the Monday before. And by the way, I asked her early on if she was twenty-one."

"Did she tell you she is my niece?"

"Yes, she did, and she sure reminded me a lot of you—even your voices sound alike. You both have sort of deep, quiet voices. But she really was very impressive on the phone. Extremely intelligent and polite. She seemed familiar with guns and clearly had done a fair amount of shooting. In fact, she told me that the captain's given her lessons."

I was relieved Lucy had identified herself as my niece. It told me she wasn't terribly concerned about my finding out she had purchased a gun. I supposed Marino eventually would have told me, too.

I was sad only because she had not talked to me first.

"Jon," I went on, "you said she called a second time. Can you tell me about that? First of all, when was it?"

"That same Monday. Maybe a couple hours later."

"And she talked to Rick?"

"Very briefly. I remember I was waiting on a customer and Rick had answered the phone. He said it was Scarpetta and she couldn't remember when she told me we would meet. I said Wednesday at eight, which he relayed to her. And that was the end of it."

"Excuse me," I said. "She said *what*?"

Jon hesitated. "I'm not sure what you're asking."

"Lucy identified herself as *Scarpetta* when she called the second time?"

"That's what Rick told me. He just said it was Scarpetta on the line."

"Her last name is not Scarpetta."

"Jeez," he said after a startled pause. "You're kidding. I just assumed. Well, that's kinda weird."

I thought of Lucy paging Marino, who then returned her call, quite likely from the Steiner home. Denesa Steiner must have thought he was talking to me, and how simple it would have been for her to wait until Marino was out of the room and get directory assistance to give her the number for Green Top. Then all she had to do was call and ask the questions she did. It was an odd sense of relief mingled with fury I felt. Denesa Steiner had not attempted to kill Lucy, nor had Carrie Grethen or anyone else. The intended victim had been me.

I asked Jon one last question. "I don't want to put you on the spot, but did Lucy seem intoxicated when you waited on her?"

"If she had, I never would have sold her anything."

"What was her demeanor?"

"She was in a hurry but joking around and very nice."

If Lucy had been drinking as much as I suspected she had for months or longer, she could have had a .12 and seemed to function fine. But her judgment and reflexes would have been impaired. She would not have reacted as well to what happened on the road. I hung up and got the number for the *Asheville-Citizen Times*, and was told by the city desk that the name of the person who had written about the accident was Linda Mayfair. Fortunately, she was in, and momentarily I had her on the line.

"This is Dr. Kay Scarpetta," I said.

"Oh! Gosh, what can I do for you?" She sounded very young.

"I wanted to ask about a story you wrote. It was about an accident involving my car in Virginia. Are you aware that you were incorrect to say that I was driving and subsequently arrested for DUI?" I was very calm but firm.

"Oh, yes, ma'am. I'm really sorry, but let me tell you what happened. Something brief about the wreck came over the wire very late the night of the accident. All it said was that the car, a Mercedes, was identified

331

as yours and it was suspected the driver was you and alcohol was involved. I happened to be working late finishing up something else when the editor came over with the printout. He told me to run it if I could confirm that the driver was you. Well, by now we're on deadline and I didn't think there was a chance.

"Then out of the blue, a call gets rolled over to my desk. And it's this lady who says she's a friend of yours and is calling from a hospital in Virginia. She wants us to know that you were not badly injured in the accident. She thought we should know since Dr. Scarpetta—you—have colleagues still in our area working on the Steiner case. She says she doesn't want us hearing about the accident some other way and printing something that would alarm your colleagues when they pick up the paper."

"And you took the word of a stranger and ran a story like that?"

"She gave her name and number and both of them checked out. And if she wasn't someone familiar with you, how could she have known about the accident and that you have been here working on the Steiner case?"

She could have known all of that if she were Denesa Steiner and were in a phone booth in Virginia after attempting to kill me.

I asked, "How did you check her out?"

"I called the number right back and she answered, and it was a Virginia area code."

"Do you still have the number?"

"Gosh, I think so. It should be in my notepad."

"Will you look for it now?"

I heard pages flipping and a lot of shuffling around. A long minute passed, and she gave me the number.

"Thank you very much. I hope you've gotten around to printing a retraction," I said, and I could tell she was intimidated. I felt sorry for her and did not believe she had intended harm. She was just young and inexperienced, and was certainly no match for a psychopath determined to play games with me.

"We ran a We Were Wrong the next day. I can send you a copy."

"That won't be necessary," I said as I recalled the reporters turning up at the exhumation. I knew who had tipped them off. Mrs. Steiner. She couldn't resist more attention.

The phone rang for a long time when I dialed the number the reporter had given me. Finally, it was answered by a man.

"Excuse me," I said.

"Hello?"

"Yes, I need to know where this phone is."

"Which phone. Yours or mine?" The man laughed. "'Cause if you don't know where yours is, you're in trouble."

"Yours."

"I'm at a pay phone outside a Safeway getting ready to call my wife to ask what kind of ice cream she wants. She forgot to tell me. The phone started ringing so I answered it."

"Which Safeway?" I asked. "Where?"

"On Cary Street."

"In *Richmond*?" I asked in horror.

"Yeah. Where are you?"

I thanked him and hung up and began pacing around the room. She had been to Richmond. Why? To see where I lived? Had she driven past my house?

I looked out at the bright afternoon, and the clear blue sky and vivid colors of the leaves seemed to say that nothing bad like this could happen. No dark power was at work in the world, and none of what I was finding out was real. But I always felt the same disbelief when the weather was exquisite, when snow was falling, or the city was filled with Christmas lights and music. Then morning after morning I would go into the morgue and there would be new cases. There would be people raped and shot, and killed in mindless accidents.

Before I vacated the room, I tried the FBI labs and was surprised the scientist I intended to leave a message for was in. But like so many of us who seemed to do nothing but work, weekends were for others.

"The truth is I've done all with it I can," he said of the image enhancement he had been working on for days.

"And nothing?" I asked, disappointed.

"I've filled it out a little. It's a little clearer, but I can't begin to recognize whatever it is that's there."

"How long will you be in the lab today?"

"For another hour or two."

"Where do you live?"

"Aquia Harbor."

I would not have enjoyed that commute every day, but a surprising number of Washington agents with families lived there and in Stafford and Montclair. Aquia Harbor was maybe a half hour drive from where Wesley lived.

"I hate to ask you this," I went on. "But it's extremely important that I get a printout of this enhancement as soon as I can. Is there any possibility you could drop one by Benton Wesley's house? Round trip, it would be about an hour out of your way."

He hesitated before saying, "I can do that if I leave now. I'll call him at home and get directions."

I grabbed my overnight bag. I did not return my revolver to my briefcase until I was at the Knoxville airport behind a shut door in the ladies' room. I went through the usual routine of checking that one bag and letting them know what was in it, and they marked it with the usual fluorescent orange tag, which brought to mind the duct tape again. I wondered why Denesa Steiner would have blaze orange duct tape and where she might have gotten it. I could see no reason for her to have any connection to Attica and decided as I crossed the tarmac to board the small prop plane that the penitentiary had nothing to do with this case.

I took my aisle seat and was completely caught up in my contemplations, so I did not notice the tension among the other twenty or so passengers until I was suddenly aware of police on board. One of them was saying something to a person on the ground, eyes darting furtively from face to face. Then my eyes did the same as I went into their mode. I knew the demeanor so well, and my mind went into gear as I wondered what fugitive they were looking for and what he might have done. I raced through what action I would take if he suddenly jumped out of his seat. I would trip him. I would tackle him from behind as he went past.

There were three officers panting and sweating, and one of them stopped right by me and his eyes dropped to my belt. His hand subtly dropped to his semiautomatic pistol and released the thumb snap. I did not move.

"Ma'am," he said in his most official police voice, "you're going to have to come with me."

I was shocked.

"Are those your bags under the seat?"

"Yes." Adrenaline was roaring through me. The other passengers were absolutely still.

The officer quickly stooped to pick up my purse and overnight bag, his eyes not leaving me. I got up and they led me out. All I could think was that someone had planted drugs in one of my bags. Denesa Steiner had, and I crazily looked around the tarmac and at the plate glass windows of the terminal. I looked for someone looking at me, a woman who was back in the shadows watching the latest dilemma she had caused me.

A member of the ground crew in a red jumpsuit pointed at me. "That's her!" he said excitedly. "It's on her belt!"

I suddenly knew what this was about.

"It's just a phone." I slowly raised my elbows so they could see beneath my suit jacket. Often when I wore slacks, I carried my portable phone on my belt so I didn't have to keep digging it out of my bags.

One of the officers rolled his eyes. The ground crewman looked horrified.

"Oh, no," he said. "It looked exactly like a nine-millimeter, and I've been around FBI agents before and she looks like one of them."

I just stared at him.

"Ma'am," one of the officers said, "do you have a firearm in either of these bags?"

I shook my head. "No, I do not."

"We're really sorry, but he thought you were wearing a gun on your belt, and when the pilots checked the passenger list, they didn't see anyone on it who was authorized to carry a gun on the plane."

"Did someone tell you I was wearing a gun?" I demanded of the man in the jumpsuit. "If so, who?" I glanced around some more.

"No. No one told me. I thought I saw it when you walked past," he lamely went on. "It's that black case it's in. I'm sure sorry."

"It's all right," I said, my graciousness strained. "You were just doing your job."

An officer said, "You can go back on the plane."

By the time I returned to my seat, I was trembling so violently my knees were almost knocking, and I felt eyes on me. I did not look at anyone as I tried to read the paper. The pilot was considerate enough to announce what had happened.

"She was armed with a nine-millimeter portable phone," he continued to explain the delay as everybody laughed.

This was one upset I could not blame on her, but

337

I realized with stunning clarity that assuming she had caused it was automatic. Denesa Steiner was controlling my life. People I loved had become her pawns. She had come to dominate what I thought and did, and was always at my heels, and the revelation sickened me. It made me feel half crazy. A soft hand touched my arm and I jumped.

"We really feel bad about this," a flight attendant said quietly. She was pretty, with permed blond hair. "At least let us buy you a drink."

"No, thank you," I said.

"Would you like a snack? I'm afraid all we've got are peanuts."

I shook my head. "Don't feel bad. I would hope you would check out anything that might jeopardize the safety of your passengers." I talked on, saying exactly the right words as my mind soared in flight patterns that had nothing to do with where we were.

"It's nice of you to be such a good sport."

We landed in Asheville as the sun went down, and my briefcase quickly came off the one carousel in the small baggage department. I went back into a ladies' room and transferred my handgun to my purse, then I went out on the curb and got a cab. The driver was an old fellow in a knit cap that he had pulled below his ears. His nylon jacket was dingy and frayed around the cuffs, and his big hands looked raw on the wheel as he drove at a prudent speed and made sure I understood it was quite a distance to Black Mountain. He was worried on my behalf about the fare because it could be close to twenty dollars. I closed my eyes as they began to water, and I blamed it on the heat blasting to drive out the cold.

The roar inside the ancient red-and-white Dodge reminded me of the plane as we headed east toward a town that had been shattered without being aware of it. Its citizens could not even begin to understand what really had happened to a little girl walking home with her guitar. They could not comprehend what was happening to those of us who had been called in to help.

We were being destroyed one by one because the enemy had an uncanny ability to sense where we were weak and where we could be hurt. Marino was prisoner and weapons carrier for this woman. My niece, who was like my daughter, was head injured in a treatment center, and it was a miracle she had not died. A simple man who swept floors and sipped moonshine in the mountains was about to be lynched for a hideous crime he had not committed, and Mote would retire on disability, while Ferguson was dead.

The cause and effect of evil spread out like a tree that blocked all light inside my head. It was impossible to know where the wickedness had started and where it would end, and I was afraid to analyze too closely if one of its twisted limbs had caught me up. I did not want to think my feet might no longer be in contact with the ground.

"Ma'am, is there anything else I can do for you?" I was vaguely aware that the driver was speaking to me.

I opened my eyes. We were parked in front of

the Travel-Eze, and I wondered how long we had been there.

"I hated to wake you. But it'd be a lot more comfortable to get in your bed instead of sitting out here. Maybe cheaper, too."

The same yellow-haired clerk welcomed me back as he checked me in. He asked me which side of the motel I'd like to be on. As I recalled, one side viewed the school where Emily had gone and the other offered a panorama of the interstate. It didn't matter because the mountains were all around, blazing in the day and black against the starry night sky.

"Just put me in nonsmoking, please. Is Pete Marino still here?" I asked.

"He sure is, though he don't come in much. Would you rather be next to him?"

"No, I'd rather not. He's a smoker and I'd like to be as far away from that as I can." This was not my reason, of course.

"Then I'll just put you on a different wing."

"That would be fine. And when Benton Wesley gets in, will you have him ring my room immediately?" Then I asked him to call a car rental company and have something with an air bag delivered to me early in the morning.

I went to my room and locked and chained the door and propped a chair beneath the knob. I kept my revolver on top of the toilet while I took a long, hot bath with several drops of Hermes perfuming the water. The fragrance stroked me like warm, loving hands, moving up my throat and face and lightly through my hair. For the first time in a while I felt soothed, and at intervals I ran more hot water and the perfume's sweet oily splashes swirled like clouds. I had pulled the shower curtain shut, and in this fragrant sauna I dreamed.

The times I had relived loving Benton Wesley could not be counted. I did not want to admit how often the images leaned against my thoughts until I could no longer resist giving myself up to their embrace. They were more powerful than anything I had ever known, and I had stored every detail of our first encounter here, though it had not happened exactly here. I had memorized the number of that room and would know it forever.

In truth, my lovers had been few, but they had all been formidable men who were not without sensitivity and a certain acceptance that I was a woman who was not a woman. I was the body and sensibilities of a woman with the power and drive of a man, and to take away from me was to take away from themselves. So they gave the best they had, even my ex-husband, Tony, who was the least evolved in the lot, and sexuality was a shared erotic competition. Like two creatures of equal strength who had found each other in the jungle, we tumbled and took as much as we gave.

But Benton was so different I still could not quite believe it. Our male and female pieces had interlocked in a manner unparalleled and unfamiliar, for it was as if he was the other side of me. Or maybe we were the same.

I did not quite know what I had expected, and

341

certainly I had imagined us together long before we were. He would be soft beneath his hard reserve, like a warrior sleepy and warm in a hammock tethered between mighty trees. But when we had begun to touch on the porch in the early morning, his hands had surprised me.

As his fingers undid clothing and found me, they moved as if they knew a woman's body as well as a woman did, and I felt more than his passion. I felt his empathy, as if he wanted to heal those places he had seen so hated and harmed. He seemed sorrowed by everyone who had ever raped or battered or been unkind—as if their collective sins had cost him the right to enjoy a woman's body as he was enjoying mine.

I had told him in bed that I had never known a man to truly enjoy a woman's body, that I did not like to be devoured or overpowered, which was why sex for me was rare.

"I can see why anyone would want to devour your body," he matter-of-factly had said in the dark.

"I can see why anyone would want to devour yours," I said with candor, too. "But people overpowering people is why you and I have the work we do."

"Then we won't use *devour* and *overpower* anymore. No more words like that. We'll come up with a new language."

The words of our new language came easily, and we had gotten fluent fast.

I felt much improved after my bath and rummaged through my carry-on bag for something new and different to wear. But that was an impossibility, and

I put on the deep blue jacket, pants, and turtleneck sweater I had been wearing for days. The bottle of Scotch was low, and I sipped slowly as I watched the national news. Several times I thought of calling Marino's room, only to put the receiver down before I dialed. My thoughts traveled north to Newport, and I wanted to talk to Lucy. I resisted that impulse, too. If I could get through, it would not be good for her. She needed to concentrate on her treatment and not on what she had left at home. I called my mother instead.

"Dorothy's staying the night up there in the Marriott and flying back to Miami in the morning," she told me. "Katie, where are you? I've been trying you at home all day."

"I'm on the road," I said.

"Well, a lot that says. All this cloak-and-dagger stuff you do. But you would think you could tell your mother."

I could see her in my mind puffing a cigarette and holding the phone. My mother liked big earrings and bright makeup, and she did not look northern Italian like I did. She was not fair.

"Mother, how is Lucy? What has Dorothy said?"

"She says Lucy's queer, for one thing, and she blames it on you. I told her that was ridiculous. I told her just because you're never with men and probably don't like sex doesn't mean you're a homo. It's the same thing with nuns. Though I've heard the rumors—"

"Mother," I interrupted, "is Lucy okay? How was the trip to Edgehill? What was her demeanor?"

343

"What? She's a witness now? Her *demeanor*? The way you talk to your simple mother and don't even realize. She got drunk on the way up, if you want to know."

"I don't believe it!" I said, furious with Dorothy yet again. "I thought the point of Lucy being with her mother was so something like that wouldn't happen."

"Dorothy says that unless Lucy was drunk when they put her in detox, insurance won't pay. So Lucy drank screwdrivers on the plane the entire trip."

"I don't give a damn if insurance pays. And Dorothy isn't exactly poor."

"You know how she is about money."

"I will pay for anything Lucy needs. You know that, Mother."

"You talk as if you're Ross Perot."

"What else did Dorothy say?"

"All I know, in summary, is Lucy was in one of her moods and upset with you because you couldn't be bothered to take her to Edgehill. Especially since you picked it out and are a doctor and all."

I groaned, and it was like arguing with the wind. "Dorothy didn't want me to go."

"As usual, it's your word against hers. When are you coming home for Thanksgiving?"

Needless to say, when our conversation was ended, which simply meant I could take no more and got off the phone, my bath had been undone. I started to pour more Scotch, but stopped, because there was not enough alcohol in the world when my family made me angry. And I thought of Lucy. I put away the bottle and not many minutes later there was a knock on my door.

"It's Benton," his voice said.

We hugged for a long time, and he could feel my desperation in the way I clung to him. He led me over to the bed and sat beside me.

"Start from the beginning," he said, holding both my hands.

I did. When I was finished, his face held that impervious look I knew from work, and I was unnerved by it. I did not want that look in this room when we were alone.

"Kay, I want you to slow down. Do you realize the magnitude of our going forward with an accusation like that? We can't just close our minds off to the possibility that Denesa Steiner is innocent. *We just don't know.*

"And what happened on the plane should tell you that you're not being a hundred percent analytical. I mean, this really disturbs me. Some bozo on the ground crew's just being a hero, and you immediately think the Steiner woman's behind that, too; that she's screwing with your mind again."

"It isn't just my mind she's screwing with," I said, removing one of my hands from his. "She tried to kill me."

"Again, that's speculative."

"Not according to what I was told after making several phone calls."

"You can't prove it. I doubt you'll ever be able to prove it."

"We've got to find her car."

"Do you want to drive by her house tonight?"

"Yes. But I don't have a car yet," I said.

"I have one."

"Did you get the printout of the image enhancement?"

"It's in my briefcase. I looked at it." He got up and shrugged. "It meant nothing to me. Just a hazy blob that's been washed with a zillion shades of gray until it's now a denser, more detailed blob."

"Benton, we've got to do something."

He looked a long time at me and pressed his lips together the way he did when he was determined but skeptical. "That's why we're here, Kay. We're here to do something."

He had rented a dark red Maxima, and when we went outside, I realized that winter was not far off, especially here in the mountains. I was shivering by the time I got into the car, and I knew this was partially due to stress.

"How are your hand and leg, by the way?" I asked.

"Pretty much good as new."

"Well, that's rather miraculous, since they weren't new when you cut them."

He laughed, more out of surprise than anything else. At the moment, Wesley wasn't expecting humor.

"I've got one piece of information about the duct tape," he then said. "We've been looking into who from this area might have worked at Shuford Mills during the time the tape was manufactured."

"A very good idea," I said.

"There was a guy named Rob Kelsey who was a

foreman there. He lived in the Hickory area during the time the tape was made, but he retired to Black Mountain five years ago."

"Does he live here now?"

"He is deceased, I'm afraid."

Damn, I thought. "What do you know about him?"

"White male, died at age sixty-eight of a stroke. Had a son in Black Mountain, which was why Kelsey wanted to retire here, I guess. The son's still here."

"Do you have his address?"

"I can get it." He looked over at me.

"What about the son's first name?"

"Same as his father's. Her house is right around this bend. Look how dark the lake is. It's like a tar pit."

"That's right. And you know Emily wouldn't have followed its shore at night. Creed's story verifies that."

"I'm not arguing. I wouldn't take that route."

"Benton, I don't see her car."

"She could be out."

"Marino's car is there."

"That doesn't mean they aren't out."

"It doesn't mean they are."

He said nothing.

The windows were lit up, and I felt as if she were home. I had no proof, no indication, really, but I sensed her sensing me, even if she was not conscious of it.

"What do you think they're doing in there?" I asked.

"Now, what do you think?" he said, and his meaning was clear.

"That's cheap. It's so easy to assume people are having sex."

"It's so easy to assume because it's so easy to do."

I was quite offended because I wanted Wesley to be deeper. "That surprises me, coming from you."

"It should not surprise you coming from them. That was my point."

Still, I was not sure.

"Kay, we're not talking about our relationship here," he added.

"I certainly didn't think we were."

He knew I wasn't telling the whole truth. Never had I been so clear on why it is ill-advised for colleagues to have affairs.

"We should go back. There's nothing more we can do right now," he said.

"How will we find out about her car?"

"We will find out in the morning. But we've already found out something now. It's not there right this minute looking like it hasn't been in an accident."

The next morning was Sunday, and I woke up to bells tolling and wondered if I was hearing the small Presbyterian church where Emily was buried. I squinted at my watch and decided probably not, since it was only a few minutes past nine. I assumed their service would start at eleven, but then, I knew so little about what Presbyterians did.

Wesley was asleep on what I considered my side of the bed. That was perhaps our only incompatibility as lovers. We both were accustomed to the side of the bed farthest from the window or door an intruder was most likely to come in, as if the space of several feet of mattress would make all the difference in grabbing for your gun. His pistol was on his bedside table and my revolver was on mine. Odds were, if an intruder did come in, Wesley and I would shoot each other.

Curtains glowed like lamp shades, announcing a sunny day. I got up and ordered coffee sent to the room, then inquired about my rental car, which the clerk promised was on its way. I sat in a chair with my back to the bed so I would not be distracted by Wesley's naked shoulders and arms outside the tangled covers. I fetched the printout of the image enhancement, several coins, and a lens, and went to work. Wesley had been right when he'd said the enhancement seemed to do nothing but add more shades of gray to an indistinguishable blob. But the longer I looked at what had been left on the little girl's buttock, the more I began to see shapes.

The density of grayness was greatest in an off-center part of the incomplete circular mark. I could not say where the density would be in terms of the hours on a clock, because I did not know which way was up or down or sideways for the object that had begun to oxidize beneath her body.

The shape that interested me was reminiscent of the head of a duck or some other bird. I saw a dome, then a protrusion that looked like a thick beak or bill, yet this could not be the eagle on the back of a quarter because it was much too big. The shape I was studying filled a good fourth of the mark, and there was what appeared

349

to be a slight dent in what would be the back of the bird's neck.

I picked up the quarter I was using and turned it over. I rotated it slowly as I stared, and suddenly the answer was there. It was so simple, so exact in its match, and I was startled and thrilled. The object that had begun to oxidize beneath Emily Steiner's dead body was indeed a quarter. But it had been face up, and the birdlike shape was the indentation of George Washington's eyes, and the bird's head and bill were our first president's proud pate and curl at the back of his powdered wig. This only worked, of course, if I turned the quarter so Washington was staring at the tabletop, his aristocratic nose pointed at my knee.

Where, I wondered, might Emily's body have been lying? I supposed any place might inadvertently have a quarter on the floor. But there had been traces of paint and pithwood, too. Where might one find pithwood and a quarter? Well, a basement, of course—a basement where something once had gone on that involved pithwood, paints, other woods like walnut and mahogany.

Perhaps the basement had been used for someone's hobby. Cleaning jewelry? No, that didn't seem to make sense. Someone who fixed watches? That didn't seem right, either. Then I thought of the clocks in Denesa Steiner's house and my pulse picked up some more. I wondered if her late husband had repaired clocks on the side. I wondered if he might have used the basement for that, and if he might have used pithwood to hold and clean small gears.

Wesley was breathing the deep, slow breaths of sleep. He brushed his cheek as if something had alighted there, then pulled the sheet up to his ears. I got out the phone book and looked for the son of the man who had worked at Shuford Mills. There were two Robert Kelseys, a junior and a Kelsey the third. I picked up the phone.

"Hello?" a woman asked.

"Is this Mrs. Kelsey?" I asked.

"Depends on whether you're looking for Myrtle or me."

"I'm looking for Rob Kelsey, Junior."

"Oh." She laughed, and I could tell she was a sweet, friendly woman. "Then you're not looking for me to begin with. But Rob's not here. He's gone on to the church. You know, some Sundays he helps with communion, so he has to head on early."

I was amazed as she divulged this information without asking who I was, and I was touched again that there were still places in the world where people were trusting.

"Which church might that be?" I asked Mrs. Kelsey.

"Third Presbyterian."

"And their service starts at eleven?"

"Just like it always has. Reverend Crow is mighty good, by the way, if you've never heard him. May I give Rob a message?"

"I'll try him later."

I thanked her for her help and hung up. When I turned around, Wesley was sitting straight up in bed staring sleepily at me. His eyes roamed around, stopping at the printout, coins, and lens on the table by my chair. He started laughing as he stretched.

"What?" I asked rather indignantly.

He just shook his head.

"It's ten-fifteen," I said. "If you're going to church with me you'd better hurry."

"Church?" He frowned.

"Yes. A place where people worship God."

"They have a Catholic church around here?"

"I have no idea."

He was very puzzled now.

"I'm going to a Presbyterian service this morning," I said. "And if you have other things to do, I might need a lift. As of an hour ago, my rental car still wasn't here."

"If I give you a lift, how will you get back here?"

"I'm not going to worry about that." In this town where people helped strangers on the phone, I suddenly felt like having few plans. I felt like seeing what might happen.

"Well, I've got my pager," Wesley said as he placed his feet on the floor and I got an extra battery from the charger plugged in near the TV.

"That's fine." I tucked my portable phone into my handbag.

20

Wesley dropped me off at the front steps of the fieldstone church a little early, but people were already arriving. I watched them get out of their cars and squint in the sun as they accounted for their children and doors thudded shut up and down the narrow street. I felt curious eyes on my back as I followed the stone walkway, veering off to the left toward the cemetery.

The morning was very cold, and though the sunlight was blinding, it felt thin, like a cool bed sheet against my skin. I pushed open the rusting wrought-iron gate that served no purpose, really, except to be respectful and ornamental. It would keep no one out and certainly there was no need to keep anybody in.

New markers of polished granite shone coldly, and very old ones tilted different ways like bloodless tongues speaking from the mouths of graves. The dead talked here, too. They spoke every time we remembered them. Frost crunched softly beneath my shoes as I walked to the corner where she was. Her grave was a raw, red clay scar from having been reopened and reclosed, and tears came to my eyes as I looked again at the monument with its sweet angel and sad epitaph.

> There is no other in the World—
> Mine was the only one.

But the line from Emily Dickinson held a different meaning for me now. I read it with a new mind and a totally different awareness of the woman who had selected it. It was the word *mine* that jumped out at me. *Mine.* Emily had had no life of her own but had been an extension of a narcissistic, demented woman with an insatiable appetite for ego gratification.

To her mother, Emily was a pawn as all of us were pawns. We were Denesa's dolls to dress and undress, hug and rip apart, and I recalled the inside of her house, its fluffs and frills and little girl designs on fabric. Denesa was a little girl craving attention who had grown up knowing how to get it. She had destroyed every life she had ever touched, and each time wept in the warm bosom of a compassionate world. Poor, poor Denesa, everyone said of this murderous maternal creature with blood on her teeth.

Ice rose in slender columns from the red clay on Emily's grave. I did not know the physics for a fact but concluded that when the moisture in the nonporous clay froze, it expanded as ice does and had nowhere to go but up. It was as if her spirit had gotten caught in the cold as it tried to rise from the ground, and she sparkled in the sun as pure crystal and water do. I realized with a wave of grief that I loved this little girl I knew only in death. She could have been Lucy, or Lucy could have been her. Both were not mothered well, and one had been sent back home, so far the other spared. I knelt and said a prayer, and with a deep breath turned back toward the church.

The organ was playing "Rock of Ages" as I walked in, because by now I was late and the congregation was singing the first hymn. I sat as inconspicuously in the back as I could but still caused glances and heads to turn. This was a church that would spot a stranger because it most likely had so few. The service moved on, and I blessed myself after prayer as a little boy in my pew stared while his sister drew on the bulletin.

Reverend Crow, with his sharp nose and black robe, looked like his name. His arms were wings as he gestured while he preached, and during more dramatic moments it almost seemed he might fly away. Stained-glass windows depicting the miracles of Jesus glowed like jewels, and fieldstone flecked with mica seemed dusted with gold.

We sang "Just As I Am" when it was time for communion, and I watched those around me to follow their lead. They did not file up to the front for the wafer and wine. Instead, ushers silently came down aisles with thimbles full of grape juice and small crusts of dry bread. I took what was passed to me, and everyone sang the doxology and benediction, and suddenly they were leaving. I took my time. I waited until the preacher was at the door alone, having greeted every parishioner; then I called him by name.

"Thank you for your meaningful sermon, Reverend Crow," I said. "I have always loved the story of the importunate neighbor."

"There is so much we can learn from it. I tell it to my children a lot." He smiled as he gripped my hand.

"It's good for all of us to hear," I agreed.

"We're so glad to have you with us today. I believe you must be the FBI doctor I've been hearing about. Saw you the other day on the news, too."

"I'm Dr. Scarpetta," I said. "And I'm wondering if you might point out Rob Kelsey? I hope he hasn't already left."

"Oh, no," the reverend said, as I had expected. "Rob helped with communion. He's probably putting things away." He looked toward the sanctuary.

"Would you mind if I tried to find him?" I asked.

"Not a bit. And by the way"—his face got sad—"we sure do appreciate what you're trying to do around here. Not a one of us will ever be the same." He shook his head. "Her poor, poor mother. Some folks would turn on God after all she's been through. But no ma'am. Not Denesa. She's here every Sunday, one of the finest Christians I've ever known."

"She was here this morning?" I asked as a creepy feeling crawled up my spine.

"Singing in the choir like she always does."

I had not seen her. But there were at least two hundred people present and the choir had been in the balcony behind me.

Rob Kelsey, Jr., was in his fifties, a wiry man in a cheap blue pin-striped suit collecting communion glasses from holders in the pews. I introduced myself and was very worried I would alarm him, but he seemed the unflappable type. He sat next to me on a pew and thoughtfully tugged at an earlobe as I explained what I wanted.

"That's right," he said in a North Carolina drawl as thick as I'd heard yet. "Papa worked at the mill his whole entire life. They gave him a mighty nice console color TV when he retired and a solid gold pin."

"He must have been a fine foreman," I said.

"Well, he wasn't that until he got up in years. Before that he was their top box inspector and before that he was just a boxer."

"What did he do exactly? As a boxer, for example?"

"He'd see to it the rolls of tape was boxed, and then eventually he supervised everybody else doing it to make sure it was right."

"I see. Do you ever remember the mill manufacturing a duct tape that was blaze orange?"

Rob Kelsey, with his near crew cut and eyes dark brown, thought about the question. Recognition registered in the expression on his face. "Why, sure. I remember that because it was an unusual tape. Never seen it before or since. Believe it was for a prison somewhere."

"It was," I said. "But I'm wondering if a roll or two of it might have ended up local. You know, here."

"It wasn't supposed to. But these things happen

because they get rejects and stuff like that. Rolls of tape that aren't just right."

I thought of the grease stains on the edges of the tape used to bind Mrs. Steiner and her daughter. Perhaps a run had gotten caught in a piece of machinery or had gotten greasy some other way.

"And generally, when you have items that don't pass inspection," I interpolated, "employees might take them or buy them for a bargain."

Kelsey didn't say anything. He looked a little perplexed.

"Mr. Kelsey, do you know of anyone your father might have given a roll of that orange tape to?" I asked.

"Only one person I know of. Jake Wheeler. Now, he passed on a while back, but before that he owned the Laundromat near Mack's Five-and-Dime. As I recollect, he also owned the drugstore on the corner."

"Why would your father give him a roll of the tape?"

"Well, Jake liked to hunt. I remember my daddy saying Jake was so afraid of getting shot out there in the woods by someone mistaking him for a turkey that no one wanted to go out with him."

I said nothing. I did not know where this was leading.

"He'd make too dadgum much noise and then wear reflector-type clothing in the blinds. He scared other hunters off all right. I don't think he ever shot a thing except squirrels."

"What does this have to do with the tape?"

"I'm pretty sure my daddy gave it to him as a joke. Maybe Jake was supposed to wrap his shotgun up in it or wear it on his clothes." Kelsey grinned, and I noticed that he was missing several teeth.

"Where did Jake live?" I asked.

"Near the Pine Lodge. Sort of halfway between downtown Black Mountain and Montreat."

"Any chance he might have passed on that roll of tape to someone else?"

Kelsey stared down at the tray of communion glasses in his hands, his brow wrinkled in thought.

"For example," I went on, "did Jake hunt with anybody else? Maybe someone else who might have had a need for the tape, since it was the blaze orange that hunters use?"

"I got no way to know if he passed it along. But I will tell you that he was close to Chuck Steiner. They went out looking for bear every season while the rest of us hoped they didn't find none. Don't know why anyone'd want a grizzle bear coming their way. And you shoot one and what're you expectin' to do with it except make it into a rug? You can't eat it 'less you're Daniel Boone and Mingo about to starve to death."

"Chuck Steiner was Denesa Steiner's husband?" I asked, and I did not let my voice show what I felt.

"He was. A mighty nice man, too. It just killed us all when he passed on. If we'd known he had such a bad heart, we would've sat on him more, made him take it easier."

"But he hunted?" I had to know.

"Oh, he sure did. I went out with him and Jake a

number of times. Those two liked to go out in the woods. I always told 'em they ought to go to Aferca. That's where the big game is. You know, I personally couldn't shoot a stick bug."

"If that's the same as a praying mantis, you shouldn't shoot a stick bug. It would be bad luck."

"It's not the same thing," he said matter-of-factly. "A praying mantis is a whole 'nother insect. But I think the same way you do about that. No, ma'am, I wouldn't touch one."

"Mr. Kelsey, did you know Chuck Steiner well?"

"I knew him from huntin' and church."

"He taught school."

"He taught Bible at that private religious school. If I coulda sent my son there, I would'ave."

"What else can you tell me about him?"

"He met his wife in California when he was in the military."

"Did you ever hear him mention a baby that died? An infant girl named Mary Jo who may have been born in California?"

"Why, no." He looked surprised. "I always had the impression Emily was their only young'un. Did they lose a little baby girl, too? Oh me, oh my." His expression was pained.

"What happened after they left California?" I went on. "Do you know?"

"They came here. Chuck didn't like it out west, and he used to come here as a boy when his family vacationed. They generally stayed in a cabin on Gray Beard Mountain."

"Where is that?"

"Montreat. Same town where Billy Graham lives. Now the reverend's not here much, but I've seen his wife." He paused. "Did anybody tell you about Zelda Fitzgerald burning up in a hospital around here?"

"I know about that," I said.

"Chuck was real good about fixin' clocks. He did it for a hobby and eventually got to where he was fixin' all the clocks for the Biltmore House."

"Where did he fix them?"

"He went to the Biltmore House to fix those. But people in the area would bring theirs directly to him. He had a shop in his basement."

Mr. Kelsey would have talked all day, and I extricated myself as kindly as I could. Outside, I called Wesley's pager with my portable phone and left the police code 10-25, which simply meant "Meet me." He would know where. I was contemplating returning to the foyer to get out of the cold when I realized from the conversations of the few people still trickling out that they were members of the choir. I almost panicked. The very instant she entered my mind she was there. Denesa Steiner waited at the church door, smiling at me.

"Welcome," she said warmly with eyes as hard as copper.

"Good morning, Mrs. Steiner," I said. "Did Captain Marino come with you?"

"He's Catholic."

She had on a black wool coat that touched the top of her black T-strapped shoes, and she was pulling on black kid gloves. She wore no makeup except for a

361

blush of color on her sensuous lips, her honey-blond hair falling in loose curls over her shoulders. I found her beauty as cold as the day, and I wondered how I ever could have felt sympathy for her or believed her pain.

"What brings you to this church?" she next asked. "There's a Catholic church in Asheville."

I wondered what else she knew about me. I wondered what Marino had told her. "I wanted to pay my respects to your daughter," I said, looking directly into her eyes.

"Well, now, isn't that sweet." Still smiling, she did not avert her gaze.

"Actually, it's good we just happened to run into each other," I said. "I need to ask you some questions. Perhaps it would be convenient if I did that now?"

"Here?"

"I would prefer your house."

"I was going to have BLTs for lunch. I just didn't feel like making a big Sunday dinner, and Pete's trying to cut back."

"I'm not interested in eating." I made very little effort to disguise my feelings. My heart was as hard as the expression on my face. She had tried to kill me. She had almost killed my niece.

"Then I guess I'll meet you there."

"I would appreciate a ride. I don't have a car."

I wanted to see her car. I had to see it.

"Mine's in the shop."

"That's unusual. It's quite new, as I recall." If my

eyes had been lasers, they would have burned holes in her by now.

"I'm afraid I got a lemon and had to leave it at a dealership out of state. The thing conked out on me during a trip. I rode with a neighbor, but you're welcome to ride with us. She's waiting in her car."

I followed her down fieldstone steps and along a sidewalk to more steps. There were a few cars still parked along the street and one or two pulling away. Her neighbor was an elderly woman wearing a pink pillbox hat and a hearing aid. She was behind the wheel of an old white Buick, the heater blasting and gospel music on. Mrs. Steiner offered me the front seat and I refused. I did not want her behind my back. I wanted to see everything she did at all times, and I wished I had my .38. But it had not seemed right to take a gun to church, and it had not occurred to me that any of this would happen.

Mrs. Steiner and her neighbor chatted in the front seat and I was silent in the back. The trip lasted but a few minutes; then we were at the Steiner house, and I noted that Marino's car was in the same spot where it had been parked last night when Wesley and I had slowly driven past. I could not imagine what it would be like to see Marino. I had no idea what I would say or what his demeanor toward me would be. Mrs. Steiner opened her front door. We went in, and I noticed Marino's motel room and car keys on a Norman Rockwell plate on the foyer table.

"Where's Captain Marino?" I asked.

"Upstairs, asleep." She pulled off her gloves. "He

wasn't feeling well last night. You know, there's a bug going around."

She unbuttoned her coat and lightly shook her shoulders to get out of it. She glanced away as she took it off as if she were accustomed to giving anybody interested an opportunity to look at breasts no matronly clothing could hide. The language of her body was seductive, and it was speaking for my benefit now. She was teasing me, but not for the same reasons she might tease a man. Denesa Steiner was flaunting herself. She was very competitive with women and this told me even more about what her relationship with Emily had been like.

"Maybe I should check on him," I said.

"Pete just needs to sleep. I'll take him up some hot tea and be right with you. Why don't you make yourself comfortable in the living room? Would you like coffee or tea?"

"Nothing, thank you," I said, and the silence in the house disturbed me.

As soon as I heard her go upstairs, I looked around. I went back into the foyer, slipped Marino's car keys in my pocket, and walked into the kitchen. To the left of the sink was a door leading outside. Opposite it was another one locked with a slide bolt. I slid back the bolt and turned the knob.

Cold musty air announced the basement, and I felt along the wall for a light switch. My fingers hit it and I flipped it up, flooding dark red painted wooden stairs. I went down them because I had to see what was there. Nothing was going to stop me, not even fear of her finding me. My heart was beating hard against my ribs as if it were trying to escape.

Chuck Steiner's worktable was still there, cluttered with tools and gears and an old clock face frozen in time. Pith buttons were scattered about, most of them imprinted with the greasy shapes of the delicate parts they once had cleaned and held. Some were on the concrete floor here and there, along with bits of wire, small nails and screws. Empty hulls of old grandfather clocks stood silent sentry in shadows, and I spotted ancient radios and televisions, too, along with miscellaneous furniture thick with dust.

Walls were white cinder block without windows, and arranged on an expansive pegboard were neat coils of extension cords and other cords and ropes of different materials and thicknesses. I thought of the macramé draped over furniture upstairs, of the intricate lacework of knotted cords covering armrests, chair backs, and cradling plants hanging from eye bolts in ceilings. I envisioned the noose with its hangman's knot that had been cut from Max Ferguson's neck. In retrospect, it seemed unbelievable no one had searched this basement before. Even as the police had looked for little Emily, she probably had been down here.

I pulled a string to turn on another light, but the bulb was burned out. I was still without a flashlight, and my heart was drumming so hard I almost couldn't breathe as I wandered. Near a wall stacked with firewood coated with cobwebs, I found another shut door leading outside. Near a water heater another door led to a full bathroom, and I switched on the light.

I looked around at old white porcelain spattered with paint. The toilet probably had not been flushed in years, for standing water had stained the bowl the color of rust. A brush with bristles stiff and bent like a hand was in the sink, and then I looked inside the tub. I found the quarter almost in the middle of it, with George Washington faceup, and I detected a trace of blood around the drain. I backed out as the door at the top of the stairs suddenly shut, and I heard the bolt slide. Denesa Steiner had just locked me in.

I ran in several directions, my eyes darting around as I tried to think what to do. Dashing to the door near the woodpile, I turned the lock on the knob, threw back the burglar chain, and suddenly found myself in the sunny backyard. I did not see or hear anyone, but I believed she was watching me. She had to know I would come out this way, and I realized with growing horror what was happening. She wasn't trying to trap me at all. She was locking me out of her house, making certain I couldn't come back upstairs.

I thought of Marino, and my hands were shaking so hard I almost couldn't get his keys out of my pocket as I ran around the corner to the driveway. I unlocked the passenger's door of his polished Chevrolet. The stainless steel Winchester was under the front seat where he always kept his shotgun.

The gun was as cold as ice in my hands as I ran back to the house, leaving the car door wide open. The front door was locked, as I had expected. But there were glass panes on either side of it and I tapped one with the butt of the gun. Glass shattered and lightly fell to carpet on the other side. Wrapping my scarf around my hand, I carefully reached inside and unlocked the door. Then I was running up carpeted stairs, and it was as if someone else were me or I had vacated my own mind. I was in a mode that was more machine than human. I remembered the room lit up last night and ran that way.

The door was shut, and when I opened it she was there, sitting placidly on the edge of the bed where Marino lay, a plastic trash bag over his head and taped around his neck. What happened next was simultaneous. I released the safety and racked the shotgun as she grabbed his pistol off the table and stood. Our guns raised together and I fired. The deafening blast hit her like a fierce gust of wind, and she fell back against the wall as I pumped and fired and pumped and fired again and again.

She slid down the wall, and blood streaked the girlish wallpaper. Smoke and burned powder filled the air. I ripped the bag off Marino's head. His face was blue and I felt no pulse in his carotids. I pounded his chest, blew into his mouth once, and compressed his chest four times, and he gasped. He began to breathe.

Grabbing the phone, I called 911 and screamed as if I were on a police radio during a mayday.

"Officer down! Officer down! Send an ambulance!"

"Ma'am, where are you?"

I had no idea of the address. "The Steiner house! Please hurry!" I left the phone off the hook.

I tried to sit Marino up in bed but he was too heavy.

"Come on. Come on."

I turned his face to one side and slipped my fingers under his jaw to keep it pulled forward so his airway would stay clear. I glanced around for pill bottles, for any indication of what she might have given him. Empty liquor glasses were on the table by the bed. I sniffed them and smelled bourbon, and I stared at her numbly. I saw blood and brains everywhere as I trembled like a creature in its agonal stages. I shook and twitched as if in the throes of death. She was slumped, almost sitting, with her back against the wall in a spreading puddle of blood. Her black clothes were soaked and riddled with holes, her head hanging to one side and dripping on the floor.

When sirens sounded they seemed to wail forever before I was aware of many feet hurrying upstairs, of the sounds of a stretcher banging and being unfolded, and then somehow Wesley was there. He put his arms around me and held me hard as men in jumpsuits surrounded Marino. Red and blue lights throbbed outside the window and I realized I had shot out the glass. Air blowing in was very cold. It stirred blood-spattered curtains of balloons flying free through a sky pale yellow. I looked at the ice-blue duvet and stuffed animals all around. There were rainbow decals on the mirror and a poster of Winnie the Pooh.

"It's her room," I told Wesley.

"It's all right." He stroked my hair.

"It's Emily's room," I said.

21

I left Black Mountain the next morning, which was a Monday, and Wesley wanted to go with me but I chose to go alone. I had unfinished business, and he needed to stay with Marino, who was in the hospital after having Demerol pumped out of his stomach. He would be fine, at least physically, then Wesley was bringing him to Quantico. Marino needed to be debriefed like an agent who's been under deep cover. He needed rest, security, and his friends.

On the plane I had a row to myself and made many notes. The case of Emily Steiner's murder had been cleared when I had killed her mother. I had given my statement to the police, and the case would be under investigation for a while. But I was not worried and had no reason to be. I just did not know what to feel. It bothered me some that I did not feel sorry.

I was aware only of feeling so tired that the slightest exertion was an effort. It was as if I had been transfused with lead. Even moving the pen was hard, and my

369

mind would not work fast. At intervals I found myself staring without seeing or blinking, and I would not know how long I had been doing that or where I had gone.

My first job was to write up the case, and in part this was for the FBI investigation, and in part it was for the police investigating me. The pieces were fitting together well, but some questions would never be answered because there was no one left to tell. For example, we would never know exactly what happened the night of Emily's death. But I had developed a theory.

I believed she hurried home before her meeting ended and got into a fight with her mother. This may have happened over dinner, when I suspected Mrs. Steiner may have punished Emily by heavily salting her food. Salt ingestion is a form of child abuse that, horrifically, is not uncommon.

Emily may have been forced to drink salt water. She would have begun to vomit, which would only have served to make her mother madder. The child would have gone into hypernatremia, finally a coma, and she would have been near death or already dead when Mrs. Steiner carried her down to the basement. Such a scenario would explain Emily's seemingly contradictory physical findings. It would explain her elevated sodium and lack of vital response to her injuries.

As for why the mother chose to emulate Eddie Heath's murder, I could only imagine that a woman suffering from Munchausen's syndrome by proxy would have been intensely interested in such a notorious case. Only Denesa Steiner's reaction would not have been like someone else's. She would have imagined the attention a mother would get if she lost a child in such a ghastly fashion.

It was a fantasy that would have been exciting for her, and she might have worked it out in her head. She might have deliberately poisoned and killed her daughter that Sunday night to carry out her plan. Or she might have carried out her plan after accidentally poisoning Emily while enraged. I would never know the answer, but at this point it did not matter. This case would never see a courtroom.

In the basement, Mrs. Steiner placed her daughter's body in the tub. I suspected it was at this point she shot her in the back of the head so blood would go down the drain. She undressed her, which would explain the coin Emily had not tithed that night because she had left her meeting before the boy she loved had taken up the collection. The quarter inadvertently slipped out of Emily's pocket when her pants were being pulled off, and her bare buttock rested on top of it for the next six days.

I imagined it was night when, almost a week later, Mrs. Steiner retrieved Emily's body, which essentially had been refrigerated all this time. She might have wrapped it in a blanket, explaining wool fibers we found. She might have placed it in plastic leaf bags. The microscopic traces of pithwood made sense, too, since Mr. Steiner had used pith buttons in the basement for years when he worked on clocks. So far, the blaze orange duct tape Mrs. Steiner had torn off in strips to tape her daughter and herself had not turned up, nor had the .22-caliber gun. I doubted they ever would. Mrs. Steiner was too smart to hold on to those items, for they were incriminating.

In retrospect, it all seemed so simple, in many ways so obvious. For example, the sequence in which the duct tape was torn off the roll was exactly right for what had happened. Of course, Mrs. Steiner would have bound her daughter first, and there would have been no need to tear off all the strips and stick them on the edge of a piece of furniture. Her mother did not need to subdue her, since Emily wasn't moving. Both of Mrs. Steiner's hands, therefore, would have been free.

But when Mrs. Steiner bound herself, that was a little trickier. She tore off all the strips at once and stuck them on her dresser. She made a token effort of taping herself, so she could get out, and she did not realize she used the strips out of sequence, not that she would have had reason to know it mattered.

In Charlotte, I changed planes for Washington, and from there I took a taxi to the Russell Building, where I had an appointment to see Senator Lord. He was on the Senate floor voting when I arrived at half past three. I waited patiently in the reception area while young women and men answered telephones nonstop, for everyone in the world wanted his help. I wondered how he lived with the burden. He walked in soon enough and smiled at me. I could tell from his eyes he knew everything that had happened.

"Kay, it's so good to see you."

I followed him through another room with more desks and people on more telephones; then we were in his private office, and he shut the door. He had many beautiful paintings by very fine artists, and it was clear he loved good books.

"The Director called me earlier today. What a nightmare. I'm not sure I know what to say," he said.

"I'm doing all right."

"Here, please." He directed me to the couch and faced me from an unimposing chair. Senator Lord rarely put his desk between himself and others. He did not need to, for as was true with every powerful person I had known, and there were but a few, his greatness made him humble and kind.

"I'm walking around in a stupor. A weird state of mind," I went on. "It's later I'll be in trouble. Posttraumatic stress and that sort of thing. Knowing about it doesn't make you immune."

"I want you to take good care of yourself. Go someplace and rest for a while."

"Senator Lord, what can we do about Lucy? I want her name cleared."

"I believe you've already managed to do that."

"Not entirely. The Bureau knows it couldn't have been Lucy's thumb scanned into the biometric lock system. But this doesn't entirely exculpate my niece. At least that's the impression I've gotten."

"Not so. Not so at all." Senator Lord recrossed his long legs and stared off. "Now, there may be a problem in terms of what circulates throughout the Bureau. The gossip, I mean. Since Temple Gault has

373

become part of the picture, there is much that cannot be discussed."

"So Lucy will just have to hold up under everybody's stare because she won't be permitted to divulge what happened," I said.

"That's correct."

"Then there will be those who do not trust her and will think she shouldn't be at Quantico."

"There may be those."

"That's not good enough."

He regarded me patiently. "You can't protect her forever, Kay. Let her take her licks and suffer her slights. In the long run, she will be the better for it. Just keep her legal." He smiled.

"I'm going to do my best to do that," I said. "She still has a DUI hanging over her head."

"She was the victim of a hit-and-run or even an attempted murder. I should think that might change the scenario a bit in the eyes of the judge. I also will suggest she volunteer to perform some sort of community service."

"Do you have something in mind?" I knew he did or he would not have mentioned it.

"As a matter of fact I do. I wonder if she would be willing to return to ERF? We don't know how much of CAIN Gault has tampered with. I'd like to suggest to the Director that the Bureau use Lucy to follow Gault's tracks through the system to see what can be salvaged."

"Frank, I know she would be thrilled," I said as my heart filled with gratitude.

"I can't think of anyone better qualified," he went on. "And it will give her a chance for restitution. She did not willingly do anything wrong, but she used poor judgment."

"I will tell her," I said.

From his office I went to the Willard and got a room. I was too tired to return to Richmond, and what I really wanted to do was fly to Newport. I wanted to see Lucy, even if only for an hour or two. I wanted her to know what Senator Lord had done, that her name was cleared, her future bright.

Everything was going to be just fine. I knew it. I wanted to tell her how much I loved her. I wanted to see if I could find words that for me were so hard. I tended to hold love hostage in my heart because, if expressed, I feared it might abandon me as many people in my life had. So it had been my habit to bring what I feared upon me.

In my room I called Dorothy and got no answer. Next I called my mother.

"Where are you this time?" she asked, and I could hear water running.

"I'm in Washington," I said. "Where's Dorothy?"

"It just so happens she's right here helping me with dinner. We're having lemon chicken and salad—you should see the lemon tree, Katie. And the grapefruits are huge. I'm washing the lettuce even as we speak. If you would visit your mother once in a blue moon, we could eat together. Normal meals. We could be a family."

"I would like to speak to Dorothy."

"Hold on."

The phone clunked against something, then Dorothy was on.

"What's the name of Lucy's counselor at Edgehill?" I asked right off. "I'm assuming they've assigned someone to her by now."

"Doesn't matter. Lucy's not there anymore."

"I beg your pardon?" I asked. "What did you just say?"

"She didn't like the program and told me she wanted to leave. I couldn't force her. She's a grown woman. And it's not like she was committed or something."

"What?" I was shocked. "Is she there? She returned to Miami?"

"No," said my sister, who was quite calm. "She wanted to stay in Newport for a while. She said it wasn't safe to come back to Richmond right now, or some nonsense like that. And she didn't want to come down here."

"She's in Newport alone with a goddam head injury and a problem with alcohol and you're not doing anything about it?"

"Kay, you're overreacting, as usual."

"Where is she staying?"

"I have no idea. She said she just wanted to bum around for a while."

"Dorothy!"

"Let me remind you she's my daughter, not yours."

"That will always be the biggest tragedy of her life."

"Why don't you just for once keep your fucking nose out of it!" she snapped.

"Dorothy!" I heard my mother in the background. "I don't allow the F word!"

"Let me tell you something." I spoke in the cold, measured words of homicidal rage. "If anything has happened to her, I will hold you one hundred percent accountable. You are not only a terrible mother, you are a horrible human being. I am truly sorry you are my sister."

I hung up the phone. I got out the telephone directory and began calling airlines. There was one flight to Providence that I could get on if I hurried. I ran out of the room and kept going just as fast through the Willard's elegant lobby. People stared.

The doorman got me a cab and I told the driver I would double his fare if he could get me to National *fast*. He drove like hell. I got to the terminal as my flight was being called, and when I found my seat, tears welled up in my throat and I fought them back. I drank hot tea and closed my eyes. I was unfamiliar with Newport and had no idea where to stay.

The taxi from Providence to Newport was going to take more than an hour, the driver told me, because it was snowing. Through water-streaked windows I looked out at dark faces of sheer walls of granite on roadsides. The stone was lined with drill holes and dripping with ice, and a draft creeping in from the floor was damp and miserably cold. Big flakes of snow spiraled into the windshield like fragile white bugs, and if I stared too hard at them I started to get dizzy.

"Do you have any recommendations for a hotel in

Newport?" I asked the driver, who spoke in the manner peculiar to Rhode Islanders.

"The Marriott would be your best bet. It's right on the water and all the shopping and restaurants are within walking distance. There's also a Doubletree on Goat Island."

"Let's try the Marriott."

"Yes, ma'am. The Marriott it is."

"If you were a young lady looking for work in Newport, where would you go? My twenty-one-year-old niece would like to spend some time here." It seemed stupid to pose such a question to a perfect stranger. But I did not know what else to do.

"In the first place, I wouldn't pick this time of year. Newport's pretty damn dead."

"But if she did pick it this time of year. If she had time off from school, for example."

"Umm." He thought as I got caught up in the rhythm of the windshield wiper blades.

"Maybe in the restaurants?" I ventured.

"Oh, sure. Lots of young people working in the restaurants. The ones on the water. The money's pretty good because the main industry's tourists in Newport. Don't let anybody tell you it's fishing. These days, a boat with a thirty-thousand-pound hold comes back in with maybe three thousand pounds of fish. And that's on a good day."

He continued to talk as I thought about Lucy, about where she would go. I tried to get into her mind, to read it, to somehow reach her through my thoughts. I said many silent prayers and fought back tears and the most terrible of all fears. I could not deal with another tragedy. Not Lucy. That loss would be the last. It would be too much.

"How late do most of these places stay open?" I asked.

"What places?"

I realized he had been talking about butterfish, something about them being used in cat food.

"The restaurants," I said. "Would they still be open now?"

"No ma'am. Not most of 'em. It's almost one A.M. Your best bet if you want to find your niece a job is to go out in the morning. Most places open by eleven, some earlier than that if they serve breakfast."

My taxi driver, of course, was right. I could do nothing now but go to bed and try to get some sleep. The room I got at the Marriott overlooked the harbor. From my window the water was black, and the lights of men out fishing bobbed on a horizon I could not see.

I got up at seven because there was no point in lying in bed any longer. I had not slept and had been afraid to dream.

Ordering breakfast, I opened curtains and looked out at a day that was steely gray, water almost indistinguishable from sky. In the distance, geese flew in formation like fighter planes, and snow had turned to rain. Knowing not much would be open this early did not stop me from trying, and by eight I was out of the hotel with a list of popular inns, pubs, and restaurants I had gotten from the concierge.

For a while I walked the wharfs, where sailors were dressed for the weather in yellow slickers and bib pants. I stopped to talk to anyone who would listen, and my question each time was the same, just as their answers were all the same. I described my niece, and they did not know if they had seen her. There were so many young women working in places along the water.

I walked without an umbrella, the scarf around my head not keeping out the rain. I walked by sleek sailboats and yachts battened down with heavy plastic for the winter, past piles of massive anchors broken and eaten with rust. Not many people were around, but many places were open for the day, and it did not occur to me until I saw ghosts, goblins, and other spooky creatures in the shop windows of Brick Market Place that today was Halloween.

I walked for hours along the cobblestone of Thames Street, looking in the windows of shops selling everything from scrimshaw to fine art. I turned up Mary Street and passed Inntowne Inn, where the clerk had never heard my niece's name. Nor did anyone know her at Christie's, where I drank coffee before a window and looked out at Narragansett Bay. Docks were wet and dotted white with sea gulls all facing the same way, and I watched as two women walked out to look at the water. They were bundled up in hats and gloves, and something about them that made me think they were more than friends. I got upset about Lucy again and had to leave.

I ducked inside the Black Pearl at Bannister's Wharf, then Anthony's, the Brick Alley Pub, and the Inn at

Castle Hill. Callahan's Cafe Zelda and a quaint place that sold strudels and cream could not help me, and I went into so many bars I lost track and wound up in some of them twice. I saw no sign of her. No one could help me. I wasn't sure anyone cared, and I walked along Bowden Wharf in despair as rain fell harder. Water swept down in sheets from a slate-gray sky, and a lady hurrying past gave me a smile.

"Honey, don't drown," she said. "Nothing's that bad."

I watched her go inside the Aquidneck Lobster Company at the end of the wharf, and I chose to follow her because she had been friendly. I watched her go into a small office behind a partition of glass so smoky and taped with invoices that I could see only dyed curls and hands moving between the slips of paper.

To get to her I passed green tanks the size of boats filled with lobsters, clams, and crabs. They reminded me of the way we stacked gurneys in the morgue. Tanks were stacked to the ceiling, and bay water pumped through overhead pipes poured into them and spilled onto the floor. The inside of the lobster house sounded like a monsoon and smelled like the sea. Men in orange bib pants and high rubber boots had faces as weathered as the docks, and they spoke in loud voices to one another.

"Excuse me," I said at the small office door, and I did not know that a fisherman was with the woman because I had not been able to see him. He had raw red hands and was sitting in a plastic chair, smoking.

"Honey, you're drenched. Come in and get warm." The lady, who was overweight and worked too hard, smiled again. "You want to buy some lobsters?" She started to get up.

"No," I quickly said. "I've lost my niece. She wandered off or we got our directions mixed up or something. I was supposed to meet her. Well, I just wonder if you might have seen her."

"What does she look like?" asked the fisherman.

I described her.

"Now, where was it you saw her last?" The woman looked confused.

I took a deep breath, and the man had me figured out. He read every word of me. I could see it in his eyes.

"She ran off. They do it sometimes, kids do," he said, taking a drag on a Marlboro. "Question is, where'd she run off from? You tell me that, and maybe I'll have a better idea about where she might be."

"She was at Edgehill," I said.

"She just got out?" The fisherman was from Rhode Island, his last syllables flattened as if he were stepping on the end of his words.

"She walked out."

"So she didn't do the program or her insurance quit. Happens a lot around here. I got buddies been in that joint and have to leave after four or five days because insurance won't pay. A lot of good it does."

"She didn't do the program," I said.

He lifted his soiled cap and smoothed back wild black hair.

"I know you must be worried sick," said the woman. "I can make you some instant coffee."

"You are very kind, but no, thank you."

"When they get out early like that, they usually start drinking and drugging again," the man went on. "I hate to tell you, but it's the way it goes. She's probably working as a waitress or bartender so she can be near what she wants. The restaurants around here pay pretty good. I'd try Christie's, the Black Pearl over there on Bannister's Wharf, Anthony's on Waites Wharf."

"I've tried all those."

"How about the White Horse? She could make good money there."

"Where's that?"

"Over there." He pointed away from the bay. "Off Marlborough Street, near the Best Western."

"Where would someone stay?" I asked. "She's not likely to want to spend a lot of money."

"Honey," said the woman, "I'll tell you what I'd try. I'd try the Seaman's Institute. It's just right over there. You had to walk right past it to get here."

The fisherman nodded as he lit another cigarette. "There you go. That'd be a good place to start. And they got waitresses, too, and girls working in the kitchen."

"What is it?" I asked.

"A place where fishermen down on their luck can stay. Sort of like a small YMCA, with rooms upstairs and a dining hall and snack bar."

"The Catholic church runs it. You might talk to Father Ogren. He's the priest there."

"Why would a twenty-one-year-old girl go there versus some of these other places you've mentioned?" I asked.

"She wouldn't," the fisherman said, "unless she don't want to drink. No drinking in that place." He shook his head. "That's exactly where you go if you leave a program early but don't want to be drinking and drugging anymore. I've known a bunch of guys to go there. I even stayed there once."

It was raining so hard when I left that water coming down bounced off pavement back up toward the loud, liquid sky. I was soaked to my knees, hungry, cold, and with no place left to go, as was true of many people who came to the Seaman's Institute.

It looked like a small brick church with a menu out front written with chalk on a chalkboard and a banner that said EVERYONE IS WELCOME. I stepped inside and saw men sitting at a counter drinking coffee while others were at tables in a plain dining room across from the front door. Eyes turned to me with mild curiosity, and the faces reflected years of cruel weather and drink. A waitress who looked no older than Lucy asked if I would like a meal.

"I'm looking for Father Ogren," I said.

"I've not seen him lately, but you can check the library or the chapel."

I climbed stairs and entered a small chapel that was empty save for saints painted in frescoes on plaster walls. It was a lovely chapel with needlepoint cushions in nautical designs and a floor of varying colors of marble inlaid with shapes of shells. I stood very still looking around at Saint Mark holding a mast while Saint Anthony of Padua blessed the creatures of the sea. Saint Andrew carried nets, and words from the Bible were painted along the top of the wall.

For he maketh the storm to cease so that the waves thereof are still. Then are they glad because they are at rest and so he bringeth them unto their desired haven.

I dipped my hand into a large shell filled with holy water and blessed myself. Praying a while before the altar, I placed a gift in a small straw basket. I left a bill for Lucy and me and a quarter for Emily. Beyond the door I heard cheery voices and whistling of residents on the stairs. Rain on the roof sounded like drum rolls on a mattress and beyond opaque windows gulls cried.

"Good afternoon," a quiet voice behind me said.

I turned around to find Father Ogren, dressed in black.

"Good afternoon, Father," I said.

"You must have had a long walk in the rain." His eyes were kind, his face very gentle.

"I am looking for my niece, Father, and am in despair."

I did not have to talk about Lucy long. In fact, I'd scarcely described her before I could tell the priest knew who she was, and my heart seemed to open like a rose.

"God is merciful and good," he said with a smile. "He led you here as he leads others here who have been lost at sea. He led your niece here days ago. I believe she's in the library. I put her to work there cataloging books and doing other odds and ends. She's very smart and has a marvelous idea about our computerizing everything."

I found her at a refectory table in a dim room of dark paneling and shopworn books. Her back was to me as she worked out a program on paper without benefit of a computer, the way fine musicians compose their symphonies in silence. I thought she looked thinner. Father Ogren patted my arm as he left, and he quietly shut the door.

"Lucy," I said.

She turned and looked at me in astonishment.

"Aunt Kay? My God," she said in the hushed tone of libraries. "What are you doing here? How did you know?" Her cheeks were flushed, a scar on her forehead bright red.

I pulled up a chair and took one of her hands in both of mine.

"Please come home with me."

Lucy continued to stare at me as if I had been dead.

"Your name has been cleared."

"Completely?"

"Completely."

"You got me my big gun."

"I said I would."

"You're the big gun, aren't you, Aunt Kay?" she whispered, looking away.

"The Bureau has accepted that it was Carrie who did this to you," I said.

Her eyes filled with tears.

"What she did was horrible, Lucy. I know how hurt and angry you must be. But you are fine. The truth is known and ERF wants you back. We'll work on your DUI. The judge will have more sympathy since someone ran you off the road and the evidence proves that. But I still want you to get treatment."

"Can't I do it in Richmond? Can't I stay with you?"

"Of course you can."

She looked down as tears spilled over.

I did not want to hurt her further but I had to ask. "It was Carrie you were with in the picnic area the night I saw you out there. She must smoke."

"Sometimes." She wiped her eyes.

"I'm so sorry."

"You wouldn't understand it."

"Of course I understand it. You loved her."

"I still do." She began to sob. "That's what's so stupid. How could I? But I can't help it. And all along . . ." She blew her nose. "All along she was with Jerry or whoever. *Using me.*"

"She uses everyone, Lucy. It wasn't only you."

She wept as if she would the rest of her life.

"I understand how you feel," I said, pulling her close. "You can't just stop loving somebody. Lucy, it will take time."

I held her for a long while, my neck wet with her tears. I held her until the horizon was a dark blue line across the night, and in her spartan room we packed up her belongings. We walked along cobblestone and pavement deep with puddles as Halloween glowed in windows and the rain began to freeze.

The following is the intriguing prologue to

FROM POTTER'S FIELD

The new Dr Kay Scarpetta mystery from
PATRICIA CORNWELL

Available in its entirety in October 1995
as a Little, Brown hardback

TWAS THE NIGHT BEFORE CHRISTMAS

He walked with sure steps through snow, which was deep in Central Park, and it was late now, but he was not certain how late. Towards The Ramble rocks were black beneath stars, and he could hear and see his breathing because he was not like anybody else. Temple Gault had always been magical, a god who wore a human body. He did not slip as he walked, for example, when he was quite certain others would, and he did not know fear. Beneath the bill of a baseball cap, his eyes scanned.

In the spot – and he knew precisely where it was – he squatted, moving the skirt of a long black coat out of the way. He set an old Army knapsack in the snow and held his bare bloody hands in front of him, and though they were cold, they weren't impossibly cold. Gault did not like gloves unless they were made of latex, which was not warm, either. He washed his hands and face in soft new snow, then patted the used snow into a bloody snowball. This he placed next to the knapsack because he could not leave them.

He smiled his thin smile. He was a happy dog digging on the beach as he disrupted snow in the park, eradicating footprints, looking for the emergency door. Yes, it was where he thought, and he brushed aside more snow until he found the folded aluminum foil he had placed between the door and the frame. He gripped the ring that was the handle, and opened the lid in the ground. Below were the dark bowels of the subway and the screaming of a train. He dropped the knapsack and snowball inside. His boots rang on a metal ladder as he went down.

[ ]	POSTMORTEM by Patricia Cornwell	£5.99
[ ]	BODY OF EVIDENCE by Patricia Cornwell	£5.99
[ ]	ALL THAT REMAINS by Patricia Cornwell	£5.99
[ ]	CRUEL AND UNUSUAL by Patricia Cornwell	£5.99

Warner Books now offers an exciting range of quality titles by both established and new authors which can be ordered from the following address:

Little, Brown and Company (UK),
P.O. Box 11,
Falmouth,
Cornwall TR10 9EN.

Alternatively you may fax your order to the above address.
Fax No. 0326 376423.

Payments can be made as follows: cheque, postal order (payable to Little, Brown and Company) or by credit cards, Visa/Access. Do not send cash or currency. UK customers and B.F.P.O. please allow £1.00 for postage and packing for the first book, plus 50p for the second book, plus 30p for each additional book up to a maximum charge of £3.00 (7 books plus).

Overseas customers including Ireland please allow £2.00 for the first book plus £1.00 for the second book, plus 50p for each additional book.

NAME (Block Letters) ....

....

ADDRESS ....

....

....

[ ] I enclose my remittance for _____
[ ] I wish to pay by Access/Visa Card

Number

Card Expiry Date